Griffey was barely inside the castle
when he met the first death trap.

<> CHASE QUEST <>

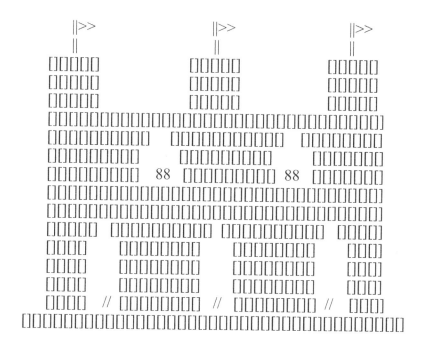

<><> M. Ray Roberts <>

08.06.2023

<>M. RAY ROBERTS<>

Thanks to the brilliant Willy Christie

for the cover art.

@willychristie [*Instagram*]

Thanks to Ted, who edited out the curse words and

gave wizard-level guidance.

ISBN: 9798699923427

◇CHASE QUEST◇

◇ Third Edition. ◇

This book was written in honor of John F. Kennedy and Jerry Litton.

Thanks to my delightful beta-readers and brave cover actors:
Bill and Nancy, Kyle and Paul.

The author also wishes to thank J.R.R. Tolkien. No one told me
what *The Hobbit* was. I had to stumble across it in my middle-
school library. Also, I am indebted to Brian Jacques, whose
Redwall books inspired the opening scene of *Chase Quest*. I've
carried the imagery of that scene with me ever since my youth, all
the way to my thirtieth year when I wrote the first draft on a bus
with my father, riding through Denali National Park.

Also, I need to thank my D&D group—Andrew, Ben, Drew, Jay
and Paul. If our hectic schedules had never derailed our games,
maybe I wouldn't have been forced to create the adventures
you're about to enjoy.

Thanks must also go to Nick, who, in the backseat of a Colorado
road trip, gestured at a distant peak and proclaimed it:
Further Mountain.

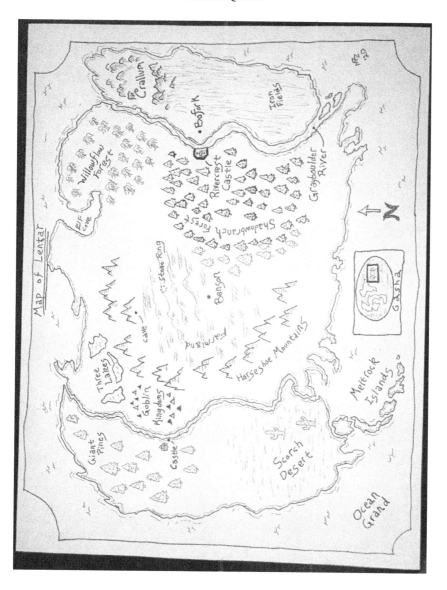

BOOK

◇ I ◇

THE QUEST.

◇ CHAPTER THE FIRST. ◇

◇Midnight Watchtower.◇

A pair of summer moons hung in the sky tonight. Two crescent sisters, embroidered upon a tapestry of starlit wonder.

The light deployed by the lunar twins sent shadows of trickery dancing through the forest. It was that Frishkadammed forest which Alkent was tasked with watching tonight. He was to keep an eye on the trees—from the depths of which, any time now, danger might come forth. Raving, barbaric, bloodthirsty.

Majestic spruce trees were dense in Shadowbranch forest and only a stuffy meadow kept its outskirts from the stone exterior of Rivercrest castle. So, at least he didn't have to look very far.

Alkent Johns grew up in a gritty fishing village back east, across the river from the castle. The greasy hamlet of Bofork held no acquaintance with buildings higher than a single story. At first, being posted on tower duty three stories high felt impressive and empowering, but that faded fast. Replaced with sweaty palms and desperate, distracting thoughts. He never expected to die up here.

Alone in a roost, staring at some trees.

Back in Bofork, it was basically bred into all the babies that they needed to seek out a life in Rivercrest. *Just across Grayboulder river, there awaits a blissful existence bursting with something called 'prosperous opportunity'*, the weary elders of

Bofork (who were all bent, burnt, and broken to a degree ten years past their age) often assured each other. When the grind of the iron-forge workday finally lapsed into the tranquil chirp of night, the elders of Bofork would huddle in their cramped, musty kitchens and whisper about their Rivercrest aspirations—always loud enough to be overheard by the bashful young'uns, constructing and toppling miniature forts in the next room.

As a child, Alkent never managed to decipher what *prosperous opportunity* was, and, as an adult, he'd searched for such a creature for years and years. Relayed by his own parents and the parents of his friends and even the shrunken, twitchy, mole-faced teachers at school, was the same vivid dictum: *get out of Bofork, get across the river. You either taste that Rivercrest life or you waste the life you've got.*

Existence in Bofork was dull and dirty, and Alkent never had reason to expect some momentous life moment would bounce him to Rivercrest and land him a job there. Yet, no matter how often people snickered about the stone soup sloshing around inside Alkent's skull, he was one lucky guy. When his smarts would sputter and he'd be flirting with failure, Alkent's reliable reservoir of luck usually stepped in to bail him out. And if luck wasn't prosperous opportunity then he was a mule.

Also, what was luck without some muscle to back it up?

Three years ago, Alkent's raw strength was on display at the Log-Drag River-Crossing contest on Grayboulder river. He had annihilated the competition, courtesy of a mighty grip, fearsome biceps, and godly lower-body power. His luck had flexed muscles of its own that day, as captain Trunk, head of the River Guard, was in the audience and hooting with appreciation when Alkent won the contest.

While it was nice having the captain in attendance, the most cherished witness in the crowd was a certain strawberry blonde. A beautiful maiden in a blue-with-white-spots dress. In a crowd of smiles during his blubbering victory speech, hers was haloed. Her adoring smile was meant for *him*, not for his log-dragging athleticism. Her name was Marynda. She was training as a Druid beneath her grandmother's gaze and the woman's towering bookshelves. Marynda alighted upon Alkent's big muscles and soft heart. He was awed by her smart, peaceful aura. It wasn't long before they married.

Getting the call across the river had been a surprise on a humbling spiritual level, springing a sheepish blushing grin to Alkent's chubby face. The bludgeoning of initiation camp had been authentic punishment, but the reward of a position on the River Guard made it all worthwhile.

His marriage to Marynda was worthwhile, as well. But, sure as a knave resides in every deck of cards, they had some troubles. She complained about his neck-beard and his muscular body gone plump. He retorted that *all* bodies faded at twenty-four suns (or, as some called it: *second-plateau plus-four*). When she got him too far fired up, he would decry her inhuman Druid ability to transform into animals. However, no matter how much squabblin' and jabbin' got going between them, both adored their freshborn baby girl. The bow atop their young family was named Hazel, and she seemed to never cry when Alkent held her. She would go calm and smile. Made his heart swell with something akin to delight.

Working the night shift way up high in a tower, however, drained Alkent's supply of delight. He was the kind of guy who preferred going to bed before sunset to greet the dawn with a chipper grin. Alkent would rather splash around in Grayboulder river or wrestle his loud idiot cousins in the dirt. He preferred any activity which kept him at ground-level. That's where his family was. His beloved Marynda and precious Hazel. Being up high, where only birds belonged, made him dizzy and sweaty and sad. Way up high on a corner tower, he felt divorced from his native grounds, as a puppy must feel when cast out lonely upon the countryside, far from the warmth of its home.

Shadowbranch forest gave him queasy knees. Men told tales about those woods. Tales which sounded absurd and unsettling but were also true. The Rivercrest economy was based around the river, as shipping and trade were its lifeblood. Lumber was needed to support the haulers and the naval protection vessels. That stock was acquired from Shadowbranch forest, right in the backyard of the castle. A few times a month, a tree-choppin' squad of dwarves (few others would take the job) would venture out, as soon as the sun hit its zenith, high and bright, and they would haul back the lumber. However, following every trip out, at first light of the next day, all the trunks severed by the blades of the dwarves… would be fully-grown once again. Restored to their full height. As if they'd never been chopped.

While it was tempting to gloat over this convenience, to boast over their access to an unlimited resource, the people of Rivercrest got quiet and nervous about the whole thing. Alkent couldn't blame them. Any system with the power to regenerate itself overnight was probably not meant to be messed with and chopped at in the first place. So people took what they needed and hoped it would last.

Rivercrest castle was built of stone, and was squat rather than tall and imposing, as if taking a penitent kneel. The perimeter security structures were recent construction projects, crafted in wood to save both time and coin. The castle was an octagon, with two of the rear eastern sections removed to meld with the river, which meant Alkent was one of six guards stationed in the patrol towers tonight.

He was desperate to be part of the team here in Rivercrest. He'd not only earned his way over from Bofork, but he'd also earned a spot on the River Guard. Being part of a team was a concept he could both define and abide. But, from what he'd seen here, there were fissures on this particular team. Information was kept separate and compartmentalized, just as the guard towers— and the six men yawning in them tonight—were split out wide from each other.

The wooden bones of the security structures weren't the only new things around here. Back when Alkent was a kid, aspiring to dream about sniffing life across the river, there had never been a need for intense overnight security in Rivercrest. Simmering tension and paranoid suspicions thrived here, and Alkent never expected to find such forces polluting a place as proud and upstanding as Rivercrest. But the general unease felt across the city was beginning to infect him, as well.

The timing did not go lost on Alkent. His arrival in the city, and with the River Guard, coincided with the gloom beginning to permeate the city. Maybe his luck was running out.

The crickets fell quiet. The chirping chorus went still. Shadowbranch forest was eerie and silent. For some reason, the trees seemed taller and the thought of something taller than his current post left Alkent woozy. He felt the wooden planks creak beneath his feet as he shot a nervous glance next door.

He couldn't see anybody over there at that station. That absence irritated him more than it worried him. He got a wretched jealous feeling he was being left out of some late night snack or something. He often fell victim to an itch of paranoia. After all, his bosses never even told him what kind of danger he was supposed to be watching for. This lack of clarity left him feeling empty. And his paranoid mind was hungry to fill that gap.

The ominous reticence of the crickets persisted. The eerie silence a prickly, smothering blanket.

Alkent shuffled his feet uncertainly. The planks groaned and screeched beneath him. His eyes snapped out at Shadowbranch forest—those shadowy secretive spruce trees, so unalike from the civilized society within the castle walls. He held his breath for a five-count, hoping that maybe the critters were pausing their whistling so they could offer up animal prayers to the moons or something.

The cricket noise did not come back. Either they'd all gone

mute... or there was something out there. Something to frighten them. Alkent glanced once again at the next guard station over, the one on his right. Fifty yards away, that wooden oval-bulb watchtower post was... empty.

His head twisted so fast to double-check the one to his left that he was whipped with vertigo.

That station was also vacant.

Feeling his pulse quicken, Alkent tried to slow his beating heart. *It's a shift change, acho? A shift change. Or a piss break. Or maybe nap time. It's a shift change.*

Alkent managed to resist the urge to climb down from his post, go trotting across the channel, and attempt to locate his missing neighbors. But the Rivercrest folk might call him nosy for doing that. Maybe even cowardly. He shuffled his feet again, wiped a cold sweat from his face. With a gulp, he felt the edginess shiver into his fingertips. He tightened his grip on the bull horn.

The security system up here hinged upon noise. If the guards spotted danger, they were to stand tall in their lookout towers and blow their horns. In addition to taxing the lungs of the poor guard playing the instrument, the action was intended to wake the entire city.

It was a policy of openness, implemented three years ago and proposed by the Second King (a leader whom Alkent just happened to support and believe in). The philosophy behind the alert system was a symbolic gesture; an "agenda of openness," as some of the more scholar types put it. What it meant was: *if there's a threat on the city, every citizen will have the same measure of warning.*

Except, well, Alkent figured, *since I control the horn, I'm gonna have a few seconds more warnin' than anyone else.* No matter how people tried to keep things equal, they never really were. Deep in his chest, he longed for his wife and daughter, the most precious beings in existence. If anyone deserved an early warning of encroaching danger, it was them.

For a Night Guard, circumstances on the battlements carried significant pressure. No one wanted to wake the whole city on the basis of a false alarm, produced from a dazed sleepy panic. No one wanted to trust their instincts too much, blow the horn, and live forever with the label of *The Fool Who Blew the Night Horn and Woke the Whole City*.

Alkent didn't think he could live with the shame of such a title. He knew his dear Marynda would get playful and tease him about it, but everyone else would stare him down wherever he went in the city. And the ferocious distaste within those glares would be genuine.

To Alkent, and all the wisdom swirling within his soupy brains, the entire concept of this security system was ridiculous. Blowing a horn on a tower was an exercise in naive optimism.

They got Sorcerers workin' in this castle, he thought bitterly, for the two-millionth time. *Yet the best security system they got is havin' Alkent try and play an instrument?* He shook his head and sighed.

Gradually, Alkent's throbbing panic melted away. He began to breathe normal again, began to relax. He took a moment to appreciate the calm double-moonlight and the soothing breeze bristling through the hushed corridors of the forest. Perhaps it was just his luck which cleared away all the cricket chatter. Spared him the headache of nature's jabbering while he was up here trying to work. While he already didn't care for heights, such things were much easier to endure without a ball of hot iron rolling around and frothing inside his skull. As he breathed deep and exhaled, he realized something further. His daily dosage of fortuitous intervention must have done him good, for he was cured of the gulps and sweats and shuffles. How nice it was to just stand up here and not be nervous.

The stations next door are on shift change right now, he reasoned.

His eyes caught movement.

Down in the forest, straight out from his post.

A tall figure stepped between two tree trunks. A shape wrapped in a cloak of rich, impenetrable blackness. The ghost raised its hands before its chest, palms curved and facing each other, as if cupping an invisible sphere. Sure enough, snug within the gap of its palms, a globe of light twisted into existence. The light was crimson, swirling and interloping with thick ribbons of black.

The orb fired up at the castle. It streaked with shocking speed—right at Alkent's post. Images of his wife and daughter blazed through the soup of Alkent's brains. His eyes shot wide with alarm. His grip on the bull horn tightened. He raised it to his lips. This was no idiot's alarm. This was a moment when he could warn the city and become a legend.

The glowing red-black orb **bashed** into Alkent's chest, demolishing his ribcage with a bursting, sickening *pop*. His body collapsed with a *splat* into a gory puddle of its own former contents, and the horn fell from his bloody grip. The horn went unblown. The crucial warning never sounded.

Silently, mischievously—moving slower now, more meticulously—the stealthy shining orb slipped over the battlements. It whispered across a vacant courtyard lit beneath a shine of double moonlight. The orb was out in the open for a clip, but its evil progress went unseen…

◇ CHAPTER THE SECOND. ◇
◇The Corpses of Dreams.◇

Sweeping down a shadowy hallway with walls the shade of maple syrup, the hovering red-black ball flowed with the warps and grooves of the floorboards. From its left, there was heavy noise—booming shouts, pounding drums, tapping feet, clanking beer mugs—but the corridor was deserted. Keeping low, the orb slipped past the side-entrance to Brumble tavern. Inside, a bloody brawl was erupting, hogging all the attention in the room, leaving no eyes available to spy the assassin creeping by outside.

Further down on the left, the sphere drifted past the kitchen. There echoed out the sounds of clattering plates, crackling fires, slicing knives, and hooting Cooks. While a few of the workers were focused on their dishes and assorted cleaning duties, most of the others were abandoning their ovens and cutting boards. They went scrambling from the kitchen to watch the brawl unfolding next door in the tavern. Again, no eyes were free to look out and mark the assassin as it passed.

At the end of the hallway, the spell-ball had the choice of veering right and venturing deeper into the city or slipping left, down a dusty, cob-webbed stairway of stone. Still keeping low, the orb turned left and zipped down the stairs—tracking its target and avoiding witnesses.

The blue-gray steps bled past; rows and rows of cracked, faded teeth.

At the bottom of the stairs, another hall spilled out to the right. This one was much broader than the one upstairs, and it was far less lively. This area was used for storage, a function which manifested as a basement dusty with neglect. Dozens of large rooms branching off the hall, each one crammed with crates and barrels and sacks of supplies—all of it buried and forgotten.

The devilish spell-ball spun and floated and cast eerie splays of light strobing along the musty walls. Down here, the only eyes to mark its progress were tiny, black, and beady, residing in the furry skulls of cellar rats. Some of the critters glanced at the flickering entity, then darted into sockets and crevices to hide and shriek. The others, the ones that stared too long, felt their hearts explode.

Screeches of dying rodents peppered the backdraft of the spell-ball as it sped onward with quiet assurance.

The storage hall bled into an expansive archery range and swordplay gymnasium. Unlit torches were mounted on the walls with no souls to boast, wrestle, and punch within their glow. At this late hour, the only attendees were the corpses of dreams. Bright and zesty when they were first brought down here, most of the dreams got stuck in the dungeon to rot forever.

Generation after generation, boys on the doorstep of manhood would march down here, huffing cloudbursts of youthful idealism out from beneath their stomping leather bootheels. Before leaving for the basement to sign their lives away, the boys would pretend not to see the smug pride of their fathers, and would ignore their weeping mothers. They carried with them dreams of glorious knighthood, and deposited them in the cellar to die. Precious few ever became actual Knights.

The instant before the wicked spell-ball smacked into a cold wall of stone, it changed course, and raced up along the face of the obstruction. Without shedding a single lick of momentum, it rode a kissing inch away from the stone surface until it rose eleven feet high. There, it blitzed inside a pipe as broad as a bakery pie encased within the wall. The orb split through the puny crossbars of a rusted steel grate, then reclaimed its spherical pulse on the other side.

When the cylindrical shaft cut right or swerved left, the black-scarlet spell-ball did the same. The orb of light moved without a sound. It moved with a purpose. A thirst.

All throughout its journey, the ball's vapors spilled glinting circular spotlights into the rooms with outlets from pipeline gridwork, but the brief stamps of these taunts went unnoticed.

The path through the pipes was a conduit to the soul of Rivercrest castle.

Unseen by anyone who could've stopped the damnation before it dropped, the spell-ball rode the underground system of arteries and ventricles network into the very heart of the kingdom.

Far above its clandestine migration, the entire city and all its iterations of life slept and snuck and sang, oblivious. From distraught mothers bobbing in rocking chairs to the screeching babies in their arms to the neglectful fathers pounding mugs of ale and trying to be louder than their buddies at the taverns. From bone-weary laborers in coma-deep sleeps, too exhausted to care about the delicate balance of peace upon which their world rested, to the spellcasters thrashing in their sheets, infected with worry over tomorrow's problems and challenges. From the nobility in their bedchambers with partners whom shared no vows with them, to the thieves slinking up the alleyways. Oblivious, all.

The wicked globe traveled a total of seventeen-hundred-and-seventeen feet before it finally slowed to a cautious creep. Blood-red with a disgusting giddiness, the roll of the orb hushed to a halt. The assassin's eye peered down into a room with books and maps and scrolls stacked in towers upon every flat available surface. A broad can-shaped chamber with a moose-antler chandelier dangling way up above and a thick puffy rug of bug-bear fur warming the floorspace.

The Second King was standing at the door, whispering with urgency to someone in the hall.

"*...a good man died to get this here,*" the visitor hissed as he handed something over.

The Second King nodded with genuine understanding and offered some words.

With delicacy the door was closed, then John Parker, the Second King, walked over to settle at his desk. For a long moment, he stared into space, his face grievous and pensive, rolling the secret scroll absently between his fingertips. Soon, his mind returned to his ancient roll-top desk. As he had done so often in recent days, he hunkered over the map the dragonfolk had gifted to him. He studied it intently.

John Parker always cared for the business of this office more than the adornments. Beyond politics and prestige, that included the garnishes of his chamber. This was a man who respected the animals of the sacred wilderness and considered them exempt from dying to become decorations. But he left the bear on the floor and the antlers up high because people expected those things in place.

The Second King was a tall thin man, with a core of well-disguised muscle and strength stashed beneath his robes, and a buzz of black-silver hair atop his scalp. King Two had reached the sixth-plateau in years and considered himself wise enough to ignore the sneers when his back was turned. Some political tongues spoke of him as poor and petty for choosing to house his offices in the basement. He figured it more important to be productive than to look good for his peers. Yet he'd even compromised on *that*—the bear was on the floor and the moose was on the ceiling, after all.

He ignored the words and shed the wounds. It was tranquil down here. Peaceful.

As this man saw it, the basement of Rivercrest was the fire which forged him into the man he was tonight. The spillover scrolls from the upstairs library stacks all resided down here; a limitless well of documents and resources which went neglected by a city which much benefit from the insights. Plus, the humble truth was that he was once one of those proud recruits who marched down here to train. He'd tromped on down, carrying a dull spear stolen from his uncle's shack, and deposited his dream. Working down here in the dark kindled a kind of cozy homegrown nostalgia in his heart.

Knighthood had eluded young John Parker, as his career path was diverted by a horrid knee injury near the start of his second-level years. He had long-since forgiven the rival party responsible for that wound, for he'd found knowledge to be a fine substitute for anger. Coupled with a generous helping of adventure and ambassador travels, the Second King considered his life thus far to have been a remarkable and satisfying meal.

More than the countless swipes with death he'd dodged during his younger days of journeying across the countryside, and more than his eventual ascension to one of the highest leadership roles in Rivercrest kingdom, John Parker was the most proud of his family. His wonderful wife, daughter, and son. His kids were both well-past grown, and he could see their lives moving fast. For all the power invested in his position as Second King, he was helpless to slow their growth. His daughter, Sho'pa, was studying to become a spiritualist Monk. She'd insisted on cross-training as a Warrior Monk, but her temple frowned on such aggression. (When asked what her career was, Sho'pa phrased it as "spiritualist with an emphasis on Warrior.") Meanwhile, John's son had opted for the vagabond lifestyle of a Ranger. Admittedly, these were not John Parker's preferred professions for his offspring—both seemed rather frivolous to him—but he was still proud they'd found their paths.

Second King John Parker peered at the map before him and felt a dribble of sweat slick his brow. It was cold in these chambers during the summer, so this was no natural sweat. He'd obsessed over the map given to him by the dragons for these past few days, so it was strange to feel so uneasy about it now.

Fingers trembling, he tore the wax and unfurled the secret scroll. As he read, his eyes grew wide. The Second King felt his breath cut short and his heart squeeze with fear. It was astounding.

A lofted rustling *hiss* tore his eyes up with a snap.

The black-crimson spell-ball did not hesitate. It struck down from its perch, lightning fast, gashing John Parker's head clean off his shoulders, spraying an appalling mist of blood.

Almost as an after-thought, the spell-ball zapped a spring of fire to the scroll upon the Second King's desk. The paper had spooled into dueling curls, and it now caught aflame and sizzled to ash.

The spell-ball fled to the pipe in the wall and began its escape attempt…

◇ CHAPTER THE THIRD. ◇
◇The Ranger and the Cook.◇

The brawl began with a boast across the barroom. But before that, there was heavy drinking.

The band of guitars, flutes and bongos wound down its opening set, clearing the air for the two friends to chat without screaming. All around, the rowdy crowd of Brumble tavern chirped and cheered.

"Do the trick, do the trick," Griffey Parker urged his friend. "There's ladies watching."

"That belongs in the kitchens." Brisk Koja barked laughter across the booth. His playful smile betrayed how much he wanted to satisfy the request. After some further prompting, Brisk snapped the fingers on his right hand and produced a tiny spark and flame. They both hooted and roared.

"When are you gonna quit working in those kitchens and spread that spark to the world?"

"Aww, that can't be useful outside the castle. 'Cept for lighting fireworks, I guess."

Griffey only nodded, for the majority of his attention was torn away by the breasts of a passing bar maid. Her hips rocked as she conveyed sloshing ale glasses and suggestive eyes across the room.

Griffey Parker was in the early years of the third-plateau, with long, thick black hair falling to his shoulders. His blue-green eyes lit up his otherwise weathered, lightly-bearded face, which carried a share of rugged charm for any ladies who dared take notice. All his life, he'd been quick with a smile and fast with a joke, but the grins and the gabs had grown rarer and grimmer in recent years.

Brisk, his counterpart across the table, was a squat Black man with a patch of curly black hair and a beard of salt sprinkles. The dimples on Brisk's cheeks stood out and danced whenever he chuckled his infectious chuckle, and those generous dimples seemed to cut ten years off his age.

A commotion drew Griffey's eye—a dispute over a game of checks-and-bones. From there, he glanced at the bar—an ashy block whose operation was overseen by a fat orange cat drowsing on the liquor shelves, and facilitated by mister Brumble himself. The owner of Brumble tavern was a rotund bald man with a wild red beard who seemed forever irritated. He wanted to be crouched in the seclusion of a dark room brewing up rich porters and grassy hoppy ales instead of spewing and swapping gossip with his brainless customers. Some said mister Brumble really set the mood for this place.

The ale house was back-lit with torches mounted on the walls, patterned between grimy windows and the dull faces of moose heads with broad antler spreads. The tables were erratic squiggles of walnut (in Brumble's, even the tables were a drunken swerve). Framed in the flickering light, eschewing the chairs, most of the attendees were men—booming, boisterous and bordering on stupid-drunk.

Brisk gulped some beer, slapped his glass to the table, and his face lit up in a cheery smile. "Yo! I just remembered! I whipped up a delicious pan of apple bread this afternoon. Wanted to gift it your way or perhaps throw it at your face as a kind of good luck charm. You're headed back out in the morning like some madman with aspirations for death. As I may never see you again, and Rangers need all the sugary battle-strength they can score, I wanted to give you a snack for the outbound trail!"

This casual mention of his looming departure triggered a mournful dip in Griffey's mood. It was a pang of guilt, Griffey supposed, and he had to gulp a swig of beer to help dull the pain.

He always got nervous before swapping the comforts of the castle for the ruggedness of the wilderness. But the feeling was usually a brand of nervous excitement. Giddiness, almost. This time, however, he felt different. As if he were leaving before addressing crucial business. Which, tragically, he was.

Instead of attending to such business, he was sitting in Brumble tavern, getting his nostrils assaulted with sweat and getting drunk with a childhood buddy. It felt wonderful, yet it also felt wrong.

"A pan of your apple bread, eh?" the Ranger slapped his own mug down, striking the latticework of ring-shaped puddles with a splash. "Dunno if getting shelled with a case of stomach poison is the best way to enhance the experience of a long hike through the woods."

"Strong words. Strong. Words. Pretty funny words you got there, o' mighty Son of the Second King. I would expect nothing less from a poet who's got poetry flowing from his fingertips."

"*Shh!*" Griffey hissed, fighting back laughter. "Quiet, man! People don't know I write poetry!"

"I suppose that's why you really signed up to go wander around in the woods," Brisk mused. "So you could be a poet in peace." The Cook wagged his finger in Griffey's face. "Now, if I can get you a case of the fire-shits off a pan of under-cooked bread, then you can't leave the castle. You won't risk dyin' every ten seconds out there in Shadowbranch forest. Plus, ole Brisk will be there to heal you up!"

"You got a cure for the fire guts, do ya?"

Brisk puffed his chest in a boast while Griffey signaled a blonde pigtail bar maid for more beer. "I've been busy these last six months while you've been gone," Brisk hooted. "Been taking night classes for the Healer's craft. Got on the good side of the master with a helping of my prized apple bread, in fact. Despite my humble kitchen background, I've made it pretty far in the craft. I can diagnose illnesses, examine broken bones. Soon I may even be whippin' up elixirs and such!"

"I'm proud of you, pal. I'm envisioning you snapping your fingers next to the face of one of your patients." Griffey grinned. "I've got an upgrade in my job, as well. I'm a Runter now."

Brisk arched an eyebrow. "Don't tell me that's a combination of *Ranger* and *Hunter*?"

"It pays double when I visit the penny booth every month."

"Huh." Brisk tossed his eyes. "I line up at the penny booth for pay every month, same as everyone else, and I don't recall them handing out extra gold for creative job titles. Self-applied."

"What can I say, Brisky. It pays to stand out from the dreary Rivercrest crowd."

"A *Runter*? Seriously? If you really get paid more for that drek, I think you owe me a beer."

"There are languages and delicacies of the tongue far more diverse than you are aware of. You see, Brisky, there's a vast, exciting world beyond the walls of that dusty oven you live inside."

Brisk buzzed his lips with a mocking snort. "That right, Mister Delicacies of the Tongue? You know, I imagine residing in an apple bread oven smells better than the Frishkadammed forest."

Griffey Parker spotted their waitress on approach with fresh sluggers of ale, and his eye caught upon a figure in the crowd. Standing at the bar, scowling over the slow drink service, was a tall figure wrapped in dark red robes. The humanoid's facial features appeared to be the consistency of rock, with harsh lines sketching a stern forehead, a flattened arrowhead nose, spiky cheekbones, and a jabbing pointed chin. The creature's large fiery eyes, shining with dragon intensity, met with Parker's. Griffey offered a nod which was not returned. Or, well, perhaps it was imperceptibly returned. Griffey's sharp Ranger's eyes marked a neck-chain hanging to the dragonman's muscular chest. A golden amulet with a scarlet-jewel center. *A Paladin!* Griffey realized. *Pretty noble for a dump like this place.*

"Listen, I get it," Brisk was rambling, accepting the mugs of beer from the pretty bar girl, "you're having second thoughts about being a Ranger. You rushed into it, like everything else you do. That's why you're trying to rename the job already. Look around, no one in here likes their job."

"How do you know that?" Griffey challenged. "You haven't been to Brumble's in months."

"The faces in here are ugly as mud, but they tell a pretty story," Brisk explained with an eloquent belch. He waved at a group of dwarves, clustered around a battlefield of empty and broken beer glasses. "See this gang of dwarves over here? They got a table in this busy place with no problem. Of course, dwarves don't like the booths, like the one we've got, because they can't squeeze in here, but they get all the tables they want because of something I call: *unspoken social stratification*. It's pretty rare in this city when a fella from the squat and brawny bloodline gets on with a construction crew or the River Guard. The only work the dwarves can get in this city is either with the lumber crews or out on the docks. Dwarves are mountain folk and hate water, so most go chop the trees. Well, Shadowbranch forest is really creepy, so people have a kind of quiet respect for anyone who does that job."

"So all the men in this castle, who are bitter arses all day long, become sympathetic once they start ingesting alcohol," Griffey finished in a dry, sarcastic tone, taking a swig of beer. Griffey didn't much care for the topic of social theory, and kind of wished Brisk would shut up about it. The pang of guilt was returned to Griffey's stomach, as he was reminded once again of his own social commitment—the one he was skipping out on to be here getting drunk. "I can see why you'd think it's that simple, ole friend, but there's another layer to it. A much darker truth." A suspicious, uneasy look twitched across Brisk's face and he had to slug some ale to hide it away. "The men in this bar," Griffey continued, "enjoy standing while the dwarves take the tables because it makes them feel superior. They're already taller to start with, but this gives an added layer to their silly bloated egos. As if having the good jobs in this city was actually something to be proud of. Plus, the common saying in this kingdom is: *I get my ass kicked by kingdom taxes all day and it's too sore to sit on.* Oh, and let's not forget the fact that, standing up, they score easier views of the serving ladies' breasts."

Brisk looked sour, sad, and uncertain, and his contorted expression made Griffey feel bad. Griffey knew he shouldn't have undercut his friend's theory so sharply, and knew he was being pissy instead of just playing along. Yet the burning hitch in his guts wouldn't go away. That argumentative element was telling him that Brisk needed a wake-up splash from the reality bucket. *The man's too sheltered in this castle*, Griffey thought with an acid bite. *Too sheltered in his kitchen.*

Griffey felt a shiver—a sign that he was projecting anger at his friend when he was too scared to confront his own problems. His nervous eyes shifted around the bar, peeling through the drunken mob. If there was danger lurking in this horde, he preferred that it announce itself and just commit to a fistfight already. He had no patience for subtlety and there was nothing subtle about a bar brawl.

Ever since he'd entered the city three days ago, Griffey knew he was being followed. As a Ranger, tracking things was his business, so it wasn't hard to tell. The worst part was that Griffey's spirit was so defeated that he hadn't done anything about it. Hadn't set up a little trap encounter or smoked out the tail or even tried to shake it altogether. Instead, he'd just hid from the problem. Hid in plain sight. He'd let the paranoia eat him. Let himself get weak. Vulnerable to insults.

And a crippling insult was only minutes away from striking Griffey in the chest.

"Listen, I'm sorry," Griffey said in an awkward mumble. "Please. Continue. Who's next?"

The jolliness pounced back to Brisk's dimples with a quick spring and a gamely smile. Brisk resumed his crowd analysis, but this time he didn't bother with a boisterous wave. "You've seen the elves, peppered throughout the bar tonight, I'm sure?" Brisk's voice was now a hush.

"Brother, I'm a Ranger," Griffey supplied. "I try not to miss much."

This wasn't exactly true, of course. Griffey didn't have much patience for observation and gathering information. And, of all the Rangers, he wasn't the most accomplished at discipline.

Still, Griffey had marked the elves in the crowd. These creatures stood lofty and golden with soft faces and long, silky white hair. Sometimes their slender bodies and lightweight feminine appearances drew in a drunk looking for a fight. But provoking an elf was terrible for one's health.

"By my count, there's five elves in here tonight," Brisk went on. "They make everybody uneasy with their empty gazes and eyes that don't blink much. Plus they don't drink beer and only drink hot cider, so that doesn't inspire much trust at all. They get ignored because they're not fun to talk to and they're not fun to drunk with. Not fun to pick a fight with, either. I heard that, a few weeks ago, a fella entertained himself by insulting one of the elves' mothers. Got his ass shot through a wall."

Brisk nodded, eyebrows up, as if to say, *crazy, right?* "The elves in this city have trouble finding work, as well, and the only job they can usually get is getting apprenticed as Sorcerers. Which means they work for the High Sorceror. That's one spooky Mage, by the way. So, my theory is that the High Sorcerer stations these guys around the castle and they cast spells of *Mental Calm* or something. Basically, they're a secret force that keeps everybody in line." When Griffey tried to speak, Brisk waved him off. "Ho now, I'm not saying these elves are terrible people. They probably hate that job. They're forced to stand around and observe the humanity of Rivercrest all day and night. Buncha people grumbling all day about the economy and the taxes. Not a fun crowd to hang around."

Griffey's drawn, wearied face wasn't a fun thing to be around right now, either. The Ranger gave a heavy sigh and said, "Frishka knows this castle's got a lot of problems, that's for sure…"

Brisk took a gulp of ale, then massaged his mug between his palms. His tone turned serious. "Now don't get upset over honesty here. I know you had your reasons for signing on with the Rangers and striking out across the countryside… but, sometimes I fear you may be losing your connection with humanity. I mean, the wilderness is the *wilderness* for a reason. You've got so much here in the castle for you, if you'd only just take it. Lord Frishka knows we could use you…"

Griffey's eyes had dropped away from his friend's face to study the grooves and wrinkles of the tabletop, filled with rivers of foamy liquid. He also noticed an unwanted warmth threading up within his eyelids. "I still believe my father can fix it all…"

Brisk nodded with somber agreement. "I think so, too, brother. You know I still believe…"

Their words crumbled into a reflective silence of sorrowful fragility.

To fill the gap, they clanked their mugs together in a wordless toast.

That sensitive reverie was shattered by a boast across the barroom…

◇ CHAPTER THE FOURTH. ◇
◇Barroom Brawl and Broken Bones.◇

In the span of time between the mug meeting Griffey's lips and the cup smacking back down to the tabletop, many things transpired.

First, Parker drained the final swig of his beer.

Second, his mind rang clear.

As it so often happens, a pang of guilt woke him right up. Forced him to see how Frishkadammed selfish he'd been. How childish. He saw that the only solution, the only way to fix the last three days, was to excuse himself from the company of his buddy Brisk and free himself from the gruff, sour confines of Brumble tavern. From there, he would go visit his father.

Even more guilt ate at him as if it were acid hissing on metal. During his six-month assignment in the woods, he'd never settled on the right thing to say to his father when he met with him in the castle. Now his mind replayed his woeful behavior over the last three days.

He'd been up north, exploring the lowest reaches of the Willowflow forest, and it rained upon his return to Rivercrest. Slumped and drenched, he and his brown-with-white-spots horse trotted down muddy, sloppy, empty streets. *So much for a party bursting with kisses and hugs and songs.* He'd sought shelter at a place where he knew he could stable his horse, secure a beer, acquire a room, and not be noticed. Such a locale did not equate to insightful conversation or delightful company, and he knew exactly where to find it. After a hot bath, he shacked up and shook the sheets with a woman whose name he forgot.

The second day delivered a similar itinerary. This one included no rain but oppressive clouds, a visit to the armory to sharpen his swords and replenish his arrows, and a meeting with his superiors to deliver his report. That afternoon, he shacked up and shook the sheets again, this time with a blonde whose companionship cost considerably more than the previous brunette and her extreme prices left little time for introductions.

His mood on the second day was not much of an improvement over the downcast and drizzle featured on the first. Meeting with his captains on the River Guard and delivering his report only reinforced his general lack of merriment. He'd relayed what he'd seen, what he'd discovered, on the trails through the willows, and he'd done so with the articulate grace of a poet. While his vivid descriptions impressed one of the captains, the other two were snippy and suspicious. Quite fast, it became clear that Rivercrest policy was not much concerned about distant threats anymore. There was a palpable sense of isolation, of *drawing in*, and it sucked the air from the room.

With his report and suggestions disregarded with calm appeasement, Griffey knew what he could've done next. *What I should've done next, Frishkadammit.* He should've gone straight to the Second King. But that was when pride slithered its tentacles onto his shoulders to hold him down, keep him restrained, keep proximity to his throat in case he tried anything. Anything that would make him look weak or predictable or embarrassed. Or make him feel heat on his face.

He'd met with his sister yesterday evening and Sho'pa took care to encourage him to meet with the Second King. Her newfound path as a Warrior Monk allowed her a high level of sensitivity to the thoughts and concerns of others, but her training also left little care for politics. Ultimately, their father was a politician now—freely elected and held accountable—and, for Sho'pa, apparently, this overrode any family ties. She still loved their father fiercely, but only pushed Griffey to visit him for personal catch-up good-time reasons. He'd offered a pledge to do so and the lie stung his tongue.

Perhaps more than the rest of his behavior, he felt the most guilty over his prevailing attitude of: *my father should come visit me, why the hell do I have to go visit him!* No matter how many times he justified it or mentally sold it to himself, it was a lie. He knew damned well that his father was supremely busy. Plus, neither John Parker nor an Oracle nor anyone else really knew the schedules of the Rangers. When to expect their returns, when to meet with them.

I've been here for three days. I'm leaving at sunrise. And, Frishka-be-damned, I'm going to see my father. He resolved to quell his self-loathing and do something positive instead.

As his mug slapped the table, he waited anxiously for Brisk to guzzle the remainder of his beer. Griffey's brain was buzzing. He flirted with fantasies of not only redeeming the past three days, but also helping his father save the realm. He considered where his father might be found tonight. Where the scene would be, the location of his vindication. *Maybe the tower, perhaps he's in the tower. More likely the cellar chambers. In the study. The man works late. Works too hard.*

Randomly, a childhood memory popped into his head. It was a resting day in Rivercrest, yet John Parker still insisted on working, busily scribbling out scrolls and sealing up envelopes. Young'uns Sho'pa and Griffey scampered into their father's office and, for once, the man put away his quill and sealed up his ink. He led them on a romp out the door and a quest across the castle. A quest for pets! By sundown, John Parker had purchased a yellow frog for his daughter and a puppy for his son. While Sho'pa's critter was not only equipped with tremendous leaping abilities, it could also walk on the walls and the ceilings! Griffey wasn't jealous. He was too busy rolling on the rug and galloping warmly about with his furry newfound companion. On that fine day, John Parker was an everlasting hero.

Brisk lowered his mug with a hearty **bonk** and unleashed a thunderous burp.

For a moment, the two friends just stared at each other in silence across the table.

"Hasn't been a proper tavern in this damn castle since the Basement King stole the crown."

The deep voice was so syrupy smooth it was almost languid. More of a dessert than a meal.

Whatever Brisk saw overtake Griffey's face, it must not have been pleasant. The Cook began to shake his head with furious, frail concern, as if begging, hoping, to divert and dissuade the Ranger's expression from morphing into anger and spawning trouble. As for which specific expression Parker's face now wore, the man who owned it could not even say. It was as if his body and senses were struck numb, and all that remained was a fire in his chest. When feeling finally did return, it only surfaced in his fingers, knotting his hands into sweaty fists. He hauled a breath of hot air deep into his lungs.

The Ranger shoved back from the table and stood. The feeble, dismayed protests of the trembling Cook went completely ignored. Brisk could only watch as his friend turned away.

As he pivoted, Griffey felt a wobble in his knees and recalled how many beers he and Brisk had pounded. Or, well, his recollection of the precise number was pretty fuzzy right now.

The shoulders of two bystanders split out wide, revealing a devilish creature with a smooth grin and a casual lean. One elbow planted on the bar, a glass chalice spinning upon his fingertips, purple liquid swirling inside. Over seven-foot, he wore all black—chain-mail, trenchcoat, boots, and trail hat. His face was an elongated half-moon, a carrot nose pierced with spikes, cheeks and chin devoid of facial hair, eerily smooth. Every inch of his visible skin was stained with a twist of borlog tattoos. Borlogs were similar to (and uglier than) vampires—in all Griffey's years of education, that was the closest comparison he could manage.

Ulkar. The man's name shot through Griffey's mind with bitter recognition. As was his habit while in the castle—a people habit, a city habit—he quickly rattled off what he knew about the man. *Mercenary. Dual-weapon combat. Usually favors a dagger and hatchet. Human... with borlog blood.*

"Lookit, folks. There's a sperm-splat offspring of our Cellar King, right there."

Ulkar's drawl was lazy, almost playful. The tone was nearly more infuriating than the words.

Griffey Parker breathed deep. Though he didn't know it, had he left right then, ignored the taunts and exited into the starboard hallway, he would've been there to not only witness but possibly stop the red-black spell-ball assassin. Instead, he balled his fists.

"Frishka would die if he knew how many jobs your father cut from this kingdom," Ulkar oozed silkily. "Of course, you prefer vagabond employment where civilization ends and deer shit begins."

It was more than displeasure over his last three days which propelled the Ranger into the fight. And it was more than compensating for his current mood. It was also blind pride for his family crest.

Griffey was at the man in a flash. He covered the distance in the split of a blink. He faked a jab at Ulkar's face with his left hand—knowing the mercenary's attack would come from that side. Sure enough, a blade slipped magically from Ulkar's sleeve and into the man's gloved right hand. Parker was able to dodge by weaving out wide-right. As he did so, he shoved up at the chalice in the offender's hand, smashing the goblet into Ulkar's face. The shattered glass sliced his cheeks and cut his forehead and slit his lips and sprayed a mist of blood and elicited a shriek of painful watery outrage.

A tall man grabbed Griffey's arm while another dealt a

slug to his jaw. The Ranger reeled drunkenly and crashed into a cluster of people, whom proceeded to domino into a table of dwarves. A full mug of ale—freshly deposited by a pretty bar maid only seconds prior—toppled over and dumped a deluge across the cards of a money game unfolding with tension in every flip of the cards.

The dwarf currently winning the card game was incensed, while his opponent was content to slip away with a humble shrug. The winning dwarf stamped down hard—stone-sole boot with a mighty weight behind it—onto the foot of the stumbling man responsible for ruining the card game. Gripped with insanity over his broken foot, this man fell forward and flipped the dwarves' table completely over—sending it crashing side-long into an elf, drifting calmly past.

By now, Griffey Parker was back on his feet, though he was still dizzy from the shot to his jaw. One of Ulkar's gigantic muscle-mountain side-kicks drew out a pair of nunchucks and advanced, whipping the sticks and snapping the connector chains. Cursing his courteous, responsible decision to leave his weapons back in his room, Parker grabbed a wooden barstool. He hoisted it up just in time to greet the attacker's onslaught. The sticks and chains instantly entangled with the protruding roots of the stool. While Ulkar's side-kick gawped with dumb fascination at the knotted cluster of furniture and weaponry, the Ranger swung out wide and bashed him in the face.

Ulkar must have enchanted his side-kicks—some kind of defensive reinforcement spell—because Parker's right hand felt as if it just collided with an invisible metallic exoskeleton.

A jolt of pain quivered through the bones of his hand. His eyes clamped shut, tears spilled down his cheeks, hot breath seethed through his teeth. He cradled his throbbing paw, curling and hunching.

He opened his eyes and saw Ulkar stomping towards him, framed within the screaming chaos.

The mercenary's face was hideous. Scars with haphazard streaks of bright scarlet glistening atop a glare of rage. While it was terrifying to have such a bloodthirsty force approaching him, it also made him forget his pain. For an absurd instant, he actually felt a pang of sympathy for the man. Sure, Ulkar had intended to provoke the Son of the Second King, but, ultimately, Ulkar had done nothing more egregious than say words. No one guilty of speaking simple words deserved to be disfigured so publicly, so permanently. That wasn't what the Parker family aspired Rivercrest to stand for.

All extensions of tenderness and empathy vanished as Ulkar lifted a dagger in one hand and a hatchet in the other. He growled, baring a rack of bloody teeth. In that charming moment, his half-portion of borlog heritage really seemed to shine. Griffey wasn't scared, but he still chose to turn and flee. He didn't choose to run because he was defenseless and there were no more barstools around. He tried to run because he had to get to his father. The urgency of a visit to John Parker was overwhelming.

The Ranger smacked into a wall of bodies and rebounded back into the path of Ulkar and his weapons. Griffey stared back at the borlog, then glanced over and spied a golden amulet trailing from a neckchain, winking a scarlet eye. *Paladin!* The fiery eyes of the dragonborn locked on Parker's face.

"Help, Paladin! I beg you!" the Ranger cried desperately. He imagined the creature stepping in and roasting Ulkar with a belch of fire. But the Paladin only stared. Did not flinch. Did not intervene.

This crushed Griffey's hope in the final seconds before the half-borlog hacked him to pieces.

Then the elves took action. The elf who was blind-sided by a flipping table (which had flung beer in his face along with wet, soggy playing cards) was especially inspired. From the splayed fingertips of outstretched hands, they hurled spells of debilitation into the crowd in a rapid-fire spree.

One tall man was struck with a *Paralyze* spell and fell with his body as stiff and rigid as one of the floorboards he smacked into. A fat bearded man was *Frozen* in stone, his expression of shock immortalized. One guy actually ran into his shoulder and was knocked unconscious. One of the dwarves was bound with *Unseen Ropes* and dangled from the ceiling. Another dwarf felt the alcohol content in his system get doubled and he lost both his passion for fighting and his ability to stand.

Griffey was rocked with a *Stun* spell and stood there, helpless, with his hands outstretched. Ulkar was socked with a charm of *Restraint*. Ulkar's muscles numbed and his movements were slowed, but he still inched closer as the mayhem in Brumble tavern began to die out. The charm of *Restraint* kept Ulkar from killing Griffey, but, with a final gasp, Ulkar spun his hatchet so the blunt backside of the blade was facing out. Once again, Griffey saw the Paladin nearby, and, once again, the dragonborn did not come to his aid. The flat of Ulkar's hatchet **cracked** Griffey's right hand and shattered it.

He did not scream, he did not twitch, but the pain was cosmically exquisite.

Soon, all was calm. Shuffling feet, weary groans, a blurt of protest from mister Brumble behind the bar, and the muffled *thump* of the fat tabby cat abandoning his post to trot indignantly away.

Meticulously, the elves began to sort and process, dealing sentences as they saw fit.

Still stunned, and riddled with pain, Griffey found time to be surprised by the elves' operation. Much had changed since he'd been away these last six months. *Looks like Brisk was right.*

While elven secret forces didn't bother him, being unable to move certainly did.

Suddenly, his good buddy Brisk appeared before him, shoving the stiffened Ulkar aside.

The dark-skinned Cook shook his head and clicked his

tongue disapprovingly before leaning in to examine Griffey's hand. "Y'know, lad," the Cook hissed, "just because ole Brisk tells you that he's been getting training as a Healer, that doesn't mean you need to go and test his skills!"

Brisk squeezed the knuckles on Parker's right paw and a bolt of dazzling pain erupted. He fell unconscious a moment later—and the elves tossed him in the dungeons shortly after that—but, first, he heard Brisk distantly and morbidly inform him: "Brother, these bones are busted…"

Shortly thereafter, the dragonborn named Konragen grew restless and turned away. It was part of his Paladin pledge to not interfere in the business of others, yet he was also growing bored with the flavorless procedural drawl of the elves interrogating witnesses and sorting out the brawlers from the bystanders. Konragen was certainly not opposed to violence, but the circumstances had to be ideal. The fight he'd just seen was a pitiful display of ego and the aftermath was just as sad.

Opting for fresh air, he stepped out into the western courtyard. Beneath the dual moons, within the scrawl of starlight, he spied the constellation of Kraven. An omen of mighty struggle and change. He spied the dot of a planet with tiny lights buzzing and glinting around it, as if it were some brilliant beehive. His heart bloomed with wonder. His pulse fired with surprise. Across the tranquility, a thing hurtled through the shadows, tying to stay hidden. For a bleak moment, the culprit slipped into view.

Konragen's volcanic eyes gaped as the red-black spell-ball vanished in the night…

◇ CHAPTER THE FIFTH. ◇
◇Death, Fire, and Smoke.◇

Rivercrest castle was on fire.

Save for the literal presence of flames, this was certainly true. Similar to death, fire possesses both both demolishing sadness and extreme value. The downside of death, both naturally and obviously, is the loss of friends and family. The value of death is demonstrated on every battlefield—where the corpses of the enemy translate to ensuring your country's way of life shall continue to flourish uninterrupted. Such stakes, and the hopes that hang on their hooks, are incredibly high. Death has an affinity for getting people to buy in.

Fire holds the power to rally up the multitudes, as well. This is manifested every time weary travelers huddle around the crackles of their campfires and when families cluster near the hearth on chilly nights. Fire emits comforting warmth, just as the body heat of a parent eases a child's fears or the hot skin of a lover elicits ecstasy. Fire boils water, keeps it safe. Fire cooks food for the dinner table.

Conversely, the customs of fire, the traditions it worships, tend to destroy the fragile bonds which hold life together. The majority of people, even in this dark age, assemble in castles. From there, they further divide themselves and settle into houses. Fire is known to eat both homes and cities.

People hold uneasy alliances with both death and fire, yet such contracts are inevitable.

While death is rather unpleasant, and fire often gives birth to death, smoke is the most egregious actor of the triumvirate.

Perhaps what makes it such a loathsome enemy is the subtlety with which it swims. When a house burns, none of the onlookers gape at the black cloud up above the action, for the roaring orange of fire draws and hogs every eye.

While smoke is an enemy whose passage goes mostly unnoticed, its insults are guaranteed to be felt. Often, by the time its wicked fingers reach nightbound nostrils and shatter peaceful slumbers, the encroaching smoke is usually too thick for it to be repelled. While the flames are still dancing carefree in the kitchen, smoke advances, trespasses, and fortifies. Upon arrival in a tranquil bedroom, before it begins its nasty tickles, smoke poisons the air. This villain claims one of life's most vital substances and pollutes it with death. The crusty chalky coal taste of smoke infects more than just the unsuspecting lungs who suck it down for sustenance. Smoke stitches its way into the fabric of clothing, it asserts parasitic dominance in the fur of dogs and cats, and it even sours the taste of ale sealed in tankards and barrels. Even if the fire is defeated, the assassin known as smoke still lingers and gestates.

In Rivercrest castle, on this fateful summer night, the news of the death of the Second King—and all the weeping, horrified hysteria entrenched in the black gums between its fangs—spread with the same abrasive tenacity as smoke.

Shortly after his death, John Parker's body was discovered...

◇ CHAPTER THE SIXTH. ◇
◇Spreading Smoke.◇

Raysmith was in his sixth year of apprenticeship, and was serving under his second consecutive Second King. He'd begun his service under the previous King Two and assisted that man for four years before having his contract carry over into the current administration. The term of a freely-elected Second King happened to be a total of six years—but the good ones were allowed a chance of two additional years, also through open election in the public courtyard.

The last Second King had not been a very good one, and thus failed to win a seventh and eighth year of power. Raysmith could testify to Second King Carpenter's poor qualifications. He'd witnessed the man's crippling indecision, sputtering vacuity, and conniving fondness for shady backdoor dealings. The man was known to shave tallies off the gold sheets, spend his evenings romping through the whorehouses, and hire out mercenaries using public funds.

Though the results had been limited—and his support amongst the other rulers was mild and, at best, lukewarm—the new Second King had a chance to achieve something special. At least in Raysmith's humble estimation, anyway. From his viewpoint, John Parker's heart was a noble one.

Raysmith was in his early second-level years and believed he could be spending his youthful energy in far more entertaining pursuits rather than what he was doing tonight. For the past several hours, he'd been scuttling through the halls of the Rivercrest catacombs, digging up old scrolls from candlelit chambers, hustling them over to the office of the Second King, only to watch with wide eyes and cold sweat on his forehead as

John Parker scrutinized his document deliveries and told Raysmith they weren't the ones he was looking for. As a gesture of good faith, Parker would give this denouncement in a soft tone with a kind, weary smile, and even stash the unwarranted scrolls in a pile just so Raysmith wouldn't feel so guilty about having brought the wrong one over.

Rather than embarrassment over such mistakes, Raysmith often just felt frustrated by the Second King's sympathy. Still, he would keep trying. Would keep fetching—or trying to fetch—whatever item or piece of information Parker thought would help improve this world. Raysmith believed in the man. He certainly wouldn't have been down here working so late for the last King Two.

Yet Raysmith was thinking about none of that tonight. His mind was buzzing over what he'd witnessed a few minutes ago. A Ranger man, weary from the trail, tromped towards John Parker's office with a scroll in his clutches and a worried, determined look upon his weathered face.

Juggling four scrolls under his left arm—each long and awkward and comprised of ancient parchment which was a constant threat to crumble into dust—plus a lantern in his right hand—with a squeaky handle and hot wax dripping from its leaky base—Raysmith reached the door of the Second King's office. Using his shoulder, he gave it a shove and found it unmoving. That was odd.

He stood there, dumbstruck and puzzled, hoping he wouldn't accidentally acquaint the lantern with the scrolls and burst them stupidly aflame. From behind him came a hiss through the darkness. He snapped over that way with a rasp of breath. For a long moment there was nothing but dead silence.

For the two-thousandth time, he cursed King Parker for choosing to work down here in this awful basement. He redoubled his grip on all his items and planted another firm shoulder at the door. This time, it relented with a bitter screech.

Something inside fell to the floor with a clatter. It sounded close, as if his entry caused the disruption. He rammed the door wide enough to fit an elbow in the gap.

Something was blocking the door. After a few more seconds of squirming, straining, slipping, and struggling, he was able to see inside a little bit. Books were heaped inside the door; a mound of heavy red leather volumes spewed out by an overturned oak bookcase. This served as his first stab of alarm. The Second King was indulgent with his reading material, and often clumsy and forgetful, but the man was far from negligent. Books meant to be on shelves would not remain long on the floor under the watch of John Parker. No matter his other concerns, he would fix that problem first.

"Master… Parker?" the scribe grunted with irritation.

There came no response from inside. A cold sweat of worry and fear streamed across Raysmith's forehead. As it dribbled down his cheeks and stung his eyes, he felt his palms begin to sweat, as well. Hating the feeling of *going backwards* at such a crucial time, the scribe dipped back into the hall and deposited the four scrolls and lantern on the stone floor. Those items didn't seem as important now as they had so recently.

With his hands now free, he went back to shoving at the door and got it open.

He staggered inside and immediately slipped on something. He grabbed hold of a statue but his slick fingers betrayed him and dumped him to the ground, scattering papers like pigeons.

"*Frishkadammit!* Master Parker! Do you hear me, Master Parker!"

Ignoring the pain of his landing, pulsing in his ribs and hip, Raysmith scrambled to his feet and dodged around giant globes and cluttered tabletops and suits of armor as he raced across the confines.

When he saw the blood he nearly screamed. But all the air

was sucked from his system. Instead, he was filled with soundless, crippling dread. Eyes wide, tears mixing with the sweat on his face, he ran to the cabinet in the far corner of the room. He fished his keyring-necklace up from his collar and unlocked the cupboard. Levitating inside was the magic bell. The signal to the Sorcerer…

◇ ◇ ◇

"The blood was, uh, stained all on the lookout tower. One could even see his, uh, innard pieces and bones and such. Oh Frishka, it was Hell. No witnesses. No eyes on the crime. So much blood—"

The scratching of the quill abruptly stopped. The account of Captain Nettle had been flowing smoothly across the parchment, with the enchanted feather pen twitching and writing unassisted. But now, the transcription halted. The quill lifted with a *scritch* and hovered briefly in the air, as if unsure what to do with itself. Soon enough, it elected to float over for a dip in the ink bottle.

The man seated across the desk from Kozard had ceased his narration so that he could weep.

This intermission made Kozard shake his head in disgust.

The High Sorcerer was deeply aged, but not nearly as seasoned as High Sorcerers were typically known to be. Kozard's strict, pointed, braided beard was still yellow-brown in color. His beard hadn't even faded to a shade of wisdom white or commendable gray. Plus, his face was growing fat around the edges, unlike the youthful faces of most old elves. Kozard even had a beer gut developing, and this trait, especially, was unbecoming of a creature with dominant elf blood.

While the High Sorcerer did not appreciate being bothered at any time of the day, he definitely did not approve of being interrupted at this time of night. Elves didn't actually need to sleep at night, as four solid hours of meditation was enough to leave them fully refreshed, but Kozard hated both sleeping and meditating. In fact, he saw those as marks of weakness and a waste of time. Thus, he often worked overnight, secluded in his high-tower office, hunkered over spell scrolls, his heavy eyes blinking shut and snapping open until his overtaxed mind lapsed into a restless snooze.

Ultimately, forcing himself to work the late hours never really earned the High Sorcerer mastery of very many charms, but, still, he did not enjoy being interrupted. He especially did not appreciate being forced to listen to a sobbing report from a post as far beneath his feet as the Night Captain of the Second Unit River Guard. *Why do I need to be here right now*, Kozard mentally grumbled. *Couldn't the Frishkadammed quill do the recording without my supervision?*

Of course, it was a decree of the kingdom that such transcriptions needed to be overseen by a member of the ruling class. But Kozard had ascended to *High Sorcerer.* He could ignore petty decrees.

Kozard's attentiveness was not helped by the fact that listening to Night Captain Nettle talk was torture for an educated mind. Nettle was prone to jumping randomly from thought-to-thought and inserted "*uh*'s" and "*um*'s" between the rest of his words with a grating, infuriating frequency.

During the Night Captain's tale, the High Sorcerer's eyes kept flicking away from his desk. To the black-crystal shelves which lined the dark walls of his upper-tower chamber. Upon those shelves sat rows and rows of dense old books, a handful of grinning skulls (mostly of the elf and human variety, plus one horned borlog skull), a tantalizing array of vials aglow with grape and green liquids, and a neighborhood of enchanted hourglasses plump with violet sands which always recycled and flowed.

But Kozard's gaze flipped right past all that senseless paraphernalia and locked upon the item which so fascinated him this evening. (Everyday, and often every night, the High Sorcerer's aggressive manner would latch obsessively onto one particular item or spell scroll. After a few hours' time, he would grasp the secret of the item or wield the spell ability or discard it as a useless child's toy rather than admitting defeat.) Tonight, his passion was focused on a monocle with a black lens.

Each time he wore the eyeglass, the High Sorcerer gained an elevated level of sight. He could see special things, acquire information. Plus, the circular monocle was tinted, polarized, and darkened to an admirable level which made him feel like a pirate when he wore it. This image made him feel confident and rather proud. *Pirate Sorcerer!*

"Um, excuse me, High Sorcerer," Captain Nettle said, wiping his eyes, clearing his throat and making other filthy hacking noises which further disgusted his host. Between them, the quill raced back to its station and resumed its scribbles. "I don't, uh, usually cry when I'm on duty, but, you see, sir… this is three of my men that got killed tonight. All of 'em got families. All of 'em under my docket. Oh, dear Frishka. We didn't find no tracks or nothin' from a killer leading up there, so…"

"So…?" the High Sorcerer said, waving an impatient hand.

"So, uh, we believed maybe magic was involved here. Dark magic, at that."

"You *believed*, eh?" Kozard taunted testily. "When something strange or something sad happens, blaming magic is the first platform peasant-brains such as yourself leap to. It sickens me."

Captain Nettle bristled at this. "Well, how almighty else would *you* explain it?" he snapped. (If there was one good thing about Nettle getting angry, it was that the dreaded "*uh*'s" and "*um*'s" vanished from his speech.) "There weren't no tracks. No signs of an intruder up there."

Kozard clapped his hands as a devilish smile split his doughy face. His pointy ears lifted high.

"My my, now now, it seems you *do* have a little fire in

your fireplace after all, Night Captain Nettle. Perhaps you aren't just a ball of sobs and stutters, after all."

The River Guardsman paused, gulped, raised an eyebrow. "Indeed, I've got some fire in my veins over this issue. These is my men who was killed. One fella, in the top-west tower, named Roninson. Then, uh, in the lower-west tower, a man named Polla. Um, in between 'em, a fella named Alkent. Didn't know him much, but still. Tragedies, all of 'em… Now, I need you to tell me how three Guardsmen in three consecutive towers got killed so quickly with no sign of a killer."

"I'll tell you no such thing," Kozard harshly declared. "Have you told anyone else of this?"

The Captain proceeded to gibber and babble and it gave the elf a headache.

"Why did you come to me with this information? Why not your River Guard superior?"

"Well, um, he's asleep. And, uh, there was dark magic involved in the murders so I figured—"

"Who else knows of this?" Kozard demanded, his bark dropping to a whisper.

"Well, um, only me and two Guardsmen who made the discoveries… But it, uh, the fraternity of knowin' ain't gonna stay so small for long. Uh, you see, I'm gonna need to assign someone to clean out them watchtowers. And I'm, um, gonna need to call in off-duties to fill those empty shifts. We, uh, can't have those posts unmanned. Uh, especially at night. And you know, um, how people talk…"

"Yes, yes. I know how people talk. What I need is for you and your men to quit talking."

Captain Nettle was positively puzzled at this remark. He didn't see why the High Sorcerer wasn't taking this issue more seriously. The damn castle was under attack yet he was talking nonsense.

Between them, on the broad desktop, the quill went on

scrawling its cursive swells.

"The two River Guardsmen who discovered the bodies, where are they now?"

"Them? Well, uh, they're right outside this room! They's waitin' in the hall f—"

"—Good. Assign them to the vacant watchtowers. They're going to complain about standing in puddles of blood from their fallen comrades, but I don't really care. I have memory wash potions. You'll only have two of the three empty towers staffed, but that will have to work for now—"

"—but, uh, what about—"

"—Frishkadammit, Nettle, isn't it clear by now? I've got solutions to all your miserable problems. You're concerned about the mess. About cleaning the damn towers. I'm going to send for a low-level Sorcerer. One I've got in training. His name is Ramsey. He's an underachieving Seventh Year who is too stupid and too scared of failing my program to say too much about what he sees when he cleans the towers."

Nettle shook his head with a sad, disdainful frown. "You're gonna be usin' dark magic to clean up the murders of my men... murders which was done with dark magic in the first place..."

Kozard could sense resentment wafting off the River Guardsman in rich, stuffy waves. The tone of the man's voice left the elf incensed. No guest in his office should sit at his desk and insult him.

"If you want to keep your job as Captain of the *Second Unit night shift*, you will remain quiet. Right. Now. Kozard the High Sorcerer has delivered your orders. Now go."

"Uh, just so's you knows," Nettle stated defiantly, "this here paper with the, um, the floating writing pen is recording every awful thing you say—"

"—Did you know that paper burns, Captain? Were you aware of this fundamental fact?"

The Captain gulped. The statements from this elf were simply astounding. It was tough to control his furious disbelief over the elf's casual, drawling implication that destroying an official record might be standard procedure. Three of Nettle's men had been slaughtered tonight, and this nettlesome elf was creating more problems where more problems weren't needed. It was beyond belief.

Captain Nettle thought again of his dead soldiers and saw he didn't care about risking the wrath of this bastard. "The last High Sorcerer was a friend of the River Guard. It kept him alive."

"That fool wasted his talents on gardening. A plant is nothing next to a spell."

Suddenly, a shriek rang out from a cabinet in the corner of the room. Both elf and man shot looks of shock in that direction, hearts hammering in their chests. "*Master elf! High Sorcerer!*" a shrill voice cried out, the sound transmitting from the levitating bell inside Kozard's cupboard. "It's apprentice Raysmith at the Second King's office! *Oh dear Frishka! Please come now!*"

Kozard and Nettle locked eyes. Without a word, the Captain stood and left.

"*Utzil*," Kozard muttered, and the feather quill dropped dead on the table as if shot from the sky. For a long time, the elf considered slotting in his magic monocle, then finally left for the basement.

Out in the hall, Nettle broke down and bled honesty to his men. His mood was sour after meeting Kozard, and he held zero Frishkadammed interest in discretion for the sake of the elf. He told his men about the distress call from the Second King's office. En route to stand on the bloody lookout towers, those men sent urgent messages to their wives. Reassuring, placating, *informative* messages.

And, thus, the spreading of the smoke cycled into full swing…

◇ CHAPTER THE SEVENTH. ◇
◇The Quest Response.◇

"**Y**ou saw the body, Kozard?"

The First King was standing at the window, facing away from the anxious jitters of his advisors. His face was lined with mid-age-years yet still handsome. The dusting crop of a beard sat upon his stern jawline, and his soft brown eyes dealt swift judgment. His brown hair had begun to go silver on the sides. His nose an inch from the glass, he was seeing more of his own reflection, a slurred, blurry, watery version of his face, than he was actually seeing what the window was intended to reveal—the shining moons and the sleeping city and the ominous forest looming out beyond.

Rodrick Callister stood facing away from his advisors—staring at his own distorted pond-surface dream-face—because he was afraid of displaying the emotions which were imperiously threatening to devastate his face. He'd been woke in the middle of the night and hadn't been sleeping very well in the hours before that, so, naturally, his mind should've been exhausted right now. But he was instead brutally focused.

No First King (or King of any grade, for that matter) wanted to be disturbed in the hours buried between dusk and dawn. Because such a disturbance was undoubtedly a nightmarish emergency.

At first, the knocks at Rodrick's door were timid. The King rolled over and found his wife, Queen Sheeva, also awake. She was on the outside stretch of her beauty and entertained as many extra-curricular lovers as Rodrick did, but they still loved each other. He respected her opinion enough to include her on his advisory council. They went to the door together. By the time they got there, the intensity of the knocks had become a pounding. Knocking at the door was Halderman, the duke of Rivercrest, Cal's top advisor. Had it been anyone less, they would've been looking at a dungeon wall.

Ten minutes later, the Top King and his small contingent of councilors were locked away in the command room. The confines held a wide desk, curved as a crescent moon, and were complete with a floor-to-ceiling window overlooking the streets of the castle. It was in that room, an overbearing oven of tension, that Rodrick Callister learned of the death of the Second King.

"Yes, Master, I witnessed the body," Kozard replied, his tone appropriately somber. The High Sorcerer was squirming on his feet, partly because he preferred sitting on his rump rather than standing and there weren't any open chairs left in here. He also wanted to get back to his darkened eyeglass.

Rodrick's shoulders sagged and he surprised himself by speaking his thoughts aloud. "So close to Midsummer's Eve… this is a terrible omen for the nobility of Rivercrest…" As soon as he'd said it, he instantly regretted it. He felt the others grow tense. He knew no one would comment on his superstition. They were all processing how weak it made him sound. It wasn't easy, but he forced out a gruff, professional request: "Kozard, give your best estimation as to the cause of death."

While the King stayed at the window, the rest of the heads swiveled to stare at the Sorcerer elf.

Kozard's tall pointy ears turned visibly red and the sight sent the group into an uproar. As this was a gathering of egos whom loved to hear their own voices talk—no matter if they had something important to say or not—a storm of objections churned up. *"This elf is not qualified to speak, he doesn't even have a chair!"* *"My King, I know you value Kozard's opinion, but the High Sorcerer deals in magic, not reality."* *"I should speak instead, I was actually born in Rivercrest!"* And so on.

From his stance at the window, breath gently fogging the glass, the First King sighed. His eye caught a flicker of movement in the window. For an empty, thoughtless moment, the source of that movement occupied his entire universe; his mind was focused on nothing else. Quickly, he discovered the movement was not outside, but rather reflected in the glass. It was a fly. A tiny creature, yet a profound annoyance. He grimly reflected that even First Kings weren't immune to pests.

Not even the blessing of Frishka and lordship over the kingdom could insulate him from the nibbling persistence of mankind's tiniest foes. From a practicality standpoint, such inconveniences bonded his existence with that of the common people. But Rodrick lacked the ability to coherently express the emotion of that connection. He would be publicly derided for even trying. He didn't enjoy concocting and delivering inspirational addresses to win friends to his side. He preferred the instant companionship of Rascal. Rascal was the source of another tiny movement in the glass, and Rascal was also not immune to the pests which plagued them all. Rascal had fleas scurrying in his fur.

Behind the King, curled beneath his desk, was his dog. Rascal was an old shaggy brown fella whom the Queen had gifted to him years ago. A source of loyalty with the kingdom on his shoulders.

In this current moment, Rodrick gladly would've cleared out the room, swept away the responsibilities of the kingdom, and cuddled up with the loving, uncomplicated company of his dog. If those were the circumstances, he would have space to calmly think. But the pup would stay stashed and cowering beneath his desk, and the clamor in his ears would continue. Until it got resolved.

It was rare for a First King in Rivercrest to work well alongside his secondary counterpart. The First Kings held their thrones for life, appointed to such heights via bloodline, while the Seconds were elected by the people, and were swapped out for another every six or eight years. This revolving door made working relationships difficult, for both Kings were expected to be equally as powerful yet only one was in for a limited term. Thus, everyone knew how imbalanced power was at the top.

Rodrick had been First King for ten years and had seen three Second Kings stand at his side. By far, John Parker had been the most professional. Unlike his predecessors, Parker wasn't ancient and stubborn, nor was he devious and corrupt. For their first year together, Callister was wary of him, but eventually came to value his input. Parker was an adult at the post; full of virtue and self-awareness. Parker knew his time on the high stage was a limited window, and he knew he would never get to be First King, either. The man held an ease of simplistic realism, plus an urgency to get work done.

Grateful to have a Second King that wasn't senile or evil, Cal actually came to rely on Parker.

"The office of the High Sorcerer received a report less than an hour ago," Kozard declared, "delivered by the Night Captain of the Second Unit River Guard... Three soldiers were killed tonight. In the watchtowers, west side of the castle. The side which faces Shadowbranch forest..."

"It was illegal for you to receive that report before I did," growled the River Guard Captain, a muscular bearded man named Trunk. "You're lucky you're not in chains right now, elvish filth!"

First King Callister massaged his face with his hands. "Continue, Kozard..."

"My dear Master, and my dear councilmen," the elf went on, "in my estimation, dark magic was employed in these killings. Most likely a green-blue spell-ball killed the Guardsmen in their towers..."

"Elf!" Trunk spat. "Tell us your theory for how *Parker*

perished!"

The High Sorcerer squirmed some more. "Well, I would suppose a duplicate green-blue spell-ball... I believe we can say with confidence that the four deaths are all connected. Thus—"

"—thus the caster of these spells is still out there!" Sheeva cut in. It was nice to have the First Queen present here tonight. But Rodrick's wife, with her tightly-braided brown hair, was all business. "In the forest, directly west of the castle. From my understanding of magic, he'll be weakened—"

"—Weakened, yes," Kozard agreed, "casting killing spells leaves the 'caster diminished. For a time, at least. He'll be traveling slowly—"

"—so we must act quickly!" Sheeva resumed. "And hope he has no assistance waiting for him!"

"*Assistance?*" Trunk mocked. "What about '*army*'? This Sorcerer assassin... what if the bastard *wants* us to chase him! Could be aiming to lure us into a trap in the trees of Shadowbranch! A massacre!"

First King Rodrick Callister finally turned to face the room and the chatter fell silent.

"This is not good, my friends. Not good at all. The kingdom looks weak right now. By association, *I* look weak right now..." His hands were sweaty and clammy and clenching.

His face twisted in morbid reflection. "It's been forty-two years since an in-office Second King was killed. Master Updike. Served at the shoulder of grandfather, Fred Callister. Death by poison."

"...poison leaf of *rumjin*..." a voice whispered softly across the room.

Chairs croaked and necks creaked as everyone pivoted to stare at Kozard.

The High Sorcerer faked a cough. "A herb from Meltrock Islands. A coward's tool."

They gaped for a while at the elf with the braided yellow-brown beard, then turned away again.

The Top King took a seat at his desk, reached underneath and appeared to give a distracted yet adoring series of scratches and pats to his dog. From there, his face turned deathly serious. His soft brown eyes locked on the Sorcerer. "If we capture the spellcaster... could this be reversed?"

Kozard hesitated. Then stammered, "... it would be difficult, Master... but not impossible..."

An insurrection of grumbling began to rise, so Callister continued.

"Duke Halderman... what is the procedure for handling such a dreadful tragedy?"

The older man with white primly-combed hair and a sharp white beard cleared his throat. "Rivercrest law states that, in cases of abrupt expiration of leadership, succession is to b—"

"I don't give a Frishkadamn about *succession*, Halderman," the First King seethed.

The duke of the kingdom, the head of the navy, paused for a moment. "According to Rivercrest law, once caught, the accused is to be brought to trial... That trial is to be overseen, not by the head of the River Guard, but by the closest family members of the victims whom were killed..."

"We haven't caught any killer yet, you fool," Trunk informed the duke.

"Which is why we must act quickly!" Sheeva injected, getting flustered at the lack of urgency.

"If the killer flees the scene-of-crime," the duke went on, "then he is to be pursued."

"I doubt Rivercrest law dictates who can pursue and who cannot," Sheeva scoffed.

"It does, actually," Halderman said. "The quest is to be run by those sa—"

"—those same people selected to oversee the trial," Rodrick finished for him.

Duke Halderman shrugged, nodded, and raised a hand to give the King credit.

"A Response Quest..." the First King whispered.

"Well, we can't do *that*," Sheeva griped. "That's crazy. Send a bunch of sad, sleepy, weeping people? That's the same as sending a goose."

"Every man and woman in the River Guard is needed where they are," Trunk stubbornly asserted. "Watching from the battlements and running the riverfront. Shipments are more valuable now than ever. Our enemies on the waters are ferocious. The squid-pirates alone are killing us."

There was a pause. Then Rodrick couldn't help but put forth more superstition. "Is it true what they say? Magic stains the waters wherever the squid-ships sail? From what I've heard, in the water around their ships, time is distorted..." The room went rigid with tortured discomfort. Bodies squirmed. Fingers tapped and fidgeted. Eyes flicked and foreheads sweated as they waited it out. "Trunk. Is it true that the River Guard has conducted experiments on samples of that water? That some men are heaved as much as a year into the future?" Trunk avoided eye contact. The air grew stiff and stuffy.

Rodrick sobered, and resumed with a commanding tone: "We won't be sending River Guardsmen. We will follow the code of Rivercrest. I want the expedition assembled and supplied and I want them on the trail by dawn. Before dawn would be preferable. No matter how weak this dark spellcaster is, I grant him no advantages."

"*Advantages?*" Sheeva spouted. "You're sending weeping widows after him!"

"One capable representative from each offended bloodline," Halderman corrected. "And the presence of a Rivercrest Sorcerer is needed, as well. For purposes of safety and medical support."

"He—you—no—he made that last part up!" Kozard cried,

sweating with strangled disbelief.

"You're already involved," the King said. "Same with your apprentice, whom you had clean up the blood on the watchtowers." The High Sorcerer was visibly surprised that Cal knew about that.

"The filthy elf has made it clear that he's acquainted with dark magic, too," Trunk added.

"And a Paladin is also required," duke Halderman threw in, almost as an afterthought.

"We aren't sending twenty people out there, are we?" Sheeva complained.

"They won't be as many as you think, darling," the King assured her. "And they won't be as weak as you think, either. Neither weak nor leaderless. I believe John Parker's son is actually in Rivercrest tonight. He's a fighter, that one. An accomplished Ranger. He will go for his father…

"May Frishka shine upon our decisions here tonight. Dismissed."

◇ ◇ ◇

When the fist landed with a knock upon his door, Rodrick Callister was sitting on the carpet, hugging his dog, face buried in the creature's comforting fur. The First King took a moment to calm his emotions and wipe his eyes, then called for them to enter. He watched helplessly as his dog struggled from his grasp and ran to the door. That was strange. And it started growling. Even stranger.

There was a muffled kick and a heartbreaking *yelp* from his dog. King Callister shot up, turned, and recoiled with shock. The man's tattooed face was hideously scarred. The red wounds were fresh.

"*Ulkar…*"

◇CHASE QUEST◇

◇ CHAPTER THE EIGHTH. ◇
◇The Dragon in the Doorway.◇

It was still dark in the city, though the eyelids of dawn would soon draw open.

Ramsey the Green was tempted to conjure a *Torch* spell to light his path through the twisting labyrinth of stone-wall alleyways. But he resisted the urge, because this was not a part of town where one wanted to draw attention. Especially an elf. Especially an elf of the higher class.

So Ramsey relied on his night-vision instead. It wasn't quite as good as illumination from an actual fire-torch, because his night eyes merely threw a forest green color upon the surfaces around him and the edges of corners tended to blend in with turns and backgrounds. But he could see well enough.

He'd never been to this part of the city, though, and maybe a torch to announce himself wouldn't be so bad. Just beyond these alleys, in a cluster of round-topped cottages, lived the dragonfolk. Feeling nervous, he clung to the fact that all dragonfolk in Rivercrest were required to adopt the sacred oath of the Paladins. (According to his history studies, he gathered that this mandate was a kind of forced *balance-out*, meant to smooth over memories of the fiery hell the dragons' ancestors once rained upon elves, dwarves, and men.) The Paladin oath tied one's life to the pursuit of honor, peace, and justice, but there was always room to doubt how closely such vows were followed.

It was hard to remain dedicated to keeping things peaceful while blind-drunk on wine or mystified on herbs or dizzied with enchantment dust. Such vices were all too common in the realm Ramsey was about to enter. As he saw it, the dragonfolk could be forgiven for such addictions. Work was hard to get for the dragon-people, and this left a high demand to feel good any way they could. Grudges over their ancestors helped to hold them back and history wasn't changing.

Work on the docks was hard for the dragons to get. There was a lot of manual labor involved, which definitely wasn't a problem for the muscular creatures, but, with exertion there was always the risk of mistakenly exhaling a puff of flame and destroying precious cargo. Such accidents always resulted in the worker going into debt to pay for the loss. Beyond this, spots on the River Guard were also tough to get, because the pledge for that sector conflicted with the code of the Paladins. The city required every dragonborn to take the oath, and the Paladin oath bound them for life.

Ramsey the Green would've been pondering why anyone would willingly live under such conditions, but he was too busy silently cursing his boss. The High Sorcerer Kozard may have a seat in lofty circles, but he belonged in the dungeons for the way he treated his workers.

Every single day in service of that headache bastard made Ramsey miss his home. He did not particularly enjoy being cooped up in a stone chamber, hunkered over a table, staring at scrolls, or sweeping up broken glass from a mess he didn't make while getting screamed at, or having his peace time interrupted with Kozard's roaring command that he go clean up pools of blood and gore on the lookout towers (*three of them!*). Ramsey wanted to be back in the forest. Wanted to be back home.

The Willowflow forest, up north of Rivercrest. Where the air was fresh and all was peace. Well, that's the way it was supposed to be. All was not well in Willowflow. His homeland was under siege.

But he didn't want to think about that right now. The

dragon he was going to visit would not take him seriously if he was shuddering and weeping.

The cobblestones beneath his feet faded out and his slippers crunched on grass. The section of the city where the dragonborn resided was connected to a grassy park area used for training drills and archery try-outs (which was even further evidence of the blatant disenfranchisement. The dominant races in Rivercrest couldn't resist carving out room for their own recreation within the dragons' small corner of the city). Their circular cottages numbered twelve in total, and each one had flames and smoke gurgling up from rooftop gaps. Ramsey wished he had a fire of his own. A torch, perhaps.

Heart pounding in his chest, the tall Sorcerer elf weaved through the array of cottages, slipping past windows and wishing he'd cast a charm of *Invisibility* upon himself. But that would've made him feel like some kind of thief or intruder and he certainly wasn't here for mischief. He needed help.

It was no secret anymore that the Second King had been killed tonight, and this calamity left Ramsey the Green stricken with a deep, shaking sadness. He'd been an ardent believer in John Parker's ascendance to the throne, and was proud to be working within the structure of the man's vision. Thus, it was with an unbelievably heavy heart that he'd needed to climb up three separate towers on the battlements and apply a collection of cleaning spells to clear away the hideous vats of blood. And the compatriots of the dead men stood around watching while Ramsey levitated the corpses down.

When he finally arrived at the doorstep he was seeking, Ramsey thought of the Second King and all the man's sadly wasted potential and this gave him the courage to knock on the door.

A moment later, the door swung open. The door was not slightly, timidly cracked so an eye could peer out and safely gauge the unexpected guest. No, no, this door boomed open wide and proud.

The dragonborn standing there was even taller than Ramsey (who stood at seven-feet, as men measured height), and his shoulders were impressively broad and spiked. Spikes seemed an essential characteristic of the figure in the doorway. Spikes adorned his forehead and cheekbones and his forearms and knees. The man's face was as rigid as lava cooled into rock and Ramsey wondered how the man could ever possibly convey any visible emotion. A simple comparison which put the size of this monster into perspective was the fact that the dragon's hands were the size of cooking pans.

Most surprising, given his scary aura, was the prim white cat, swishing and purring at his feet.

The dragon wore red robes, brightened by the fire roaring behind him, and he stank something awful. Ramsey spied the glint of a golden amulet with a red eye hanging from his necklace.

The creature's fiery eyes matched that necklace jewel, and those eyes beheld a tall, thin elf in a faded green cloak with frosty green eyes, long blonde hair and a non-wrinkled, absurdly smooth face.

"Are you called Konragen?" Ramsey the Green inquired in a surprisingly steady voice.

The dragonman offered only a gruff nod, and Ramsey figured this qualified as a response.

Ramsey stumbled over what to say next. He thought of the firm scripted instructions given to him by Kozard (who was too bitter and lazy to assemble the Quest Squad himself). But Ramsey shoved all that oversight away. The pretentious, nagging, demanding words of Kozard simply would not be persuasive or appealing to a man like Konragen. So Ramsey spoke from his heart.

"The Second King is dead," he told the dragon. "A dark magic wizard villain has killed the leader of our city. The villain in question has fled. West of the castle into Shadowbranch forest."

No response from the dragon, but Konragen's red-orange eyes seemed to glimmer.

"John Parker was elected freely by the people," Ramsey explained, "not given the throne as a birthday present. He may be gone, but I intend to honor his memory by catching his killer."

Konragen's shoulders seemed to slump and his face looked downcast.

"I am a member of the Quest Response to hunt down this assassin and bring him to justice," Ramsey went on. "We're meeting at the western courtyard and leaving at dawn. Rivercrest law dictates we are joined with at least one Paladin. And we would be honored if you would be our Paladin."

Ramsey the Green stopped talking. There was nothing left to say.

A long, long silence followed.

Finally, the man with dragon blood spoke. His deep voice was scratchy yet gentle.

"What you know about... Second King's assassin?"

The Sorcerer elf gulped. "Not much. Only that he is probably weakened. Moving slow…"

Konragen nodded thoughtfully, and Ramsey got restless. Ramsey was firmly stranded in uncharted territory now. He'd forgotten all the precise details of their supplies and the specifics of their travel plans. He hoped the dragon just wouldn't ask. He knew he should get a commitment from the Paladin, otherwise he would face the insufferable Kozard with an "I'm not sure." He could straight-up ask if he would be seeing Konragen in the western courtyard at sunrise, but his nerves were failing and he imagined his voice squeaking high when he spoke. *What if he demands to get paid or something?*

With indecision surging and spiking through his veins, Ramsey decided to just turn and go.

But the dragon-man grunted again. "What are you called?

What is name?"

Ramsey blinked at this, and felt stupid. *I forgot to introduce myself!* He swept out his left arm, pressed his right hand to his breast, and bowed with a flourish. "I, sir, am Ramsey the Green!"

"*Green...?*" Konragen murmured. "Green...? Why is called *Green?*"

"Oh, well, that's a family title for a forest elf of my age-years... I'm a, uh, forest elf!"

Konragen only stared at him, fearsome eyes narrowed with instant suspicion.

Feeling stupid once again—having danced himself into danger—Ramsey sputtered. Looking at the huge man with chalky-black skin, he considered how things like forests were probably nothing more than snacks to dragonfolk. *Roasted* snacks, at that. The elf nodded, turned, and began to walk.

"Why choose me?" the raspy, rumbling voice called. "Of all Paladins, why Konragen?"

The elf turned back to face the dragon in the doorway. He chose his words with care. "I read about your bloodline in the archives. Your father fought bravely at the battle of Bock's Top... I guess I figured that if anyone took their Paladin vows seriously, it would be you..."

Once again, the young Sorcerer elf turned to leave.

"Ramsey Green!" Konragen called after him.

As he turned back, he tried to restrain himself but impetuous habit forced the correction.

"It's, um, it's Ramsey *the* Green, actually..."

For a long, curious moment, the dragon studied him as one might ponder a boot in a tree.

"Ramsey Green," Konragen finally declared. "I shall join your Quest."

Then he slammed the door.

◇ CHAPTER THE NINTH. ◇
◇The Widow's Wish.◇

The dark of night still held, but the threat of dawn was already etching watery streaks low across the eastern skies. It was in the courtyard facing the western skies where Ramsey the Green would soon be expected to have assembled the full staff of the Quest. To deliver the impossible. It was obvious that time was running out, and it was also obvious that he was failing miserably in his duties, but the Sorcerer elf tried his best to swallow his creeping doubts.

Ramsey's horribly detailed imagination was hyper-active tonight. In his mind, he saw the rising sun painting the summer sky canvass with easy pinks melting into mild oranges, giving way to furious reds, exposing his defeats for all to see.

All these worries—compounded with his worries *about* those worries—left Ramsey wanting a nap. And elves never nap. This was a mental exhaustion that no meditation could cure. But Ramsey didn't want to meditate right now. During trance dazes, his thoughts still churned. With a nap, he might be able to just forget everything. Escape, for at least a little while. Flee from all of Kozard's pressures.

Sure, the commitment of Konragen the Paladin was a charming surprise, as well as a success. But it was nothing to stay awake for. The dragonman was a brute with a bucket of dirt for a personality and Ramsey was scared of him. Plus he wasn't even related to those who lost their lives in the attack.

Ramsey's meeting with the Paladin seemed so distant now

that even the dragonfire felt cold.

The Sorcerer elf was now winding through a series of cobblestone streets in one of the city's poorer, wood-built neighborhoods. Despite his frustrations he was still resisting the urge to utter a *Torch* spell and light up his path. What if he tripped and accidentally caught someone's home aflame? The loss of the Second King, alone, was enough catastrophe to deal with tonight.

The night air was hot, and Ramsey's glow-vision caught glimpses of grungy rats scuttling in the gutters and big, fuzzy cats slinking after them. He passed rows of shops and parlors, bursting and bustling with shadows. Occasionally, a drunk would stumble out from an alley to gape at him, or a woman in an extravagant dress and ten layers of makeup would flirt at him as he passed. These encounters didn't leave him enthralled with local culture; they just made him feel sad and empty.

He rounded a corner and was confronted with a rickety set of switchback stairs. He clambered up, offering thanks to Frishka for elves being blessed with weightlessness—otherwise, any amount of human weight would surely send this pitiful, spiritless riser crashing and crumbling to the ground.

Once he reached the third floor balcony, he knocked confidently on the wrong door. An old woman with thick white hair and one missing eyeball screeched and smashed the door shut in his face. Shaken and embarrassed, he drifted to the next one over and gave a few feeble knocks.

His knocks were answered pretty fast, and he beheld a beautiful young strawberry blonde.

Her fine looks, however, were spoiled with tears of sadness and her hair was frazzled with stress. Her bleary hazel eyes met Ramsey's frosty green eyes, and, for a moment, he was certain she was going to close the door with a smash. Right in his face. Such would fit the trend he'd been experiencing at every stop tonight.

Ramsey could tell the woman had been crying hysterically and his heart went out to her.

"You..." she sobbed, staring at him in wonder. "You... you're a forest elf..."

He nodded at this, swallowing his mild disbelief that she wasn't demanding his name.

"Yes, madam," he replied. "I... I was born in Willowflow... the forest up north."

His words seemed to weaken her. But he didn't sense it as a bad thing.

"Oh..." she cried in a breathless, awestruck whisper, "oh, how I long to visit there..."

The Sorcerer elf wasn't sure what to say, so he filled the silence with a shrug and a nod.

"Yeah, um, it's a really special pl—"

"Either come inside or get out of here," she suddenly snapped. "Stay or go."

Babbling out a bunch of hushed nonsense, Ramsey shuffled in and she quietly closed the door.

The awful sweaty stench of the city (a disgrace which the elf's sensitive nose was always keenly aware of) was swept away, replaced with the soothing smells of flowers. His eyes quickly adjusted to the candlelit scene and he saw vines and leaves flowing along shelves on every wall in this small apartment. It seemed every inch of the wall-space was sprouting fingers and petals of vegetation.

This setting was, for Ramsey, a most blissful surprise.

"Are you going to tell me who you are?" she demanded, wiping her eyes.

"I am called Ramsey the Green," he proclaimed, drooping for a bow. "Sorcerer's apprentice!"

She looked unimpressed, crossed her arms, let her eyes slip shut, and sighed with exhaustion.

The elf coughed. Then drew out a scroll, fumbled it,

flipped it in the air, and crunched it as he caught it again. He unrolled it, saw the text was upside-down, spun it back the other way, then cleared his throat, and recited: "You are Marynda Johns. Druid's apprentice—"

"—it's Marynda," she corrected, pronouncing it "Marr-*inn*-dah."

"Ah, yes," he agreed, deciding the scroll's information wasn't very helpful and stashing it away once again. "And, as a Druid—or, shall I say, *Druidess?*—you convene with nature. Which means you and I should get along splendidly, as I would much rather be in the forest than in this nasty city."

"When I was a girl, I studied under my grandmother at her hut in the forest down south. She said there are too many dangers in this world to get hurt by being called *Druid* and not *Druidess*. We lived within nature. We spoke with the animals. Shared secrets with them…" Her voice was still a whimper but reminiscing seemed to help. "Then, when she got sick, we had to move into the castle to get her medicines. She died a month later. It wasn't all bad, coming here, because I got to meet Al—"

Alkent, the elf thought with heartbreak. *Killed in the western watchtower.*

Marynda collapsed into a fit of choking, shuddering sobs. Without even realizing it, Ramsey stepped forward and embraced her. She hugged him back, weeping into his faded green cloak. Her fingers gripped the fabric of his clothes as if he were a raft on a perilous river. Her wails seemed subdued somehow, as if she were holding back, as if trying not to wake someone in the adjacent room. Ramsey thought of Second King John Parker, killed in his prime, and nearly cried right along with her.

Then he thought of the woman in his arms. What she was going through. It was just too much.

Marynda stepped back from him—and it was just in time, or else he would've started to cry.

"Ramsey the Sorcerer," she rasped, wiping her eyes. "Tell

me why you're here."

Ramsey wasn't sure what made him spill his life story right then. Maybe it was sympathy for this beautiful woman in mourning. Maybe he just felt comfortable with her. More comfortable in her presence than with anyone in this castle. She wouldn't judge him, wouldn't laugh.

"As I said... I was born and raised in Willowflow, north from here, up Grayboulder river. The first one-hundred-and-eleven years of my life were blissful carefree adventures through the forest."

"People here don't say *one-hundred-eleven*," Marynda cut in. "It's *eleventh-plateau-plus-one*."

Ramsey nodded and continued. "Casting innocent charms to change the colors of leaves, swinging through the treetops, dealing minor enchantments to make my brothers and cousins fly... Anyway, it all fell apart on my one-hundred-and-twelfth birthday. (You know what year I mean.) It was on my birthday that the first symptoms of disease appeared in our village. A mysterious plague tore through my family and friends... but, for some reason, the sickness only affected the girl elves. Women elves. Mothers, sisters, grandmothers. There was a long stretch of miserable weeks filled with coughing and hacking and wretched bedside gatherings and desperate spell-casters who always seemed to fail...

"Through it all, I blamed myself. As if I were somehow responsible. As if the plague were my birthday present. Inevitably, others made the same connection... When the tension got unbearable, it was decided that I would be sent south. To Rivercrest castle. To enter the Sorcery school and endure whatever punishment it took to get through the twelve-year program." Ramsey sighed, shook his head.

"Sure, I could stand here and tell you I'm altruistic and I came to Rivercrest with the noble goal of becoming a Healer to save my people... but the truth is: I got in an ugly fight with my father. One day, I rebelled against the old elf and his weakness and ineffectiveness. Looking back at it, I feel terrible. That shouting match drives me every day to succeed. To return home and save them all…

"Before I left, I was also charged with finding an elf woman and mating with her. So, here I am, a Seventh Year Sorcerer, barely past the halfway point, and I've accomplished nothing. I haven't unlocked the Healer's powers and I haven't found a woman to bond with. I'm apprenticed to the High Sorcerer—who only accepted me because of my elf heritage and that's the closest thing to a compliment I'll ever get from that cruel bastard. High Sorcerer Kozard puts restrictions on my research. Keeps me away from learning about diseases and elixirs. Threatens to expel me…"

Marynda said nothing. She only stared at him with her sad hazel eyes.

"I'm part of a Quest Response," he told her, hoping he hadn't just rambled too much. Trying to stay focused. "We're tasked with catching the dark wizard who attacked our castle."

This must've triggered some sad thought, because her face scrunched up, bruised bulges rising beneath her watery eyes. "Good for you, Ramsey the Green. I wish you luck. Now, please leave."

He held up his hands, palms out in surrender. "We need you with us, Marynda."

"I'm sorry, Sorcerer, but, honestly, why would I care about what you need?"

"You are blood-kin with one of those we lost tonight. This mission needs your blessing."

She waved her hands in the air. "Great. Fine. My blessing you have. Now—go!"

Marynda shoved him, and both seemed surprised at how light he was, how easy he was moved.

"What I meant to say is—we need you with us," he

rasped. "You have to come along."

Her hands shot up to clutch at her hair, while her face twisted with impossible exasperation.

"Frishkadammit, Ramsey, I can't go on a Quest right now! I lost my love tonight, and… I…"

The next moment balanced upon the tip of a sword's blade for an anxious, eternal moment.

"I visited two other kin-bloods before you," he said, needles of emotion threading a desperate quilt. "Two wives, grieving, just as you are, and both refused their duty. And, rightly so. It would be crazy to leave at such a sensitive time. But there is nothing convenient in this ugly world of ours. The Second King was lost tonight, as well, and his son is locked in the dungeons. So, our Quest has no kin-blood. That is an ill omen… Be our good omen, Marynda. Bring this bastard wizard to Rivercrest justice. Do it for Alkent. For your blood who was taken…"

"I don't care about omens and I don't care about the King. And revenge won't bring my Alkent back to me." She spoke sternly, but it sounded impulsive, as if she truly wanted to say something else.

After a heavy breath, her eyes met his and held them strong. "I wish I could join your Quest, I really do. I'm a widow now, and escaping this dreadful castle for the fresh air of the forest might just be the healing that I need. But, no matter how hard I wish, nothing can heal this scar I carry now… You claim to be a Sorcerer, and I'm a widow with many wishes. Are you the one to answer them, Ramsey?"

Ramsey the Green opened his mouth to reply, but a cry interrupted him—

—the cry of a baby, echoing gently up the hall to the main room where they stood.

Marynda's wide eyes flicked rapidly to the sound, then back to Ramsey. It was as if she were gauging his response. Evaluating, in that instant, whether or not she could trust him.

Verifying that it was safe for him to know the whereabouts of her infant child. *Who could blame her?* Ramsey thought. *The poor woman's family has been hurt once tonight already. She's just protecting what's left of it.*

Without another word, she reached to a nearby tabletop, swept up a saucer with a lit candle on it, then fled up the hallway, leaving Ramsey standing in the front room, wondering what to do.

Soon enough, he scurried after her.

Fortunately, elves were able to move with great stealth, so he didn't risk startling her. Under any other weight, the hallway floorboards would've creaked and groaned. Ramsey was charmed, yet again, by seeing ivy vines trickling along the hallway walls.

The apartment was just as small as he expected. The hallway was a sad abbreviation. He found her in a little bedroom on the right-hand-side. She was kneeling next to the bed she once shared with Alkent, addressing something on the floor. On closer inspection, he saw it was a child's pillow basket.

Marynda didn't even glance at the elf when he knelt beside her. She was too busy crinkling *leaves of soothing* between her fingertips and letting the tiny crumbs sprinkle down to the face of her adorable baby girl. The cries of the baby, who looked to be a few months old, faded to tender gabble.

"Her name is Hazel," Marynda said. "Now, do you see why I cannot join your Quest?"

The elf stared quietly down at the child. The baby's name reflected her mother's eyes, but the girl's eyes were bright blue and her hair was a spark of black against Marynda's strawberry blonde.

"Though, still, I wish I *could* leave this castle and help you. After my husband died here, I don't exactly feel safe here anymore." She looked at him. "Are you ready to hear my wish, Ramsey the Green?" He offered a faint nod, his eyes slipping shut. "I wish I could take my baby girl with us."

"There is a spell I could cast..." he said, after some deep thought. "It would create a room inside a handbag. Baby Hazel could be placed inside that room and you would hold the handbag. Baby Hazel could sleep undisturbed while you carry her unseen in our world. She would still need to be fed and cared for, of course, but she would have air to breathe and could travel safely and out of sight."

Marynda looked at him for a long time with a severe, exacting expression.

Then, she whispered, "Tell me more..."

◇CHASE QUEST◇

◇ CHAPTER THE TENTH. ◇
◇Cold Dungeon Stone.◇

Griffey Parker snapped awake as a splash of cold water smacked him in the face. Right after that—just as shocking and startling as the water—he felt the whistling sting of brutal pain in his right hand. He rolled wildly on the prison cot and, though his right hand made contact with nothing more offensive than the meager slab of the mattress, an alarming jolt of pain still hit him.

He barked in pain—"*Gaaarrrgh!!*"—and his Ranger training instantly chastised him for the outburst. When awakening in a strange place, only a fool would draw attention to himself.

An episode of thrashing kicks tumbled him to his knees, where he twisted around and leaned onto the sweaty, soggy cot, cradling his injured hand against his chest, breathing with the intensity of a snorting bull. Cold water dripped and streamed from his hair to his forehead to his eyes. Now that the initial shock of the chilly water was passed, the liquid actually felt consoling upon his aching head.

His headache was a thunderous rumble. His skin grew hot, then instantly icy cold. Since he was already in a kneeling position and leaning forward, he figured now was as good of a time as any. He vomited all over the cot.

The acid slop fired up his throat, abused his taste buds, exited his system, and splattered all over the ragged yellow mattress. He whirled away from the mess and slumped to a sitting position.

"My sympathies and apologies," he mumbled, "to the next

occupant of this cell."

His foggy vision cleared. Three walls of mushroom stone and one rack of iron dungeon bars. It was cramped, but he was too drunk to bother with claustrophobia. A few guards stood gaping at Griffey with mute fascination. They were six feet away, beyond the bars, and blurry. He noticed one of the men in the middle was holding an empty bucket with water dripping from its lips.

"What the Frishka are you guys staring at?" Parker grunted as he rubbed his forehead.

Since he'd puked, his headache felt slightly less like a hyena with its fur on fire bashing around inside his skull. He felt a little better, but not really. He felt dehydrated and hungry. His bones hurt and his muscles ached.

He tried to rattle his memory and reclaim last night's events, but that just made his head hurt.

"You guys gonna talk or what," he groaned at them, feeling groggy and goofy.

The group continued to gawk at him in idiotic silence.

From what Griffey's hazy drunk-battered vision could discern, there appeared to be four of the nosy loitering bastards. They were just kids. Fat little cream puffs with spotty neck-beards which didn't extend north of their jawlines. They wore brown sleeveless tunics, which were just bags hanging from their shoulders to their knees, tied off with leather belts and straps across their chests. In their belts they carried swords they'd probably never swung, and all their helmets were the wrong sizes.

"You fellas should trade helmets or something. Maybe you'll end up with one that actually fits."

The sudden need to piss grabbed hold of Griffey. With his left hand, he grabbed the metal frame of the cot for support, then snatched his hand away again as he recalled how gross the cot now was. Lacking assistance, he miraculously grumbled to his feet and staggered over to the piss bucket in the corner of his cell.

He stood woozy in the musky sector, swaying perilously, afraid
he might knock into one of the stone walls next to him. Or both of
them. He closed one eye to help his balance, to unclutter his
visual field. He peered back at the guards, then decided that he
didn't care.

A moment later, he was pissing in the bucket with a loud
satisfied moan.

When it was done, he turned back again, leaned against a
wall, and managed to stay standing.

"Y-Y-You're…" one of the guards sputtered. "Y-You're
Griffey Parker, ain't you?"

The Ranger spat on the floor, then realized he should've
spat in the bucket, so he did that, too.

He gave a wheeze, then admitted, "I'm a prisoner with a
hangover, nothing more."

"The Son of the Second King?" another asked in an
anxious, boyish squeak.

Griffey gave a shrug. "Don't tell anyone you saw me puke
on a cot, alright guys?"

"We've been charged with releasing you from the
dungeons," the one who'd dumped the water proclaimed. He
seemed to be the leader of their group. The kid held up a big key
ring and rattled it.

Parker nodded at this pleasing sight, yet he couldn't
suppress a yawn.

"I dunno, fellas," he told them. "I'd settle for a slammer of
coffee."

He was expecting minimal laughter from this, but didn't
even score a chuckle.

"Before we grant you release," the leader amended, "we're
s'posed to tell you two things."

"Two *important* things!" another chimed in.

"You gonna tell me what the Frishka happened to my
hand?"

"You broke your hand in the bar-fight," someone proclaimed in an informative tone.

In a hideous rush, all Griffey's memories from Brumble tavern screamed back into his consciousness and he nearly sagged to the floor. He remembered pounding endless ales with Brisk. He remembered feeling regretful and hollow over neglecting his own father. He recalled being an absolute ass, and escalating someone's insults into physical assault. That someone was called Ulkar.

Ulkar. Oh dear Frishka. He imagined the borlog, out there, somewhere, stalking the halls of the castle, his fury brewing over what Parker had done to him. *Disfigured his face with a beer glass, that's what you did*, he reminded himself. *Oh dear Frishka, **why** did I go and anger a borlog mercenary?*

"What time-of-clock is it?" he demanded of the guards, stepping forward.

"It's pushing dawn," the leader replied. "You've been a'sleepin' for about five hours. Ever since the elves dropped you down here. We tried to wake you up... S-S-Sorry about the cold water."

"If you're granting me release, let's get to the granting."

The leader held up his hands in a harmless gesture, also lofting up the over-sized key ring. "Sir, we're not authorized to release you from the dungeons until we've told you two important things."

Griffey stood there, arms crossed, eyes traveling from face-to-face, gauging them all.

One chin at a time, they each turned to gaze expectantly at their leader, standing in the center. The head of this band shuffled his feet and his face went radish-red with blush. He looked at the floor.

"Listen," Parker said quietly. "Whatever you've got to say, it's probably not your fault. So I'm not going to kick blame on your boots over this. Just tell me what it is, so I can get out of here."

Finally, the kid's bright blue eyes locked on his. "The Second King was killed last night…"

The words struck Griffey with a forceful *thump* to the chest. The wind left his sails, the feeling fled from his legs, the world faded to an unfathomably hopeless pin-prick of inky black blood.

When his conscious mind returned, when his boots reconvened with the cold dungeon stone, he felt impossibly light. As if all the weight he'd earned throughout his life now had to be paid back.

He hadn't fallen on his ass, but he was leaning against the iron bars, left hand steadying him.

"We are to escort you to the western courtyard. You're expected there," the voice of the leader was saying. "You're to be part of some sort of Quest. To go and hunt down the assassin of the King."

There was a jingling, the scrape of silver kissing iron, and the click of a lock…

◇ CHAPTER THE ELEVENTH. ◇
◇Escort Posse.◇

With the intrusiveness of curious children, blades of sunlight began to glide over the tops of the castle walls. Spilling light began to fill the bowl of the western courtyard, dispersing the shadows.

Though he was arguably the most important member of the Quest, Griffey Parker was the last member to arrive at the meeting plaza. He strode in slowly—not because he wanted everyone to watch him make a dramatic entrance, but because he still felt drunk. Though his River Guardsmen escorts had given him jug after jug of water to chug, he still felt dehydrated. He had to concentrate on each step he took to avoid toppling over, and now he had the pressure of an audience.

It was strange. He'd focused on every step taken to get him up from the dungeons and all the way over here—with the group of young, awestruck prison guards following behind him in posse formation—but he could remember none of the journey. It was as if his mind now belonged to an animal. A carnivore with minimal needs and no affiliation with complaining.

If he'd been asked, when a splash of cold water woke him up in the dungeons not long ago, to supply a list of his basic needs and requirements, Griffey's demands would've been pretty basic. He'd needed some coffee. A bath. An acquaintance with some cleaning paste for his teeth. In absence of the paste, he'd settle for something more heavy duty, but he wasn't even sure that a

Sorcerer's spell could eliminate the nasty taste of burnt coal, kitchen grease, and tobacco layered upon his tongue.

News of his father's death—relayed to his ears through a rack of prison bars, delivered by a kid too young for the uniform he was wearing—had simplified his existence. Whittled him, with a woodworker's mastery, into a smaller, more condensed statue-version of himself.

With the rugged, measured life he now ran, he didn't even consider coffee nor contemplate a bath. He'd trotted straight up here, with the guard posse forming up and hustling along a few steps behind. He didn't have to ask them to come along. This was probably their most thrilling day in weeks.

On the way to the courtyard, he'd streamed questions to his buddies as they galloped and wheezed after him. "Where are my supplies? My armor, weapons, and horse?" One guard replied: "It's all been collected and it's waiting in the western courtyard. I dunno about the horse, though. Don't think they're gonna let you bring her along. You're heading into a part of Shadowbranch forest that ain't got a trail through it."

"Water?" he inquired. "Fellas, I'm gonna need some water if I'm heading for the forest."

"We got water-skins!" huffed a guard, slapping a bag onto Griffey's shoulder. He grabbed it and chugged water as they walked. "We got dried jerky and rice and other tasty provisions for you, too!"

"What about my hand, fellas?" he called out. "I've got a broken hand on me."

"There's s'posed to be a Sorcerer travellin' with you. I figure he could fix your hand."

"I heard there was *two* Sorcerers involved!" one of them yelped in excitement.

"Break your other hand and you got double the doctors!"

Griffey heard muffled curses as the kids slapped and *shooshed* the dumb one into silence.

Their path was a slow rise through a smooth stone tunnel, then wove the sleepy streets, and the gates to the western courtyard appeared. The Ranger's sharp eyes peeled into the confines long before any of his pals even saw the fence. What he saw waiting in there made him stop at the gates.

A group of four was clustered at the heart of the grassy yard. Two men, each over seven-feet, one woman, and an elf with a yellow-brown braided beard and a black-shaded monocle in one eye.

On the right, flanked by a troop of River Guardsmen, stood both Griffey Parker's mother and sister. Seeing them— standing there, nervous, fidgety, expectant, tearful—made him feel as if he'd just stepped off a cliff and down a waterfall. The air left his lungs, and he felt weightless again.

Griffey held up at the gates and his puzzled posse shambled and stumbled and stopped just short of crashing into their leader. Pausing there, as yet unseen by those inside the yard, the Son of the Second King let his eyes slip shut. The sick feeling of guilt was back again—yesterday, he'd nearly left the city without seeing his father, and, this morning, he hadn't even thought of visiting his mother.

Before he could enter that arena, there was one thing he had to do.

"This is where I leave you, gentlemen." He turned back to the Guardsmen, and looked them each in the eye. "A thousand thanks for your service and assistance. You spoke freely with me, you helped me when you knew me no further than my name. Now, please, tell me your own names."

Down the line, they rattled off: "Fisher," "Crawberry," "Rich," and "Garver."

Garver was the one who'd dumped the ice water bucket. The one with the keys. The leader.

The posse would stand there and spectate upon all his activities in the plaza, and when it was all over, they would exaggerate and aggrandize the tale for years. *The day they took the Son of the Second King from jail to his journey.* But this would be where he left them. There would be no waving once he breached the yard. Parker tried on a smile which felt wrong, so he gave them a nod and turned away.

He entered the western courtyard, trotting in the first rays of day…

◇ CHAPTER THE TWELFTH. ◇

◇Daybreak Departure.◇

A knight stepped up immediately on Griffey's left. Without a word, this person handed him his armor, belt, two short-swords, and a knife. The man even threw in a burlap pack of food, free of charge, with no conversation required. Parker accepted these items with a distracted yet appreciative nod. Part of him wanted to cry out in need of his missing bow and quiver, which he'd left at the inn he'd been shacked at. He walked over to the most important women in his life. His eyes were on them for the entire stroll, so he was blind and one-handed while trying to slip on his armor and strap on his belt and sheath his swords. When he got there, his mother and his sister gave him brief critical looks, then they both helped him settle his accessories into their proper places.

As he met with the ladies, their Guardsmen protectors—a troop wearing helmets and full knight armor—stepped respectfully back. *They'd show more respect by coming on the Quest with us,* Griffey thought bitterly. He shook it off. He could only worry about himself and his family right now.

"Oh! There he is! Dear Frishka—it's about time!" a voice cried across the expanse. The plaza was a sprawl of rich green grass spotted with stone benches and fountains, the space compressed into a trapezoid by the fifty-foot ramparts. He spied the exit to Brumble tavern and thought it strange how soon he'd come full circle. One of the lookout towers beckoned overhead with silent brooding regard. A man named Alkent, Guardsman

from Bofork across the river, had been killed in that very tower last night. Arguably, the journey of the Response Quest had begun up there in that same steeple, so it was appropriate that the watchtower's shadow was cast in the direction of their travels— out from the familiarity of the castle and into Shadowbranch forest. As if attempting to drag the dark reputation of that woodland over the barrier and smear civilization with it, someone was yelling at Griffey Parker.

"**This** *is the pride of Rivercrest, eh? Shows up late on a day as crucial as this??*"

It was irritating to listen to those remarks, but Griffey stayed rigid. No amount of screeching from any man could make him turn from his mother right now.

Before he'd entered the courtyard, he'd marked High Sorcerer Kozard. The elf who occupied such a lofty rank while somehow managing to avoid becoming tall like the rest of the elves, and while also developing a glaring beer gut. One of the elf's eyes was dark today, and it wasn't a bruise.

"*I heard the kid spent the night in the dungeons for attempted theft, that's what I heard!*"

"He's been bitching like that for the last ten minutes," Griffey's sister, Sho'pa, seethed.

"Ignore that dreadful elf," Griffey's mother, Jessyn, advised her son with a mutter. She shot a reproachful sidelong glance at the caller. "His black eye is an unnatural shine."

Mother Parker was a proud woman, always careful with her words. She was shy yet pretty; always short on words yet quick with a genuine smile. Her brown hair was fading gray and wrinkles he didn't recall now severed her gentle face. It was rare that she made public appearances other than those in support of the Second King, for she was at peace in her private chambers with her beloved flute and books of poetry. The thought of this reminded Griffey that it was his mother who'd first inspired him to craft poetry when he was ten and chained up one summer with a broken leg. The thought nearly made him cry. As if to match the sensation he was feeling, fresh jets of tears glistened in Jessyn's eyes as she grasped his arms. She pulled him into a hug. When she leaned back, her face was strained and sad.

"Mother... I don't know what I'm doing. It's all been so horrible. All happened so fast."

"He loved us all," Jessyn whispered, "and... he would demand that we be strong right now."

"I shouldn't be going. There's nothing strong about me leaving you at such an awful time."

The sting of guilt resurfaced with a spike to the Ranger's gut. He'd stomped up here from the dungeons, blind and barking at some kids foolish enough to follow him. Though he'd been off the drink for hours, he'd been drunk on vengeance. He'd forgotten that his mother and sister shared his grief.

If given a quill and some paper—and if his hand wasn't broken—Griffey would've drafted out his thoughts with elegant prose. Instead, all he could sputter was: "I loved him so much. Yet I never really let him see that. And now... now I can't even see my own path. It's there, but I can't see it..."

"You will find your path," Mother Parker assured him softly, boldly. "Because the lives of these people depend on it. These innocent people who've volunteered to go with you into that wretched forest. They will need your guidance, son. That is your duty now. Your father would want you to do your duty. He would want you to go on helping people. That's all he ever wanted..." Her voice broke.

"Dear Frishka," Griffey wheezed. "What about you, mother? What can I do for you?"

She stared at him for a long, arduous time. "What I want can't be given, my son. So, all that's left is for you to catch the rat responsible." Her eyes dropped to his right hand, snuggled weakly against his chest. She gave a motherly squint. "What's happened to your hand? You need to fix your hand."

After hugging Mother Parker once again, Griffey moved to embrace his sister.

Sho'pa was four years younger than he, and she was in spectacular shape from a disciplined diet and a career apparently spent with activities more physically demanding than constant meditation. She was a foot shorter than he, her skin was a deeper tan than his, her brown eyes shown with bright, thoughtful, piercing intensity, and her hair was done in traditional female Monk style—shaved on the sides with a long braided brown ponytail trailing down her back. She wore a simple brown one-piece garment and her feet were in slippers that made it tempting to believe she'd be crazy to attempt kicking anyone. But such a belief would be a dreadful mistake. Griffey knew his sister was an agile fighter.

"I'll keep it brief, big brother," Sho'pa uttered. "I'm breaking my silence vows as it is… We all loved father and he loved us in return. Go catch the filth who did this. The one who hurt our family…"

Griffey knew it would be foolish to ask her to come along. Her pledge to the temple forbade her from partaking in actions connected to politics or family. She was married to a misanthropic life.

He opened his mouth to say something, but she stopped him. "The guards are listening to us—or, at least trying to," she said in an impossible whisper. For a moment, Griffey thought he was imagining her speaking. *Maybe her vow of silence is still intact and this is just an illusion,* he wildly thought. But then she spoke again: "At this stage of my training, I am forbidden from leaving the castle. Still, I would break my pledge this very morning if it meant we could bring father back to us. But we can't do that. So I can't come with you, big brother. But that doesn't mean I can't help you." She grasped his left hand, pried it gently open, and placed a coin in his palm. She curled his hand shut and clasped it with her own hands. "This is a coin of Grulva. If ever you find yourself trapped with precisely no hope of escape—toss this coin high in the air and recite the words: *Grulva Vitiera*."

With that, she hugged him heartily, stepped back, and would say no more.

He nodded to her and pocketed the strange copper coin.

*"Not only did he try to rob somebody last night—he's robbing **us** of our precious time!"*

Griffey frowned. He was ready to go make Kozard shut the hell up, but his mother made him stop by lofting up her hand. She turned and waved to the metallic row of knights behind her. Their ranks split apart and a civilian bounded forth—a squat Black man with a mop of dark curly hair.

"Brisk Koja!" Griffey breathed. On other occasions, such a surprise would've been evident by a gleeful glow in his voice, but now his voice was as dry and as enthusiastic as a chunk of wood.

Parker's childhood buddy slipped past the begrudging Guardsman—who obeyed the wife of the Second King, yet did not appreciate indulging anyone else (Griffey distantly feared that creatures such as they might not revere his mother for too much longer). As Brisk squirmed through the gap in their ranks, his brown backpack snagged on the hilt of one of their swords. He was embroiled in a brief, horribly awkward struggle to free himself. Once he was liberated, Brisk dusted himself off, cast a disparaging look at the knight with the offending sword, then huffed over to Griffey.

He collected his composure, exhaled heavily, then looked Parker in the eyes.

"I've brought more than apple bread this morning, old friend," Brisk said in a dutiful tone. "I've brought my knife and my boots and my pots and pans and I'm coming with you on your Quest."

Struck with mild shock, Griffey raised his left hand in a *"hold up"* gesture.

"Look, I'm a Cook. You're gonna need to eat," Brisk bellowed at him. "And I've got training as a Healer, too, so you can justify my inclusion." His tone softened and his stern, affronted expression melted. "I heard about what happened... what happened to your father. And I truly want to help."

A thousand thoughts flew through the mind of the Second King's son. He considered dissuading this recruit because it was dangerous beyond the castle walls. He contemplated critiquing Brisk's lack of supplies and lack of experience in the wild. He even pondered the convenience of the Sorcerer in their group. *Kozard could probably do all the cooking duties with the snap of a spell.* But he said none of this. There was no time. Brisk was committed and the man was intensely stubborn.

"Endless thanks, brother." He raised a fist and the two knocked their knuckles together.

Griffey nodded once more to Jessyn and Sho'pa, then he turned and strode across the courtyard. Towards Kozard's blaring mouth and the rest of the assembled Quest. He tried consciously not to fiddle with the adjustment straps for his belt and his pack and armor. Brisk fell in stride beside him, which helped him focus. Both of their hickory-colored cloaks swished and sailed out behind them.

"I imagine this'll be the fist time," the Ranger whispered aside to the Cook as they walked, "that the beasts in Shadowbranch forest have ever done battle with an apron man."

"A pox on you, Parker," Brisk shot back, but his response carried a tepid tone and lacked its usual inspired flavor. Griffey could tell his friend was absolutely frightened to Frishka right now.

He decided he would do all the talking, to spare his friend the embarrassment of a potential tremor in his voice. He also hoped there would be minimal talking. The loquacious Kozard was obnoxious, but the elf did raise a good point. This expedition should've departed long ago.

In the seconds before the Ranger and the Cook reached the line of four people staring back at them, Griffey's eyes strayed up to the watchtower, looming overhead. He was struck by how this time in his life would bury itself in his memory. Soon, the gritty authenticity of his every footstep would dwindle, and the day would become defined as a whole. Though the details would die, the impact, the *feeling* of this moment would never fade. *This is eternal.*

In the span of his introspection, it was as if his senses were kicked to a higher tier of the castle. He felt the blades of grass crunch beneath his boots, heard the soft pitter-patter babble of Brisk's cooking pans, smelt the delicious scent of baked apple bread, felt a mellow breeze wisp his brow.

He spied a bearded watchman in the lookout tower, staring back down at him with a worn leathery face and a grave expression. They exchanged subtle nods. Then it was back to business.

The Ranger and the Cook halted six feet short of the group.

Griffey Parker surveyed the volunteers, appraising each one.

At the left-end of the line was a tired woman with strawberry-blonde hair who looked drained and weary, as if she'd much rather be by herself right now. She wore a light blue shirt, brown patched pants, with a sapphire cloak pressed beneath her knapsack and bedroll. She featured no visible weapons, and didn't look like she could use one, anyway. Instead of defensive measures, she clutched a black leather bag, which looked honestly empty. She tried to make shielding the bag look casual.

Next up, there stood a smooth-faced elf-man with crystal green eyes, long blonde hair, and a faded green cloak. He was tall with a gnarled six-foot staff the shade of gingerbread-wood. A bulging brown haversack rode astride his slim shoulders. A cylindrical scroll-case and various pouches draped from his belt and cross-belt, plus a graceful coil of hemp rope. Yet—*again*—with no weapons in sight.

The penultimate recruit held far more promise than the others. A dark, towering dragonman who made the tall green elf look short. His face was carved from rock, with orange-fire eyes, and spikes up his arms. He wore a huge tent-pack, a deep crimson cloak, with pouches, hooks, and hammers trailing across his chest. And—*thank Frishka*—he was noticeably armed. With his broad red shield, he wielded a massive dual-bladed battleaxe. Coupled with his height, it was intimidating as hell.

Parker recognized the man, of course. *The Paladin from the bar fight. With the gold necklace with the red-eyed amulet. The one who heard me plea for aid and did nothing. Just stood there.*

Finally, there stood the High Sorcerer Kozard, grasping a tall black staff, with a longsword in his belt. This powerful elf was acting menacing, and his black eyeglass didn't make him any friendlier.

Frishka, the Ranger thought. *Two of these people are useless, one I can't trust, and one is crazy.*

"Oh great, he's got a broken hand! Can you believe that?" Kozard scoffed. "They sent us a wounded man. By how slow he moves, you'd think his leg was broken, too."

The Ranger nearly bit back the words. But his sudden anger was too radiant. It was the same heat he'd felt last night, when Ulkar insulted his father. Only now, his family name was being assaulted while wounded. "For an elf who rarely leaves the cushion of his high-tower office," his words were beyond his control, off to the reckless races, "you're quite anxious for departure."

Very soon, the gates were opened and they stepped outside.

It wasn't long later when Griffey came to regret his remark…

BOOK

◇ II ◇

THE FOREST.

◇ CHAPTER THE THIRTEENTH. ◇
◇Disappearing Trails.◇

Morning was only a few minutes old and it was already obvious that today would be blazing hot. The summer sun cleared the peaks of the castle and began to brazenly infiltrate the landscape.

Once the small group of three humans, two elves, and one dragon-man, were outside the castle walls, the tall iron gates squealed, then shut with a mighty *clang* of finality. For a few nervous moments, they lingered. The grass was much higher than back inside the plaza; a glaring microcosm of just how much their lives were destined to change from this day forward.

They stood in a meadow which encircled the parts of Rivercrest castle that didn't touch the river. Beyond this little clearing, there lay the depths of Shadowbranch forest, rich and imposing.

"Well, I suppose we should offer introductions now…" Ramsey tentatively opined to his ruffled compatriots. He glanced around at the loose circle they'd formed. Kozard still looked moody over the insult from the Ranger. Both Marynda and the ebony man with the cooking pans kept shooting longing glances back up at the gates, as if they'd forgotten some critical item back at their apartments. Konragen looked bored. The Ranger looked as if he didn't even hear Ramsey's attempt at conversation.

"F-F-Fair enough," the young elf sputtered. He decided to engage the black gentleman and tried his best at a hospitable smile. "I am Ramsey the Green." He gave a bow which went quirky as his heavy haversack tottered. "This here is Marynda

Johns, Konragen the Tall, and Kozard the Hi—"

"*Enough of this drivel!*" Kozard snapped. "*We've no need to practice tongue-flapping!*"

After a tense moment of silence, the High Sorcerer turned away, shaking his head and hissing through his teeth. With the toxic elf's back turned, Brisk finally found the courage to speak. It was Kozard's rudeness, actually, which inspired him. Snapped him from his daze. "I am Brisk Koja, crafter of fine dining!" His mood didn't match his spirited words, but he sounded convincing enough to spite Kozard. "Drinker of fine ales! Practitioner of the Healer's arts! This here is Griffey Parker."

(*Is there a reason you list 'ale-drinker' before 'Healer'?* Ramsey thought but didn't say.)

If he were to drink a potion of *Honesty*, Griffey would've admitted he lacked faith in all of his companions being able to move fast through the trees. Kozard was too fat, too out of shape. Marynda looked distracted, frazzled, worried. Brisk was always a threat to drop down, curl up, and nap. Yes, the Paladin was grand, but he wouldn't be able to intimidate endless trees and vines and thorn bushes out of his way. The dragon was big, but he'd be slow without a trail. Ramsey appeared to be a forest elf, which was a promising finding, but the elf looked as if he hadn't left the library in a decade.

Parker spared few further thoughts for these people, as his focus was on the profuse tangle of tree branches marking the edge of the forest. His mind ran calculations for moving efficiently through there, and the scant thoughts he did give to his companions were concerned with how poorly they might move through the congested woods. He pondered how long until they reached the trailhead.

The Ranger scampered across the meadow towards the trees. The rest hung back for a long leery moment, as if the castle walls were a campfire on a chilly night. Soon enough, his action galvanized them to follow. Griffey called, "Sorcerers! Do you detect a magical residue of our quarry's back-trail?"

The Ranger halted at the edge of Shadowbranch forest, using his specially-acquired Scout Sniff ability, first hinting left, then tracking right.

Both Sorcerers arrived at the same time. Ramsey closed his eyes and cast a silent spell of *Detection*. A few seconds later, his eyes opened, and he knew exactly where the dark wizard had fled into the woods. However, before Ramsey reached this conclusion, Kozard had closed his left eye and peered through the black glass lodged in his right eye-socket. The glass mystically filtered the scenery into categories of peripheral and useful—the trees went gray and the path of the assassin lit up gold.

While it was impressive how quickly the Sorcerers worked, they announced none of their findings. Meanwhile, the Ranger scented out the spot they needed without the aid of magic. However, when he reached out to spread a gap in the branches, he earned a searing bolt of pain in his broken hand.

The Ranger managed to choke down a cry before it escaped his throat. With strict, measured movements, he faced the castle again. Before he stepped away, he dealt a quick nod at the entrance point, hoping the people would look at that instead of him. He was afraid there might be a tint of tears in his eyes, as his broken right hand hurt extremely bad. Brisk hopped to his side, worry on his face.

All Parker wanted to do was get going. The threat was out there, with its trail just begging to be burned. Maybe he would catch more than just a dark wizard. Perhaps he'd also snare some answers. But his urgency had blinded him, yet again, of his need to fix his broken hand.

Though it was inevitable that he would take control of the expedition at some point, Kozard seized this moment to do so. With a mighty puff of his chest, Kozard stepped up and gestured after the Ranger. "Clearly, our man is not only wounded but he's also scared to lead our little pack!"

While the High Sorcerer bellowed hearty laughter, Brisk, trying to help, squeezed Griffey's broken hand, eliciting yet another strike of pain. The cackling in the background was far from soothing.

Ramsey the Green noticed the Ranger was discomfited and felt guilty that his boss was laughing at the man's misfortune. The young elf strode forward, his gnarled brown staff marching with his feet.

"I would be proud to lead our way, High Sorcerer! To detect any dangers which may await us!"

"Shut your mouth, you lousy Seventh Year!" Kozard snapped. The older, fatter Sorcerer shook his head with defiant disgust. "I'll not see this mission inaugurated with an idiot child." He sighed dramatically, as if accepting some noble sacrifice. "Only *I* am qualified to lead us. To keep us safe."

"B-But-But..." Ramsey spluttered. "But you *hate* nature! You despise the forest! The trees..."

"*You're damn right I do!*" Kozard roared back. "It's filthy and uncivilized and governed by bear manure instead of intelligence—but it scares me not! It is *I* who must master this place. Prove our kingdom superior to these worthless woods. You, Ramsey, couldn't even assemble the roster as called for!"

The younger elf faded back, head bowed, feeling foolish and ashamed.

During this exchange, Marynda looked sick and Konragen continued to look unentertained.

Now standing alone, his power unchallenged, the High Sorcerer surveyed the loose group before him. "The best my apprentice could muster is this pathetic assembly," he spat. "If we are to survive—not only against our foes, but against the forest—my powers will be doubly needed."

A dark silence dragged past. A breeze swept away their edgy breath, leaving only tension.

Kozard turned and stomped into the forest. To the

observant hawk-eyes of Marynda Johns, however, he didn't move as a boastful invincible conqueror, but rather with the picky hesitancy of an agitated grandmother. Of course, she wasn't about to say this joke aloud. She would probably be withholding comments from these people, altogether. The only assemblage of words she needed to consider was what she would cry out when she turned around and called up to the soldiers manning the gate, demanding to be let back inside. *Can't go back inside. It's not safe in the castle anymore.*

Marynda blinked and realized a few seconds had skipped past. The angry, bossy elf had disappeared into the trees. Broken Hand Ranger was ducking inside with Loquacious Little Cook helping to hold back the obstructive flap of the branches. The Cook (she thought his name was *Risk* or something) was motioning chivalrously to her. "Madam, would you care to venture forth?"

The recent widow shook her head automatically, without even thinking about it. The Cook frowned and nodded with regretful acceptance. With a look that said he'd rather keep a thick buffer of humanity between himself and whatever lay beyond, the Cook sighed, and trudged on in. Marynda wondered why the Cook hadn't asked the other two to go first, after her refusal. She turned back and saw the blonde elf pouting, and the enormous, terrifying dragon-man glowering at nothing.

Marynda's first instinct was to defer to Ramsey the Green, because he was the most familiar person here. He was the one who'd knocked on her door and given both her and her handbag an escape from the castle. But the defeated look which now dirtied Ramsey's image did little to inspire. Her eyes drifted past those two, to the walls of Rivercrest, one final time. She gulped. She'd met Alkent in there, lost her grandmother in there, given birth to Hazel in there. She hugged the black leather handbag tight to her chest. *But not too tight!* With a flick of panic, her grip went from **CRUSH** to *caress* in a snap.

Fearing she might go insane if she stood around thinking much longer, she darted in the woods.

Soon, Ramsey followed. Then Konragen. Neither turned back to wave goodbye.

The first ten paces were the most tangled and difficult, filled with snags and scrapes to their faces. After that, the woodsy obstacles gave way to a labyrinth of tree trunks coated with frizzles of branches. The thickets encasing each trunk were far fatter than the trunks themselves. Clear blue sky was visible overhead, piercing through the canopies, but none risked looking up at it, as they were constantly dodging and ducking and twisting and pivoting. The ground was a wet, squishy carpet. The air was humid and no cool breeze glided in. Birds chirped, merrily indifferent to their struggles.

Once she had some breathing room, Marynda heard the others ahead. Not only could she hear their crashing footfalls, but she could also hear them talking. Her hearing was attuned for distance and clarity, but she didn't need that now. The technical degree of the hiking terrain forced them to squirm through gaps in the vegetation, so they cheated after each other and scrunched together.

"Kozard!" Griffey Parker called ahead, his tone obviously restrained. "High Sorcerer!"

It took a while for the elf to reply. He was too engrossed with the imagery in his dark eye.

"What is it, Son of the Second King?" the elf relented.

"I've calculated that we'll reach the trailhead with two hours' hike time."

"Calculated, eh? I thought you were a Ranger, not a practitioner of mathematics."

"He's a *Runter*, actually!" Brisk announced. "A Hunter *and* a Ranger!"

"*Frishkadammit, Brisk.*" Griffey blinked with theatric frustration. He'd managed to conceal his right hand by pressing it beneath the form-fitting chest-plate of his armor.

"You should've calculated a trail for us to walk upon," Kozard hissed. "I saw you arrive three days ago in the rain astride a brown-with-white-spots horse. Clearly there's trails out here."

Fear prickled across Parker's brain. *No one saw me arrive three days ago in the rain... Just the Guardsman who let me in.* Suspicion rippled through him as he forced himself to think faster and more intently about how Kozard may have witnessed his arrival. *What exactly* **is** *that black eyeglass he has?*

"*Oy!*" a woman's voice cried out. "Did you guys say there's a trail?"

Both the Ranger and the Cook turned to look at her with faces of mild surprise.

Marynda looked back at them, her face slightly red. She offered a shrug, then resumed picking her way through the brush. She figured, *If I'm not going back to the castle, if I'm going to stay with them and hike, then I can't let them make all the decisions.* Sneaking through the trees was challenging, but it only irritated her because she feared for her handbag. Overall, being in the woods made her calm.

Parker turned back to navigating his own feet, and found himself responding in the automatic informative manner of a forest guide. "There are few trails through Shadowbranch forest, because they are so difficult to keep. In the early days of Rivercrest kingdom—forty-two years ago, during the reign of First King Fred Callister—many trails were cut out here. Most took months to complete, and none of them made it all the way across the forest. For each trail, there came a day when the workers would head back to their stations and find all the trees completely regrown. All their work erased...

"The trees grow back on certain trails while others are left intact. There are only two remaining trails which begin at our castle. They head north and south—not west, where we're heading. But," Griffey paused, "there *is* one western trail. And we can pick up its trailhead two hours from now."

"I think our dark wizard went that way, too," Kozard whispered, peering ahead, licking his lips.

Another dark tide of unease surfed through Parker. *What is the High Sorcerer really after?*

"Why the hell would a trail begin two hours deep into a forest?" Brisk asked, swatting at a bug.

"Shadowbranch forest does as it pleases," Parker shrugged. "Some say the trails even shift."

"We aren't going to be able to just step onto this trailhead, are we?" Marynda quietly asked.

The Ranger shook his head. "You're right... We'll have to contend with the Trail Guardians..."

"And...?" Brisk wondered, "... uh, what the hell are *those* exactly...?"

"Let's just get there first," Griffey said, which sounded trite, so he addressed their leader instead. Now that he'd been shoved into a secondary role, Parker didn't refrain from asking tough questions. "Kozard, what do you know about this dark wizard? Is it true that he is weakened?"

For a while, it seemed as if the High Sorcerer wouldn't dignify them with an answer. But, ultimately, answering made him feel more important. "The three tower guards and the Second King were killed with a green-blue spell-ball. That means the caster of that spell is of wilderness origins. Which means he'll be in recovery for more than a day. He'll be drained of energy, moving slow."

"Who said it was a *he*?" Marynda muttered quietly.

At the back of the line, the eyes of Konragen the dragonborn lit up. He shivered and shook his head in disagreement. Ultimately, he stayed silent. Did not interfere. And it filled him with dread.

Marynda's sharp eyes caught the movement of a large creature in the trees...

◇ CHAPTER THE FOURTEENTH. ◇
◇Warning Signs.◇

The Ranger swung around a bramble of thorny shrubbery, ducked beneath a tangle of lanky tree branches, then scrambled across a fallen log, its bark covered in a smattering of turquoise mushroom saucers. He hopped down from the log and his boots splashed through a puddle which they usually would have avoided. His mind was distracted as he edged closer to the High Sorcerer.

Frishkadammed fool, Griffey Parker! he cursed himself, with another pang of guilt (the feeling was becoming disturbingly recurrent) which hurt as much as his hand. *You're lucky enough to be with someone as powerful as a High Sorcerer, and you insulted the man! Called him a cushion elf!*

Kozard's left eye was clenched shut (he'd considered cutting the useless thing out). He was consumed with the dark glass in his right eye. All the peripheral scenery was a smoky coal-dust gray, and the path before him was a glowing, sparkling gold. As if the monocle knew he was uncomfortable out here, and it wanted to help him, his black eye guided him. It sent him checking left to avoid spikes disguised as leaves and skipping right to avoid sharp rocks hidden in moss. He felt like an entirely new elf when the glass was in his eye. Stronger. More capable. More informed. Best of all—most *intoxicating* of all—his precious monocle was delivering him to the dark wizard. Dark wizards were beings of boundless prominence. Kozard envisioned and anticipated meeting a being smart enough to appreciate his crafty capabilities. Maybe they would even team up.

His witless superiors back at Rivercrest were wasting his

potential out here in the woods. The elf suspected they'd sent him out here to get him out of the way, to conspire behind his back.

Speaking of conspiring behind his back, the High Sorcerer sensed the Ranger behind him.

"Why are you sneaking so close on my trail, Ranger Parker?" Kozard sneered back at his follower, not bothering to turn. "Is this a pathetic attempt to regain control that once was yours?"

"I just wanted to remark upon your spectacular leadership."

"Well, you've remarked upon it," the Sorcerer spat, still not turning. "Let's back off then, shall we? I'm doing some serious hunting work up here. Wounded men belong back with the women."

"That's what I wanted to discuss, actually," Griffey exclaimed, bounding past a clog so he was close enough to clap his left hand on Kozard's shoulder. The elf's progress halted in the middle of a little clearing. He went rigid. "Sir, I apologize for my earlier comments. My mind has been a mess since… since my father died. You see, sir, if you want me to contribute fully to this endeavor, it would be best if I were at full strength." He withdrew his right paw from its cozy nest, pressed between his armor and his chest. "You are advanced with the Healer's arts… Please, can you help heal my hand?"

Up close, Kozard's face looked old, weary, and dangerous. His left eye was squeezed shut, spilling wrinkles out across that region of his face. His right eye was adrift in a swirling blackhole.

In Kozard's vision, Parker's face was not lit up gold. It was a dull, ugly, *time-wasting* gray.

When he spoke, his voice was a hiss: "I don't recall this endeavor needing you to be at *full strength*. I don't recall *needing* you at all. Nay, sir, I will not be fixing your Frishkadammed *hand*. Kozard does not fixate on the background while he's thriving in the foreground."

The High Sorcerer could keep his vision off the path no longer, so he ripped his face away and remounted the golden carpet. It felt glorious for Kozard to dismiss the Ranger. Griffey Parker was no different from the fools in Rivercrest's ruling class. Out from the stuffy shadows of the castle's social structure, Kozard finally felt free. It was appalling, of course, to associate such a blessing with a place as dreadful as a forest. Still, as he hustled deeper in, shoulders thrown back, the elf allowed himself a wicked grin. Behind him, frozen and shaken, Griffey soon had reason for a grin of his own.

Kozard was salivating so closely over his path that, ten feet along, a tree-branch-bystander reached out and snared hold of his long braided beard. The old Sorcerer was yanked rudely back and twisted for good measure. Brisk stepped up at Griffey's side and viewed this with a snicker.

With a bark of gruff dismissal, the High Sorcerer thrashed the tangle free, and tromped away.

As the sounds of the elf's violent departure faded, a chill settled upon the Ranger's bones. It was rare that he felt uneasy in the wild, but it wasn't the forest that concerned him. He and the Cook stood alone, trapped between the leader and the rest of the group. Both sections worried him to some degree, but it was top-heavy. The High Sorcerer was extremely powerful—*and* mentally unstable—and the elf was now out from beneath the umbrella of Rivercrest justice and had marked Griffey as an enemy.

Griffey couldn't help but imagine the old elf cackling while slaughtering them all at nightfall.

"Old lousy jester won't help you fix your hand, eh?" Brisk uttered.

"With no High Sorcerer to assist, that boots the ball to your doorstep, o' Great Healer."

"You know, if you're gonna put weight on my shoulders," said the Cook, "then you need a different sort of injury. This one you've got just needs to sit on a pillow and heal."

Griffey exhaled heavily. "I don't anticipate much pillow time on this mission, Brisk." He shook his head, glanced behind them, and let out a sigh. "Brother, I've gotta get to full-strength."

Brisk followed his gaze, nodded, and clicked his tongue. "Why don'cha ask that green fella?"

The tall green elf had yet to trudge into view, but the Ranger didn't need to see him. "He's just another Sorcerer, same as the last. How can we trust an elf working in service of Kozard?"

"Well. Frishka." Brisk tossed up a meek wave. "How about the huge dragon-man? What if he grew up on some distant mystical island where all the kids get to learn some ancient Healer's magic?"

"Can't trust him, either."

"Why in the hell *not?*"

"Last night at Brumble's, I called for his aid and he just watched me get my ass kicked."

"Last night at Brumble's, you smashed a man's face into a beer glass. Maybe you deserved it."

Marynda slipped around an imposing knot of vines and came into view of both the Ranger and the Cook. Her mind was racing. She'd spent years living in a forest with her grandmother, so she was not about to panic over whatever creature she'd seen moving in the trees a few seconds ago. But, she had her black leather handbag to think about. She had to protect it at all costs. Which meant she would be more than willing to make the men perform any necessary battles with the local wildlife.

She held up a moment and waited for Ramsey the Green to circle around the ivy clump. Out of all of them, she'd spoken with the green elf the most. She remembered him telling her about how he preferred the woods to the castle—a sentiment she shared—so, she figured he might be experiencing her same feelings.

"Ramsey," she whispered at his saggy face. "I saw

something out there. A big animal."

His wide green eyes shot over and scanned the trees, and, for a moment, his face almost lit up. But then he offered her a shrug and his posture drooped, his expression morose and pathetic once again. All the energetic sympathy,he'd offered her last night was gone.

Ramsey's timid dismissal filled Marynda with breathless disbelief and frustration. Last night, Ramsey had been the second one to visit her during her life's darkest stretch of hours. The first visitor had informed her that her beloved Alkent was murdered in a guard tower. So, in comparison to that horrid relay of information, everything the green elf said to her had a particular shine to it. Now she just felt betrayed. Maybe that was too harsh; maybe she should empathize with him getting publicly scolded by his teacher. But, no. He needed to be strong. He needed to deliver the same vigor he'd displayed to her when he convinced her to join this Frishkadammed Quest. Instead, he seemed weak and it made her want to get away from him, as if his lukewarm fragility might be somehow contagious.

As if she needed further motivation to move on, the giant spiky dragon figure rounded the corner behind Ramsey. With an exasperated exhale, she turned away, tightening the shoulder strap of her black bag as she did so. She noticed that the fat, boisterous elf was gone, so she hurried over to warn the two men. She hopped over a clog of rocks, gripped a dangling vine and swung expertly across a slim sunken trench. Her movements were automatic actions, because her mind was occupied elsewhere.

From the way she treated the obstacles as secondary, Griffey could tell she was alarmed.

The dread embedded in her face made Griffey gasp. Though his own face didn't betray the feeling, Parker's left hand went digging in his pocket to massage the Grulva coin his sister gave him. It was the closest connection he had to his family, and it was kind of close to comfort.

Marynda didn't speak until she was standing right before them.

"I saw something." She nodded to her right. "A big creature. Rustling in the woods."

Both men looked anxious. On instinct, Parker tried to draw his sword and he used his right hand to do so. This reflex gave him yet another spike of quivering, needling, horrific pain.

While the Ranger could see nothing through his tears, Brisk squinted and surveyed the wash of leaves and tree trunks. Nothing moved, yet his own unease did not fade. Still, he forced a smile and a chuckle. "I'm sure it was just a trick of the light, young madam."

This placating remark triggered nearly as much ire as Ramsey's own lack of action. "No no no," she snapped, her nerves too raw to output anything but authentic emotions, "don't you say *trick of the light* to me. I've lived in the woods before, Mister Risk. I lived in the forest for over ten years. I know the sound of a beast. And tricks of light don't make those sounds."

"Woah woah woah," he raised his hands, "I didn't mean t—Risk? Look, it's *Brisk*, lady."

"I thought I was a madam, not a lady." She knew this senseless retort would accomplish nothing, but the words were out before she could stop them. She was beginning to feel hopeless. Her eye caught upon the injured Ranger, squatting with watery eyes, air seething through his teeth. Ramsey was asleep on his feet, the fat elf was pouty and aloof, the Cook was not helpful, and she'd yet to hear the dragonborn utter anything more intellectual than a grunt. Whenever the monster attacked, *she* was probably going to have to be the one to fight it away.

Unless running's an option. She eyed the thick, snarling web of the forest and doubted it.

Uncertainty flooded back in on her, and she raised her own hands to match the Cook's surrender. Just as suddenly as it had sparked, her anger was gone. There wasn't time to squabble.

She was conditioned to the way the forest breathed, and she could sense the beast slinking towards them.

"Brisk," she softly pleaded. "If this thing attacks us, we can't run. We have to fight."

His face was nothing less than a gape. He choked, then coughed, then sputtered, "I heal people from fighting, I don't do the fighting myself. I work in the kitchen. I've used a sword one time."

A stick cracked behind Marynda. She whipped her head around, and her hand was a dart to the empty black bag riding at her hip. Brisk noted the empty sack, and raised a puzzled eyebrow.

Ramsey and Konragen appeared and paused five feet back, the top of the dragon's head obscured by branches. The elf's green eyes flicked from the kneeling Ranger to the bewildered Cook to Marynda's look of fear—and the frost upon his soul dissolved. Still, he didn't know what to say.

Marynda the Druid was caught in the same frantic spell of silence.

With a tremendous **_CRASH_**, a monster burst from the trees...

◇ CHAPTER THE FIFTEENTH. ◇
◇Attack of the Zodak.◇

Tree trunks shattered and canopies tumbled and thick branches bashed. Dirt and grass and leaves churned up as tree roots erupted from the earth. The pointed face of an enormous lizard monster sprang into sight, shoving the scenery aside. A pair of nostrils were the first to appear—fuming volcano craters. The head rolled back from there at a slant, bright shamrock-green and speckled with scales the size of a soldier's chest armor. The scale pattern was a honeycomb formation, patterned with turquoise gems, decoy eyeballs. Its authentic eyeballs were golden orbs, side-set in the arch of its skull, gawping stupidly down at the stinky intrusive humans. The black line of its mouth drooped with a forever frown. Yellow spines thrust atop its crest and waggled upon a skin-flap draping from its jaws.

The beast encroached behind the kneeling Griffey Parker, and it arrived with absolutely horrendous timing. Not only was the Ranger's busted right hand throbbing with pain, but that pain was steadily getting compounded with the effects of last night's drinking. Through the pain, he still managed to find things to feel bitter about, including a raving anger for his father's killer. In addition to some rage for Ulkar, who caused his broken hand, and for Kozard for not helping fix it.

But there was no time for any of this. Not when trees were smashing down with showers of splinters directly behind him. He pitched over into a roll, hugging his broken paw to his stomach, bouncing his left shoulder off the ground, and popping to his feet. Dispelling the misery of a hangover was surprisingly easy when one's life was in danger.

The first instant-reaction to flash through Griffey's mind was how naive he'd been. *Should've heard this beast approaching! Three days in the city has made me a bedtime weakling!* Second, he thought, *It's not here to hurt us! It's just being inquisitive! Sniffing us out!*

He wanted to holler: "Give it food! No aggressive moves!" but only a croak escaped his throat.

Marynda ducked, flung her leather bag around behind her, and grabbed a stone off the ground.

Brisk Koja fell on his ass, pots and pans clanging inside his pack and smacking off his back.

Ramsey reeled backwards, gripping his staff, rebounded off Konragen, and plopped to the dirt.

Konragen's typical brash stature broke from statue-mode, down into a defensive stance, dual-bladed battleaxe thrust out before him. He rumble-growled as his orange eyes locked on the invader. The sight of a looming beast did not intimidate the dragonborn. Rather, it invigorated him. He'd spent the last four years of his life in that stiff, awkward, stuffy castle, trying to earn some glowing karma, and every minute of it was boring as hell. While his outward manner was always calm, and he avoided all confrontations (depleting his anger with physical tasks), he'd been dying for a challenge. The circumstances would have to warrant his own violent intervention, of course (he respected his Paladin vows, even while drinking ale), and his opponent would have to be an equal—someone either his size or a group of people to match him. There were plenty of dragonmen his size, but all were drunk and lazy—plus he was forbidden from fighting his own kind. *So many rules just to pick a fight.*

Marynda sensed the same thing that Parker did. This big iguana wasn't here for anything more sinister than curiosity.

Nothing more deadly than sniffing foreign creatures who had breached its territory. *It could still trample us*, she reasoned. *And what if it eats what it smells?*

Across the scene, Griffey's heart sank as the scent of fresh apple bread reached his nose.

Brisk lay on the ground, doing a turtle-shell wobble in the dirt, with his eyes wide. Brisk wasn't much concerned about the lizard (*just a big dumb animal*). He was, however, exquisitely mad that he'd squashed his supply of apple bread. He flopped over onto his knees, and hauled his backpack around for inspection. While he was fidgeting and muttering, he didn't notice the silence.

Everyone stopped breathing. Konragen's growling faded. The birdsong went deathly still.

Heat rushed down the back of Brisk's neck. The brown fabric of his shirt and cloak ruffled and rippled as a gust of hot wind rushed at him. Suddenly, the status of the provisions in his pack didn't matter so much. Where he knelt, he slowly turned. The white nub of the lizard's face was inches away.

"*It's a Zodak...*" Griffey managed to hiss. "*It just wants food. Be quiet. Don't spook it.*"

Brisk felt a kick of insanity, in which he prissily did not want to give up his bread. His recipe for apple cake wasn't dignified by the High Chef back at the castle, and thus Brisk had to bake the dish in secret. He'd put up the risk so he could gift the bread to his friend, not serve it to a big dumb reptile.

Brisk relented, and slowly brought his pack around, keeping his eyes on the threat. The Zodak tilted its head so one of its side-mounted eyes could look down at the Cook. The spikes on the skin-flap hanging from its jowls dragged across the grass. The hint of a large tongue—thick as a python—snapped out from its pale lips, forked and purple and tasting the air. This wretched sight distracted Brisk at a crucial moment. His hands fumbled with the pack, and two cooking pans fell out.

Not only did the duo of pans have a loud, clattering mid-air battle, but they smacked each other on the ground, as well. The clamor startled the humans, the elf, the dragon—and the Zodak.

Suddenly incensed, the head of the Zodak drew back and its jaws split open.

Brisk dumbly gawped at the pointy teeth and pink-black gums.

From where he lay in the leaves, Ramsey the Green was frozen with shock. He'd seen a few Zodaks in his youth, up north in Willowflow forest. They'd always been peaceful herbivores, but he'd once read that some were omnivores. The sound of the pummeling pans snapped his rambling brain back on track. He watched in horror as the lizard reared back and prepared to chomp down on the Cook. Ramsey wrenched up his staff, whipped it around and aimed at the beast.

He had to think quickly, and act even faster. He didn't want to kill the animal but he absolutely had to stop it. He propped up his left elbow, braced the long brown cane, and uttered a *Frozen* spell beneath his breath. The right concoction of syllables coalesced in his brain, swept past his lips, sent his eyes flipping to the whites, and his arms juddered as he launched the spell.

The elf Sorcerer's aim was perfect—but the magnitude of intensity was far too docile.

In the instant before the giant iguana snapped at the quivering Cook—an invisible spell-ball socked into the left side of its skull. It recoiled in shock, felt its left eyeball and the left side of its face go numb. It twitched and *yawped* a squawking cry of alarm—but it did not collapse.

It did not go down. Instead, the lizard became enraged.

It's sights fell on Griffey—a low, injured target—and its long-clawed feet fired in a mad scurry.

Parker drew one of his shortswords with his left hand, but

the motion was awkward, and the Zodak was at him very fast. He dealt a pathetic slap, which slit the creature's lip and spilled out thin scarlet ribbons of blood, but it certainly didn't kill it. As its massive jaws snapped at him, the Ranger turned and dove into a glob of bushes—a clean escape by mere inches.

Annoyed, the Zodak swung its sights back to Brisk—just as Marynda threw a stone. Her Druid's training had sharpened her athletic skills in both knife-throwing and the humble art of throwing rocks. Her aim was ideal—and the force was admirable, as well—but the stone smacked against the numbed portion of the Zodak's face.

The Zodak's lone active eye locked on Marynda. Its mighty python-tongue ejected from its mouth, flew with an arrow's pulse, and *thumped* Brisk in the chest. The wet, soppy impact rammed the air from the lungs of the Cook and tossed him backwards.

The monster scampered towards Marynda, its mouth sagging open, tongue reeling back in.

She stared back at the oncoming lizard, and options cycled fast through her mind. She considered the *other* ability her Druid training had afforded her—far more extravagant than tossing rocks at targets. In the seconds before it reached both her and her black handbag, her eyes flicked first to the mossy yellow-green carpet down low, then up to the woodsy rafters. Her first option was to go small. Tiny enough to scurry unseen into the bushes, maybe down a rabbithole. Her second option was to fly. Go high enough and flap far enough so that she'd clear the chomping range.

But neither option meant she could take the handbag with her. She froze up. Hesitated.

The roaring mouth of the Zodak drew so close that she could feel sizzling heat on her face.

Konragen watched this all unfold, and his mind ran a cycle of its own. As mandated by the Paladin's pledge, he needed to analyze everything before stepping in. The bloated iguana had established itself as a threat when it knocked Brisk with its tongue. And, just by showing up, the Zodak had demonstrated that its possession of strength and power matched or exceeded Konragen's own. In addition to all that, the life of the young blonde woman was framed with imminent peril.

The dragonborn leaped forward, swung his battleaxe, and pounded it with thunder. One of the digits on the lizard's left foot was lopped off with a bloody *crack*. The Zodak screeched and reared up on its hind legs, smacking lofty branches. Its broad tail slashed out, slammed Konragen ten feet through the air, and he collided with a tree and collapsed. With lightning speed, the monster struck down at Ramsey the Green, snatched him in its jaws and rose up with a roar...

◇ CHAPTER THE SIXTEENTH. ◇
◇Powerhouse and Floor Chips.◇

Though Ramsey's earlier *Frozen* spell-ball lacked a potent punch, casting the streak had left him tired and weak. His biggest complaint about studying under High Sorcerer Kozard was that he was overloaded with books, and rarely put the arts in practice. Endurance was tied to being able to summon the energy for multiple consecutive spells, and Ramsey was feeble in the fortitude game.

In the last desperate instant before the behemoth crunched him to a gory pulp between its fangs, Ramsey knew he was too weak to cast an attack. His eyes rolled back white, and he encased his body with a protective *Bubble* spell. The magic formed an invisible exoskeleton, tightly enshrouding his body, along with all his possessions. While he and his staff were shielded, nothing was done to repel the colossal iguana and stop it from taking him. Ramsey felt his stomach drop out as he was torn upwards, and he even felt the heat of sickening steam rising from the lizard's gullet. The tips of the teeth halted less than an inch from touching him, held steady by the unseen barrier, but he still vividly imagined the puncture wounds. The mouth itself was large enough to park a wagon inside, the roof was gashed with pink grooves, and brown chunks of meat were stuck, flapping between the incisors.

With a gash of fear, Ramsey realized two horrible things. The first was that he couldn't fight back in any way, couldn't even wriggle his staff free to fire. He would be immobilized until the magic faded. The second awful realization spawned from the sight of the lizard's nasty investigative tongue scraping and sliding over him. *It can't taste me! The Bubble tastes bland! It's going to sp—*

Annoyed by this tasteless snack, the Zodak spit him out. Ramsey was loose—racing, tumbling, plummeting through the open air. Had the *Bubble* given his jaw any flexibility, he would've wailed and screamed. The ground rushed up at him, and he smacked down in a flurry of sticks and leaves.

Nearby, Griffey Parker struggled to his feet and became instantly entangled within a maddening mob of vines. He was poorly coordinated with his left hand, but he managed to hack his way free. He stumbled out, sheathing his shortsword, feeling woozy, battle-drunk and wild. A thirsty commandment to join the fight drove the Ranger to not only spot the pointed tail of the Zodak, but to run and scamper up it onto the back of the beast. At its thickest point, the tail was as plump as an elephant and it roamed in a dull, lazy wag. He made it about seven feet up the slant when the region of his mind blurting, *This is a great idea!* was rightfully shouted down by its counterpart calling him an impetuous fool.

The iguana raked its hind-quarters around with a quack, nearly flinging him into the brush. He lurched forward and grabbed hold of a spike—the first of a long line of spindles, dotting the knobs of the creature's spine from its tail to its skull. He doubled-down on his forward momentum and lunged forward to snatch the next station. He squirmed one further—hooked his right arm around the next horn, buried his injured fist beneath his chest plate, and held on tight—when the tail began to whip.

Gotta reach the head! The decoy eyes are pressure points! Punch the blue scales on its face!

The Ranger's goal was doomed. The swinging tail collided abruptly with a solid wood column and launched Griffey through the air. He actually glimpsed Brisk down below—turtle-bobbing on his back, shrieking about getting licked by the Zodak's tongue—then crashed down into the trees.

The mighty lizard thrashed about, cracking its tail against the trees and unleashing a bellow of triumph. It pivoted, churning dirt beneath its bulk. Utterly by accident the Zodak lifted a large errant foot—one of the digits was a bloody scarlet nub from Konragen's chop—and brought that foot down to annihilate Marynda, kneeling in the weeds.

In the instant before her pretty weeping face was mashed to a gory pulp, a piercing *SNAP* bashed through the forest, riding astride a walloping breath of wind of insistent silence. The wide leathery sole of the Zodak's foot stopped close enough to buzz the strands of strawberry blonde atop Marynda's head. That foot— and the entire iguana body attached to it—was yanked *up*. The big lizard shot directly vertical, up through the branches, to kiss the sky of blue.

The entire attack unfolded in less than a minute, and in less than five seconds the creature was blasted up past the highest reaches of the trees and completely disappeared.

One second later, the vacuum rebounded, bringing with it a clap of rushing air as noise rushed back in to bombard everyone's ears. Leaves fluttered and branches cascaded, as if loosened by the destructive breath of a thunderstorm. The peaceful, natural rhythmic sounds of the forest were slit with maniacal laughter, steadily building to a monstrous echoing cackle.

"Heh Heh Heh Heh Hahhh *Hahhh Vooo Ahhh Haaa* **Haaa** **HAAA HAAA HAAAA!!!**"

Since she was kneeling out in the open, Marynda was the first to spot the source of the laughter. She raised her chin, tears glistening in her eyes, and sucked down a shivering gasp. Twenty feet away, Konragen climbed to his feet, stretching his aching back before looking over to identify the laugher. Brisk quit rocking and whining and sat up, his face lit with alarm. With a groan, Griffey rolled over in the bushes, and got up to look over. Ramsey couldn't move in order to look, but he didn't need to.

High Sorcerer Kozard stood at the edge of the little clearing, arms raised. His physical height hadn't changed, yet he seemed impossibly tall. He held his long black staff high in his right hand and purple fingers of jittery electricity swam out from there in crackling waves, down his sleeves to criss-cross his body. His beard went from blonde to black and his eyeglass grew as black as a thundercloud.

At that moment—with an unlimited flow of arrogant dominance surging through the mortal fibers of his being—Kozard could've boomed out anything he wanted. He could've named all of the onlooking adventurers to be servants forever in his debt. He could've declared himself a demigod, beyond question and immune from defiance. In the end, he said nothing. Didn't need to say anything. It was clear where the edge resided. He was the powerhouse and they were the floor chips.

His cackling suddenly stopped. He gave a wicked one-eyed grin filled with bright crooked teeth. Then, he turned and vanished in the trees; striding the golden path lit by his black eyeglass.

One second later, a bass-drum *thud* pounded in the distance as the Zodak finally hit the earth.

Griffey Parker exhaled. Though half his body stung from landing hard on the ground, he was kind of grateful for getting tossed by the lizard. At least it had put distance between himself and Kozard. It would've been lethal to lounge too close during the Sorcerer's flexing power display.

The Ranger limped back to the clearing, which was now cluttered with leafy fallen branches, spotted with stubs of broken tree trunks, and cratered with sunken pits from the big iguana's footsteps.

Griffey found Brisk and helped him to his feet.

Brisk realized he was drenched with a clear liquid, goopy

and slimy.

"*Frishkadammit, Parker!*" wailed the indignant Cook. "Damn lizard got me with its tongue!"

In Parker's eyes, things had changed. He was no longer concerned about the other people in this Quest gang. He still didn't trust all of them, but, in the face of the raw deadly strength possessed by the possibly insane High Sorcerer, the Ranger saw these people as far less threatening.

Konragen marched over to where Marynda was still crouched. Unsure what to do, but knowing he wanted to try and convey comfort and grace, the big dragon-man leaned over and patted her on the shoulder. The Druid woman nodded at him.

Next to that pair, there resounded a ***POP!*** followed by a groan and the soft grating crinkle of someone thrashing about in the grass. Konragen looked over and began to laugh.

"Why is Ramsey Green wet?" his deep voice rumbled.

As if to evidence this observation, the elf sat up and shivered, sending droplets flying from his clothes and hair. Agitated yet informative, he snapped, "*Bubble* spells exude moisture when con—"

More hearty chuckles from the dragonborn interrupted him.

"Ramsey Green, birthed fresh from mother's womb!"

This tasteless comment was enough to snap both Ramsey and Marynda to their feet.

"I can't believe you haven't spoken this entire trip, and these are the first things you say!"

"Have only been out of castle twenty minutes. Not much to talk about."

Marynda began to pace, hugging her black leather handbag to her chest.

Brisk tried to shake away the lick of the Zodak with a twitchy dance.

Griffey noted that Ramsey was near to having a meltdown.

The elf's seven-foot frame was hunched as he pranced nervously about, hands switching between rubbing his arms and seizing his hair. His green frantic eyes kept shooting between where Rivercrest castle was and where the High Sorcerer had just disappeared. He was breathing too fast.

"Why don't you two calm down," Marynda suggested. "It's hot out here. You'll dry off fast."

"I don't give a Frishkadamn about the *moisture!*" the green elf retorted, his hysteria hitting a high note. "I'm worried about us getting back to the castle!"

"Runter Man say trees jump around in this forest. Ramsey Green may get lost."

Parker gave this a nod with a frown. It felt good to hear the stoic blockhead dragonman reference his earlier lecture and it felt rather funny to hear himself called a Runter.

When the elf didn't reply and continued to fret, Konragen scratched his pointed ear and offered, "Big Lizard gone. Surely Ramsey Green not still afraid of Gone Big Lizard?"

Ramsey finally paused, looking at Kon with enormous eyes, bloated with ghastly disbelief.

"I'm not concerned about the *lizard!*" the elf wheezed, astounded by the allegation, as if he honestly hadn't even considered it. Then, all he could do was gesture after Kozard and sputter.

He finally managed to choke out, "H-H-He's... He's c-capable of horrible things..."

Everybody's gaze twitched in that direction. After the High elf. The direction they were headed.

But their eyes returned quickly to each other, as if it were safer there.

Nobody wanted to talk about their imperious leader. At least not directly.

Brisk complained, "If anyone's got a gripe with the lizard, it's the one who got the sloppy tongue treatment." This made

Konragen laugh, which didn't break the tension, but it helped.

"Zodaks aren't meant to fly," Marynda rasped as she paced. "They're peaceful roaming cows. People are too big to be their prey. It would've left us alone soon enough. Didn't need to make it fly."

"Hey, at least the spell didn't explode the thing," Brisk exclaimed, slapping his leg, a jolly smile lit upon his face. "Can you imagine *that?* Guts and bones and blood just drenching us?"

Marynda was wrapped too tightly in her worries to respond to that. She wasn't spooked about almost getting absently squashed by a Zodak's foot. And she wasn't particularly afraid of being trapped out here with a volatile elf equipped with advanced Sorcery skills. (After all, Kozard *had* saved her life. He'd stopped the monster while they were all helpless. The elf's odd pompous taunts didn't change that.) No. More than anything, she was worried about herself. *I froze up. Oh dear Frishka, I froze up when I should've acted.* For one raving moment, she wanted to accuse Ramsey of casting some kind of spell on her when she was in the lizard's path. But she would just be hiding from her problems.

She knew it wasn't the young elf's fault. It was her own. She'd encountered big beasts in the woods many times before. But she'd never faced such a menace while carrying her only child. *Was it the pressure? The pressure to preserve what's left of my family? Is it just too much for me? Has three years living in the pampered city weakened my survival skills?* With a cold prickle of certainty that quickly turned to stone, she knew she would never escape another razor as close as that one.

When the chatter settled down and it became clear no one else was going to speak, the Ranger cleared his throat. Griffey's lake water eyes locked on Ramsey's frosty green ones. "I understand why you're afraid," he told the elf. "And I think we all have reason to share that fear. But going back to the castle is not an option for me. I've got nothing left to live for, besides catching the catch out here."

Marynda's gaze froze upon Parker as if she were seeing him in a fresh new frame. His words hit her in the heart. She wasn't just out here to preserve her family. She was out here to avenge it, as well.

"It's true," Griffey continued, "we're sharing this forest with many dangers—some more intimate than others—but at least our residency won't be a lonely one. We can fight them together." He gave a shrug of mild acceptance. "I will not blame you for going back. It took courage to assemble this crew and enter the woods today. A thousand thanks for that, Ramsey the Green."

The Ranger dealt the elf one further nod, then turned and began to pick his way through the brush. With his left hand he pulled back the flap of a bush and eased through the gap.

Marynda gave her handbag one more hug of reassurance, then slipped over to help hold back the vegetation and assist the one-handed man. With a sigh, Brisk followed them.

Konragen patted Ramsey on the head, then turned to scoop up the Zodak claw he'd chopped off.

"There no adventure waiting back at castle," the dragonman advised before romping on ahead.

After a long empty moment, Ramsey nodded and followed.

◇ CHAPTER THE SEVENTEENTH. ◇
◇The Spirit of a Chef.◇

A few minutes later, Brisk Koja realized that technical hiking—filled with lunges and ducks and pivots and strain—wasn't much fun. If he could only do some talking, he figured he could assuage the challenge. Five feet ahead of him, Marynda and Griffey seemed pretty committed to a silent brooding brand of movement. So he turned back and felt a small glow of approval because the elf was still with them. "Ramsey!" he hollered back. "We both got soaked, but it was I who got slimed!"

"You smell worse, too," the elf replied. "I can smell you all the way back here."

"Ah, that's why Brisk carries fresh apple bread in his pack! Cancels out the stench!"

The dragonman looked up at this, his spiky head smacking a few branches aside. He hoisted up the severed Zodak digit and lightly tapped it against his palm like a club. "Konragen eat no breakfast," he informed them with a grunt. "Munching apple bread would much please Konragen."

On the outside, Brisk looked calm and accommodating as he stopped, swung off his pack, and knelt to dig around. But inside, he was actually nervous. The enormous dragonman, with his spikes, dark complexion, deep-red cloak, and heavy snorting breath, loomed over him while he fidgeted.

Brisk extracted a square-cut of apple bread and thrust it up to Konragen, who accepted it and popped it in his mouth. The Cook gave a slice to Ramsey, as well, but he kept his eyes on the dragon, hoping to see a glowing smile light up his face. The best he got was a subtle nod and a beckoning hand demanding "more." The Cook complied, as the elf complimented him, "A fine dish, good sir."

When he stood up, Brisk noticed Marynda had stopped and was staring back at him.

"We've taken enough breaks already," Parker muttered. "We're moving too slowly."

"But I'm hungry," Marynda told the Ranger, "and your friend's food smells good."

Griff shuddered, keeping his attention forward, while Mary eased over to the others.

Seeing smiles all around—well, except for Konragen, whose face was made of rock, and Griffey, who was facing the wrong direction—ignited a bloom of satisfaction in Brisk's chest.

The Cook stretched and yawned. Making people happy through the magic of food was the Cook's calling in life, and he felt relaxed enough to spout off any thoughts which entered his head.

"Gonna be a hot one today, folks," Brisk announced, a humble attempt to shift the attention off his bread so he could save some of the stash for later. He ignored the dragon (who would probably beckon for "more" until he'd eaten every slice), then sealed up his pack and strapped it back on.

"Hot is how Brisk prefers it," the Cook declared. "Needs to be as hot outside as it is in the kitchen. That way there's some consistency, you see. As long as he's got heat, Brisk is a happy Cook."

"I tend to agree with Bread Man," Konragen admitted. "Hotter much better."

"Are you saying that because you're dragonborn?" Ramsey inquired.

"I think it's funny," Marynda told Brisk, "how you use the kitchen as your baseline temperature."

The Cook only offered a shrug and sighed, "Lovely day, hot lovely day."

From where he was standing, still facing away, Parker felt a shiver of sadness race through him. Personally, he thought this day was awful. It did not at all fit his mood. He felt the overcast gloom of the past three days—his days in Rivercrest castle—would've been far more appropriate right now. It just didn't feel right to have the sun shining, birds chirping, and enemy lizards vanquished, when he felt so sad. Not only had he neglected to visit his father over the last three days of the man's life… but here he was today, trudging through the woods, going to miss the man's funeral this afternoon. He imagined his mother and sister standing at that somber gathering with no one there to comfort them.

Without thinking about it, the Ranger hopped back at it, hiking forward through the thick maze of brush. The others adjusted their gear, pulled one last stretch, and reluctantly trekked along.

"Sorcerer!" Griffey called back. "Thanks for sticking with us. Could you come up here, please?"

Marynda actually felt the same as Parker did. She didn't think there should be bright pretty sunshine on the first day with her beloved Alkent gone from the earth. Still, it felt good to be moving. To be making progress, no matter if their goal was still hazy and undefined. Eating some food had made her feel a little better, too. She decided that talking more would help keep Alkent off her mind.

Ramsey trotted past, looking nervous and confused.

Marynda turned to Brisk as they walked. "So why are you a Cook and not a Chef?"

"Ahh milady, there's the spirit of a Chef in every Cook!" Brisk proclaimed. "While it's true, my job is to follow the recipes and make the orders, I still thrive on creating new dishes! How do you think that apple bread originated? Ole Brisk had to work late, had to wait until his boss was gone."

"Well, it was very tasty, thank you," she said with a shy smile. "So, how did you become a Cook? Or, um, a Cook with the spirit of a Chef, I guess."

"*Story time it is, then!*" The Cook clapped his hands with joy as they walked. "Well, you see, madam, it's almost Midsummer—the hottest time of year, and Brisk's favorite time of the year. But, once, when Brisk was a boy, a great challenge fell on his shoulders on the opposite calendar date.

"It was Midwinter's Eve, about twenty years ago. The Koja household had a full horde of rowdy relatives and loud friends coming over that night. It was early in the morning when my mother fell ill. My father cared more for metallurgy and sitting silently in a rocking chair and staring at the wall, so he wasn't going to be cooking up a meal. My sisters certainly weren't up to the task—they would rather have had no food in our house, so all the guests would be prompted to leave sooner.

"In the end, the job fell *smack* onto Brisk's plate. I snatched up my mother's recipe book and set out across the castle—an adventure to gather ingredients! When I finally returned to the house, I had quite the task ahead of me, and I even managed to enlist my sisters to help! Under my direction, we fashioned up a wonderful spread of cranberry sauce, spinach dip, cinnamon bread, cheesy potato mash, corn-and-carrot hot soup, pumpkin crumb pie, and some delicious applewood turkey—oh my!

"All our guests were endlessly dazzled, and it turned out to be a fine fine day, indeed. Young Brisk, of course, deferred all the compliments to his mother. I let people believe she was responsible, for that dear woman deserved the praise. Still, I knew I had done a good job when I saw their faces light up at the dinner table. It felt good to make them feel good, and the thrill has never left!

"Now, jump ahead a lotta years, and Brisk is working in

the main Rivercrest kitchens. I get to eat whenever I want, all day long, and that's very convenient. My boss, however, is an ugly grump-troll who gives me a horrible schedule every week, and I don't particularly enjoy making the same recipe day after day, year after year. That's kind of why I made a life decision six months ago. I parlayed my love of helping people and began training as a Healer! Now I give people good taste and good health!"

Marynda was nodding, clearly impressed. "That's excellent, Brisk. Both a Cook and a Healer, eh? It seems you'll be a very handy man to have along for our journey."

Brisk wiped sweat from his forehead. "Ooo-hoo, milady, I'm hoping we can wrap up these festivities pretty soon. Maybe catch the ole dark wizard this afternoon, scoot home by suppertime."

Marynda stayed quiet on that subject. She wasn't nearly as optimistic as the Cook.

◇ CHAPTER THE EIGHTEENTH. ◇
◇The Ranger and the Sorcerer.◇

Up ahead, Griffey Parker was also interested in timetables and the prey they were chasing. The tall green elf was walking alongside him now, a recalcitrant student wary of his instructor.

"Once again, Ramsey the Green," the Ranger said, hoping he could make this guy relax and trust him, "thank you for staying. Our Quest can certainly use you."

Ramsey waved it off. "Leaving would've risked my status in Kozard's Sorcery program."

"How advanced are you in that program, exactly?" the Ranger pressed, probably too soon.

The elf froze up. He kept his pace alongside Griff, but his movements were rigid.

"Listen," Parker sighed. "We're stuck out here together, so we need to be honest with each other. We need to know what each of us is capable of. That way we cover our blind-spots, acho?"

"Acho, Ranger," Ramsey relented with an eventual sigh. "I am a Seventh Year Sorcerer, but don't get too excited. Kozard is a classroom goblin. He's more interested in limiting my knowledge than encouraging my advancement. I've been studying a lot of scrolls and cleaning up the messes he makes… Still, I have managed to harness several spells. One is, *Decipher Languages*—either written or spoken. I can also do *Lesser Illusions*—limited to about the size of a dinner table and—"

"—Don't be offended, master elf," said Griff, "but those

don't sound very useful in a battle."

Ramsey sputtered and nearly tripped. He felt his smooth pale face grow hot, as if he were being ushered to a cliffside. He sensed the Ranger was trying to determine who was useful and who wasn't.

Trying not to sound indignant and petulant, the elf revealed, "I've harnessed *Fire Bolt*, as well."

Parker shot him a grin and a shoulder pat. With that one simple exchange, the elf's anxieties eased away. In that moment, he felt more accepted than he ever had in Kozard's classroom.

"You've only *harnessed* those spells, not *mastered* them?"

The green elf shrugged. "That's apprenticeship without practice, I guess…"

"Do you need that staff of yours to cast these spells?"

Ramsey held up the indicated staff, a gnarled cane of gingerbread-wood. He nodded. "If this device is taken from my possession… I will be reduced to only performing very minor magic…"

"Always seemed strange to me..." the Ranger mused, "...entrusting your power to an *item…*"

"What is a warrior without his sword? Or his shield?"

"Fair enough." Griffey's eyes danced up to the wash of ivy and branches, pulsing with birdsong. "Have you ever considered that Kozard has been doing you a favor?" Before the other could interject, he went on, "I suspect you're a forest elf, which means you draw your power-flow from nature. And you've been training inside the walls of a damn castle. Not much nature to draw on there. No matter how poor you felt, you would've felt worse if none of your spells worked. If you constantly failed…"

"The only *favor* Kozard ever did for me was isolating me from his other students. That way no one else had to witness my humiliation." The elf glanced at Parker. "I was allowed to start a garden. A tiny one. In a closet with a window. I used that to draw power from. But every day, the High Sorcerer would laugh at me for that. Would remind me of how weak it was to rely on leaves and sticks.

"That fat elf insulted my homeland every day for seven years," Ramsey softly stated. "First thing in the morning, actually. He would bless that day's lesson by proclaiming that: *Willowflow forest is filth, just as all forests are filth.*"

"If he made you jot that phrase on the blackboard, I hope he let you use magic to do it."

The young Sorcerer sadly shook his head. "No magic. Had to write it myself each time…"

Griffey scratched his neck with discomfort, decided to push the conversation elsewhere. "My Ranger's training exposed me to a bit of magic, as well," he revealed. The elf shot him a curious glance, and he cleared his throat. "Just one trick, really. Harnessed or mastered, I dunno."

"I presume Rangers draw their power-flow from the same natural sources as forest elves?"

Parker nodded. Then he forced himself to smile. (Just as before, it felt wrong on his face and it didn't stay for long.) "I have the ability of *Scout Cast.* I can transmit up to a hundred yards' distance, but I'm automatically returned after sixty seconds. Mostly use it for hunting, tracking…"

Before the Sorcerer could express his acclaim, the Ranger's nostrils twitched. He squinted with strain, as if the scent of piss had just flirted across his face. His jaw set firm and he stopped in his tracks, sending Ramsey striding a few steps past. Parker pivoted back the direction they'd come from.

"You're attuned to this forest, aren't you?" Ramsey breathed. "More so than I am."

*I'm attuned to **danger**,* Griffey corrected in his mind, but not aloud.

"Just because you're bragging about your magic doesn't mean you need to demonst—"

Parker's eyes slipped shut. He raised his left palm, facing

outward. Then he vanished.

The tall green elf was left standing by himself, stunned by the suddenness of the flourish, but irritated, as if abandoned. He dusted off his cloak and breathed some fresh forest air, and then—

—the Ranger reappeared, his boots smacking right back where he'd last been standing, only now he was facing forward. He took a moment to catch his breath, then shot his elf companion a wink, as if to say, "*You and Kozard aren't the only ones with magic out here, fella.*"

"What can we expect from this dark wizard we're chasing?" Griff smoothly ventured, as if there'd been no interruption, as if he'd never left. They even resumed walking without a hitch. "He's been weakened from casting the kill spells. But how long until he can generate a portal and escape?"

Ramsey's eyes went cold, and they grazed across the woods ahead of them, wary of Kozard.

"Look," Parker said, "I know you're not trained in dark wizardry. And neither one of us is particularly fond of the High Sorcerer. All I need is your best estimate here. Some sort of target."

With a gulp, Ramsey relented once again, "I think he'll hit full strength by tomorrow night."

The Ranger didn't scoff, didn't get in his face and yell. He merely nodded and walked on.

Grateful for being treated as an equal, the elf felt obliged to ask, "How can I help you, Parker?"

It was difficult for Griffey to hide the relief on his face. Finally, he was having a conversation with someone with both the potential to help him and the willingness to listen. He withdrew his mangled right hand from its protective pouch, in between his chest and armor. He held the paw up so the tall green elf could examine the swollen flesh and purple worm-veins ranging across his knuckles.

"I don't suppose you can help fix my hand?" the Ranger modestly requested.

From the severe scrutiny the elf gave his paw, there was actually a moment of hope.

The Sorcerer's words were meticulous and steady. "I'm due to attain full Healer's powers once I've ascended to the next stage of my training… But… But I can't fix your broken bones right now…"

For an irrational flash, Parker was convinced his earlier suspicions were correct. His thirsty paranoia raved, *This little Sorcerer is under orders from Kozard to obstruct my mission!*

"It wouldn't be proper for me to attempt it. I'm not certified and can't be held accountable."

Griff gutted the urge to punch the elf in his smooth unwrinkled face. *There I go again*, he thought. *My first reaction is to get angry*. He took a deep breath and looked Ramsey in the eyes.

"Listen, Ramsey…" he calmly spoke. "I'm in rough shape here. I lost my father last night. Went to jail last night. Lost my right hand last night…" He trailed off, hoping his words held enough heartfelt eloquence to adequately inspire without further effort. Yet the elf looked unconvinced.

"Ramsey the Green," he tried again, clearing his throat. "Why are you out here with us?"

The elf looked surprised, then his defenses seemed to melt away as a look of sadness overtook him. "You weren't the only one who lost your father last night. Our whole kingdom lost him…"

There was a moment of strained silence and held breath.

All Griffey did was raise his right hand.

Ramsey decided to help this man. There were reasons beyond this being the son of John Parker. Griffey didn't treat people like dung on his boots, as Kozard tended to.

"What I *could* do," the elf told him, "is create… an area. A contained environment, off the plane of our reality, yet still connected back here. We could place your hand there. It would be shielded from further harm, cause you no more pain, and you'll be able to retrieve it unchanged when you need it."

Parker stopped walking and his eyebrows raised. "You're talking about the sub-world…"

The elf offered a shrug and a smile. "Well, it *is* free real estate."

Park actually chuckled. "If you're sure I can get it back later, I consent to your assistance."

The elf didn't look excited because his magic was being trusted. Didn't look ecstatic at being given a chance to prove himself. His was a look of serious business, exactly what Griff wanted to see.

Ramsey concentrated. Leaned forward, his left hand braced beside Griffey's injured hand, with his staff hovering on the other side. There was a brief flash of white-light intensity, and a crackle of grape-wine electricity… and Griffey's hand vanished. His right arm now ended in a nub at the wrist. It felt as if a fat invisible cylinder was appended to his wrist. There was nothing there, but he could *feel* the weight of the cylinder. Eyes wide with amazement, he tried to clap his hands and hit empty air.

"I know what you're thinking," Ramsey said, his words quick, as if he were afraid Parker might turn angry. "When my skills are advanced enough to attain Healing powers, we can extract your missing hand from the sub-world. It will reattach to your arm. Undamaged. As if it never left."

"And then… then, you'll be able to actually mend the broken bones?"

The tall green elf gave a solemn nod, as if he wished he could be anywhere else right now.

Griffey felt a worrisome knot tangle up his guts. He'd begun their conversation hoping to gain an advantage over the situation they all faced. Now he felt even more crippled. Maimed, even. And he was filled with the same separation anxiety that a child feels when his brother borrows his favorite toy for the day. His hand was safe, but he wanted to be able to *see* it. To verify its safety. To know if it even *existed* anymore. He'd also begun their conversation convinced he could get Ramsey to see his way of thinking. It was obvious the young Sorcerer detested his superior Sorcerer, so that left room to maneuver. However, he now feared that Ramsey had out-paced him. It felt wrong to think that Ramsey—and *only* Ramsey—could now locate his hand. He'd trusted the elf enough to let him perform the act, but that trust carried the same caution as the kid whose brother absconded with his toy for the day.

Parker was about to mumble out a word of thanks when the blunder-and-crunch of shambling footsteps approached. A moment later, the other three members of the crew emerged.

Marynda and Konragen could be seen in the back, idly conversing.

Brisk was in the lead, walking alone, and huffing to himself.

The Cook looked up, spotted Griffey, and hooted, *"Holy Frishka! Where's your hand??"*

◇ CHAPTER THE NINETEENTH. ◇
◇The Chamber in the Handbag.◇

The chamber was the shape of an egg tilted on its side. The floor was cold gray stone, cross-hatched with a faded pattern of graded sand mortar. The curved walls were a thick silver mist which gave the space the illusion of an oval shape. The curtains of the mist convened at a circular cloud, directly overhead, about the size of a soldier's shield. This cloud was a swirl of cotton throbbing with sunlight. That round elevated window spilled a soft frosty glow into the chamber, keeping at bay the sensation of eerie-dank-dungeon.

From where she lay on the floor, wrapped in a warm padding of thick wool blankets, the human baby spent the hours staring up at that peaceful churning cloud. The human baby's hair was a jolt of thick black, her eyes were a bright dazzling blue, and her demeanor was one of calm. She rarely ever cried. Only last night, the night her father was murdered, did she let the tears flow and the squalls fly.

She did not feel the trembles of the outside world as her mother's handbag was tossed about during the hike through Shadowbranch forest and the battle with the Zodak lizard. Nor did she feel the worry—the constant nagging *worry*—ebbing from her mother's every breath. So, in a sense, she was lucky to be encased in this place. Still, Hazel was such a mellow baby, she might not have even cried had she been in Marynda's arms during the dash through the woods or the showdown with the iguana.

In here, the only thing to entertain her was the heavenly

plate of cloud swishing overhead.

Suddenly, an object **popped** into existence and hovered, unmoving, five feet above her. The eyes of Baby Hazel shot to this new arrival and studied it. At first, her primitive mind saw it as a bird. **Must** *be a bird. One without feathers.* Then details began to trickle in. The sketchy contours of the levitating item began to clarify. She realized it was a hand. A man's hand. Like her father's.

Only it was bruised. Swollen. An ugly purple, stained with crispy brown blood…

◇ ◇ ◇

"That's excellent, Brisk," Marynda said with a nod. "Both a Cook and a Healer, eh? It seems you'll be a very handy man to have along for our journey."

"Ooo-hoo, milady, Brisky is actually hoping we can wrap up these festivities pretty soon. Maybe catch this dark wizard this afternoon, get home by nightfall."

Marynda looked unconvinced, and eventually said, "Your friend… the woodland Ranger. The, uh… the Son of the Second King… he behaves as if this will be a prolonged enterprise…"

Brisk trumpeted a chuckle. "Griffey is pretty in touch with things like the woods and the animals, but you'll find he runs with his head in the clouds and his boots off the ground."

"He's too gruff and humorless to be an idealist."

"Well, it's been a rough couple hours for the ole chap…"

"S-Same…" Marynda sputtered. A sudden weight heaved upon her heart and she didn't think she could stomach much more conversation. She forced out, "H-How do you guys know each other?"

Brisk recognized that, for the next little while, the Druid woman was going to be a patient listener instead of an active contributor. "Let's see here. More story requests from Brisky, eh? Gotcha hooked as if I were serving cheesy po'taters, eh? Hmm. Oh! I was—*ooo, I dunno*—about three years past ten, I believe.

I'd brought a pan of my famous pumpkin bread to Academy class (hoping to impress the instructor, you see). A gang of thieves stole the bread from me, left me beaten in a corner. When I was at my lowest point, I raised my chin and watched a boy named Griff beat up one of the villains and win back my bread. It was smashed and ruined, but he returned it to me. Been friends ever since!"

Brisk noticed she was rubbing her black handbag and nodding, still not going to say anything, so he babbled on. "Anyway, it's not perfect, but being a Cook has its perks. Every day, I get to go to work and contribute to the finest cuisine in the region. Far better than that slop served in Bofork—"

Konragen grunted loudly.

The pair felt a spray of heat on the backs of their necks.

Both Brisk and Marynda turned to make sure the dragon wasn't about to roast them.

"Bofork may serve nasty food, but at least Bofork music isn't out of tune and horrid!"

Brisk squinted and sputtered. Marynda nodded with a smile.

"I agree, mister dragon. I have a fondness for Bofork myself. Are you from there?"

Sensing he was about to lose his audience, Brisk tried to make it sound like he wasn't lunging, but he was definitely lunging. "I assure you, milady, the music in Rivercrest is not so horrid—"

"Konragen been in Rivercrest four years. Lived in Bofork for one year before that."

Marynda fell back in line to walk next to the dragonborn.

Brisk was left feeling stupid, regretful, and somehow unclean. The blonde was pretty and it felt wrong to have her displeased with him. For an absurd moment, he considered offering up more apple bread just to get attention. Maybe even walking backwards through the sticks and rocks and mud, just so he wasn't shut out. In the end he just trotted on alone, wishing he hadn't made the Bofork joke.

"Why are you carrying that?" Marynda asked the dragon, trying to hide her disgust.

With his orange eyes, Konragen gave her the look of a confused puppy dog, then realized what she meant. He was carrying the claw he'd chopped off the foot of the giant Zodak lizard. "It smells worse than a bugbear circus tent," she complained (this was probably true; Kon wasn't good at smelling things). It was a pointy blackened cone with a gnarly glob of spoiled flesh stuffed inside.

Kon lofted it up, gave it an adoring pat, and declared, "Trophy from lizard defeat!"

"Yes, but *we* didn't really defeat it," she admitted. "And surely you have a purpose for it?"

The dragon looked confused once again, as if unsure whether she was making fun of him. He decided to let the feeling slide; he enjoyed her company. "After Zodak is dead," he explained, "Zodak skin hardens to hard as stone but still very light. Konragen will hollow out claw, use as arm shield."

"You're gonna hollow that nasty thing out? And put your arm in there?"

As if anxious to exhibit that he knew what he was doing, Konragen drew a machete from his belt. He stabbed the blade inside the cone, churned it around, and dumped out the mushy contents. With what passed for a sly grin on his rigid face, he then slipped his right arm inside it, sliding to his elbow.

"What did you do while you lived in Bofork for a year?" Marynda asked.

Konragen rumbled laughter. "Same as everyone else," he said with a wave of his claw arm. "Get dirty and work for blacksmith." Then, the dragon's mood turned quieter, more reflective. "City of Bofork very kind to dragonfolk. No discriminate because of what our people did in past. Always somewhere to work, just not enough pay. Konragen even fell in love in Bofork… for a short time…"

Marynda surprised herself by opening up. She sensed the dragon didn't want to elaborate further, so she figured it was safe to speak. "The love of my life came from Bofork, as well, actually. We met when he won a strength contest on Grayboulder river—"

"—*Log-Drag River-Swim??*" Konragen cut in with a vibe of excitement.

The Druid woman smiled, a single tear glistening in her eye.

"Konragen nearly win Log-Drag River-Swim four years ago!"

Marynda shone her sad smile upon her companion. It felt somehow comforting to know this dragon held the same interests and a similar background as her beloved Alkent. But that comfort wasn't enough to hold back the tears. She realized that if she let Konragen rattle off the story of his work in the Grayboulder contest, then there would be nothing for her to do except listen… and cry. She needed to do the talking herself. Needed to stay occupied. Stay strong. That's what Alkent would've wanted.

"I met Alkent three years ago," Marynda told him, her wobbly voice gaining balance and traction as she persisted. "We were married shortly after that. It was the only option, really, and we both knew it. We were in love. I forced him to be spontaneous, and he forced me into relentless laughter…

"Anyway, a year after we met in Rivercrest, he took me back to Bofork for a visit. It was a remarkable little day trip adventure—mainly because of him. Alkent seemed to get lucky at every turn. We got a late start that morning and missed our ride across the river. But we ran into an old friend of Alkent's on the shore of Grayboulder river, and that man owned a boat and escorted us across for free. As if that hadn't left me giddy enough, once we reached the town, we passed a vendor with one doughnut pie remaining in his stock. (Doughnut pie is my absolute favorite.) A line formed up behind us while Alkent bought it for me—you see, had we been a few seconds later, we would've missed out!

"We strolled through Bofork, he regaled me with amusing tales of his childhood—making me laugh with every one—and we ran into one of his cousins. That man's name was Bokent and he took us to the stable he owned. Bokent explained that his horse, Ginger, just received new shoes and he needed someone to ride her out into the country and back just to test her out. We graciously accepted, and scored a scenic ride for free! The day was hot, but the breeze felt wonderful as we rode Ginger together, laughing the entire way. Eventually, we broke in a wide-open meadow of yellow flowers and made love in the beautiful sunshine…" She trailed off, but had successfully defeated the weeping urge.

Marynda's flurry of gleeful memories did not last for long, and perhaps that was a blessing. Any more reflection upon her Alkent would only inevitably remind her that he was dead now.

The Druid woman and the dragonman had been walking in silence for a few companionable moments when a sudden *pop* erupted in front of them. Griffey Parker appeared from the empty air, his boots bouncing a flurry of leaves. He appeared as if birthed from nothing, plucked from a portal.

With a look of desperation on his face, the Ranger seized hold of Konragen. The Ranger's right hand was concealed, so he had to grab the dragon's arm with his left hand, but it didn't seem to limit his power. Despite the size difference between the two men, Parker hauled Kon off to the side.

Marynda froze in her tracks, looking at both of them in shock, afraid they'd start fighting.

Towering over Griffey, Konragen glared down at the man and growled low in his throat. Parker felt sweat slick his face as he imagined the dragonborn punching him and pummeling him to death.

With a frantic expression, Griff gestured urgently over to where Kon had just been walking.

Marynda's eyes followed the Ranger's direction and it was her call that stopped Kon's fists.

"*Konragen, hold up!*" she hollered. In that moment, Griff found her to be amazingly attractive.

Kon glanced over and saw how seriously she was studying the ground. It must've been a good performance, as her focus was enough to convince him. Kon drug Parker by the arm over to where she was peering at the forest floor. At first, there was nothing but grass and dirt and leaves and sticks. But, just as Kon began to growl again, the ground… changed. Whatever the enchantment was, it dissipated and revealed, sure enough—right where Konragen had almost stepped—a hideous pit. A gaping hole, a tunnel down to a dark, musty pile of skulls on spikes, squirming with snakes and spun with spider web.

Marynda gasped with fright. Griff exhaled with relief (*if my intuition had been wrong…*).

The dragonborn's evaluation was drawn-out for a few long dramatic seconds, but Griffey knew that, as soon as Marynda was convinced, he was in the clear. The concrete grip on Griff's arm released.

Konragen stepped back, gave Parker an up-down look of amazement, then he did a curious thing. The dragon drew his right arm out from the Zodak claw, then pressed his right fist to his left breast. He even bowed his spiky head. The gold chain with the red jewel squiggled out and dangled.

"Griffey Parker, Runter of Rivercrest," Konragen exclaimed. "You just saved life of Konragen. In honor of Paladin oath, I am indebted to you for one favor."

With that done, Kon stood back to his full height and resumed the trek which the Ranger had interrupted. The dragon was careful to avoid the skull pit as he passed, but otherwise acted as if nothing had disrupted this pleasant morning stroll. Left standing there, Griffey's eyes flicked over and made brief contact with Marynda's hazel gaze. He offered a shrug and a helpless smirk, then—

—his sixty seconds were up, Griffey vanished, and fired back to rejoin Ramsey up ahead.

Marynda found herself staring at the forested scenery which was now devoid of Parker. She blinked and looked over just in time to see Konragen pause in his tracks and look back at her.

"I will join you in a moment, Konragen," she told him, "but first I must attend a need."

The big dragon huffed with annoyance, but he felt honorbound to stay there and wait for her.

The Druid woman scurried into the bushes, but not too far from the general area they'd adopted as their trail. She squatted in the bushes and attended to her needs. Then, she peeled open her black handbag, and, clutching a water-skin, dunked her hand inside…

… inside the egg-shaped chamber, Baby Hazel continued to gape up at the human hand floating stationary above her cuddle of blankets. Then a woman's arm breached the swirl of sunlit cloud directly overhead. The woman's arm absently nudged the mangled hand out of the way—sending it endlessly spinning, a captivating twirl which would go on to dazzle the baby and ease her into a dreamy snooze. The new hand brought the nipple of a water-skin down to Baby Hazel's lips. Once she was sipped and happy, the woman's hand tickled Hazel's tummy, then retracted to face the dangers of Shadowbranch forest.

◇ CHAPTER THE TWENTIETH. ◇
◇Battle Positions.◇

"**H**oly Frishka! Where's your hand??"

Griffey Parker shuddered. He knew it was Brisk making the comment, but he was still slightly annoyed at having his vulnerability poked and prodded so publicly. He gutted the feeling, and reminded himself that everyone was going to find out eventually that his hand was totally gone. Which meant, no matter how ashamed he was, he could never hide it; the discovery was inevitable. On another level, he commanded himself to be grateful. After all, the Sorcerer had granted him what he needed.

Ramsey had given him a reprieve from the pain, and had done so with excellent timing.

The Ranger knew that, very soon, they would enter an arena of supreme danger.

The Trail Guardians drew near.

"Our Sorcerer friend was kind enough to take my hand away," Griffey told the Cook, then instantly scrunched his face with embarrassed regret. "Er, I mean, took it away and will Heal it soon."

"I know how it looks and I know how it sounds," Ramsey quickly inserted. "But I know where the hand is, and I can easily retrieve it once I've attained the necessary level of Healing powers."

"You're a Healer, eh?" Brisk challenged. "Well, so am I." The Cook was still grumpy over losing his conversation with Marynda; the dragon stole his spotlight. Plus, he was irritated at the dragon for eating his apple bread and never even thanking him. The heat and humidity out here didn't bother him, but he *was* getting annoyed at the scratching branches and prickly insects. He paused, then couldn't resist picking a fight. "You know, I've gotta say—your Healer's skills can't even fix a hand?"

"Excuse me, sir!" Ramsey quacked, appalled. "I didn't see *you* fixing his broken bones!"

Griffey, caught in the middle, felt his pulse spike.

Were he encamped alone in the forest on a tranquil summer evening—with a window gap in the treetops just wide enough to admit some starlight, shining down on the pages of his journal—then he would've undoubtedly been able to articulate what he needed to say. Hell, there even would've been some musical—perhaps even poetic—eloquence to his words. Yet, instead, his temper ran hot. It was just baffling how these two buffoons wanted to argue when there were bigger worries and bigger goals.

"*Quit bickering!*" Parker blurted.

Brisk felt pretty insulted by that. *Griff shouldn't say that when all he's done today is moan about his busted hand—which got broke because he was being a bum at the bar last night!*

The Ranger stopped him from saying those words aloud when he jabbed a finger in the Cook's chest. "*You're not a Healer!*" Griff jabbed Ramsey next. "*And **you're** not a Healer!*"

He let his words sink in for a moment, then started speaking again just before a flurry of objections erupted. "But that doesn't mean you can't be. Doesn't mean you won't be soon."

Their faces began to dawn with understanding and this served to ease Griff's own nerves. "We're a team," he reminded them. "We work together. And, here very soon, we're gonna have some serious business to go to work on." He pointed up ahead, along the back-trail of the High Sorcerer. "We're nearing the trailhead. It will be well defended. Maybe the dark wizard got caught there."

Griffey saw Marynda and Konragen appear around a corner, dodging around an umbrella of tangled branches. He waved them over, then addressed Brisk again, just before the Cook started to complain. "Brisk, all you've got is a knife, so I want you to borrow one of my shortswords." Parker gestured at the hilt of his sword by trying to grab it with his right hand, which was, of course, absent. With his left, Griff drew the sword, handed it over.

By now, Marynda and Konragen had approached and paused to form a rough circle with the others. Both of these fresh arrivals felt enough respect for the Ranger to give him their attention.

Griff addressed the newcomers, "We're getting close to the trailhead. I've never been here myself, as my Ranging has been restricted to mainly Willowflow forest. But I know we're going to be facing some opposition here. Plus, the dark wizard may have gotten snared in the trap."

"You can sense it, can't you?" Ramsey asked. "You can sense the danger up ahead."

Parker nodded. "Yes, but I can't define it. That's why we need to be ready for anything."

He could also sense resistance and reluctance in the crowd. Yet nobody vocalized their doubts, so he just went on talking. "Brisk and Marynda, I want you two to stay in the back. Seeing as Marynda doesn't have any weapons—Brisk, it's your job to protect her, acho?"

"Acho, Parker, I got your back," the Cook offered, raising the shortsword.

Marynda looked offended, but she stayed quiet.

"You'll be safe at my side, milady!" Brisk declared. "Together, we'll safely observe."

The Druid woman felt insulted and nearly fired off a demand to be part of the battle. She bit it back, though, thinking of her child. With a sigh, she exhaled her pride and turned to the

Cook. He gave her a charming smile which didn't ring with a warrior's confidence, but she managed to smile back.

"Now, Ramsey," their impromptu leader went on, "I want you walking ahead of those two. Cast that *Fire Bolt* you told me about, and cast it often. Just choose your shots carefully. Don't hit us."

"Runter Man want to be on front lines with Konragen at his side," the dragon observed.

Parker gave him a nod and confirmed, "You and me will lead on this one."

"Why is Runter Man our leader?" Kon pointed at Griff's amputation. "He single handed."

"Yeah, uh…" The Ranger actually tried to wipe his forehead with his missing hand.

"What about the High Sorcerer?" Ramsey hissed.

Before Parker could reply, Marynda spoke up. She may have been banished away from the action, but her voice still needed to be heard. "Let's look at what we know for sure. The High Sorcerer obviously cares about our mission, or else he wouldn't have saved us all from the Zodak—"

"—his maniacal laughter says *killer lunatic* more than *caring chaperone*!" Ramsey barked.

Marynda looked frustrated by the interruption, but nodded. "That's correct, Sorcerer, I was just about to add that in. Thing is: we don't know what to expect from him. With us or against us."

"We may be all alone," Griff exclaimed, "so prepare for the unknown."

Before there could be anymore talking, the Ranger turned and began the hike. Konragen, also not a big fan of talking, fell in stride beside him. The others clearly sensed they weren't being allotted as much power as those two, and felt that arguing amongst themselves wouldn't accomplish much.

The landscape began to rise to an uphill slant, and the thickness of the trees and brush slackened and fell away. Even the richness of the branches overhead thinned out, gradually birthing a view of flawless blue summer sky. Birds flapped past and whistled in the trees.

It felt good to be able to stretch their arms without smacking vegetation obstructions, and it was encouraging to be able to spread out a bit. They were all glad to trade that for an uphill slope.

Soon, the trees relented and they spotted Kozard, standing on the outskirts of a clearing.

The powerful elf was facing away from them, staring down the challenge…

◇ CHAPTER THE TWENTY-FIRST. ◇
◇Whisper Rush.◇

Now that the trailhead drew near, now that he was almost reunited with Kozard, now that the dark wizard who'd killed his father was potentially within his grasp, now that he had everyone adjusting to following him… Griffey Parker felt it all cave in on him. The company had agreed to act upon his wishes, but had he given the right directions? Had he chosen the best path to keep them safe? *Couldn't I have easily commanded them all back to the castle? Rather than marching them into what could possibly be a trap?*

It was so crushingly obvious to him now. He'd elected to cast these poor peoples' lives—those who'd volunteered to help him avenge the assassination—onto a game board where they were undoubtedly favored to lose and die. Whether at the hands of the Trail Guardians, or Kozard, or the dark wizard—all three of those threats were viable. *My father was the natural leader, not me.* Realizations unk in—he'd just used the past-tense in reference to his father.

His confidence was far from peaking as he stepped shakily up next to the High Sorcerer. He'd barely even pondered the decision to walk over here, as his capacity for contemplation was bereft. On some subconscious level, he'd processed that Kozard was no longer uttering maniacal cackles and that was all it took to make the elf less threatening. That meant it was safe to approach. It didn't mean Kozard wasn't their enemy, but it did mean the

Sorcerer had bigger concerns.

Quite possibly it was just curiosity that drove Griffey's feet to shuffle his way to the crest of the hill. He was very intrigued to see what form the Trail Guardians would take—here, at the start of the western path through Shadowbranch forest. He'd encountered Guardians in other forests, and they were often in animal form. Giant cobras, giant wolves. *They're usually giant-sized, I guess.*

The Ranger halted next to the Sorcerer elf. He surveyed the field and saw little to impress him.

The most imposing feature stood beside him. Griffey was a half-foot taller than Kozard, yet he somehow felt inadequate. The rest of the fellowship hung back, leaving Griffey to feel very much alone.

Did my father ever feel so solitary?

He felt a special stab of anger for Konragen, whom he'd assigned to be by his side in battle. He'd selected the dragonman for that position for obvious reasons. Kon was an eight-foot hulk covered in spikes wearing a Zodak claw on one hand and clutching a battle-axe in the other. Meanwhile, John Parker's son still possessed a gnawing headache and was short one hand.

Not having the dragonborn at his side only seemed to magnify his insecurities.

Sprawling out before him, the Ranger saw a circular field a hundred yards in diameter; a disc carpeted with luscious bright green grass, ringed on its circumference with unforgiving chain-links of gnarly tree branches. Positioned at the heart of the field were enormous round shrubs, three abreast. Boxwood bushes; clumps of shamrock towering over twenty-feet high. They weren't full spheres, as their bases were compressed, so each resembled a witch's gazing ball resting atop a lip-curled saucer.

The giant scorpions or giant grizzly bears, he smugly thought, *are lurking beyond those bushes.*

With his mind satisfied on that topic, Griffey gave his

attention to the other crucial case. He shocked himself by speaking his thoughts aloud, "The dark wizard didn't get trapped here, did he?"

"If he were here, you'd be dead.

"Stay out of my way, Ranger," Kozard growled. "Stay back with the other children. Make sure that excuse for a Seventh Year doesn't cast any spells, because he's the worst spellcaster I've ever seen. Oh, but, if you *do* get yourselves killed, I'll gladly catch the wizard on my own..."

The fat elf's voice faded out, his last words conveying a cutting edge. As if there were nothing more the High Sorcerer desired than to do just that. Catch the dark wizard on his own.

For the first time since he'd been standing there, Griffey looked at the elf next to him. The elf's pointed-braided beard was now black. But Griffey's focus went to the black glass clenched in Kozard's right eye-socket. Wrinkled skin slashed out from there; a mimicry of shattered glass.

The High Sorcerer flinched his staff and a gust of impossible wind flung Griff down the hill, flipping and rolling, kicking up a screen of dirt and rocks. He smacked to a halt against the stone-statue shins of Konragen. "Hey!" Griff barked. "Thought I told you to stick with me up there!"

Konragen leaned over and extended a pan-sized hand to haul the Ranger to his feet.

"It is rare that dragonfolk give favor debt to humans. Don't waste on something silly."

Instead of arguing with the dragonman, Griffey felt hot resentment rush through his veins. Murderous rage for Kozard. He felt like a toddler tossed off a playtime haystack and laughed at.

A hand grabbed his shoulder. It was the tall green elf. "I see that look on your face. Only the High Sorcerer can anger someone that much. Believe me, I'm acquainted. He'll kill you if you try."

Parker shook Ramsey off, but did not run. Breathing heavy, he stared bitterly uphill. Kozard's billowing cloak disappeared as the elf strode into the field. The sun was bright in the pure blue sky.

"Frishka," Brisk submitted. "Let's hide out in the woods and let the big elf handle it."

"The trail we need is on the other side of the field up there," Griff said. "I'm not hiding from it."

Marynda shrieked and everyone turned to look. Behind them, the tree branches began to wriggle and move like the arms of an octopus. They squirmed and grew and thickened and began weaving and knotting with their neighbors. In seconds, an impenetrable screen shut them out.

Recovering fast, the Druid woman exclaimed, "We run along these trees. Sneak around while the High Sorcerer kills whatever it is that needs killing." It took a moment, but they all nodded.

They moved along the treeline, which rode up the hill, leveled out, and banked around the meadow's edge. Their heartbeats were pounding bass-drums. Their footsteps were a whisper rush.

With irresistible snaps, five sets of wide eyes gaped across the meadow.

Just as the tree branches in the forest had animated, the three towering spherical bushes were quivering to life. Shaking without a breeze. The High Sorcerer was still thirty yards short of them.

To the right of the three large bushes, the Ranger's sharp eyes spied a shadow that shouldn't be there. *Given the position of the sun, that spot should be lit up clear and green.* Instead, it was a blackened crust. Circular in shape. A gentle cloud of steam rose from it; the upward smoke of flames.

Did the dark wizard do that? Did he clear out the fourth bush? That means—

"The bushes are the Trail Guardians??" the Druid woman breathed, finishing Griffey's thought.

Movement in the bushes grew from a quiver to a violent rattle. With a grotesque series of *pops*, dozens of tentacles burst from all three Guardians. As thick as tree trunks, yet as loose as bull whips, the black arms screeched out from their hosts; writhing demon-snakes cutting the crisp blue sky.

◇ CHAPTER THE TWENTY-SECOND. ◇
◇The Trail Guardians.◇

With amazing quickness, three arms belched out from the center bush and fired at Kozard. The High Sorcerer boomed a command in some unknown language, streaks of fire hissed from his staff and met the snakes mid-air. Ten feet burnt off each tentacle—those sections evaporated in ashy-gray dust-clouds. Undeterred, more footage spilled from the host and the arms advanced without a hitch.

Kozard emitted a squawk of surprise which alarmed the others. Caught off guard, the elf tossed a *Protection* spell. The three snake-arms sizzled and smoked as if they'd hit an invisible inferno.

Running along the outside ring—yet watching intently with every step they took—Griffey realized his company had fallen into the order he'd originally drawn up—he and Konragen, then Ramsey the Green, followed by Brisk and Marynda. Only his plan had broken down. They were running side-long, not straight-on, so they were all left equally vulnerable. And they were certainly vulnerable.

If the High Sorcerer's having trouble out there, we aren't just gonna sneak past!

If this meadow were a sundial, then their party had traveled a quarter-hour before the Guardians registered their presence and dispatched a welcome party. One snake-arm for each of them.

Griffey drew his sword. With an awkward left-hand hack,

he managed to chop off the tip, but stumbled off-balance. The arm slithered around him and rung him up.

With a beastly roar, Konragen spun to face the assault. Not only that, but he also side-stepped over to intercept the tentacle intended for Ramsey. Both the dragon's arms went to work, one attacked while its counterpart defended. The dragon's right arm powered his dual-bladed battleaxe, steadily chopping at one of the snakes—*Ch-Ch-Ch-Cha!* The dragon's left arm—shielded within the shell of the Zodak claw-cone—intuitively blocked danger.

The tip of the snake split open, a mouth with an array of flower-petal lips. Konragen jammed the pointed cone right down that throat. Latched on, the tentacle shook wildly, but he held on.

Granted this reprieve, Ramsey the Green tossed up a *Protection* bubble around himself, Marynda, and Brisk. The two remaining snake arms slapped the lucid bulb and began encircling it.

Mary knew this was her chance. She couldn't flee into the woods. She was trapped. So she knelt in the grass. Folded her hands on her lap, bowed her head, and closed her eyes. Her bizarre behavior—compounded with the ghastly claustrophobic sight of the black tentacles rapidly encasing them and shutting out the sun—caused Brisk to panic. He flailed about and shrieked nonsense.

The Druid woman's blue cloak and brown knapsack fell away as if worn on the shoulders of a ghost. Her physical human form dropped away as she squatted down on all fours. Her body shrank as it sprouted a coat of rough black fur split with streaks of white. She unleashed a snarl and pounced.

From where they were standing, both Brisk and Ramsey yelped. The elf nearly lost his spell.

Churning her vigorous fore-paws, the badger dug furiously at the ground. While her nearest companions gaped at her with stunned, befuddled expressions, she drilled four feet deep—slinging heaps of dirt up to bounce off the *Bubble* and smatter all over her observers. The badger climbed up from its freshly-dug pit, scampered to the pile of Marynda's clothes, drug out her black handbag, clutched in its teeth, deposited the sack down the chute, then started shoveling the dirt back in.

Snapped from his paralysis, Brisk knelt down to help her fill the hollow and smooth it over.

With every passing second, with every toss of dirt, they thought of the enemies outside.

At the same instant the dirt hit level, Ramsey's strength failed and the *Bubble* spell died.

Guardian tentacles—the texture of cornstalks—seized Brisk and Ramsey. While the Sorcerer meekly collapsed, hugging his staff for fear of losing it, the Cook fought back, slashing with his sword.

Once again, Marynda bowed her head, closed her eyes, folded her front paws together. (She was pleased at how smooth the endeavor was, given she hadn't *Transformed* since before Hazel's birth.) Just before the snake-arms grabbed her, she loosed a cry from her razor beak and spread her wings. With a furious flurry of flapping feathers, the giant red-tailed hawk bolted to the skies, talons tucked in.

Now skybound, at least thirty feet up—where the air actually swished, as opposed to staying still as it did in the bowl of the trailhead clearing—Marynda's lethal eyes swept the scene below.

The dragonman's activity was by far the most entertaining. His left arm was stabbed down the throat of a thrashing tentacle, while he relentlessly bashed another vine with his axe. In contrast to that action, the Ranger, Cook, and Sorcerer were all captured by snakes and lofted off the ground.

Her every instinct cried out demands that she *dive-attack-assist* but Marynda Hawk claimed a brief split-moment for her own enjoyment. Soaring high, a gliding grace upon the thermals, she felt the warm embrace of the sprawling world. A landscape of majesty; a clumped, bumpy carpet of rich shamrock; spruce trees flowing with the hills in all directions. In that awe-struck moment, she felt both a sensation of extreme strength and a vivid unbreakable bond with the natural world.

Marynda was quietly infuriated because Griffey Parker had asserted control of their group and publicly declared her as rescinded to the background of this battle. Admittedly, she probably belonged back there. Indeed, she had frozen up during the Zodak encounter. She had a baby child to worry about, as well. Plus, it was logical that Griffey's eyes saw her as defenseless. Still, she did not appreciate the feeling of being judged just because she was an unarmed woman. She was armed, *Frishkadammit*. Heavily armed. Her weapons were just conveyed as teeth and wings and talons.

She hovered for a sliver longer, her lavish hazel eyes gulping scenery.

Down below, a blinding flash of lightning tore across the field. The High Sorcerer—the elf who, to Mary's beak, stank of rotten cabbage—launched a series of spells at each Guardian. The impacts lit each boxwood bush on fire and the flames spread ravenously; hurricane clouds enshrouding entire globes. Remarkably, the snake arm stalks were severed at the source, and they all collapsed, then vaporized into clouds of dust. The captured adventurers tumbled to the turf; castaways in the grass.

Kozard began to cackle. But the charred stratum of each bush peeled away, just as a snake sheds its skin, exposing fresh green layers underneath. New tentacles sprouted and ejected almost instantly. This time, clearly annoyed, the Guardians delivered other gifts along with those. With belching *popping* noises, thorny balls hurled out from the bushes and soared through the air. One of the cockleburs—as large as a rolling-lane game-ball—pounded down a foot away from where Brisk was sprawled, and another bur grazed Ramsey's shoulder as it whistled past. Konragen raised his Zodak arm and deflected a spike-ball away from his face. From where he lay spread-eagled and startled, Griff tracked a missile all the way down to **smack** the vacant plot where his right hand used to be attached.

By this time, the fresh tentacles were already fully-grown and halfway across the field.

Now, however, Griffey's group was not only ready, but focused.

Griffey ran at the Guardians with a battle cry and was pleased to notice Konragen charging right along with him. Despite the hysteria, Griff found time to feel conflicted about this. He couldn't shake a feeling of distrust for Konragen. At a moment such as this, it was completely absurd to fixate about last night at Brumble tavern. But that'd been his first impression of the dragon. Kon could've helped Parker but didn't. Let him suffer instead. *What kind of Paladin ignores the pleas of a suffering man?*

This internal argument helped to power his blind run; a fuel of dumb frustration.

A shifting, weaving snake-arm raced out to meet the Ranger and—at the last second before the impact of his sword— the vine jaunted up high and arched down for an aerial strike. A pocket of blazing orange whizzed and sizzled past on Parker's left and struck the host at the perfect spot to kill the vine attacking him. The Ranger shot a nod of thanks back at Ramsey before dashing onward.

Konragen galloped along with the same feverish focus as Griffey—these conditions met his Paladin requirements for interference, mandating all members of their group being threatened—but he was a far slower runner than Parker. This subtle thought—the glaring fact that he was slower than Griffey implied he was also weaker than the Runter. Or maybe that was just his own foolish pride.

What he lacked in speed, he compensated for by being deadly with two weapons as opposed to Griffey's one. With a punch of the Zodak spike on his left arm, he impaled a snake-vine and held it flapping uselessly an arm's length from his face. The dual-bladed axe in his right arm mutilated any snakes that got close. But he missed one. One that slipped in low, wrapped up his ankle and rudely whipped his feet out from under him. He yelped in surprise as the bulk of his body slammed to the ground. An instant later, two other vines entangled him and hauled him up high.

Further back, both Ramsey the Green and Brisk the Cook were experiencing similar reactions. Though neither would ever admit it aloud, they both felt a sour blend of irritation. They'd witnessed Marynda morph with startling efficiency into a badger and then into a bird, and then she flew away. It aggravated them because she'd hid the ability from them, never mentioned it. Plus they were both rather jealous of her rare and special talent. Envious of the ease with which she'd escaped.

The scrape on Ramsey's shoulder—a flicker-burn left by the spike-ball—shook him into action. As he unleashed a stream of *Fire Bolts*, the young Sorcerer elf felt a surging confidence. The adrenaline was totally unlike anything he'd felt in his seven years locked in that broom-closet castle. It was exhilarating to step up and shell out streaks of fire. Ramsey watched with glee as his shots struck their targets, eliciting squeals of pain from the big bushes. Just as he felt a grin of pleasure touch his lips, he saw Konragen go down. His next target was the trio of snakes which were lifting the dragon up to shake him in the air. His sensation of glowing aplomb was rooted in his surprise attack, and that advantage expired fast. The Guardians sent their own version of heat back at him—a total of six snake-arms deployed. Startled, Ramsey's green eyes shot wide. He shot a *Bolt* but only hit two of the snakes.

In a valiant display, Brisk stepped in to defend the Sorcerer. That wasn't his full motivation, as he found Ramsey the Green to be pompous and annoying. Honestly, Brisk was angry at these bushes and vines because they'd made him feel puny by knocking him down earlier. And the path ahead of the Sorcerer just so happened to be filled with candidates for Brisk to focus his fury on.

Wielding a shortsword in one hand and a frying pan in the other, the Cook proceeded to batter the snakes, knocking them off course. He inflicted no serious damage, but gave Ramsey time.

Brisk's interference gave the young Sorcerer a gap, but there was no clear designation for how that window was to be used. Ramsey could have hurled a parade of fire in at the Guardians, turning their offensive tentacles to dust and freeing Konragen and saving Brisk from his inevitable capture. But the elf was inexperienced on the battlefield. The blooming courage he'd enjoyed only moments earlier evaporated, replaced with an icy gut-twisting throat-mashing alarm. An implacable demand for self-preservation. After all, Ramsey wasn't certain that his *Fire Bolts* would actually help kill the Guardians. Plus, he didn't really know any of these people well enough to risk his life for them.

Ramsey the Green threw up a bubble, dropped to a coward's crouch, and tears of shame stung his eyes. Plus, he felt drained and exhausted. As the tentacles slapped the outside of his encasement (and others gripped the helpless Brisk and bore him away), Ramsey's wandering eyes saw… many things.

Ramsey saw Kozard in action. Time slowed down. Ramsey felt a strange rippling sensation quiver through his mind. Though he'd only read about such occurrences, and they were very rare, Ramsey knew this was a telepathic Sorceror's connection. A link built in a time of high stress, high focus.

The young green elf saw Kozard's mind. He saw Kozard's plan. A scheme to betray their party and ally with the dark wizard. Pledge himself to the machinations of the evil assassin.

Time snapped back in. Air rushed through Ramsey's hair.

High Sorcerer Kozard, from the safety of his own *Bubble*, reached up to the sky, where the ugly chunk of a dark gray cloud appeared, and he drew down a booming crash of blue-purple lightning. This *Freezing Bolt* struck the great boxwood bush furthest down the line and instantly trapped the plant inside a form-fitting ice-block, severing all its active tentacles down to frigid stubs.

Kozard began to cackle once again, his voice vibrating with presumed invincibility. His shield collapsed and his laughing stopped. Vengeful tentacles from the remaining Guardians struck in at him. One snake spiked him in the stomach, doubled him over, and another flipped him roughly to the dirt.

The elder elf face-planted with a *whump*, then lay unmoving, his staff clattering at his side.

Overhead, there tore out a tremendous "*scraaaaawww!!!*" A giant red-tailed hawk swept down, impressive wings flung out wide as her talons lashed at the two tentacles which had captured Brisk. With an echoing howl of his own, the Cook plopped down to the grass. Fresh snake-arms appeared and snapped at her feathers, so Marynda soared back up high, out of reach, before diving back to the action.

Her brilliant eyes—that wonderful hazel color, so reflective of her human form—flicked across the field. Both Griffey and Konragen were being hoisted into the air, flailing and hurling useless objections. She swept down towards them, weaving, bobbing and dodging through a screen of snakes.

Griffey Parker was certain he was about to die. And, on some limited level, he knew he probably deserved it. He was an impetuous dasher. Prone to barreling into conflicts he was sorely incapable of surviving. One tentacle was wrapped securely around his waist, while another was latched on his left leg. He thought these two vines might rip him apart as they rollicked him through the air. One second, he swung so low that blades of grass brushed his brow and chips of dirt speckled his eyes. The next second, he was flying to the clouds, then dropping back down in a cork-screw of insanity.

The cracks of hideous mouths began to split across the bald faces of the Guardians. Black yawning pits, lined with yellowed fangs, the openings were wide enough to chew a country shack.

Both Griffey and Konragen were reeled in. Drawn to a doom of horrid digestion.

◇ CHAPTER THE TWENTY-THIRD. ◇
◇Raindrops on the Fire.◇

Konragen's crimson cloak trailed out behind him in a frantic flap while he sailed with the vines. Most of his other belongings—a tent-pack, backpack, Zodak claw, and battleaxe—had tumbled away during his capture. He didn't mind losing the bags, as they weighed him down and restricted his fighting style, but losing the rest of the stuff had rendered his fighting style extinct. A Paladin balance, he thought with uncommon sarcasm. Despite his losses, he thought he might have a little fight left.

Air whipped past his face as he raced at the towering spherical shrubs. His eyes discovered that the vines entangling him belonged to the closer of the two remaining Guardians. Which meant he would be dying about thirty seconds sooner than the alternative. Because the surfaces of the bushes were no longer smooth shamrock green. Just as the sun peeks over the horizon in the morning, mouths of mustard-stained fangs peeled open on their faces. He was headed for the closer cruncher.

Suddenly, the coppery-feathered figure of a big bird swept in, a flick of red on its tail. Its talons snipped clean-through the snakes holding the dragon-man hostage, leaving him to free-fall. As he plummeted, he glimpsed the Runter Man also getting the freedom/free-fall treatment. Kon shielded his head and curled into a ball. A crash landing didn't discourage him, as his body was outfitted with a natural cushion of rock. He was just glad to be free. Ecstatic, even. He hated feeling trapped.

Just before he smacked the turf, two more tentacles darted

out and snagged him. The indignity of being a hostage again so soon enraged Konragen. Filled him with such fury that he felt heat rumble deep in his guts. His jaws opened wide, fully intending only to roar out some frustration.

A gust of red-orange flame burst past Konragen's lips, appearing as a stream and expanding to a cloud. The fire engulfed the Guardian, not only annihilating the tentacles which held him, but all those jutting from the surface of the plant. In a last gasp, the bush inhaled the fire down its throat and burned from within.

Though he was not typically attentive while blinded by one of his fiery moods, Konragen traced the path of his flames. He watched the column of fire swirl down a gnarly tunnel with slimy, warped, and knotted walls. The arrow of heat was drawn all the way down to torch the roots of the Guardian, and beyond that to the dweller creatures which powered the monster's surface movements. The ghastly seeds, buried deep in the earth.

With an abhorrent squalling crackling sound, the bush turned black and imploded.

The repugnant scent of burnt hair hit Konragen's nostrils, but he wasn't good at smelling things. Beyond that, given what he'd just done, he knew that food would be tasteless on his tongue for at least the next three weeks. He'd just willingly rendered all his taste-buds useless and cursed his throat with coughs. Thoughts of these repercussions only intensified his anger and led to more discomfort.

Unleashing a roar, Konragen marched forward, shoulders thrown back, bright red cloak billowing out behind him, feet stomp-crunching across the char-black patch of the dead Guardian.

The lone remaining bush actually squealed with fright and attempted to seal its mouth closed, hastily stitching thousands of woody stem fibers back together, but it didn't act fast enough. The next gush of flames churned from the mouth of the dragonman fired right down the Guardian's throat.

All the snake-arms dropped dead, and the bush shrank away, a smoldering desiccated husk.

In the immediate aftermath there were no joyous sounds or boasts of triumph. Instead, Konragen fell to his knees, clutching his throat and begging wordlessly for a drink of water. His throat ached with the heat of an active lava tube. Worst than his inability to cry out with wretched thirst, was the knowledge that this suffering was his own fault. Soggy with regret, yet bone-dry in every other fashion, the dragon-man began a humble crawl across the field. His fading vision made it hard to see where his backpack had landed during the hysteria. His pack with the water-skin inside. *Water. Please. Water…*

Nearby, Griffey Parker sat up and rubbed his head. Beneath the throbbing pain in his skull, he felt a dull amazement over witnessing Konragen burn down two imposing foes. He'd eliminated them so fast it was hard to take in. Meanwhile, Griffey had been freed by the hawk, dropped to the ground, and tried to shield his face with his nonexistent right hand. *Hope no one saw that.*

The Ranger forced himself to stand, and quickly checked on everyone else. Brisk was sitting on the grass, dusting off his clothes and fussing with his backpack. Ramsey was on all fours, breathing heavily, his staff lying next to him. Sudden movement caught Griffey's eye. The sleek arrow of a hawk hitting the ground. As soon as it landed, the bird's body bloated, elongated, and shed all its feathers in favor of fur. Now Griffey was staring at a black-white badger, which proceeded to scamper over near Brisk—who hooted with alarm, but had nothing to fear. The badger then began digging at the dirt, rifling a thick detritus haze in the air. The mammal disappeared down the hole it made, then popped back up, with a black handbag snared in its jaws. After that, the badger changed again.

Changed into a beautiful woman with strawberry blonde hair… who was utterly naked.

Griffey gaped at the woman's exposed breasts and tanned, athletic body. His gape lasted merely a second, before her eyes found him. She looked annoyed. He blushed and looked awkwardly away.

While Marynda dashed over to the pile of her discarded clothing, Griffey felt ashamed with a tringle of befuddled excitement. *Did I just see a bird become a badger and a badger become Marynda?*

It hurt his brain to think about the implications of that right now, so Griffey shut it out.

With a natural gravitation, Griffey strayed to the far side of the field. He looked past the crusty graveyard garden, left by the Guardians, to where the ring of trees broke. He saw the gap marking the western trailhead. He could actually see the dirt path snaking away, weaving behind the trunks of the trees. His heart rapidly thumped. He thought he spied movement. A shape slinking through the trees. It may have been a cloaked figure turning away and leaving. Or it may have been nothing.

Griffey felt a desperate desire to run over and investigate, but a cry for help stopped him. He swiveled and spied a large man with a red cape crawling across the field, inching at a pitiful pace.

Given that he'd recently taken a beating, Griffey needed to see the full picture before taking action. At least for now. He tracked ahead, to a black lump in the grass. He didn't know what was so important about that backpack, but he knew he could get there faster than the dragonman could. He staggered drunkenly, resisted the call of the trailhead, and jogged to the bag.

Along the way, the Ranger picked up his shortsword, stuck it on his belt, then reached the dragon's rucksack. From his spot on the ground, Konragen was outraged over this thievery. Then Griff trotted over and knelt before him. The dragon was shocked by this generosity, but was too thirsty to comment. Kon gobbled inside his pack, drew out his water-skin, and began slurping greedily from it.

"Breathin' all that fire dried you out, eh?" Griffey remarked. He wasn't sure why he said this, and was relieved when the dragon ignored the joke. "Listen, uh... thanks for saving us all."

Konragen still made no reply. He drained the water source, shook the empty flap with disbelief, then his body began shaking with a nasty cough. A pained expression dominated his rocky face, and this got Griffey's attention. "Let me find my pack. I've got more water in there, acho?"

The inside of the dragon's throat felt as if it were being probed with a scalding poker.

As he stood back up, Griff's eyes darted back to the trailhead. No movement over there now.

Griffey's travels took him near Brisk, so he helped his buddy to his feet.

"Parker..." the Cook murmured as he dealt a bewildered nod at Marynda. "Woah..."

The Druid woman was fully-clothed now, and she was ignoring them all, crouching in the grass, peering inside her black handbag. Griffey wasn't sure what to do or say, so he slapped Brisk on the shoulder, then chased down his backpack, plucked out his water-skin, and ran back to Konragen.

Since the dragon had just saved all their lives, and Griffey was, in turn, quenching his thirst, he figured he and Konragen were now bound together. It was sure to be entertaining when they talked with Marynda and begged her to spill her secrets. It was only courteous to assume Konragen wanted to be included in that. But, as Griffey slipped an arm around him and tried to boost him to his feet, Kon yawped with objection, shoved him off, and fell back down.

Griffey backed off and stood there, dumbly watching while all his water was gulped away. The Ranger quickly saw a larger problem developing. Their Paladin was in serious choking trouble.

By the time the Ranger hustled back to Brisk, he found the situation had shifted. Seeing as Marynda was still shunning them all—keeping her back turned while she consulted with that obsessive bag of hers—Brisk's attention was elsewhere. First, the Cook's eyes came to the green Sorcerer elf. Ramsey was staring at something, and appeared to be frozen with shock. From there, Brisk rolled his gaze over and saw a body crumpled in the grass. For a moment, he didn't recognize it.

Griffey stepped up beside the Cook and could sense there was something greatly amiss.

"Park..." Brisk whispered, still not moving his gaze off the corpse. "The High Sorcerer is dead over there. Oh Frishka's severed skull, what are we gonna do now??"

"Hold up, are you sure this guy is dead? Have you gone over there and che—"

"I'm not getting close to him. He's not breathing. And even if he was alive, none of us got the Healing skills to fix him." Brisk took a sharp intake of breath, signaling a panicked rant was coming.

Despite the Ranger's efforts to interrupt him, the Cook talked on, blaring his words and breaking the cold, stiff silence that hung over the field. "Frishka! The High Sorcerer is *actually* dead over there. How are we gonna survive out here now? He's the only one equipped with spells!"

By this time, Marynda stepped up on Brisk's left, her gaze matching theirs. "Brisk is right," she murmured, "losing him really hurts our chances of staying alive out here..."

Griffey's eyes moved off the corpse of Kozard, his eyes moving to the same place Brisk and Marynda were looking. At the young green Sorcerer elf. The one who would need to adopt Kozard's responsibilities. The one whose spells they would rely on the next time they hit a deadly jam.

As if crippling under the unspoken pressure, Ramsey the Green began to tremble and shake.

It was a sad thing to watch, so Griffey brought up something more important.

"To all," he called out, "Konragen needs water. Please get your water-packs out and bring em over." The ensuing puzzled silence really annoyed the Ranger. "Frishkadammit, guys. Water, let's go!"

Now everyone was staring at him and shooting nervous, uncertain glances over at Konragen.

Just as Griff began to bark again, the paralysis broke. Mary and Brisk checked their bags.

Ramsey the Green climbed shakily to his feet, rubbed his face, and hollered, "It's not gonna be enough. Whatever water you've got is not gonna be enough." The other three shot him curious looks. "Konragen's got the *dragon's throat*. Trust me. He's gonna need more water than what we've got."

Before people could start complaining, the Sorcerer raised his staff, uttered some words. A cloud the size of a sleeping cot appeared ten feet above where Konragen lay hacking in the grass. Raindrops dribbled from the cotton ball, then increased to a steady flow and didn't let up. The dragon sucked down the moisture and was soon kicking with relief. Griffey and Brisk nodded their approval.

Marynda and Ramsey made eye contact. His eyes flicked to her black handbag. Her eyes flicked to the corpse of Kozard. Their eyes reconvened. Both stayed silent with their secrets.

◇CHAPTER THE TWENTY-FOURTH.◇
◇Tension in Pairs.◇

Seeing that their Paladin was saved, Griffey turned his attention to the body of the High Sorcerer and started edging towards it. He felt it was his duty to go inspect the dead elf, but all he could think about was sprinting across the field towards the trailhead. After his father's murderer.

As Griffey wavered and walked, Ramsey the Green appeared at his side, which all but solidified the need to go investigate Kozard. Under other circumstances, Griffey likely would've felt a swell of pride within his chest. He was about to stand over and stare down at the body of a Rivercrest councilmember. Griffey never cared for any of those people, as they were almost universally fawners on the carpet of King One. Such bias always left King Two to assemble his advisors from the remainder of available people, a populace less influential than the upper tier. So, grudgingly, Griffey understood why Kozard had given him no respect. At least the High Sorcerer never insulted his father, and had also saved their lives. Plus, relishing the elf's death would waste time.

Griffey and Ramsey knelt next to the fallen Sorceror, who lay face-down. They did nothing but stare for a moment, the Ranger clearly detecting that Ramsey would not be reaching over and turning the dead elf face-up. Instead of embarrassing his companion, Griffey leaned in, and flipped the body over.

The snow-pale skin-shade on Kozard's face was instant confirmation of their fears and suspicions. Flecks of grass clung to the elf's long braided beard. For some reason, Ramsey's eyes caught upon that haphazard collection of clippings. The flecks of green were glaring aliens entangled in the mat of brown hair. A smattering of disorder; a besmirching reminder of Kozard's fate.

"Ramsey the Green," the Ranger submitted, "do you wish to say any words here?"

"The High Sorcerer built his career by insulting the natural world. He always insisted the source of his magic came from the heavens. From the stars. From the constellations. He berated me every day during our studies over the worthlessness of my forest homeland...

"... despite all his power, he couldn't see an obvious enemy. Both his eyes went blind..."

This statement rang strange in Griffey's ears, but he shook it off. There was too much else to do. "Speaking of eyes... I'm gonna give you *that*." The Ranger thrust a finger at the black eyeglass, glinting a golden flourish in the sunlight. "And you're gonna be responsible with it, acho?"

Ramsey's own eyes shot wide with shock. "No. Absolutely not. It's dark magic. It's—"

"Kozard's death has imperiled our Quest, wouldn't you say? And his eyeglass was an asset to him." When his companion sputtered senselessly, Griff continued with decisive grit, "So we need every asset and advantage we can get. And, a Rivercrest councilmember would be delighted to help our cause."

Ramsey was desperate to look away from Kozard's black eye-socket, so he changed the subject. "The bodies of elves disintegrate after a half day's passing. Our avatars elevate to whatever source of magic we're tied to. So... so, we won't have to spend time digging a grave."

Griffey nodded appreciatively at this. "And his staff? What about his staff over here? Can you pick that thing up and start to use it? Gain its powers and wield its powers or somethi—"

The young green elf furiously shook his head. "No. I

absolutely cannot. Each Sorcerer's staff is matched to its particular owner. I have my own already. And, no, one of the rest of you can't just pick it up and suddenly gain a Sorcerer's spells... You should let me snap it over my knee."

Not wanting to argue about it, Griffey waved his hand in assent. Then he sighed and his tone lightened. "Listen. Ramsey. I know this is a difficult moment for you, but I need you strong. His duties are yours now, acho? The Sorcerer is an important part of a Quest, and I know you'll do just fine."

The Ranger slapped the elf on the shoulder, then stood up and turned to face Marynda and Brisk. In the near-distance, Konragen was lounging beneath his own personal rain cloud, happily lapping at the drizzle. "Kozard perished in the battle," Griff announced. "Ramsey is our new Sorcerer. Let's be patient with him, acho? And, just so we're clear on this, I'm entrusting Kozard's black eyeglass into Ramsey's care. He'll be using it to help us any way he can. As for Kozard's longsword, that will go to Brisk. And, Brisk, that shortsword you've got should go to Marynda if she wishes it."

Griffey turned back to find Ramsey was still kneeling in the grass. He gave him a nudge. "Sorcerer," he hissed, "we gotta go. I need you to acquire that eyeglass and gather your belongings."

The tall green elf stood up, and snapped the black staff of Kozard across his knee. Despite the brightness of the day, sparks were visible in the storm of bursting splinters.

Brisk hollered out, "I don't think it matters who's got what weapons. A member of our group is literally dead in this field. I think we've proved our point out here. It's time to go back." The Cook felt his breath snag in his throat, and he tried to hide how winded he was. He resisted stating what seemed so obvious to him: *Parker, we're not gonna catch the dark wizard who killed your father. He's definitely escaped through a portal by now. That's what dark wizards do.* Instead of those grim thoughts,

Brisk proclaimed his optimism, "We defeated the bushes, so the path behind us should be freed up—"

Brisk twirled to face down the slope they'd climbed to get here, and all the hope faded from his face. A painful knot clenched in his chest as he saw the branches of the trees were still tightly bound together. Scampering down there to walk their back-trail would be the same as running into a wall.

Suddenly, the presence of Marynda was gigantic beside Brisk. As large and hot as a duplicate of the summer sun overhead. He tensed and felt sweat on his face, inevitably thinking of glimpsing her naked a few minutes ago. While that had been a lovely sight, it made him feel ashamed, as if he'd pried on her privacy at a vulnerable moment. His eyelids fell heavily shut as he tried to distract himself with calming thoughts. This, naturally, brought up his cozy castle apartment and the peaceful, familiar clattering sounds of the kitchens. Those things made him even more homesick. He tried to be positive by thinking, *at least I'm stuck out here with a beautiful woman.*

That beautiful woman, however, was standing next to him and looking at him as if he were a child. Brisk did his best to tamper his pride, accept her sympathy, and grow from it.

"Marynda," he said, "you can have the longsword from the dead Sorcerer if you want it."

"I think that's the most romantic thing a man's ever said to me." Her tone was sarcastic and playful, but Brisk could tell it was a show only for his benefit. He sensed she was distracted and sad.

"No, really," he explained, "you're clearly a better fighter than I am. I'll keep the shortsword."

"I don't fight with steel," she said with a shrug. "I prefer to kill with claws."

"Thanks for what you did. You really saved us all. Without you becoming that bird, Konragen would've gotten eaten and he wouldn't have burned those bushes."

"I imagine you've fried plenty of vegetables in that kitchen of yours." This response, plus the way she turned away, showed her insistence for deflecting. She didn't want to talk about herself.

Brisk actually found her chilly response to be frustrating. He had so many questions. *How does she turn into animals? Was it true that Druids could do things like that? Druids aren't just frauds, are they? Was there an adjustment period or learning period when she changed from a ground animal to a flying one?* His mind veered back on-course. *I can't say the word **fraud** to her! Frishka!*

In place of all those question marks, he had a disturbing memory. A feeling of claustrophobia while trapped inside Ramsey's *Protection* bubble. Marynda (as a badger) had furiously buried an item, presumably precious, in the ground, and he'd even helped her do it. He knew she didn't want to talk about herself, but it was irresistible. "What's in that black handbag of yours?" he asked her softly.

Her wide hazel eyes shot to him, a startled look on her face. *Frishka's severed skull*, the Cook thought uneasily, *she looks more affronted now than when she caught me looking at her naked.*

"I… It's…" she stammered, shaking her head. She would not be talking about that.

Marynda felt unbelievably foolish. Here she was, fresh off a significant contribution in defeating a threat to their Quest, and all her confidence had deserted her. This was in sharp contrast to the showdown with the Zodak, as she'd frozen up while that battle was unfolding. Now she was getting skittish in the aftermath. On one shoulder, she enjoyed Brisk's company and appreciated him helping her to bury the handbag earlier. On the other shoulder, she thought he was too intrusive and nosy.

All she could do was back away, and raise her hands in what, she hoped, communicated surrender and peace. She thought of her little girl, all alone inside that handbag. Reminding her that her daughter would grow up without a father.

Oh, dear Frishka, how she missed Alkent.

Tears in her eyes, she walked off towards Konragen and the trailhead beyond.

Brisk raised his own hands with disbelief and an astounding lack of understanding. He chalked it up to a lifetime of poor luck with women, but he still felt as if he were under Konragen's rain cloud.

Griffey stepped up to him, shoved the longsword at him, and demanded his shortsword back.

None of them had much to say, so they trudged after Marynda towards the trailhead. Griffey reluctantly accepted the call of leaning into the isolated downpour to help the dragon to his feet.

Some of them dealt brief glances back at the field. Konragen saw the patches of his fire, where he'd saved his friends yet cursed himself. Marynda saw something similar in the hole she'd dug. Ramsey saw his fallen mentor, and felt the vastness of that vacuum. Griffey only looked ahead.

◇ CHAPTER THE TWENTY-FIFTH. ◇
◇Uneasy March.◇

With one footstep, blades of grass crunched beneath the boots of the travelers. With the next footstep, their path became a rumpled pavement of dirt, pebbles, and sticks. Along the sides of the trail, the trees were no longer linked together in a menacing screen. Now, their sandy-brown trunks were spaced with breathing room, their leaves shone a mellow green, and rich grass padded their roots.

Konragen had collected his battleaxe, backpack and tent-pack, plus he'd slid the Zodak shield into a snug position upon his left arm, then he'd led the procession up the trail. For the first stretch of minutes, the dragonman strode with his head up, occasionally tilting back to let some cool water run down his throat. Soon, though, his shoulders slumped, sagging in the unrelenting downpour.

Ten feet over the spikes of his head, the coal-black cloud floated along, perfectly matching his pace so as to always spit on him. The fingers of tree branches leaned out and scraped the passing cloud, flinging out mossy wisps but always failing to dismember or disrupt the mass. No physical intrusion could halt its showers. A healing benefit, for Konragen would often cough, feel a vile burn rise in his aching throat, and would need to lean back and gulp from the cloud. The infusion of cool, clean water was refreshing and soothed his pain… but the pain always returned.

Konragen ended up walking faster than the others and leading the group. It was a blind action; casting for hope that some resolution may lay ahead. An answer to the oppressive yet relieving solution that hovered over him.

"*Ramsey Green—*" the dragon called out, before getting racked with a cough.

"Ramsey *the* Green," the elf irritably corrected from where he walked at the back of the line.

While Konragen's coughs continued, Marynda saw that the dragon intended to say something important and was unable to do it, and this saddened her heart. She turned back to Ramsey and hoped her sympathetic guess was correct. "He wants to know if you can turn the rain off."

"Why would I do that?" the elf grumped at her. "Can't you hear he's still got the cough?"

"Yes, but, maybe you could just ease the sprinkles for a while? Give him a break?"

Ramsey threw up his arms and exhaled. "I can't. I can't shut it down and I can't make it disappear. All I can do is create the cloud, not control it. It's not mine anymore. It's beyond me…"

The elf's words faded, as a sense of helplessness engulfed him. Ahead of him in line, Marynda looked away, disappointed that Ramsey wasn't willing to try harder—at least *try*—to help the Paladin.

Feeling irritable himself, Brisk looked back at the elf. "You're the new High Sorcerer, eh?"

Ramsey let this insult pass. His staff, gnarled and gingerbread brown, tapped lightly in-stride with him. He felt the fingertips of his off-hand steal into his pocket to caress Kozard's black eyeglass. He hadn't tried it out yet. Had resisted the temptation to put it in his eye. He felt lousy just having it.

Griffey Parker rumbled up ahead, admonishing Brisk. "We're a company. Remember that."

The Ranger's gaze fell upon the crimson cloak of Konragen, soaked and sopping and drooping and dragging. He didn't know what made him attempt to make a joke, but the impulse felt similar to the rising glow of inspiration that often preceded him fumbling out a journal and jotting down poetry.

Griff nodded at Kon, said to Marynda, "He got his thirst quenched, but got his attire drenched."

She didn't laugh. Didn't even smile. She shook her head and sighed, exasperation fuming from her nostrils. Her reaction made Griffey feel stupid. If he'd gained any perception of stable leadership by reprimanding his friend Brisk, then he'd just robbed himself of those earnings. By making a silly jab at the misfortunes of Konragen, probably because the dragon was an easy vulnerable target right now, Griffey had just undermined his own respected social standing. *No way my father would've done that…*

Walking behind Konragen was awful. First off, it felt wrong for Griffey to know he was faster than the dragon, yet the dragon was setting a faster pace than he was. Beyond that, the constant drizzle from the dragon's cloud was turning the trail soggy. While beautiful sunshine gleamed on the rest of them from a flawless blue sky, and the feel of a prestigious summer's day hung in the air, their feet were being met with sloppy mud. Their boots stuck and sucked at the groggy surface, wobbling their balance. This discomfort only increased the sullen mood of their group.

"Konragen, halt!" Griffey eventually cried. He regretted having to do this, but knew it was warranted. "Please let us walk ahead of you, acho? Water from Ramsey's cloud is destroying the trail."

"It's not my cloud anymore, didn't I explain that?" the green elf yelped.

The dragonman paused and they all slipped past him— dodging and ducking through the temperature-dip of the rain cloud and back into the sun. Griffey nodded an apology back at Ramsey. It wasn't his intention to demean the Sorcerer and his cloud, but he felt it had been a necessary sacrifice to make Konragen agree to stop and switch with them. However, once Kon was at the back, things still didn't feel right. The dragonman was the sick one here. It felt cruel to leave him at the rear.

One bright spot from the switch in their marching order was that the Ranger was now in the lead. He held a prime position to spy ahead for movement. His peering eyes kept a constant watch for the signature twitch of a black cloak. They walked for a few hours, but he saw no sign of the figure.

At one point, he called for a stop so they could each scurry into the trees and relieve themselves. Then they clustered back together and ate a light lunch. There wasn't much talking, and it was all strained. They took turns shuffling over to Konragen's personal space and shyly requesting permission to consult his rainshowers to fill up their canteens and water-skins. It was uncomfortable business.

The remainder of their hike that day was nothing short of unsatisfying. Especially in the wake of their victory over the Trail Guardians. They had won the right to not struggle through the imposing tangle of the woods anymore; had traded the rough for the smooth. Yet they still felt unfulfilled.

During the trek, the Ranger considered jumping ahead. He envisioned using his *Scout Cast* ability to leap one-hundred yards up the trail—skipping the nearest curves and switchbacks of their snaking path. This was tempting because the group wasn't fun to walk with. But, he'd only escape their sour grumbles for sixty seconds and then he'd be right back with them. It was also tempting because he could look for the assassin. But facing the enemy, alone, even for sixty seconds, was stupid.

On the other side of a blink, a dazed, foggy dusk settled upon the sky. The crisp yellow sun morphed to an autumn orange and left streaky fuzz across the horizon. The ocean of overhead blue relented to a woolly gray, which tumbled into inky blackness. Lonely pinpricks of stars bejeweled the heavens before the sun fully dipped, and full galaxies soon advanced their armies.

As the rest of the Quest group flowed to an unspoken stop, Griffey Parker chugged on for a dozen paces, then quit, eyes locked forward. Shadows gobbled the scenery, bleeding from the trees to the trail, absorbing all hope of glimpsing the shifting movement of the dark wizard's creep. Griffey didn't want to believe the assassin had already escaped through a portal. He wanted him crippled and crawling.

◇CHASE QUEST◇

◇ CHAPTER THE TWENTY-SIXTH. ◇
◇Legacies.◇

Eventually, Griffey gave up on staring pensively at the distance. By the time he turned and walked over, there was a flurry of activity, a campsite under construction. Brisk unfurled a blanket, mushed his backpack into a pillow, then wandered off to gather sticks for a fire. Ramsey settled all his stuff into a neat arrangement, then spread his cloak out as a bed blanket. Konragen, working alone in the drooling rain, slung his supplies into a pile, then gruffed his tent to life and disappeared inside.

Far more entertaining than the rest, were the actions of Marynda. She lodged all of her stuff into a humble huddle, then hastily transformed into a wolf. With her ears pricked up, and ashy fur shining in the twilight, she gauged her human companions with fierce golden eyes. She seemed to evaluate them, one-by-one, to see if they were threats. Everyone stared nervously back at her during this transition, frozen with fear over failing inspection. Then she darted into the woods and vanished for ten minutes.

Griffey deposited his possessions in a pile, let his night-vision adjust, then sauntered into the woods to help Brisk hunt.

When they emerged, heaps of logs and twisted twigs were curled in their arms, a film of powdery bark dust on their shirts. They stacked the logs and steepled the sticks and declared it a structure worthy of burning. "We gonna need a *Fire Bolt* on this one?"

Brisk smirked a dart at their remaining Sorcerer. Ramsey was fussing with a scroll, which constantly, automatically wanted to roll back up again. Griffey shot the Cook a look of warning.

"Brisk, I believe you can supply us with some sparks," Griffey said. "It's not your kitchen, but..."

With a dramatic flair, Brisk hunkered over. He didn't need to clack specks of flame from a pair of flint rocks. The Cook just snapped his fingers. A wolf burst from the forest, ran up on them. Jolted, the men nearly tumbled over on their rumps. The canine carried a dead rabbit in its jaws, and dropped the kill at their feet. Then, the pup whirled and went sniffing across the camp, weaving through the fabric mounds, until it discovered Marynda's scent. It snatched a pile of clothes, then bounded for the woods.

A few moments later, Marynda strolled up to them, wearing her blue shirt and sapphire cloak.

"I delivered dinner, lads," she announced, "now the Cook needs to cook it."

Both Griffey and Brisk were still trying to lower their blood pressure after seeing that wolf sneak up on them and they were shocked at how casual she was. Brisk laughed aloud and clapped his hands. "Acho!" he cried. "Acho!" This little outburst broke the tension. The promise of a hot meal helped, too. The gloomy atmosphere—a choking fog—finally dissipated. The mood turned light.

Griffey fed the fire, built it to a charming blossom of golden warmth. Brisk skinned and gutted their dinner, then selected some ingredients and a pot from his pack. Ramsey put his scroll away and sat with them. He even cast a *Hover* spell on Brisk's cast-iron cauldron, allowing it to hang suspended over the flames without constructing a spit. The Cook's eyes lit up with

admiration, and he shot the Sorcerer an appreciative nod. During
this episode, Marynda relaxed, resting her head on her pack,
closing her eyes, hugging her black handbag to her chest. All the
commotion caused the flaps of Konragen's tent to wave as the
dragonman peered curiously out at them. Once dinner was served,
the dragon nearly sauntered over to join them, bringing his
rainshowers with him. Everyone hooted their concerns about the
water extinguishing the campfire, and Kon morosely returned to
his shelter.

As soon as the soup was ready, Brisk hustled the first bowl
over to the dragonman's rainy tent. "You doin' alright in there?"
the Cook amiably called, waiting just short of the showers.

"Konragen hate camping," came the rumbling reply from
within the tent.

The ground beneath the pyramid was quickly becoming a
vat of slop, but Konragen was relatively dry inside. Kon was
seized with an ugly storm of shivering coughs. He leaned his head
out the opening, turned his face to the sky, and drank until the
ache released him. Then he accepted Brisk's bowl of soup and
retreated. "Thanks again for saving us all." Brisk's mumble was
met with a grunt, which was good enough for him, so the Cook
gave a winning smile and went back.

Dinner was delicious—rabbit stew with mushrooms,
carrots, grassy herbs, and singing spices.

When the bowls were cleaned and returned to their pouch,
Brisk promptly passed out and Ramsey settled in for a meditative
trance. Marynda and Griffey were left sitting at the fire.

Griffey caught himself examining the nub of his right
wrist, and Mary noticed his mournful look. It went unspoken
between the two, but they both felt the same illness. It was strange
that, at the end of such an eventful day, they were tired yet were
unwilling to lay down and sleep. A sadness had draped upon them
as the dark of night embraced them, and their ears were filled
with forest chitters and soft isolated rainfall. Griffey thought of

John Parker. Marynda thought of Alkent. Both felt their loss.

"I'm sorry about your hand," she awkwardly stated, forcing out the words just to keep her mind occupied. She wasn't ready for her first sleep without Alkent. "Ramsey helped you out with it?"

Griffey gave a sorrowful nod, imagining a hand perched on that wrist. "He stashed it in the sub-world somewhere. I'm scared that... well, that I won't be able to get it back..."

Marynda quivered, then went stiff, her eyes stark with a brief alarm. Griff pretended not to notice. She had to get past this moment, so she sputtered, "But that's not all that worries you about it?"

"You mean besides being unable to fight? Being unable to wield a sword or punch?" He raised his right arm in a shrug and chuckled. He couldn't believe he was about to admit this. But, seeing reality as it now stood, with his father gone, made him realize how precious life was. And how silly it was to keep himself sealed off from the world.

"Honestly, Marynda, the real reason why I miss my hand... is because I have so much to write." His voice was soft, his gaze distant and pensive. "I write poetry and music. Not formally trained in either, of course. And I hesitate to admit these hobbies, because... well, because Rangers are supposed to be rugged, silent, brooding characters that utter one-word responses to everything... I'm scared of learning to use my left hand, acho? I'm scared it will never properly translate what thrives in my mind. I have strings of poetry and snippets of song dance through my head all day long. I dunno what ocean that river flows from, but I know its my duty to write it all down. Either that or sing it. But I've never had the courage to sing for anyone. Other than my sister when we were kids, I guess."

"I think it's lovely that you practice the arts. Keep culture alive in this brutal world of ours." Marynda's eyes drifted up to the stars. To the pair of moons; the crescent sisters. "But I have to be honest… I never cared for poetry and music. Those things made Alkent happy, though…"

"To me, they're basically the same thing," Griff explained. "Poetry is music. And music is the dialect of the universe. Of life. Music transcends all boundaries, acho? It dances across languages, getting the message across even if the words aren't clear. It transcends the boundaries of time, too. Just try and think of a song you haven't heard for a long time. Choose something from your youth, if you can. And then—*boom*—once you've got it clear in your head, it's like… well, it's as if you're all-of-a-sudden *reconnected* with that time in your life. Music leaves legacies. Links us to the past…"

Unsure of what to say, Marynda asked, "So… what song are you working on now?"

"Something for my father..." he told her, wiping his eyes. "I'd like to write something for him."

When silence fell, Griff recomposed himself. "I think we should set a watch," he proclaimed. "Never know what danger might happen upon our camp in the night."

"I don't care about the forest," she told him. "I'm not as scared of it as I was this morning."

"Because your handbag is safe?" The words slipped out before he could stop them.

She managed not to feel hurt, and replied, "We've all got something out here that we're fighting to protect… For me, yes. It's my bag. For you… for you, I presume it's the legacy of your father…"

Griffey was surprised by the bluntness of her response, but he respected her for it.

Nearby, Brisk rolled over, sat up, rubbed his eyes, yawned, then looked expectantly at Griffey. Ramsey's eyes twitched open and he looked over, as well. Both waited for Griffey to speak.

"In a way…" Parker began, gathered his thoughts, then

restarted, "In many ways, my father was so much bigger than one man. I remember, as a child, feeling as if I could never quite impress him. Could never win his affection or gain his full approval. He loved his kids. Didn't neglect us. Took time to connect and care and create memories. But children just have too much to learn. Looking back at it, now, I can see it clearly. My sister and I, with our destructive, squabbling behavior, simply didn't offer much intellectual stimulation. And John Parker was a man of boundless intellect. Philosophically interwoven with the universe. Always thinking beyond simple problems; always five moves ahead of every action. It's just that his horizons were vaster than anything I can comprehend, even now. All his life, he truly wanted progress for the kingdom. Oh Frishka, I'm rambling."

"I think a leader like your father is exactly what Frishka would've wanted," Ramsey said. "Getting representation for the people is exactly what Frishka sacrificed himself for."

"Yes, and it cost him his skull…" Brisk breathed with sad reflection.

Griffey Parker nodded. "Frishka believed giving the people a Second King was the cure to oppression and distrust. He believed it so much, he got us across Grayboulder river and built the castle…"

"Didn't live to see its completion, of course," Brisk reminded them. The Cook looked at each of his campfire companions, circled beneath the stars, and tried his best to say something more upbeat. "What's so interesting to me—so intriguing to me—is how few people actually met John Parker, yet how many people felt devastated by his passing. I only met him three times and it still crushes me…"

"So many people," Griff spoke with remorse, "invested their hopes and dreams in that *one man*."

Inside his den, Konragen detected this sadness and felt a knot of guilt tighten inside his chest.

"Having one man, one leader, is just easier," Ramsey mused. "Rather than having thousands of voices screaming and complaining, it's best to condense the will of the people down to a single voice."

"Frishka's legacy is the funnel for the people," Mary expounded. "Too many problems, and people can't work together. So they need an ideal leader to do it for them. Someone who embodies the values people want when they're feeling optimistic. Once, I heard someone call it vicarious romanticism."

"I focus too much on my job," Brisk confessed, as if speaking to a mirror. "Always have. I shut out the world and I go cook. It's too stressful to get involved with politics beyond voting day."

"I'd say I'm a level above Brisk, but that doesn't make me better," Ramsey admitted. "I supported Second King Parker's initiatives all across the board. He routed the mercenaries into other professions. He made concessions and opened up the river trade. Helped the dragons get more opportunities for work. Myself, being a minority elf, I appreciate gestures like that. But, I feel guilty because my own actions never helped those causes. I just left all the work to Parker. All the struggle…"

"Forcing big city guilds to consider dragon workers," rumbled Konragen, his voice a volcanic fume from the depths of his tent. "That look good on scroll-paper. But jobs all pay dragons less than others."

The beastly dragon, bare-chested, emerged and stood. He tilted his face to the sky and gulped some rain. His dark figure was enchanting to look at, through the campfire haze and sheets of rain.

Everyone was silent, until Marynda said, "Alkent and I always thought the First King exists to water things down. We would talk about it late at night in our apartment—never during the day, and always in the kitchen. Strange traditions inherited from his parents, I guess. You see, the First King knows that, with every new Second King, things are going to change. The people demand it. But the First King wants consistency, so he slows things down. He lets change happen, but he controls the pace."

"Sure was nice of the Big King to show up in the western courtyard this morning," Griffey muttered. "I can't stop thinking that I could've done more to prevent what happened to my father…"

Konragen hacked a ferocious cough, then blurted, "*Griffey Parker.*"

Everyone looked at the dragonman. Griffey felt a winter's chill within his veins.

"Runter Man has Paladin's debt in his pocket," the dragon informed the crowd.

"I saved your life today," Griffey reminded him. It was ridiculous to feel defensive right now, but he'd just shared his innermost thoughts to people he barely knew. "I brought you water when you had none. You could've done the same for me. Last night, I pleaded for your help… but you did nothing."

"Paladin's oath restricts interference in conflict." Konragen didn't sound happy about it. "Especially we cannot interfere on behalf of belligerent party that starts fight. Fight uncalled for."

"*Belligerent?* I was barely *drunk*. Ulkar *insulted* my family. *And* pulled a knife on me."

Konragen gave a feeble, defeated gesture. "Cannot change past. But Paladin's debt may help."

Marynda touched Griffey's leg, gently disarming his anger. The Ranger gave a weary sigh.

"Fair enough, I'll trust you on this," Griffey proclaimed. "*Paladin*—I call home my debt."

Konragen bowed his spiky head, dramatic in the drizzle. The tension built while he prepared to speak his mighty burden. His voice was strained, yet he did not cough. "I admired John Parker. I am glad my debt is to Griffey Parker, so I can tell him and help him… Kozard said that green-blue spell-ball killed Second King. But elf was wrong. Last night, after bar fight, I went outside tavern… and saw something in courtyard… A ball of dark magic. Fleeing from castle. It was red-black…"

"*Red-black…*" Ramsey whispered, eyes wide. "That's not a wizard, that's a Warlock…"

As the party absorbed this, the flames gave a hiss.

A twig snapped beyond their camp. Heavy footsteps approached…

◇ CHAPTER THE TWENTY-SEVENTH. ◇
◇Supervisory Capacity.◇

Marynda shot instantly to her feet. And then her feet disappeared. A wash of strawberry blonde trailed out as her head shrank down the collar of her shirt. The bulbs of her shoulders merged to her abdomen just as her breasts deflated. Two seconds later, hickory-brown wings thrashed free of the bundle of her clothing and a Great horned owl shot away. The Druid woman darted for the high branches of a spruce tree. She fluttered through the gnarly maze of tree limb fingers, raced towards the dual moons, and settled in silence. With sharp, astonishing vision, she peered down and saw the scene long before her groups' eyes adjusted. From her perch among the treetops, she watched it all.

She saw Griffey surge to his feet. His Ranger training had drilled an even-flow into his nerves; prepared him to be surprised at any time. But he was trapped in a moment of heart-pounding fascination and fright, and was definitely not prepared. Not only did he stumble once he stood, but he also planted a boot in the clump of a backpack, and lunged for his shortsword with his ghost hand. The nub of his wrist hit hip instead of iron, and this incongruity nearly drug his eyes down to gawk with puzzlement. He gave an irritated grunt, drew the blade with his left hand, and stared out at the shadows.

Golden ribbons of fire were printed upon the black blanket of night and made it hard to see.

Brisk hopped to his feet, then immediately squatted back down and began fussing with the spread of his belongings until he drew out Kozard's longsword. He waved it with a brief high of triumph, then felt a jolt of panic as he whirled to face the danger. He and Griffey were closest to it.

Konragen groaned a powerful (yet arthritic) arm up to clasp the battleaxe slung across his back, realized it wasn't there, then turned and flopped towards the flappy entrance of his tent. Directly above, the charcoal-chunk of rain cloud followed loyally right along, churning out moisture everywhere he went. Before the dragon could reach his axe, the rain stopped and the axe became unnecessary.

Nearby, at the seven-o-clock of the campfire, Ramsey the Green stepped forward, raising both arms high, with his Sorcerer's staff held firmly in his right hand. A protective *Bubble* clamped down in a perfect circle around the dish of their campsite. This invisible encasement sliced through the glob of the endless rain cloud. The guts of the cloud stripped away in strings and the drizzle finally stopped.

"*Frishka!*" Griffey snarled. "How did he sneak up on us? Frishka's severed skull!"

"Parker—" Brisk sputtered, pointing, "—that's *behind* us on the trail! He couldn't—"

"—where did Marynda go??" Brisk quietly yipped. "Did she fly away again??"

"Cook Man correct," Konragen rasped at them. "Noise come from wrong direction."

Right after getting these words out, the dragonman looked to the sky. The empty sky. Nothing but ink and prickles of twinkling starlight. He didn't mind water (had participated in the Grayboulder *Log-Drag River-Swim*, after all), but, dear Frishka, he was splendidly relieved to have the rain relent. The hint of a smile on his rock-hard lips was interrupted when a flaming-hot pulse huffed up from his guts to scorch his throat. Tears slipped from his eyes as he tried to smother the cough threatening to hack its way past his tongue and knock out his teeth en route to the open air. He wanted the water back.

I chose to breathe out flames, he thought in misery. *It was me who cursed myself.*

Griffey stepped up to the curve of the *Bubble* and peered through its hazy glimmer. Ramsey's enchantment had killed the campfire, so he had to pause, breathing heavily, and let his eyes adjust. After a moment, a figure swam through the moonlight. Standing, ten feet away. No visible weapons.

The Ranger stared out at this figure for a long time. He tapped his blade against the window, sending a shimmer running across the surface of the shield, dumbly hoping for some kind of reaction, some kind of twitch that might betray a weapon in the person's clutches. The apparition didn't move.

Griffey turned back to face his friends, who looked back at him. He made eye-contact with each of them. Brisk, acquainting himself with the weight of Kozard's sword. Konragen, massaging his chest, battleaxe drooping at his side. Ramsey, arms still raised up high, face strained and determined.

"Ramsey," the Ranger softly instructed, "let the guard up."

"What the—" Brisk yawped at him, "—*are you crazy??*"

"Whoever it is," Griffey calmly stated, "they're talking, and we can't hear them in here."

"*Why do you need to talk to them??*"

"Ramsey," the Ranger said. "It's dangerous, but it's not the Warlock…"

After an arched eyebrow and a moment's hesitation, Ramsey drew back. The *Bubble* faded.

Griffey turned once again and found, staring back at him, ten feet away, a familiar face.

A horrid face. The face of a borlog. A creature from the brutal depths of some ragged mountain or swamp; some nasty, musty, forgotten pocket of the underworld. A face with fresh scars on it.

Ulkar was a tall figure with pure black attire, complete with a trenchcoat and cowboy hat. His long face, already ugly and spider-webbed with tribal tattoos, was now disfigured with rust-brown slashes. Hideous tracks were gouged across his forehead, cheeks, lips, and chin. A blackened layer of crust lay shining beneath these unnatural trenches and gory gaps. His sharp black eyes met Griffey's green ones and they stared at each other, a garden of limitless tension flourishing between them.

For a split, Griffey actually felt a pang of sympathy. Everyone knew that face wounds could be treated but never fully healed. *Imagine if I hadn't wasted my time fighting him at the tavern last night.*

Griffey felt the thick emptiness of the forest pressing in around him. Not emptiness in a physical sense, as this region was rife with trees and wildlife. Rather, there was a palpable lack of restraint. A frightening lack of *Rivercrest*. A vacuum of order. Everyone out here was out here alone. There was no support structure of civilization to steady them. To keep them safe.

Frishka's skull, Griffey shuddered, *why did I forget my bow and arrows.*

Without a word, Ulkar advanced at them. Griffey drew back into a fighting stance, blade raised.

With two vast strides, Konragen the dragonborn bounded across the ashy sizzling patch of the campfire, and stood tall at Griffey's side. This quick movement ruffled Konragen's stomach, but now he didn't resist the creeping urge to cough. He embraced it. He barked out a puff of red-orange fire.

Shock overtook Ulkar's mangled face, and he held up short, eyeballing the dragon with dismay. He hadn't expected a fire-breather. The borlog lofted his right fist and held it there with blunt intent.

"He's got two friends," Ramsey exclaimed, "twenty yards back, armed with clubs with spikes in them. Wait—both just stopped coming towards us. I think he sent them a signal to hold up. Oh, and, this guy may *look* unarmed, but he's got a hatchet in his belt and a dagger in his sleeve."

"Mercenary," Griffey recited. "Dual-weapon combat. Human with a half-scoop of borlog blood."

Ten feet behind Griffey, the green elf was kneeling in the grass, his right eye peering through the filter of the High Sorcerer's tinted eyeglass. Silently and harshly, Ramsey commanded himself not to enjoy the feeling. Not to get addicted to it. Only now, with danger close, would he use the *Sight*.

In the distance, over Ulkar's shoulder, Griffey spotted two bulky henchmen. True to Ramsey's word, both were wielding spike-clubs. Right then, a night bird swept down from above, wings thrust out wide. Its talons gored a henchman's face, prompting him to wail, "*Gaahh! My eye my eye!*"

The swell of confidence within Griffey's chest was inevitable. As was the smirk on his face. It felt blissful to have the advantage here. Ulkar may have surprised them, yes, he may have sneaked into their camp. But Konragen frightened the borlog. And Marynda just maimed one of his sidekicks.

Thus is was with a cocky edge that Griffey called out, "What is your business here?"

"Official Rivercrest business," Ulkar replied with infuriating smoothness. He flung his hands up in surrender, then slowly extracted a scroll from a pocket in his black trenchcoat. He lightly flicked it.

"Signed by Rodrick Callister himself, with full authorization of the council," Ulkar announced. This proclamation was met with hushed gaping silence. Now it was Ulkar's turn to allow himself a smirk. "That fool Kozard met with Callister last night. Must've convinced him that a Chase Quest was a good idea. Funny, eh? I went in the First King's office right after that and proposed the same thing."

"We've got it covered," Brisk hollered out. "You can head

on back, acho?"

"Apologies, Cook, but that I cannot do," came the borlog's swift response. He waggled the scroll, as if one of them might actually trust him enough to walk over, take it, unroll it, and inspect it. "The First King of Rivercrest declared a second Quest was necessary. In a supervisory capacity."

Brisk spat in the dirt.

Ulkar jabbed a finger at the Cook and, despite the distance, it actually made him flinch.

"You best watch your tone when addressing your superiors, you lowly floor Cook," Ulkar snapped. Then his tone softened, as if depicting a personal tragedy. "My two companions and I... we don't want to be out here. Trust me, we would rather be in the safety of our homes than out here in this wretched wood... But it is our duty, see? We are charged with successfully apprehending the assassin."

"That's our task," Griffey Parker asserted. "We've got it handled, thanks."

"If only the Basement King hadn't stripped us of our jobs..." Ulkar went on, "then we wouldn't need to accept work such as this. Performing dirty work others are incapable of completing."

"We'll be completing it just fine," Griffey replied, "we appreciate your concern."

Ulkar cackled. It was the garish sound of stones cracking against other stones as they tumbled down a bottomless well. "You've certainly *attempted* your mission thus far, I can't deny that," Ulkar seethed. He clicked his tongue (*tsk-tsk-tsk*) with rich condescension. "Despite having a Ranger in your ranks, you've managed to tangle with the wildlife. Not only did you kill your High Sorcerer, but you failed to report his death back to the kingdom." He shook his head. "A dreadful dereliction of duty."

"We didn't kill the High Sorcerer," Griffey stammered. "The Trail Guardians b—"

"I noticed you all settled around a campfire here," Ulkar observed. "Which is fitting, I suppose. Because you're talented at telling campfire stories. Children's stories. Stories that no rightful servant of Rivercrest might possibly believe. Yes, the Trail Guardians may have struck the final blow, but it is one of your group here that weakened Kozard in the moment before his death."

Ulkar's dark eyes shifted, landed upon Ramsey. The green elf was staring back with a stoic face, concentrating on a higher realm through the eyeglass (he saw golden lifeforms moving across fuzzy black scenery). But the borlog's accusation still made him sweat. The sweat was cold. Ramsey felt a shiver run through his bones. He couldn't take it. He removed the eyeglass and shoved it in his pocket.

"A handy tool, the *Sight* is, eh?" Ulkar said to Ramsey, tapping at his eye with a fingertip.

Does this borlog have a link to Kozard's eyeglass??

Griffey, Konragen, and Brisk all turned to briefly look at Ramsey, whose shoulders were slumped and whose head was bowed. They all turned back to the horrid borlog. The borlog who was trying to intimidate them. Who'd been in league with Kozard.

"Of course, Ramsey the Green isn't the only one within your ranks with a secret to hide," Ulkar oozed with a sneer. "The woman. The one who calls herself a Druid. Where is she? Is she flapping the trees? Is she scuttling the bushes like some worthless underbeast? She's got some secrets, too, oh my."

No one knew what to say to this, so a tense, remarkably uncomfortable silence ensued.

"There's no way the council approved you to follow us out here," Griffey declared.

Ulkar's gaze sharpened like a blade. He tossed the scroll through the air, landing it perfectly before the Ranger's boots. "It is supremely disappointing, really, but not at all surprising," Ulkar mused to himself, distractedly examining the waggling fingers of one black-gloved hand. "Parker, your company is comprised of thieves, liars, idiots, and murderers. All you've done since receiving your commission is walk around and eat rabbit stew. You lack competence, you lack discipline, you lack results. The Second King lays dead back at the castle, you've had a full day, and your accomplishments show no value. The kingdom is far from pleased, far from pleased…"

It took every ounce of restraint for Griffey to hold back from charging at the bastard. It had taken far fewer words to provoke him last night at Brumble tavern. Ulkar narrated his dilemma aloud.

"I can see you struggling to not fight me," Ulkar observed, his voice smug. "You want to hack at me with your sword. Your left-handed sword." At Griffey's side, Konragen issued a rumbling growl. This made Ulkar pause, but, then, Konragen's intimidating display tumbled briefly into a cough. Ulkar squinted at this, then threw up his hands. "But we can dodge our grudges, can't we, Parker? We can agree that you damaged my face and I amputated your hand. Let it be until the mission is done. And we'll be monitoring the rest of your mission from a distance. In a supervisory capacity, of course."

Griffey said nothing, but his pulse was thunder. Thankfully, Konragen didn't cough anymore.

"Why the sour faces?" Ulkar boasted with the sleaziness of a carnival barker. "Tomorrow is Midsummer's Eve, have you people forgotten that? It's the perfect time for change. We needed a change in leadership. It got stale. Gotta think positively, Parker. For the Basement King's legacy? What happened last night is perfect for that. There's nothing more powerful than martyrdom. The immortality treatment. Now, he'll live forever." The borlog cast a wicked grin and melted into the shadows.

Konragen wrapped up Griffey to keep him from screaming and pursuing.

Soon, a scratchy blanket of tranquility fell upon the night.

◇CHASE QUEST◇

BOOK

◇ III ◇

THE VILLAGE.

◇CHASE QUEST◇

<> CHAPTER THE TWENTY-EIGHTH. <>
<>Outrider Eyes.<>

"**D**on't think I'm gonna get much sleep after that startling experience," Brisk surmised.

But he was wrong about that. It wasn't long before he went to his blanket, yawned, and dozed.

Soon, after Ulkar retreated and disappeared along with his two shadowy companions (presumably duplicate borlogs with equally-ugly complexions), Konragen had to demand assurances from Griffey that he wouldn't run off and get himself killed. Only once those bitter guarantees were procured did the big dragonman release the Ranger from his imprisoning hug.

Griffey paced around the camp, sword in his left hand and braced down at his side, making everyone nervous as he revolved around them, glaring at the trees and muttering. Ramsey simply sat in a moody silence and eventually dropped into a removed state of meditation, legs crossed and hovering a foot off the grass. Konragen returned to his tent, curled up where nobody could see him, and tried to fall asleep before a coughing fit wrangled him to death.

Twenty minutes later, an impressive, large brown bird with a spike above each eye swooped into their camp and landed upon the clutter of Marynda's discarded clothes. Griffey paused in the course of his laps around the camp and turned courteously away while the Great horned owl transformed into Marynda.

With his back still turned, Griffey gave her an update:

"The borlog says he and his mates were commissioned by the kingdom to follow us and report on our progress."

"Owls have ears to match their tremendous eyes," Marynda informed him, snapping the clasp of her cloak across her collar. "I heard the whole thing. Did you read the scroll he threw at you?"

Griffey realized he hadn't and shook his head. "I guess I don't think it matters what that scroll says… no matter what, we're stuck out here. With a trio of bloodthirsty borlogs behind us, and a dark magic Warlock ahead. Proclamations from distant Kings don't matter out here. All that matters is how good we are at survival…" He paused thoughtfully. "Did you scratch one of their eyes out?"

Marynda laughed as she stepped up at his side. "Yes, there's a borlog cyclops out there now."

"Did you hear what he said about tomorrow being Midsummer's Eve?"

The strawberry blonde Druid woman offered a nod. "I did hear that. Really surprised me, too. I think you and I were so traumatized recently that we… well, we forgot what day it was."

"If tomorrow's Midsummer's Eve," Griffey said, "that means there's gonna be an eclipse..."

"At noon on Midsummer's Eve, like a ghost the sun shall leave," Mary recited.

Griffey cast her a surprised, critical eye. "Thought you didn't like poetry?"

"I don't." She turned and headed to her blankets. "Wake me in two hours, I'll take second shift."

The Ranger sighed, then resumed his slow pacing around the campsite. This routine lasted for about an hour, then he sank into a sitting position. He decided to face the trees on the left shoulder of the trail, that way he could turn his head should trouble arise or approach on either his left or right.

No trouble materialized. As if Ulkar's psychological

harassment was enough. Crickets sang and critters scampered through the brush and he nearly sank into sleep just before Ramsey tapped at him.

"I meditated for a few hours," Ramsey told him, as if this explained everything clearly. "So I can take the rest of the watches until sunrise. If danger shows up, I'll cast the *Bubble* and wake you."

Griffey produced a dull nod, then shambled over, plopped his head on his pack and passed out.

At the end of his watch, Ramsey the Green prodded Griffey awake. His Ranger's training told him before the Sorcerer said it—sunrise was peeping over the horizon.

"It's Midsummer's Eve," the elf informed him, then went to wake the rest of the crew.

Sleep had been far from peaceful for Griffey; an exhausted necessity he was grateful to escape from. Filled with dark stone hallways, his father's echoing voice, him running and never catching up.

With a quiet hurry, everyone packed up their belongings and prepared for the trek with the manner of hassled refugees. The moments not occupied with stuffing belongings in bags were filled with anxious glances at the woods, at the trail behind them, at the trail ahead of them.

They'd been hiking for twenty minutes when Ramsey lost patience with the silence. He couldn't stop his thoughts from flying in all directions, a continuation of the affliction he'd suffered all night watching the camp. *I should be wearing Kozard's eyeglass. What am I missing by not wearing it? That awful borlog told my friends that I killed Kozard. Are they even my friends? Are they scared of me?*

"I picked up the scroll the borlog gave us," Ramsey said, rattling his haversack. "I inspected it, too. It appears the First King *did* assign them out here. But the council's signatures weren't there."

"Ulkar is going to try and kill us," Griffey assured them, dealing a look over his shoulder. He considered jumping along their back-trail using *Scout Cast* to see what distance Ulkar's gang was following at. After that, he considered *Casting* ahead to look for the Warlock they were chasing. His eyes found Ramsey's and thought, *Can we really trust the elf?*

"We're caught in the ole iron sandwich," said Brisk. "Squeezed between two slices of trouble."

"I've been trapped between two bad options every minute I've been out here," Marynda sighed. "Every time something attacks us, I feel I have to abandon my handbag to go fight with it."

"Couldn't have been easy for you to leave it behind and become that owl last night," Ramsey sympathized, to which she nodded. Brisk, who'd only eaten a bit of apple bread this morning (a breakfast far less glamorous than what he was used to), was feeling cantankerous and nearly intruded.

At the back of the line, Konragen erupted with a hideous coughing fit. It was the lung-quivering cough of the seriously ill. Everyone marching ahead of him leaped defensively forward, as if the cough were contagious. Marynda eased back to him. "Want Ramsey to bring back the cloud?"

The dragonman shook his head. "Getting rained on gives me depressed. Can't trust cloud."

"Is it the cloud you can't trust," Brisk inquired, "or the guy who makes the cloud?"

The comment sent disquiet rippling through the group.

Konragen went on coughing.

Just as Griffey felt frustration growing over how childish these people were behaving, just before he turned from his spot at the head of the line to chastise them—

—he saw the footprint. Left by a boot. A man's. A size or two larger than Griffey's own.

He came to an abrupt halt. Ramsey stumbled into him, and

then Brisk right after that. This little collision did not improve the tension between those two. A shoving match ensued.

"*Yield, you fools, yield!*" Griffey turned and snapped at them. They both hung their heads as shamed schoolchildren. "Don't create enemies amongst us, we've got too Frishkadammed many already. Brisk, I trust Ramsey with my life. I do so because I have to. He's been helping us, acho?"

He didn't Heal your hand, Griff, he stole it away, Brisk thought but didn't say.

Griffey couldn't stop thinking about the figure he'd glimpsed in the distant trees after they'd defeated the Trail Guardians. The figure who'd deposited this boot-print. Who'd killed his father.

"I think we're getting close to the Warlock," he whispered. "I'm going to jump ahead a hundred yards. Marynda, please give your bag to Konragen. I need you to fly up and see how far back Ulkar is. The rest of you stay right here. We'll be back in literally less than a minute. We need outrider eyes."

Marynda was hesitant, but acquiesced without argument. They both vanished...

◇ CHAPTER THE TWENTY-NINTH. ◇
◇The Warlock.◇

The Midsummer sun blazed down with relentless heat. Ramsey preferred a mild temperature to this seething sweat, but the heat wasn't his only source of discomfort right now. His usual peaceful, reflective manner was transforming into one of incensed combatant. It felt eerily similar to the indignant rising outrage which boiled in him during the High Sorcerer's droning lectures— always sprinkled with insults about Ramsey's heritage.

The crooked Kozard often labeled him as too old to start over with a career in Sorcery, and somehow used this to justify treating him as a child. One day, during an elementary-level spell-ball class, Ramsey nearly hit back at the older elf. He nearly cried out that Kozard's disdain for him was because he was secretly afraid that Ramsey's forest origins produced superior magicians.

Right now, Ramsey's talents were hobbled far from superior. *I'm out in nature. My powers should be flowing freely,* his thoughts grated at his nerves. *That eyeglass in my pocket is fogging my thinking. Everybody thinks I made a mistake back at that meadow, but I didn't—*

"—I didn't kill Kozard, the Frishkadammed Guardians killed Kozard, *can't you see that??*"

Ramsey was hot, they weren't going anywhere, with nothing to do but stand around and listen to the big bull hack and sputter his lungs out. So, fighting with someone was an appealing activity.

Brisk promptly turned to accept this challenge with a grin

of sappy joy upon his face. His narrowed brown eyes, however, held a feverish temper. "Pretty fierce denials for a bystander."

"I don't think you comprehend, *Cook*. I'm a Seventh Year spellcaster. I could melt your bones."

"You look pale and sweaty and hysteric right now, you're going to cast yourself a heartkiller."

"I'm a hundred-and-nineteen years old, Frishkadammit! Nearing prime physical form!"

"You sound old as hell. Maybe that's why you aren't a real Healer. Too old to learn."

Ramsey lifted his deadly Sorcerer's staff. Brisk raised his fists in return.

Konragen shivered, his red medallion necklace twinkled in the sun, and he fell to the dirt...

<>   <>   <>

Marynda was reunited with the glorious overlook of the blissfully bright blue sky. Gone were the relentless brown sugar patterns of the tree trunks, replaced with the vivid green bristly broccoli carpet of treetops rolling smoothly across the hills. The padding of the trees stretched out to the west where it dusted the feet of a chunky rocky mountain range. Straight ahead—facing back east—she could see the spires of Rivercrest castle; from this extent, the cones resembled needles piercing the sky. She could even see the slump of the forest where Grayboulder river carved its way through.

This vantage was a gorgeous blessing—she adored flying in daytime, especially with a Golden eagle's eyes—but her heart was troubled and her glide was tense. *Flying should never be tense.*

She thought of her black handbag. The one with that weird cave inside. The cave where her only daughter resided with a severed hand roommate. (When she discovered it, Mary had nearly plucked out the bruised, purple intruder and flung it to the mercy of Shadowbranch forest, but relaxed when she realized the hand must have belonged to Griffey Parker.) Mary hated being separated from that bag; wanted desperately to get back to having Baby Hazel with her. Konragen was clutching her bag right now, and she'd agreed with Griffey's decision to entrust it to him. Of the remaining guys, Kon was the strongest, most reliable, and also wasn't on the verge of brawling.

But Konragen was also sick. Coughing. A threat to pass out.

She had to get back there. Fast. She wouldn't be able to just instantly snip back to her initial spot—as Griffey could with his envious *Scout Cast* ability—no, no, she would have to bank around, and descend and land. That whole process would take time. She needed to get this task done.

Luckily, her Golden eagle eyes were incredibly sharp and the borlog trio was easy to spot.

An arrow fired through the air, right up at her. A blade riding astride a black-feathered arrow. She dropped into a dive and the dart missed her by a few sparse inches, hissing on the open air. She loosed a *"sqwaaa!"* of protest from her beak. She did not want to be trapped out here with a borlog enraged at her over getting blinded in one eye.

In possession of the information she needed—Ulkar and his cronies were following their group at a distance of a hundred and fifty yards—Marynda wheeled around and flew back to the others...

The power of *Scout Cast* offered a maximum travel distance of a hundred yards, but, no matter how far the journey was, it always took a single breath. For Griffey Parker, that brief span was stuffed impossibly full with an eerie emotional concoction of excitement and anxiety. *You got him, Parker, you caught the assassin*, rang his confident vibe. *He should be too weak to throw any spell-balls, right??*

He landed in the same stance he'd departed with—sword

drawn, ready for attack. Users of *Cast*, however, never arrived fully ready to do battle, for the transportation process forced every traveler to blink. The rush made it inevitable. So, heart hammering, Griffey landed with his eyes closed.

His blue-green eyes snapped open, he sank to a defensive crouch, and swept the area.

A crushing sense of disappointment heaved upon his neck and shoulders. There was no sign of a shadowy figure, cowering before the awesome presence of the intimidating Ranger-Hunter.

The trees on his left and right were sparse and this paucity of hiding places exuded certainty that Griffey was alone up here. All the bushes were scraggly and thin, and the tree trunks weren't sturdy enough to admit an adult climber. Nature was meager here because he was standing on the cusp of a hill. About the only scrap of luck to be gained from this quick expedition was the fact that he hadn't gone tumbling down the slope.

His keen vision tracked across the valley sprawled out before him. He saw a village. A circular honeycomb cluster of huts and houses with dusty strips of streets. From this clot of civilization, there rose a dull drumbeat, accented with the crackle of fireworks and corresponding whoops and giggles. For a breathless moment, Griffey just gaped. Then it hit him. *It's a festival of the eclipse…*

From there, his eyes lifted to the sky. To the dual moons— two crescent ribs. Not only were the peaks and craters of the moons crisp and visible, but the orbs were lined up and chasing each other, as if marching in parade formation. Together, they were an eclipsing battering ram, charging at the sun.

Rays of golden light bled into Griffey's eyes, sinking back to his brain and causing him to squint. From the arrangement of the celestial bodies, the Ranger could easily tell what time it was. It was three hours until noon. *At noon on Midsummer's Eve, like a ghost the sun shall leave…*

There was a sudden flash, twenty feet ahead, down the

slope, on his right. It was followed by heavy, rasping breath and the rustling sound of someone trying not to fall down in a tangle of bushes.

Griffey's eyes shot to the site of this commotion, and then he understood. *The Warlock has perfect invisibility. But he's not strong enough to hold the spell for long. I can hear him, out of breath.*

Even though the Ranger's eyes went directly to the figure, it seemed as if the panting met his senses first. It was a hideous rasping scraping sound; like a stone grinding against a skull; the haggard hiss of an animal about to die. The grotesque sounds matched perfectly to the visuals.

Right there, unobscured by the jaunt of a boulder or the dangle of a tree limb, wide open, and almost pathetically vulnerable, stood the Warlock who killed Griffey's father. What instantly stood out was the creature's pale face, but, overall, there was a palpable implication of fatigue. The Warlock probably stood at over six-foot, but he seemed shrunken and hunched, all the way down to five. A thick cloak was draped over his shoulders all the way to his boots, and, under optimal conditions, it would've reflected a deep purple-black shade. Out here, however, after a day and two nights' of rough travel on-foot through Shadowbranch forest, the fabric was muddy, dusty, faded, and torn. Beneath this layer, there stood the creaking bones of a skeleton. The Ranger could see the shoulders and elbows, pointy and prodding.

The face of the Warlock was an elongated droop, as if it were portrayed on a canvas with seeping water color paints. From a high bald dome above a broad forehead slashed with wrinkles, down to prominent bulging cheekbones, his head terminated with a round chin and sagging jaw. Inside his mouth, there could be seen globs of burgundy gums which sprouted the occasional fang. Slithering about in there was a crusty brown tongue. The skin of his face was shockingly pale, and where it wasn't highlighted with this sickly gleam, there were hard-edged contours of bruise-colored shadow. The one facet on the creature that didn't seem distorted were his bulbous cyan-blue eyes, which blazed and stared and captivated with the alarming clarity of a creature whom has accumulated centuries worth of knowledge yet was now staring down death.

The most revolting part of this encounter was the pang of sympathy Griffey felt for the withered creature. The Ranger's heart was trained to care for injured animals, and that's what this resembled.

"Why did you do it??" Griffey shrieked. "Why cast that death spell? *Why kill my father??*"

The eyes of the Warlock glared back at him. The creature uttered garbled words in some filthy, repellent, unknown language (*"Bree-okk kann! Tokk brell-okk!"*). He threw a ball in the air, the ball gave birth to three knives, which stabbed down at Griffey with a flash. The Ranger ducked aside, heard the blades strike into the dirt. The Warlock turned and fled down the hill. Griffey's time was up. He *Cast* away…

◇ CHAPTER THE THIRTIETH. ◇

◇Coalescence.◇

Griffey Parker appeared out of nothing just as Brisk was about to punch Ramsey's nose and the elf was about to imprison Brisk in a giant block of ice. To keep his balance, Griffey grabbed Ramsey. This interference threw off Brisk's timing, and disrupted the elf's spellcast, as well. "Frishkadammit, quit fighting," Griff grunted at them, his eyes already settling on the bigger problem: the dragonman, thrashing lightly on the ground, clutching his burning throat.

A large brown bird cascaded down and landed purposefully next to the muffled hump of Marynda's clothes. It was odd to see such a large fowl venturing so close to a cluster of people, and this caused both Ramsey and Brisk to twirl and stare at it. Griffey grabbed them, and turned them courteously away so Marynda could become human again, then get dressed in peace.

"The three borlogs are a hundred-and-fifty yards behind us," Marynda said in a rush.

"They will surely gain on us if we have to carry Mister Dragon with us," Brisk observed.

"Ramsey the Green," Griffey exhaled with desperation.

Ramsey's frosty green eyes met Griffey's wide blue-green lakewater eyes.

"You want…" Ramsey sputtered. "Y-You w-want me to put Konragen in the sub-world…?"

"Why not?" Griffey shot back. "There's air for him to breathe. He'll be safe until we reach the village—" He saw puzzled eyebrows raise and was forced to hastily clarify, "A hundred yards up the trail, there's a hill down into a valley. In the valley, there's a village. We can get there by noon."

"We *need* to get there by noon," Marynda declared. "The eclipse of Midsummer's Eve is going to hit at noon. And I do *not* want us all trapped in the woods with angry borlogs in the dark."

"Ramsey," Griffey pleaded, "we'll move faster with him stashed. Get him help in the village."

"Acho, acho, acho," Ramsey irritably griped. He flailed flustered fingers at Griffey, then extended an expectant hand to Marynda. With a grudging surrender, she gave up her black handbag.

"Woah now," Brisk objected. "Ramsey's known the secret of her handbag this whole time??"

The Sorcerer knelt beside Konragen, staff in one hand and bag in the other. Griffey gripped the shoulders of the Cook. "We don't need questioning right now, Brisk," he implored his friend. He pointed up the trail. "I saw… I was face-to-face with the Warlock… I think he's heading for that same village."

"He can regain his strength there," Brisk filled in. "And then portal out and escape."

"Wait!" a deep voice yelled. Konragen struggled up onto one planted elbow. With a weak unsteady motion, he passed the Zodak claw to Ramsey. "Give to Runter Man. He will need it."

Ramsey provided an accepting, promising nod, then the dragon lay obediently down again.

With some murmured words and a display of blinding light, Konragen and his belongings vanished. After a breath, everyone made a tight circle around the handbag. Ramsey dutifully slipped it open so the huddled group could peep. For a brief moment of skin-rippling terror, Mary imagined the big dragon landing atop her baby girl and crushing her. But there was no such misfortune. Beyond the clasping lips of the bag, they peered down from the roof of a cave. Kon and Baby Hazel were dozing by each other on the floor. A broken human hand hovered in mid-air. Ramsey abruptly closed the bag and stood. The company reacted with mystified surprise. The elf gave the bag to Mary.

Griffey felt a bit guilty over inspecting his severed hand the entire time. Ramsey thrust the Zodak claw into his arms and this gift galvanized Griffey's spirit. He could almost feel the vibrant life of the Zodak which had once occupied this claw. He turned and led the troop in a march along the trail. The claw found its way snugly onto his abridged right arm; a perfect fit.

"There… there was a room inside that bag," Brisk muttered in disbelief. "A *cave* room. And there was a… a baby? Marynda, did your bag get any heavier after we put the dragon in?"

Clearly uncomfortable with the topic, she shrugged, emphasizing her unchanged burden.

"Thank you, Ramsey," Griffey said as he urged the party onwards.

"Can he hear us in there?" the Cook inquired. "If we shake the bag, does it shake him?"

"That cave is in the sub-world," Ramsey said informatively. "It is… very far from here."

Brisk appreciated this explanation, but he'd wanted to hear something from Marynda. He wanted to know more—even at the expense of an apology for his excessive curiosity, which was so palpable he could cut through it. When nobody was talking, he felt all alone out here. It was silly for them amble in silence when they could be building a workable rapport. No Rivercrest kitchen team could survive without ongoing communication. They needed to see that conversation was infectious. It helped keep people engaged and kept away darker thoughts.

"I won't ask about the baby, alright?" Brisk offered, lofting his palms. He hurried up to the tall green elf, walking ahead of him, head down. "Breathing all that fire really made Konragen sick?"

At first, Ramsey kept his gaze on the path, but he could feel the Cook looking expectantly at him. He assayed the Cook, and wondered if it was worth talking to him. "The dragon people gave up more than just their wings when they chose to live in the cities alongside men and the rest of society. Slowly, over the generations, they suppressed their natural fire-breath abilities. Konragen is suffering from *dragon's throat*. Basically, the fire core of his body has been awakened, and it thinks it needs to be constantly producing heat right now. We will find a Healer in the village. Or an elixir."

"Curing him from what's natural," Marynda scoffed. "Nothing more backwards than *that*."

"Are you going to keep using that black eyeglass after what Ulkar said?" Brisk asked the elf.

Ramsey hesitated before replying, as if caught off guard. Which, of course, he was. His mind had been swirling ever since the encounter with the Trail Guardians, and he'd totally forgotten about what Ulkar said last night. The borlog had tapped at an eye and said, "A handy tool, the *Sight* is, eh?"

"Skull of Frishka…" Ramsey breathed, before recovering and giving Brisk a pat on the shoulder. "Y'know, mister Cook, I feel like you give me an unfair shake pretty often out here, probably because you're jealous of my abilities, but I truly thank you for reminding me of that."

"I'm not *jealous*, I don't get *jealous*. I just feel that you've been keeping secrets from us." When the elf protested, Brisk raised his hands again. "Just being honest. But I'm also being honest when I say those spells you've got have saved us several times out here. Frishka thank ya for that."

This disarmed Ramsey and surprised him so much that he swallowed his angry retort.

Brisk continued, "I'm used to sleeping in a bed not in the dirt. Being out here is not exactly my preference of living. So, maybe that's why I get snippy sometimes…"

"Ramsey the Green," Mary injected, "what did Ulkar say to you? I must've missed it?"

"Ulkar practically winked at me and said something about how great the power of *Sight* is…" Ramsey gasped, drawing concerned looks. "I think Ulkar may have a double of Kozard's eyeglass."

That startled Marynda, who said, "You mean, he's got one that can see what yours sees?"

Ramsey gulped and nodded. Brisk was unnerved and said, "Well, get rid of it, then!"

"It is unwise to destroy or discard such a valuable magical object. One that can help us…"

That was when they reached the slope, where the trees thinned out, the trail sank away before them, and an astonishing panorama unfurled. Griffey's gaze went to the spot where he'd seen the Warlock. The rest enjoyed the visual buffet—the sprawling majesty of the valley, the nostalgic allure of the village, the breathtaking vistas of yonder mountains, the blue ocean overhead with merging moon islands which would soon force the sun into premature midnight.

"Can't get views such as this in your kitchens, can you?" Ramsey prodded Brisk.

"You may be right… but, same as the kitchens, this place has got the ingredients for sumptuous." Brisk was stunned and humbled by the breadth of the countryside. It reminded him of how small their lives really were. "Ramsey, at some point, that black eyeglass is going to poison views like this for you."

Ramsey gulped, felt his palms start to sweat. His fingertips began to creep towards his pocket.

"*Frishkadammit, Griffey!*" Marynda hooted. "Just tell him if he should keep it or not!"

This startled everyone, and even brought Griffey to a halt, looking back at her. She hadn't made a specific decision just now, but she'd been loud and decisive in identifying their leader.

Though she would never admit it, her reasons for the outburst were far from noble. Not only did she now hold the lives of Konragen and her daughter in her hands, but her earlier fears were being multiplied. The big dragon was now in position to casually roll over in his sleep and absently smother Baby Hazel to a muffled death. These glaring worries rocked her nerves.

After a moment, Griffey sighed. "I'll make a deal, acho? We keep moving, and I'll tell you."

The Ranger set a hasty pace, which was aided by the downhill travel. No one objected to the speed, as there were plenty of reasons to quickly reach the village. Shuffling down the slope spawned a greater chance of slipping and this helped them focus more and stay alert.

Ramsey jogged along behind Griffey, and for the first portion of their hike he juggled his staff back and forth, unable to find a position that agreed with the motion. Mainly, his mind was reeling. He was concerned that Griffey might permit him to keep Kozard's black glass. He was afraid that Brisk may be correct; whatever veins of magic flowing within the prism would not be contained. If he started religiously jamming the monocle in his eye socket, then it was reasonable to think the wispy tentacles of dark magic might traverse the short distance from there into his brain. He was also terrified that Griffey would make him get rid of it. Not only would the loss hurt their chances of survival, but it would essentially amount to a betrayal. He would be discarding a relic of the society of Sorcery which he'd pledged his life and legacy to. He suspected that Kozard may have used and thrown away many magic relics. This thought forced Ramsey to confront the truth that his legacy may already be doomed.

At the rear of the line, Marynda was keeping up with the others, maintaining a crazily hectic pace. She hugged the black bag to her chest; couldn't bear the prospect of letting it flap down at her side or dangle over her shoulder and openly invite an enemy arrow to puncture it. The fact that she'd clawed out one of the borlogs' eyes did not invigorate her with the confidence that she could strike that easily every time. Raving thoughts such as this produced a series of rapid glances over her shoulder. Her imagination conjured the horrifying imagery of black bootheels slurping from the dirt-brown trail into the pure-blue sky. Following these precursors would be the undersides of borlog chins just a little further upslope. She could escape from such an elevated attack, but her friends might not.

There was no resisting it. She lifted the bag to her face, opened the slit, and peered inside with reassuring hope. She was in the back of the line. No one was going to look back and catch her.

Hot air refreshingly swept over Griffey's face as he raced ahead. Soon the trees would gobble up his view of the village cottages, towards which he felt a nostalgic draw. He could hear the smoky scatter-echo of firecrackers. Just as the restorative warmth of a springtime sunrise can soothe away the dread of winter, a wash of nostalgia eased the crushing pressure of this current moment and what lay ahead. For a split, his boots were many sizes smaller and his hand was grasped in the comforting grip of his father's. His mother carried his younger sister and together they strolled an aisle of festival tents with an eclipse in the sky. His dazzled eyes gaped at swirling colors while his nose sensed a fried sizzle and a frenzy of delighted laughter filled the air.

Gentle, wonderful memories of a Midsummer's Eve festival long, long past.

Griffey sighed, his mind mercifully at peace, even as the forest thickened once again and they sank into its depths, the treetops blocking the village from sight. He brought the group to a halt. "Growing up in Rivercrest, I don't remember many tales told to me about adventurers. Men and women and elves and dragons who roamed the earth on quests. The further we get from the castle, the more I feel they kept us intentionally blinded to the world beyond. Now that we're so far removed from our home, it's almost as if we've been cut off from history. Rivercrest history, I mean. No tales are told—to little children or in Academy classrooms—about adventurers who never return. My father was one of the few to go out and roam, but he mostly stayed quiet on the topic of his travels. You see, with all the world pressing against us, I think we need every advantage we can get. Kozard's glass has value. Keep it. Trade it in the village."

"Is this your poetic side speaking?" Marynda said. "It's surely not the drunken tavern brawler."

Griffey uttered a tiny laugh. "Four days ago, I entered Rivercrest castle and Kozard was not there to greet me. Yet, later, Kozard was able to describe the scene perfectly, down to my brown-with-white-spots horse… His glass is powerful. We can trade it to a Healer to help fix Konragen, acho?"

Brisk and Marynda looked curiously at Ramsey, who only nodded and had nothing to say.

"The world seems so much different out here," Griffey mused, the previous wistfulness returned to his voice. "I've Ranged forests before, but never this one, and never under such circumstances. It's almost as if we roam a whole different planet. Speaking of that, isn't it odd how we never really talk about Gasha? Our planet, I mean… *Planet*. A funny word. I haven't heard it spoken since my youth. See there? A long-ago childhood memory instantly brought to the present. Time is malleable, and perhaps we need to think of it as not being so rigid. As a construct of the city, time has a different flow from what we see and feel out here… Perhaps we need to consider the entire *world* differently…"

◇ CHAPTER THE THIRTY-FIRST. ◇
◇The Festival of Midsummer's Eve.◇

"The borlogs are gaining on us."

Marynda's words were spoken with blunt certainty. She'd tried hard to keep any quivering emotions out of her voice, and had barely succeeded. She hoped this discretion would avert panic in the hearts of her companions, but they also deserved to know of the elevated danger.

She hadn't precisely witnessed any of Ulkar's trio on the trail behind them—so that was encouraging. But she *had* been able to briefly adopt the ears of an owl—not the full physical feathery form, just the ears. She had heard the unmistakable patter of footsteps. Footsteps emanating from boots mashing dirt. The boots of three man-sized beasts. "I've pinpointed them at ninety yards behind us."

"Surely they have generosity in their hearts," Brisk surmised. "Got a progress report for us."

"Supervisory capacity and such," Ramsey added, which made the Cook chuckle and grin.

The hill struck its nadir and the terrain leveled out once again. They walked on smooth turf for a while, the trail weaving through the blocks of trees and boulders. Soon, the ground began to creep and crawl over the humps of lazy hills. The sound of smattering firecrackers and laughter drew closer.

Griffey adjusted the cone of the Zodak claw, which was lodged snug to his right elbow. Inside, the hairs of his arm were slick with sweat from the impervious insulation, but the shield was surprisingly lightweight. The Ranger's blue-green eyes lifted up high while he jogged. Through the cascading patterns of leaves and branches and birds and squirrels, he caught a glimpse of the sky. The two lunar masses were colored a sickly thundercloud purple and threatening to turn black. The amount of sunlight was already beginning to dim. Shadows deepened upon the pits and mounds of the trail.

Griffey asked for the party to prepare themselves "to mingle," he said, "and be extremely alert." He asked everyone to explain what they planned to do in town.

"Hmm-*hmmm*," Brisk rumbled. "I'd say my tertiary goals include a hot bath, a good meal, and a loving brunette. More to the primary, I'd proclaim my goals to be the same as every Midsummer festival. A few healthy tosses at the dice table, then over to the prime rib smokers."

"I usually aim for," Ramsey revealed, "double-sour lemonade and pebble-puddle toss."

"*Double-sour lemonade?*" Brisk repeated with revulsion. "Pebble... *pebble-puddle-toss??*"

"I'd choose knife-throw over *that*," Marynda murmured. "Maybe even ball-bottle-knock."

Griffey smiled as his companions fell back into familiar behaviors. However, he chided them and said, "We need to get a plan together so we don't get killed. We'll have to split up. I'll go first into the village. I'll be looking for a Healer's tent to help Konragen and get my hand back."

"I could reattach your hand right now," Ramsey groaned, "we just need somebody to fix the broken parts." This drew a warning look, so the elf relented. "I'll follow Griffey to the Healer. I've got our most coveted trade item, after all. Maybe we'll find a potions booth, should look for that."

"I need some *food*, brothers and sisters," Brisk boomed. "Sign me up to gather up the goods." He thought for a moment longer, then added, "I want weapons, too. Maybe a knife. Ooo-ooo, er, how about a dagger? Yeah, one of those. And some kind of shield. I want to be more prepared next time…"

"To get any of that stuff, you're gonna need coin," Griffey noted. "Make those dice roll hot."

This brought a confident smile to the face of the Cook. Then, he and the Sorcerer looked back at Marynda, awaiting her contribution. "I'll go with Brisk to oversee his gambling habits. And I want to visit the weapons tents, as well. Changing into wolves and birds is nice, but I always end up naked in front of you guys… I can't believe the elf drinks double-sour lemonade…"

The misdirection of this joke succeeded exactly as she'd planned. Instead of pressing her any further, Brisk started laughing at the elf which, in turn, definitely distracted Ramsey. She didn't want to reveal exactly what destination she had in mind. Didn't want to risk the objections.

Still, further attention was inevitable. "Marynda," Griffey called softly. "I know you're not going to like this, but, if we're splitting up, we've gotta take your bag. It has Kon *and* my hand inside."

This was the moment she'd feared more than anything. Being forced to part with her bag. Which she would have to do. She couldn't tag along with the Ranger and the Sorcerer and also attend to her business undetected. Still, she feared giving up the bag. Even to a man she trusted.

"I will carry it until we enter the village," she stated stubbornly. "Then, I'll hand it over…"

The time of that transfer arrived before any of them were ready for it.

The sounds of the village met their ears in a gradual assault, steadily increasing in volume. In contrast, sight of the place appeared abruptly, with a sudden jolt. Around a casual right-hand curve of the western trail of Shadowbranch forest, two squat, humble log cabins emerged. They were spaced apart so the trail could squiggle between them, and each structure was accompanied by weakly-built fencelines encompassing snoozing goats and chickens and clumps of hay. With the borlogs on their back-trail, there wasn't much hesitation or concern about invasion of private property. The party swept around the corner and discovered that the trail they'd been walking had now morphed into a broad central avenue.

Here, on the fringe, Griffey paused, allowing the others to step up and gawk along with him. Despite the marvelous visuals directly ahead of them, their eyes were drawn to the skies—right along with all the families and festival workers who filled the street. The two sister moons were the shade of a bruise and preparing to kill the light.

An enchanted hush fell across the entire village as one final bursting ray of golden light escaped with an accusatory lash. The moons slid into place, dislodging the golden orb, bringing out the stars, drawing the drapes of night. With a palpable spike, the temperature dipped a few chilling notches. Alarm rippled through the spruce forest; robins and rodents chirped and chittered with confusion.

Griffey was the first of the group to look back to the street. He saw two rows of tall men in long black jackets with matching top hats, lining the avenue at regular intervals. In unison, these Samaritans knelt and struck flames upon matchsticks. More or less at the same time, the gentlemen lit bright candles, settled them into cradles, and removed their hands. Pale paper balloons with cut-out tops rose lazily into the air, each held in place with leashes of ribbon so they bobbed and twinkled ten feet up.

A pall of restraint persisted, yet all it took was one anonymous whistle for the congregation to blossom into a cheering, hooting mass. This gave a hearty pluck to the nostalgic strings of Griffey's heart, and he was fiercely tempted to join in and applaud with glee. His childhood gnawed at him, demanding that he participate, that he join the fun. However, now that his eyes were leveled upon the crowd, he fell into the routine of intensely sweeping faces. Searching for the Warlock.

Marynda shot a glance behind them, registered how swollen with shadows the trees were and felt a rush of fear. She hugged the bag to her chest, closed her eyes and savored the embrace, then tapped Griffey on the shoulder and passed it to him. Taking possession of the bag ended his search.

They entered the festival with caution, moving in a delicate manner. Bathed in the twilight-orange glow of the floating balloon-candles, their progress was tentative at first. They edged into the outer bands of the action, where horse manure caught their noses and the snores of a drunken bum scratched their ears. These pleasantries—combined with the sloppy mud-patch squishing beneath their boots—got them moving faster.

Nailed high on a post, a wooden plaque proclaimed: *The Hospitable Village of BENSON.*

Through occasional gaps, they caught sight of log cabins set further back. This meant the festival attractions were not only dominating the entire avenue, but also playing on peoples' lawns. But nobody seemed upset by this invasion; in fact, the people seemed overjoyed with the show. Couples, arms clasped around each other, strolled up the street, sometimes pausing to laugh or whisper or embrace, while rowdy, bawling children traced more hysteric traffic patterns, drawing flustered parents in pursuit. Scents of venison pepper-jerky and warm apple bread filled the air.

"Do you plan to challenge those bread-bakers on the quality of their product?" Ramsey asked.

"I'd rather just buy some and quietly judge later on," Brisk said. "We ate all my bread, so…"

"I think a more appropriate description might be: *the Cook consumed the crop…*"

"Frishka's broken skull," the Cook muttered, but all enthusiasm for insults vanished when the glorious, delectable scent of a pig-roast nuzzled up to his nostrils. Brisk actually blinked as he savored the treat. Eyes back open, he spied the rotisserie on the left and, right across the street, he marked the sharp resounding *thwack* of a knife-throw booth. Settled next door to that was a tent with the bright green felt of a beckoning dice-roll table. Brisk rubbed his hands together with a winning smirk. "I've found my landing, folks. First stop, at that. How convenient, eh?"

"You'll get the pleasure of meeting Ulkar and the ugly boys before the rest of us," Griffey said, still scanning the crowd. "Roll hot dice and roll 'em fast," he advised his friend, before addressing the Druid woman. "If you're staying with Brisk, be on your guard. The borlogs might try and flank you, so watch out. Head our way as soon as you've won enough money to buy food and weapons."

"Elf," the Cook exclaimed, before departing, "best of luck tossing pebbles in them puddles."

Ramsey began to protest, but Griffey gripped his arm and drug him along. The Ranger looked back and found Marynda's hazel eyes. "I will care for your bag, madam. I will guard it with my life."

◇ CHAPTER THE THIRTY-SECOND. ◇
◇Hexahedra Quartet.◇

"Brisk met the tongue of a Zodak yesterday," the Cook boasted as he romped into the tent, "and not only did he survive the encounter, but he scored some heat-magic fingertips."

Marynda followed him in. She didn't duck fast enough to avoid a slap from the entry flaps. Her awkward entrance, combined with the boasts of the Cook, were enough to make her brightly blush. It felt silly to feel embarrassed at a time like this, when she should've been more concerned with the fact that she'd openly agreed to stay back and potentially fight three borlogs with only Brisk at her side.

The brown leather tipi was coated with a thick coat of dust. Beneath the dust, there lurked symbols scrawled in some unknown language; runes shining a faint green glow.

A pair of smelly customers were seated at the lime-green table. Both were fat and bearded, one with a black eye patch, both with looks of losing bitterness; expressions which cried out for standing up and waddling away hours ago. They were either addicted to the dice or afraid of all the social crowds outside. The boisterous arrival of Brisk was the day's highlight for them, but it did not earn any smiles from them. Even the table runner shot a glare at Brisk.

"A-hem, acho, acho." Brisk coughed out a nod to the table runner, a lanky, sickly man with a thin drooping mustache and an impossible collection of wrinkles entrenched around his bulging eyes. Brisk settled into a chair, crackled his knuckles, and tried to look casual. "Let's roll, shall we?"

"Yeh'll not be a'touchin' any cubes in this tent," the runner rasped, "without coin to pay."

When Brisk hesitated, the two players and the manager shifted their gazes to Marynda. This unwanted attention made her even more uneasy. Brisk hoisted Kozard's longsword and smacked it down onto the table, effectively drawing all the eyes away from her. "Buy me in, I say!"

The host gave a grin that was equally giddy and greedy, revealing a set of jutting, crooked brown-yellow teeth. His eyes positively glowed and flashed upon the blade. A moment later, his standard scowl returned. His voice was a squawk. "Me give three gold and one silver for this sword."

"Oh dear Frishka," Marynda gasped, her face pale. "He's dragging you to the washboards—"

"Wiiiiiith your assurances," Brisk declared, "that I may buy it back for the same price. Tonight."

Mary protested, Brisk held up a hand to her. The host gave a nod of consent, and the odd little man scurried after the transaction, as if it were a mythical creature which might escape. The sword was hauled away with graceful rapidity, while the scant jingle of coins were flung carelessly at the Cook.

Marynda's head was in her hands—she wasn't talking, for fear of a quiver in her voice—because watching was just too painful. Men were such fools. They always thought games and luck could solve all their problems. She didn't see Brisk's first roll produce double turtles, but she did hear an audible groan and Brisk's sharp intake of breath. She forced herself to look and realized he'd bet one of his golds on that worthless turn. While the Druid woman's heart thundered and her eyes went wide and cold sweat slicked her brow, she watched helplessly as Brisk pushed in the remainder of his money.

"Oh, Frishka's busted brains, this is madness," she yelped. "I'm sorry, we have to go—"

"Doncha flap your fingers at a man's money on the dice

table," Brisk scolded her. The other occupants of this dreary tent sent glares of equivalent disapproval at her, and it was clear that the mood in here was against her. She didn't care about that; she abhorred whatever stupid codes men adhered to in dumps such as this. Still, she restrained herself. She stood, arms crossed; a muted spectator.

Brisk took a moment to gather himself. He huffed hot air into his hands, rubbed them together. The other players at the table leaned back with deferential respect, making it clear they were sitting out this round. The scoundrel host, however, had other plans. "Me buy in against you. Me roll against you."

With a sly, wicked little grin, the table runner dished out the requisite two gold and single silver.

Outside the tent, bells jingled, whistles tooted, children yipped, people laughed, dogs barked.

Inside the tent, the loudest domestic sounds were particles of dust sprinkling off the walls.

Everyone knew the stakes that stood. If Brisk lost this upcoming roll, the result would bounce him right into indentured servitude. Being chained to the leg of a shadowy worker in a traveling carnival was one horrid prospect for a sane person. "I accept," Brisk asserted with sly confidence.

Marynda, the host, and the duo of overweight onlookers were all equally shocked by this.

Barely repressing a snicker, the table runner produced a pair of die, grape in color, and cradled them in his palm, hovering out above the lime green landscape. "*Halt*," called out one of the bearded men, who leaned forward in his chair, bringing the front two legs down with a ***slap***. Everyone looked at him and he lit up, as if relishing the attention being on him. "Bardo is my name," he informed Brisk and Marynda. He voice was soothing and deep. "I live in Benson. I roll this table once a year. Every Midsummer's Eve, you see. You may want to consider switching cubes with him."

Brisk's eyes traveled from Bardo's face to the rodent sneer of the host to the pair of purple die framed in the hand of the host, then, finally, to the pair of scarlet cubes in his own palm.

After a breath, Brisk softly exclaimed, "I shall beat him as is." This sent Bardo leaning back in his chair once again, arms clasped across his belly with a look of intense scrutiny upon his face. His pirate patch companion, who could've been his twin, wore a look of annoyance and childish defiance.

Both Brisk and the host shook their die within the compartments of their fists, then, in unison, unleashed the dancers across the dancefloor. The quartet of hexahedra hopped and hobbled, twirled and tripped, bounced and bobbled, sputtered and spun across the smooth felt tabletop. Animal imagery, imprinted upon the surfaces of the cubes, blurred and smeared into imaginary crossover beasts.

The four cubes rebounded off the short padded walls which enclosed the arena. The blocks of destiny rumbled to shivering stops and everyone gawked down at them with ravenous gazes. Face-up on the purple dice were a basilisk and a squid. Face-up on the scarlet pair were double dragons.

The front legs of Bardo's chair *clapped* back down again. "Not only does the guest win all the coin," he narrated in a soft tone of awe, "but he also gets an extra roll without the chance of losing."

"The host can only tie…" Marynda finished for him, drawing an ugly sneer from the host.

While the bearded men whooped and applauded, Marynda grabbed a delirious Brisk by his shoulders and turned him to face her. "Brisk! You did it!" She couldn't control her schoolgirl glee, and when she saw something similar on his face, she got serious. "Cash out, get that sword back, and meet me at the supply tent across the street, acho?" She had to shake him to wake him. "*Acho??*"

Brisk finally sobered. "After I win this extra roll," he told her, "I'm only going to do one final roll after that." He saw her eyes flash. "But I'll only bet a single gold on that one."

She held up a lecturing finger, then sighed. An absurd part of her memory informed her that this is what some young parents might frame as a *learning moment*. Sadness pierced her heart.

"You meet me at that supply tent in five minutes," she managed to say, her voice level and stern.

To demonstrate her decisiveness, she plucked one of the gold coins and held it in Brisk's face. "I'm getting us food across the street," she told him, "bring the rest of the money, meet me at the weapons."

Marynda shot back outside, tent flaps flailing in her wake.

◇ CHAPTER THE THIRTY-THIRD. ◇
◇Festival Stroll.◇

A pair of drunken dwarves—the topographies of their rust-brown beards straining and pooling with rivers and lakes of spilled beer—nearly bowled Marynda over in the street. She hadn't seen them, they hadn't seen her, yet the collision was averted at the last instant. They barked, muttered, and cursed at her as they staggered away. She felt a pang of shame and heated resentment as her conscience exaggerated her interaction with the dwarves into some grand social tragedy.

She was startled by a drum-roll burst of crackle poppers, each tiny explosion giving off a flash of sparks. Children skittered in energetic circles with the unmitigated excitement that only fireworks can deliver. A shaggy pony stomped past, sending splatters of mud in all directions. Drug along behind the beast, a rickety cart swayed and croaked with a hairy toothless farmer lounging dejectedly on the throne. Once this obstruction shuffled clear, Marynda forced her feet to move.

It was an eerie feeling to be strolling the streets of a foreign village during an unorthodox nighttime. For it was indeed nighttime. Rich shadows were lumped between the tents lining the road, and flickers thrived almost everywhere else. The only reliable light sources were the balloon candles hovering and humming along the avenue, supplemented with the occasional lantern or tiny, contained fiery burst of a child's plaything explosive. *Why parents let them play with explosives is beyond me.*

Beyond these fire hazards, a dense heat permeated the air of this impromptu summer evening.

Part of her held heavy doubts that Brisk would politely excuse himself from the gambling den after one final dice-toss. Yet she detested places like that and her troubled heart had cried to get away.

She glared after the horse-drawn carriage and attempted to sort out the horde and locate Griffey and Ramsey the Green. She hoped to catch a glimpse of them, just to make sure they were safe, and at the very least, alive, but it was a hopeless exercise. A jolt of panic struck her pulse as she realized how stupid she was for looking right instead of left. Her head quickly spun to the way they'd entered town. The degree of human commotion over there was far more mild, and this actually made it scary. This meant the trio of borlogs would be walking in the open.

She saw none of those bloodthirsty brutes. Not Ulkar, nor the cyclops who would be after her. It wasn't preposterous to think that one-eyed borlog would know she had caused the ghastly injury to his face. Surely Ulkar had access to the records of their Quest. He would know who the Druid was.

Marynda darted to the opposite row of tents then scurried up the street. Her first stop was at the rotisserie, a consultation which she conducted very quickly but not without manners. Using Brisk's gold coin, she purchased six slices of salted rotisserie pork, and collected her change. Right next door, she selected a small loaf of apple bread and some vegetables and nearly ran out of money. Both booths were starved for customers, so she got full attention and efficient service, her eyes imploring them to hurry. She shoved all these provisions inside her brown knapsack and paid them no further thought.

Continuing up the street, she spied a wooden barrel with people clustered around it clutching fishing poles and expressions of exaggerated excitement. She saw a booth where kids threw trash at statues of dragonpeople and it made her sad. In the middle of the avenue, running right up the lane, was an elongated tub of water with a dozen children congregated around it. Inside the trough, mallards were lazily paddling and supposedly racing. The kids shrieked and cheered at the contestants, as if they could actually encourage or discourage the pace of the ducks. This delightfully ridiculous event was interrupted by a cascade of bright sensations on her left. A wall of shelves, packed with jelly apples, blackberry pies, bowls of popping butter corn, plus jars of pink and blue frosted sugar cream.

Her stomach growled, urging her to eat her recent purchases, yet she pressed onward.

Happiness and innocence seemed to drip from every inch of the scenery, yet the mood was not infectious. She saw fathers kneeling with their sons and executing demonstrations with wooden swords. She saw mothers holding their daughters up to bakery displays, whispering enchanting words in their ears. All of it left Marynda feeling empty. Not only did she feel the awful separation from her handbag, but there was also the dreadful reality that her family was broken. Never would she stroll the streets of a carnival with Alkent on one arm and Hazel tottering along at her side with a starstruck expression.

She spotted the weapons booth straight ahead. A concentric hub of insurance against all the injustices of this world; innocuously tucked amongst all the family fun. Though it didn't seem to be fielding many customers (most of the folks roaming through Benson village appeared contented with observation rather than consumption), Marynda saw it as somehow more honest than all the rest of the attractions. Reality was a cruel locale, and that red booth had no patience for pretending otherwise.

The exterior of the display was a deep crimson, matching the back wall inside. Mounted upon that wall was a rack of hooks from which dangled an impressive array of weaponry: wooden clubs, jagged daggers, sleek crossbows, mighty hammers, dazzling maces, shimmering axes. She needed to meet Brisk over there very soon, and she fantasized over what defense measures she might acquire.

She spied a javelin posted on that red wall. *Alkent used to throw the javelin.* He'd let her try it out a time or twice, but it always felt awkward to her. No matter what she ended up buying with Brisk's prize money, she figured Alkent would be proud to see her not relying solely on her animal powers.

Her attention snapped away as a group of kids ignited a string of firecrackers and raved with delight at the results. *Does no one in this town keep track of their children on Midsummer's Eve?* She recognized this critique for what it was: she was becoming the snooty, overprotective parent she always swore she would eschew. She balanced this out by thinking, *At least I'm out here, right? I was willing to leave the safety of the castle and bring my daughter out into the world. That says something, right?*

From where Marynda was, all it took was one step forward and her destination slid into view. To her left was the cone of a black tent, quaint, understated, set back from the festival as if it were a sulky cousin lingering on the periphery of a family reunion. This tent was so thoroughly copulated with shadows that Marynda should've missed it—but, sometimes, the animal powers she adopted through Druid transformation seemed to stick around. She'd been an owl recently, and her eyes were keen.

Without hesitating, as if being drawn, beckoned, she left the glow of the streetlights and sauntered over towards it. She saw that this cone wasn't entirely black, as a split of mysterious green light seeped out from a triangular slit in the entrance curtains. She stopped a few feet short of the threshold, felt a rush of anxiety, glanced over her shoulder and verified that no one was watching her. She leaned a bit and felt her heart lurch. There was a little round table positioned inside, and a person with a hood. She shook off the shock. *It shouldn't be a surprise to see it occupied,* she scolded herself.

Though the building was made of fabric, Marynda still had an absurd inclination to knock before just barging inside. Her paralysis was broken by a soft, compelling voice which whispered and flowed out to grace her ears and intoxicate her. "*Enter, Druidess... I have been expecting you.*"

◇ CHAPTER THE THIRTY-FOURTH.◇
◇Generosity and Revenge.◇

With a deep breath, Marynda ducked inside. The confines were cramped, the inside of the tent fabric was stained sangria wine. Shelves lined the perimeter, stocked with vials, jars, and bottles of mysterious colorful liquids, along with a human skull. An army of candles flickered along the tops of the shelves, pulsing shadows in the sockets and crevices of the skull. The round table at the heart of the tent was smooth with a black velvet cloth. The person seated at the table wore a heavy black robe complete with a hood draped over to fully obscure their face. A hand gestured for her to sit.

As she settled down onto a stool across the table, Marynda made sure the front flap of the tent was closed behind her. When she turned back, she saw the person toss back their hood to reveal a woman who'd been gorgeous ten years ago. Now, the woman was passing middle-age, with streaks of gray encroaching upon her silky black hair. Wrinkles were entrenched imperiously beneath her arresting blue eyes and snaked around the thin scarlet lips of her smile. She was, indeed, smiling.

"I am called Brishtiva," the enchantress spoke. "Oracle of the Muljane Islands."

The Druid noticed faint swirls of smoke begin to rise from someplace on the floor. Steadily, a haze cut the air with thin curtain layers. Riding upon this uprising, there came the pleasing scent of cinnamon. Marynda tensed, afraid she'd just been trapped in a mystic hallucination tent. *But that's just a rumor built to frighten children. Right?* "I am called Marynda. You already know I'm a Druid…"

"We are pleasant-met beneath the eclipsing moons."
Braced atop the table, the Oracle's palms joined together, fingers
forming their own miniature tent. "You want to know how I knew
you had Druid's blood. But you also want to know that you are
safe. Rest assured, that, while in my company you are under the
spell of my protection. No outside force can harm you here. As to
that... ahem, *other* worry of yours, you have nothing to fear from
me, either. I offer you nothing less than aid."

Marynda squirmed a little in her seat, fighting to keep her
hands and feet from fidgeting.

"In a shrewd interpretation, I am a woman of business,"
Brishtiva confided with a shrug. "I extracted myself from the
prissy, structured, limited realm of Oracle society many years
ago. Instead of that dreary footsoldier life, I elected to apply my
talents in the real world. To help real people. I use the Sight to
gaze upon a stranger and distill their aura down to a single secret
scroll which only I can read. The words written on that scroll may
depict a person in need of medicine or a love potion or a glimpse
into the future. Granted, I use this ability to further my business
interests. How could I not?"

"I see no shame in it," Marynda commented. "We all must
do what's necessary to survive."

"There's more to life than survival. Generosity and
revenge come to mind." Brishtiva grinned, which could have been
either charming or wicked, but Marynda didn't want to spend too
much time analyzing it. She didn't want to spend much time in
here at all. Ever since she left the main path, she felt the allure of
the weapons tent where she needed to meet with Brisk. She
needed to be there. *At least this current place is better than the
gambling den. And motherly advice is a rare commodity.*

"If those are your two available categories... I suppose I
need to call upon both."

"You are nearly out of coin and have nothing of value to
trade." Brishtiva gave her a critical eye, but her cold stare soon

softened. "Your friend has coin, but you worry about giving it to me."

Marynda thought of the trio of deadly borlogs which might be out roaming the village right now. Walking amongst the families. Maybe right up behind Brisk. "Madam, in my black handba—"

"Tell me, young lady," Brishtiva interrupted with a smack of her lips, "have ever you heard the tale of Vara the Prince's Daughter? Not a very famous story. Who really cares about the daughter of somebody third-in-line to the throne? *Hrrummph.* It was a distant time ago, in an even more distant kingdom, where the Prince—who was married to a maiden at the time—went ahead and impregnated another girl, despite the circumstances. The Prince's decision to do this left nobody impressed with his behavior, and even fewer people pleased. All holy hellfire was raised from the chickens of the court as they squawked and fretted over *what to do, what to do.* In the end, yelling and bickering got in the way of devising a plan, and nothing was done to prepare for the birth of the child. Vara was her name."

"Madam Oracle, I—"

"—I *know* you have concerns about enemies outside. About your friends outside. But you came to me for a reason. And I shall help you. Oh yes. I shall most definitely help you. *Mm-hmm.* The results of that help, however, may not be the dreamy glory you seek... Now, listen to the rest of this story.

"Little planning was done ahead of Vara's arrival to the world. She was raised as a bitter afterthought step-child and treated even worse. She was seen as a black-eye upon the royal family—whom were naturally far too lofty and flawless and dignified and noble to be involved with adulterous pregnancies, *tsk-tsk-tsk.* While his daughter was treated poorly, so was the Prince. Never could he escape the stain he'd brought to his house. So he took sympathy upon his daughter. Upon Vara. They became something close to kindred souls of suffering. He offered to grant her any wish…"

At this point, the eyes of Brishtiva the Oracle turned a deep shade of black and narrowed with a whip-crack. As the candles flickered, the light drew low, and the smoke thickened around them, the older woman leaned forward, drawing her guest forward to meet her. Marynda tried not to breathe, and that caused other problems on its own. Brishtiva's voice dredged to a scratchy whisper.

"Vara wished for a way out. Not to run. Not to change her name and hide. She wished to reach the age of first-plateau plus seven. The age of independence. The age when she could just walk away from it all. She wanted maturity without earning it, you see… So, under cover of night, the Prince went out and consulted with a Cleric on the outskirts of town. The price he paid is unknown, but the Prince obtained a potion. A potion of *Acceleration.* The Prince's intentions were pure… but the results were harsh. The girl drank the potion that very night and she began to grow. She aged so fast that, within a few hours, she not only shot past the seventeen mark, but was well into her third-plateau. The Prince locked the door of the chamber and howled beside the bed while Vara aged and aged. Eventually, the process came to a stop, leaving Vara a gnarled, white-haired old hag, writhing with pain and regret…"

Silence gripped the women. Marynda's hazel eyes stared across the table in a grip of horror.

"I know why you entered my tent beneath the eclipsing moons," Brishtiva breathed, staring right back at her. "Your infant daughter is hidden in the sub-world. Inside your black handbag."

"Y-Yes, her name is Hazel…" Marynda stammered. "I lost my husband two nights ago. Alkent was k… was killed in an attack on Rivercrest castle. I want vengeance upon the foul being who killed him, but I also need to care for Hazel. I… I'm just not sure I can do both of those things with her as a baby."

Brishtiva rapped long black fingernails upon the tabletop,

then she swiveled and scrutinized a shelf. She turned back and held out two corked vials of liquid; one sloshed with red while its mate glowed an eerie blue. "Potions have come a long way since Vara," the Oracle assured her. "You get Hazel to drink the blue vial and she will reach the age of independence sooner than you're ready for. Before your mind conjures a nightmare, just know: the process *will* stop where it's supposed to."

Marynda accepted the vials, a single tear in her eye. "Why… why are you helping me?"

Brishtiva issued a heavy sigh. "I was a struggling young mother once, myself, you know. Just because I've run into some success—don't let my presence at a back-country carnival deceive you—doesn't mean I've forgotten the experience of pregnancy back pain." This comment was enough to remind Marynda of the ache in her own lower back. Brishtiva went on, "I could demand that you pay me whatever you've got. I could bind you to me in the chains of some horrific lifelong debt. But I have no care to do any of that. Is it so impossible to believe I just want to see a young mother get her wish?"

Marynda had no words. Her hands trembled as she deposited the vials in her knapsack.

Brishtiva held up one bony finger and wagged it slowly before her face. "Just because I'm doing you a favor, doesn't mean I won't implore you to think double before giving that potion to your little girl… *Think* about what you're doing. You're actually looking to instantly send a girl to her seventeenth year— into the world with no childhood, no foundation, and no father." The Oracle spread her hands. "As is, I think you may be signing on for full payment, a harsh payment."

"It'd be better than keeping her in the cave. At least… at least she could defend herself." Marynda felt a raw certainty that this view was the right way to look at it. She bit her lip, dropped her eyes, and decided to say something she'd never really admitted to anyone but Alkent. "You know… when I was pregnant—er, well, when I gave birth… I pushed so hard I burst the vessels in my face.

"And," Marynda continued, "no matter how painful that was, how unsettling it was to see my face blood-red for so many weeks, no matter how awful the pain of childbirth was… none of that even compares to the pain of thinking I may not get Hazel to seventeen without this drink. May not get to see her become a strong, intelligent, independent woman. I am afraid I will fail her…"

The sorrowful Oracle nodded with a look of grim acceptance, but she did not speak.

"What's the red liquid for?" Marynda asked.

Brishtiva leaned back and stared at her, eyes alive again. "I know you're not used to fighting while you're in human form. That red liquid will heighten your senses for battle. Enhance your abilities and reaction time. Drink it when you're in danger, young Druidess. You will need it very soon."

◇ CHAPTER THE THIRTY-FIFTH.◇
◇Attackers from the Smog.◇

Looking back at it later, Marynda did not remember standing up from the table, leaving the tent, and walking back to the main avenue of the festival. Once she got there, her temper still did not mesh with the joy simmering off the games and food. She felt just as empty, hollow, and scared as she had when she was out here earlier. Meeting with the Oracle had given her new alternatives to ponder.

A voice spoke to her. It rang with the jolly confident tone of an umbrella salesman in a rainstorm. The substance of the words garbled together in her ears. All she registered was a bright crimson color which steadily swam into focus. The surfaces comprising gained texture, ranging from flimsy and delicate to rigid and solid. At about the same time, the sound and the physical elements gained coherence. Her eyes registered the red fabric of a tent enclosing a broad plank of wood painted red. Her ears heard a voice which was now seasoned with concern. "Madam, you acho?"

"I need a shield," she heard her own voice command, "a dagger, and I'll be needing a weapon, as well." The assortment of armaments fluttered into view. "I'll take the mace, please." She envisioned swinging the spiky ball at the end of the chain and, in her imagination, it was an elegant portrayal.

"Young madam, yeh can't afford *that*," scoffed the plump hairy man behind the counter as he reached up and plucked a wooden club instead. He clanked this down, along with the rest of her order.

Just as Marynda was about to protest the brutish lack of

grace inherent to a wooden club, Brisk arrived at her side, huffing for breath. Though she shouldn't have been, Marynda was surprised to see him. Brisk was stunned to find her actively engaged at the weapons booth instead of perplexed with indecision. The hairy merchant with the beady black eyes was more shocked than both of them combined when he witnessed Brisk take stock of the situation and shell out a stack of gold coins.

"Marynda, I know what you told me, but one roll turned into two rolls," Brisk placated her.

"That's it—promises to Frishka." Then, a sly smile lit his face. "All profit, pure profit, total profit."

"That's good, Brisk." She patted his shoulder while he jingled a pouch of coins inside his jacket. She warily noticed his sword. "How much did that guy charge you to get Kozard's sword back?"

"Same as I bought it for," Brisk declared obstinately. He was going to pursue the topic further, to defend his honor, but her attention had already moved on. Marynda held up her new wooden bat, adjusted her grip, dealt a look of suspicion over at the hairy merchant, then turned back to the club, gauged the weight, gave it a few preliminary waves. With a shrug, Brisk examined his own new items.

His dagger was a steel blade, almost outshone by the bronze handle which came generously complete with the swoop of a knuckle guard. *Can't wait to dice carrots and gut fish with this.* He nearly slipped the blade into his belt, hesitated, then turned and hastily purchased a leather scabbard.

Next up, the Cook examined the shield Marynda had picked out for him. It was a buckler, built of metal, rusted brown, trapezoidal, gripped by a handle in the back-middle. The weight was mild, yet enough to help bulk up his left bicep. He drew out Kozard's sword, just to have some balance and considered the shield. *Good for hand-to-hand combat, won't do any good at blocking arrows—*

A black-feathered broadhead arrow crashed into Brisk's shield, four spikes springing out with little screeches at the point of impact. Fortunately, while dancing with his hardware, Brisk had turned away from both Marynda and the booth. This oblivious motion took him back the way he'd come and put his shield right into the path of the incoming missile.

While Brisk recoiled, ducked, and looked stupefied, Marynda's eyes shot to the contents of her knapsack. She snatched out the vial of red liquid, popped the cork and tossed it in the direction of the astonished merchant. The drink was bitter and stung as it sizzled down her throat, but she gulped it all. For a horrific moment, her stomach churned but she kept it down and the results were instant. Gooseflesh rippled up her arms. All traces of weariness and foggy eyes were swept away. Readjusting her grip upon the club, she felt confident strength surge down her shoulders, arms, hands, and knuckles, all the way to her fingertips. Marynda had experienced raw power before—she'd once roamed the forests in the body of a grizzly bear, after all. But never had she felt such magnificence while in human form. While occupying her own body. With a predatory focus, she whirled and crouched.

In that moment she was very proud she'd chosen to fight in her human form. She couldn't carry her knapsack if she were running around as an animal.

Another broadhead sliced past, just overhead. Marynda's ears noted a *ping* and a squawk from the startled merchant, but her eyes were locked forward. To the trio of dark figures emerging from the blurry firecracker smog and the golden glimmer of the tethered balloon lights. *Borlogs in the fog…*

It took a moment for the bystanders to register that their party had just been disrupted. People began to clasp each other, adopt frantic faces, and at least one shriek tore out as they dispersed beneath the blackened midday sky. The borlogs shoved people out of their way and some whom were already sidelined. Marynda marked the tallest of the three as the one in the middle, though this illusion was enhanced by the trail hat atop his head. On average, the figures stood at well over seven feet. It wasn't long before their faces and features reached clarity in the candlelight. They were muscular but not aggressively so. Rather than sauntering beasts, they were more streamlined, more vampiric.

Borlogs were sun-walkers—well, that was the rumor Marynda heard in her youth—but what did it matter during a Frishkadamn eclipse? She saw their half-moon faces, dashed with spiky barbs of ink.

The troop held up twenty feet away and the scene seemed to freeze. No one breathed.

"The kingdom is far from pleased, far from pleased," the one in the middle, the one with the trail hat drawled. "Tell you what, Ulkar's in the mood for some deal-making, seeing as it's Midsummer festival and all. You two losers crawl back home and deliver news of your failure, and I'll let you live."

The borlog on the left raised a crossbow and shot an arrow at Marynda's face. She deftly blocked it with a swish of her club. She saw the shooter glaring back at her, marked him as a cyclops.

In a sudden break, the borlogs ran at them. Ulkar flung a dagger at Marynda—she managed to block this, as well. Ulkar twirled a hatchet to his fingertips and charged at Brisk. She saw what their plan was: she was to be the prey of the cyclops and only the cyclops. To stop this tactic, Marynda launched herself in a dive, sprang to her feet, and swung her club at Ulkar's head.

Ulkar ducked this blow and rocked her in the stomach with a fist. Marynda sputtered but recovered fast, wheeled around, bludgeoned the third borlog in the skull. He sank with a satisfying thud.

Brisk got in one solid swing with Kozard's mighty sword. Ulkar sidestepped this with infuriating ease, then slammed his hatchet into Brisk's shield. The impact sent the Cook reeling and the sword slipped stupidly from his hand. From there, ceaseless hatchet blows pummeled. Brisk toppled over and landed muddy yet lucky. In his grasp, some kid had left an unlit firecracker. Ulkar closed in.

Marynda spun to face the cyclops. He stashed his bow, drew out a scimitar, feinted left, attacked from the right. She raised her club for the block—her reflexes were fast, but she anticipated the worst. The scimitar met her club but went no further. She flipped forward, and kept hold of her club with the blade stuck in it. The borlog was too stupid to let go and she yanked his shoulder from its socket. The cyclops roared with pain, but managed to turn and kick her to the dirt before collapsing himself.

With a snap, Brisk produced a spark, lit the fuse, hurled the popper and the explosion in Ulkar's face sent the borlog lurching. Brisk scrambled, grabbed his things, hauled Marynda up, and they fled.

◇ CHAPTER THE THIRTY-SIXTH. ◇
◇Frigid Presence.◇

Griffey Parker raised his right hand to wipe sweat from his forehead. There was still a lot of residual summer heat out here, despite the departure of the sun, but it was cooler. Almost as if they'd just entered a clammy cellar where the damp air squeezes your lungs. When Griffey's right hand met his face, he remembered his right hand wasn't attached anymore, and what connected with his face was the rough crab-shell-texture of the Zodak claw. He saw a clown walk past, thought it was his reflection.

So far, they had failed to find a Healer nor any sign of one. The intensity of their search began to wane.

Ramsey tapped excitedly at his shoulder. "Pebble toss! I'm amazing at that game."

"Don't think they let Sorcerers with levitation powers get in on that."

A mother with her kids hustled by. She saw Griffey's black crustacean arm and looked appalled.

The Ranger squirmed his shoulders with a pang of embarrassment. *Why the hell does a Zodak arm look so strange at a Frishkadammed carnival?* As he walked, his left hand dropped to his hip and verified—for the tenth time—Marynda's bag still hung there. The bag with the cave chamber inside.

Thoughts of the people in that cave made Griffey nearly bump into an old man in a red apron pushing a cart stuffed with jelly apples, popping butter corn, and fluffy candy cones. *Konragen's trapped in there, battling for his life. There's a kid in there, too. Kid has to be terrified; she's got an ailing dragon beside her.* Griffey spied a booth decorated with red and white stripes on the fabric. Inside, shelves were lined with brown ale bottles and contestants tossed rocks at them.

Ramsey the Green gazed with fascination at a spinning number wheel. It stood ten feet high and was a pie-chart arrangement of colors and numbers. Players stared breathlessly as the wheel twirled and their numbers skated past. The number tabs flipped past the catch at the top, *fwip-fwip-fwip.*

"Elf, we're not here to play games," the Ranger grunted at him.

"Very well, then," Ramsey huffed. "I'll have you know, I moved to Rivercrest for two reasons: to become a fully-certified Sorcerer, and to find a mate. Preferably blonde. Tanned skin. Around seven-feet tall. Close to my age—around one-hundred-fifteen or so. Maybe I'll just strut off and do that—"

"—what? And miss out on the poem I wrote as a child about Midsummer festival?"

"Parker, I'm sorry, but, I don't think anyone in our group actually likes poetry."

"Let's stay focused," Griffey advised. "Believe me, I'd join you in chatting up the maidens and winning prizes. Except there's a Warlock in this village. And he could be invisible right now."

They walked in silence for the next few moments, eyes scanning the crowd. Parakeets chirped and fluttered inside a golden cage. A self-proclaimed card trick magician transfixed a tiny audience by making the dragon of hearts disappear. A mother, father, and two kids gazed adoringly at a pony.

"The Warlock could be anywhere," Griffey warned. "But he's still weak. Can't hide forever."

Griffey stopped in his tracks. He raised the black claw to halt his companion, which sent a musty, sweaty stench billowing into Ramsey's face, causing him to swat the intruder away.

"Look, Ramsey!" Griffey exclaimed, jabbing a finger. A target range was set up on the left shoulder of the avenue. Some archers stood tall and proud while others sagged with despair, mourning the precision they'd once possessed. The participants launched arrows at red-circle targets propped on easel-stands in an empty lot where no cabin stood. The sounds of the missile volleys sang out with a rhythmic *swish-**thock** swish-**thock** swish-**thock***. To Griffey's ears, it was an irresistible calling.

"Frishka's clobbered skull," Ramsey cursed. "You just said: *no games*, now you're drooling over that Frishkadammed target range? Can the Rangers abandon every pledge so easily??"

"We need coin if we're to get a cure for Konragen *and* find someone to fix my hand." Griffey's eyes scanned to the nearby tents and booths, foolishly hoping to spot a Healer's den.

Ramsey was overcome with a gnawing sensation. Heat emanated from his pocket. From where Kozard's black eyeglass restlessly resided. "What is it?" Griffey asked. "You've gone pale."

"Kozard's eyeglass," Ramsey sputtered, actually surprised that he was willing to vocalize his affliction. "It's eating at me, Parker. It's as if the thing *knows* we're going to get rid of it... I was thinking... if I put it in my eye, I think I'll be able to see the invisible Warlock..."

Slowly, Griffey shook his head. "We can't risk that. I've read about magical traps like the one you carry. You gain a short-term advantage, but you pay for it in the long term." He exhaled. "If you use it for something as serious as spotting the Warlock, you may be in its grip forever..."

Desperate for either a resolution or distraction to this awkward moment, Ramsey flapped a hand towards the archery range. Griffey gave him a grateful smirk, but his face quickly returned to its serious scowl. His eyes caught movement; a wavering radiation of rainbow colors; a serpent squirming and thrashing up the wall of a tent. His heart raced in a rampant flurry as he imagined his father's killer appearing with a sneer. He squinted and perceived the sight as an array of mirrors. Some were bent and contorted, producing blurry, bloated, jumbled images and it gave him a headache.

"It's nighttime at noon, folks!" a jolly voice blurted. "Time to test your archery skills!"

Griffey stepped up to the range officer, fully expecting to be berated for his shortage of money and lack of a right hand and the hideous claw he'd substituted for that hand. He was not disappointed, as all three issues were addressed promptly and loudly. When Griffey appeared unaffected by these challenges—coupled with the curious stares he drew from everyone else present—the officer gave him a chance to speak. The Ranger offered up his pair of shortswords in exchange for entry.

The officer looked him up and down, shook his head, briefly considered his own safety in the presence of this lunatic villager wearing a crab claw on his arm and, instead of any more snippy remarks, the officer became a showman. He threw his arms wide, boasted at Griffey without looking at him, and scooped an audience from a loose cluster of bystanders. "Our next match carries the prize of a King's crossbow. That's right, folks! Mountain peak quality! And this claw-hand man wants to try for it!"

The current match concluded surprisingly fast; the contestants seemed to hurry it along.

During this gap, Griffey had enough time to admonish himself. *Dear Frishka, why do I make such dumb decisions?? Before we entered this village, I chose to split the group to gather supplies and seek a Healer. Why not focus them on finding the Warlock? What goal am I trying to achieve out here?* The face of John Parker swam across his mind, filling him with guilt and remorse. *Now I've gone and signed myself up to get slaughtered in a game, and gave away my swords to do it.*

"Claw-Hand Man!" called the officer. "You're up—

against the masterful Grack Washencraw!"

After shoving a traditional longbow into Griffey's hands, the officer said, "shooters at the chalk line, three rounds, three shots per round, more points for deeper targets, one target level change per player." Griffey barely heard what was said. His eyes were caught upon the underside of the Zodak claw. He lifted his arm close to his face and studied it. He saw tiny tabs lining the claw's inner rift; little ribbed teeth marching along a mountain range. A plan began to hatch within his mind.

Grack Washencraw—a man promised to be *masterful* on the range—was tall and bald with a drooping mustache and condescending eyes. Since his opponent was *masterful*, Griffey had to go first.

Griffey's first attempt to fire an arrow—using one of the notches on the Zodak claw to grip the nook at the end of the shaft—resulted with laughable failure. The errant shot flubbed into the weeds, drawing clucks and chuckles from the crowd and a gaze of disbelieving hunger from Washencraw. Griffey's next attempt actually hit the target board—only it landed outside the painted circle, beyond the realm of points. His final try of the opening round hit home and accumulated a respectable amount of tallies.

While Washencraw stepped up to the launching chalk, eyes rolling with a scoff, Griffey turned to Ramsey. Seemingly feeding off the energy of the crowd, the elf was trying to look at literally anything besides Griffey's shameful performance. "My friend, you should continue to seek the local Healer."

Ramsey the Green was speechless. His hand gravitated shamelessly to the magic in his pocket.

"If that glass calls to you, resist it," Griffey commanded. "Fight the temptation, for our lives."

The tall green elf was actually rather touched that Griffey was making this moment about him. Rather than worrying over the aces Washencraw was scoring, Griff was concerned for

Ramsey. Even when the range officer tapped at Griff, he still spoke to Ramsey. "It will beg you. Just keep it at bay."

Ramsey offered, "Give me Marynda's bag." It was tough but necessary and Griffey handed it over.

A moment later, Ramsey shuffled through the crowd and out of sight, and Griffey was back at the chalk. Grack Washencraw was leading him 22-8. *"Target back two levels!"* Griffey roared.

The officer hustled to the relocation. A voice in the crowd hissed, "He'll get triple points!"

Griffey raised his bow to a lofted angle, braced the glistening black bulk of the claw up near his brow, hooked onto the arrow, drew back, breathed deep. Once the missile was loosed, there was no dramatic pause for tension. It flew with such force, it reached its target in an instant. He didn't miss, but could've used better accuracy. The first strike landed on the outer painted ring—a 2, tripled to a 6. Second, he struck a 4, tripled to a 12. Third, he relapsed, picking up another triple-deuce. He was now miraculously leading the contest 32-22. People applauded with surprise. Washencraw looked incensed.

Unbeknownst to Griffey, Ramsey actually lingered at the back, saw these results, then left.

"Target back!" Washencraw hollered. His voice hitched before finishing, "Second level."

"Brave strategy," a voice commented from within the murmuring crowd. "Thinks he was up big enough after the first round that he can win with only double points from here on out. Hmmm."

Griffey was equally surprised as the village narrator by this development. Washencraw just gave up the chance to shoot for triple points for the rest of the game. But the sensation of surprise didn't stick around long before it was replaced with dread. The supposedly masterful archer scored large gains on his first two attempts, slacked a bit on the third, and ended the second round with a fat lead: 48-22.

While Grack Washencraw fired away, the eyes of the crowd, and those of Griffey Parker, were locked upon the action. The simple fact that so many people were invested and engaged drew even more onlookers, most of whom weren't really curious about the showdown but shamelessly didn't want to be left out. At the back of the throng, there lurked invisible eyes. Watchful, diligent eyes.

The Warlock lingered on the distant periphery, hunched and snarling, occasionally bumped by passing children, whom became befuddled, speechless, and frightened. The adults whom drifted past all seemed to step out and subconsciously avoid him, as his frigid presence emitted a chilling, abhorrent pulse. His perceptive eyes had marked both the Ranger and the Sorcerer, but he was far more concerned with the tall green elf. Though the elf was a pitiful novice with a limited spell capacity, the Warlock still feared him, especially while he was weakened. When the Ranger dismissed the Sorcerer, a warm glow lit upon the Warlock's black shriveled heart. *Banished his defender. Tragically foolish.*

For a moment, the Warlock was tempted to flee. Instead, he waded forward, bony fingers flexing.

Towards the Ranger. Whose back was irresistibly turned…

◇ ◇ ◇

Beyond the world bathed in solar eclipse darkness, within a fusty, dimly-lit cave, Konragen the dragonborn lay on his back, shaking in pain. The coughs were getting worse. Sending quakes across his ribcage. He began to violently rock. The shadow of his heavy, spiky shoulder fell over Baby Hazel…

◇CHASE QUEST◇

◇ CHAPTER THE THIRTY-SEVENTH. ◇
◇From Wicker's Tabletop.◇

Ramsey the Green dodged around a sauntering elderly couple, then crashed against a barrier built of people in hats and masks. Hats with caribou antlers and masks with green goblin skin and bulging eyes. This encounter left him flustered and frantic. A tall man in a dark, trailing overcoat brushed rudely past him and it wasn't hard to imagine sly-devil fingers slipping into his pocket and extracting his prize. Kozard's black eyeglass. The crucial item which Griffey forbade him from using. *The **one** tool that could save Konragen's life right now. Could save **all** our lives right now.*

Fear enveloped him as he turned in helpless circles. Bystanders began to stare at the staff he carried. They gauged his gnarled gingerbread-brown staff, clearly pondering its classification as either a prop or a threat against their lives. For some absurd reason, Ramsey nearly sputtered out a stream of nonsensical explanations, detailing how he was considered in the cellar of his class and, thus, was equipped with a magical apparatus of the lowliest quality.

A band of deep rumbling drums, peppered with occasional trumpet blurts, began to swell the air and quicken Ramsey's pulse. A whiff of horse manure assaulted his nose. Arrow-tips struck their targets.

Kozard's eyeglass was out of his pocket, in his hand, nearly in his eye-socket. The sight of this—an inch from his eye—made him squawk and this drew more eyes to him. He stashed the glass.

"Lunatic forest elf over here," a voice muttered. "The

eclipse always churns out the crazies."

"Crazy Ranger thinks he can shoot with a claw for a hand," another complained.

Ramsey's heart continued to hammer. Time was running short and he was standing still.

For some unknown reason, an image of John Parker fluttered across his mind. The Second King, standing tall on a sunlit stage, grinning and waving to a raucous, cheering courtyard. First King Callister stood off to the side, removed. Ramsey, like the rest of the inauguration swarm, didn't have much cheering to do for the First King. The First King was there every year, every election; always the same gruff, bland personality. John Parker, however, was full of hopeful, promising character.

Or, at least, he had been. Ramsey's racing heart slowed, then proceeded to sink. Abruptly, he was pleased to be closed in by a ring of aimless bystanders. It made him feel safer. Then the words of Second King John Parker soared through his mind. It was a quick catchphrase, uttered at his inauguration, or some other time, or both. *The safest path is not always the most rewarding.*

Ramsey exhaled. His nerves calmed. His gaze caught upon a gap between shoulders. An older man with a sharp silver beard, lounging at a display table, legs crossed. The tall green elf eased his way through the crowd, excusing himself and parting people who were all pleased to let him pass and get rid of him. As he walked, he felt a chill. The sensation of paddling through a lake on a warm summer's day and trespassing upon a patch of icy cold. He moved through this anomaly, didn't think about it— didn't have *time* to think about it—and hustled onward.

The seated old man appeared handsome and gentlemanly, saw Ramsey approaching, and welcomed him with a wave. *How did we walk this way and not see him!*

"Don't give a thought, Master Sorcerer," the man called.

"People walk past me all the time."

The prospect of someone not doubting the authenticity of his staff was rather assuring.

"You recognized my power," Ramsey stammered, standing before him. "You're a Sorcerer?"

"I tried," the fella declared. "Couldn't take the pressure. This be three plateaus and five years past, or somethin' of the sort." He shook his head, looked distant and mournful for a moment, staring blankly at the crowd. Then, his face cleared. He cast up a grin with bright blue eyes. "But that don't mean I don't be stockin' supplies a Sorcerer might seek. Wicker's me name. Come ho, acho?"

Arching a doubtful eyebrow, Ramsey leaned in. The tabletop was littered with time pieces, quills, ink bottles, compasses, folding knives, jars of liquid, velvet drawstring pouches, and dusty scrolls.

"Hey now, customers are preferable to observers," the old man admonished with good humor. He displayed a welcoming grin. "Got all kindsa scrolls here, fella. Only the finest collection here with Wicker, y'see. Got scrolls on Architecture, Mathematics, and ancient philosophy. Fer that matter, got modern philosophy, too. Got scrolls on the trolls. Travels of the trolls. History of the continent. History of all sorts uh mystical beings and cultures. Even that boring Sorcery religion." Wicker glanced around, surveyed people nearby, paused until all had walked to a satisfactory distance, then leaned forward with a conspiratorial glint in his eyes. "Elf, some of these scrolls here are special ones... Enchanted, they are. By that I mean: you can absorb their knowledge without even readin' em."

"Uh-huh," the elf said with a quizzical nod. On any other day he may have been entertained, but not now. "I need a potion to cure *dragon's throat*. And a Healer's scroll for a broken hand."

"Hmmmm..." Wicker exclaimed with an exuberance and zest that tried both the patience and the ears of his captive audience. The old merchant's utterance was just as suspenseful as it was unhelpful. The noise felt overly dramatic and just as frustrating as an outright denial.

"If I got the Healer's scroll," Wicker oozed, "it ain't a fancy one. Yur gonna have to read it."

While the merchant crowded forward and began picking and tapping and scrolling through his assortment of trinkets, Ramsey turned away. He saw Griffey at the chalk. Aiming and shooting.

Ramsey chanced a look over at the merchant and beheld a fortunate sight. Wicker was twisted around, digging and rooting through some dusty box or musty chest buried in the shadows behind his seat. Ramsey's eyes dropped to the table. To the magical scrolls. A healthy heap of magical scrolls. Unguarded. Unwatched. Perhaps what followed was a last-ditch impulse from Kozard's black eyeglass in Ramsey's pocket. One final amoral jab on its way to another owner. A conclusive corruptive thrust.

Feeling his heart thudding against his ribcage, feeling his pulse quickening, Ramsey leaned forward, raised Marynda's black handbag, snapped its mouth silently open. Adrenaline fired through his veins, unlike any sensation he'd ever felt. The thrill of doing something shameful and wrong, yet potentially very profitable, with people all around. Inattentive people.

Ramsey scooped five scrolls, added a sixth, tumbled them in the bag, then turned to watch some archery. "Acho! Acho!" Wicker hollered, drawing his visitor back around. "Got not one— but both!"

Ramsey's eyebrow rose once again. *Gotta remain skeptical. That's what John Parker would do.*

The bearded merchant flicked a glass vial with icy blue liquid sloshing inside. "Here, for ye, got some *polar milk*. Eases any burnin' in the throat or the gut, heh heh. Turn the ash of yer campfire into a snowflake flurry." With a flourish, he lofted a leather-cased scroll. "This here's for busted knuckles."

Ramsey exhaled with genuine shock and appreciation. He savored the moment, eyes closed, nodding his head. "Yes sir. Very good, sir. You're a true scholar. I'll take both. I need both, acho?" Then he caught the sounds of arrows rapping on targets and corresponding cheers. When Wicker spoke, the green elf was turned the other way, wishing he could see past the people clustered with their backs turned. Wicker's skeptical voice grumbled, "I ain't convinced ye can afford *both*."

Ramsey whipped around the face the merchant. Concerned the words were true, Ramsey disguised his surprise. "How much for both, then?"

Wicker appraised the items clutched in his hands, intently looking over each in turn, face wrinkling, squinting as if he'd never glimpsed such bountiful treasures before.

Ramsey felt a surge of panic race through his system. "I've got a trade," the elf proclaimed, drawing a startled look from the seller at the table. "I've got an item of equal value…"

Wicker gave a bewildered shrug. The elf dipped his hand in his pocket… and he froze. For an instant, he was certain Kozard's glass had fallen out somewhere in the carnival mud. Then his fingers brushed the lens. An intense heat shot through his arm into his brain. Rather than comforting, it was frightening. He felt threatened but at the same time keenly alert.

"Here…" Ramsey forced his fist forward and dropped the magical shaded monocle into the old man's open hand. "This holds the power of *Sight*. Though I would advise caution with it."

Wicker reacted as if ten pounds of metal just plopped into his palm. A flash raced across the old man's eyes. His fingers curled to a close around Kozard's Seer's Glass. His other hand jutted gradually forward, bequeathing the vial and scroll into Ramsey's possession. The green elf nearly turned and left, but he was held in place by an eerie feeling. A gnawing doubt over what he'd just done.

When the silver-bearded man finally looked back up at

Ramsey, his face was far different than only thirty seconds prior. Wicker's eyes were brown, no longer that sharp original blue. His face twitched, his tongue darted out, then back in. Wicker's eyes leered out ravenously at the village.

Ramsey didn't say anything, and he doubted the merchant would respond even if he tried. He watched the old man lean back in his chair, and link his arms across his chest. Ramsey was left with an awful certainty that this man was no longer just some humble, anonymous carnival merchant. Once a failed Sorcerer, Wicker was now elevated to something menacing. Because of Ramsey.

Reality settled in. He felt guilty for stealing from the merchant but also greatly concerned that he had unleashed a sinister force.

Ramsey retreated slowly, his gaze still locked upon Wicker. Though he knew it was pointless, he offered a nod. Then, he turned and hurried away from Wicker's table. He melted into the crowd, trying hard to forget about the greedy, vacuous look which had infested the old man's face. But, no matter how hard he tried, he couldn't escape the glaring implication that he'd just traded for these cures with blood money. His guts knotted up and his hands felt clammy—but they held fast to the vial of icy blue water and the leather-packaged scroll.

The salvation for my friends, he rationalized. *That's what these little items represent.* He swung Marynda's black handbag around front. He tucked his recent acquisitions into the crook of his arm and his fingers trembled as they opened the bag. He was shaking. *The merchant didn't even look through Kozard's eyeglass and still got corrupted by it. Wicker had stared at the villagers as if they were fish in a pond. Lesser creatures than he. Once the festival is over and normal life resumes, he'll start learning peoples' secrets, tracking their actions. He'll systematically dominate this place. Or destroy it.* Ramsey paused in his tracks, exhausted. *I may have just traded this entire village for the lives of my friends…*

      Standing where he was, at the loosely-packed rear of the crowd at the archery range, Ramsey was oblivious to the foot traffic gliding past him. Looking inside Marynda's bag, he was reminded how silly it was to see a man as massive and imposing as Konragen reduced to the scale of a miniature toy. From Ramsey's perspective, outside the bag, that's exactly what Konragen resembled. Any chance for a brief giggling respite was shattered when Ramsey witnessed what was about to happen.

      The large dragonman was about to roll over and carelessly crush the helpless baby resting on the cave floor next to him. Ramsey quickly reached in. His arm was transformed to a size approximate to the scale of the sub-world. He grasped Konragen at the last second and stopped his momentum. With his teeth, he popped the cork from the vial of *polar milk*, reached in, and poured the cooling liquid down the dragon's throat. Next, the Sorcerer unfurled the scroll, read the surprisingly easy incantation, and watched with fascination as the bumps and bruises disappeared from Griffey's floating hand.

      Ramsey looked up, smiling, feeling a little better. That's when the screams began…

◇ CHAPTER THE THIRTY-EIGHTH. ◇
◇Shatter Point.◇

Losing 48-22—a more apt description might include the phrase *getting buried*—Griffey Parker stepped his boots to the chalk and raised his bow. The hollow Zodak claw was popping sweat all along his right arm. While it was a snug fit, he didn't feel entirely comfortable wearing it, as the abbreviated nub of his wrist was unable to grab anything and hold on. There weren't exactly any handholds in there. He exhaled, forced himself to focus.

Fortunately, a Ranger's training encompassed sublime focus in stressful moments. He just imagined he was on a hunt. Perched in the tranquil treetops, taking aim upon a deer. The prospects were plain enough: either make the shot or starve. Despite his fledgling connection to the Zodak claw as an extension of his body, it responded with the perfect torque as he used it to draw back the bowstring. One eye slipped shut. He acquired his target. Fired. Hit a seven. Tripled to twenty-one.

Without pause, he swiftly drew, fired again, and picked up a duplicate of his previous score. Again, without a hitch in his motion, he socked home an eight—tripled to twenty-four. As the slate now stood, Griffey led the masterful Grack Washencraw by a score of 88-48. Shocking and remarkable.

Murmurs of excitement rippled through the crowd clustered at the archery range. It was impressive that the Claw-Hand Man was shooting at a target ten feet further than Grack Washencraw and this earned many nods from the village observers. Undoubtedly, the energy from the crowd seeped into the usually even nerves of Washencraw. In this, the final round, Griffey's opponent picked up two sixes with his first two turns—each doubled for a total of twenty-four tallies. With these uninspiring results, the vocal mood of the crowd hastened into the realm of rowdy. People began to positively shout. Right in the middle of Grack's draw, loud voices hooted and some unseen child shrieked.

On his conclusive attempt, Washencraw delivered a seven, doubled to fourteen. This added up to a final score of 86-88, in favor of the man with a smelly black claw in place of his right hand.

Griffey blocked out the enthusiasm from the mob, shunned the thrill of victory, and turned to offer a respectful nod and handshake to Washencraw. Naturally, the handshake was a failure, and the nod was not returned, as Washencraw scoffed at him. There wasn't must time to ponder this, as the range officer boomed forward, anxious to close this business so he could clear his range. He shoved Griffey's pair of shortswords into Griffey's possession, then presented the King's crossbow prize (*"mountain peak quality"*). During the transfer of this award, something wonderful happened.

There was a sudden sensation of growing warmth at the nub of his right wrist. A moment later, he pulled off the iguana glove, and stared with shock at his dominant hand—not only reattached without preamble, but also no longer bruised and broken. He waggled and bent his fingers, flexing the sleep from his knuckles. His face was lit with delightful relief, but no one else saw this revelation as anything to celebrate. They all assumed Griffey's hand had resided where it belonged the entire time, and Griffey had worn the Zodak claw as a crazy festival-goer's accoutrement. Washencraw was acidic and disgruntled, as he perceived Griffey's usage of the claw as some kind of prideful insult.

The crowd started to lose interest, first swelling with chatter, then dissipating. The range officer grunted with animated displeasure over this, then cleared his throat and boasted loudly about how more entertainment was just minutes away. While the crowd looked unconvinced, Griffey returned the standard longbow to the officer's distracted hands. Right then, they both noticed that the bowstring had been clipped in two by the tip of the Zodak claw. Averting an awkward exchange, Griffey turned and slung his prizes over his shoulder. No time to admire the golden crossbow and matching arrow sleeve.

Trophies from his archery victory, while special, were also bitter reminders of failure. *I was selfish and stupid just now. I chose to seek profit for myself rather than helping my companions. Because I'm undisciplined. I couldn't shoulder the pressure of leadership, so I hid behind the comfort of a familiar game. Embracing nostalgia is just easier than seeking the enemy. Seeking the Warl—*

A shriek rose up ten feet behind him. Griffey whirled and beheld heart-pounding terror.

Appearing from nowhere—much as a Ranger does, at the denouement of a *Scout Cast* maneuver—rising up within the crowd, obscured by shoulders and sleeves, the Warlock shed his invisibility and stepped into view. Beneath the pitch of his hood, there stood a high hairless forehead, perched above bulging vivid-blue eyeballs, which dominated a bony, sagging, drooping face. A face contorted with malice; angry because Griffey had been alerted to his presence. His treat was cheated.

As if gripping an unseen pumpkin, the Warlock's palms formed a cup, and between them an orb of silver-black fog twisted into existence. Griffey didn't so much react to this developing threat as he simply felt the hot desire to kill. To avenge not only his wounded family crest, but to also cleanse from his conscience his recent leadership mistakes. While his shortswords were back at home on his hips, the Zodak claw was still held loosely in his hands. Griffey heaved the claw as if he were hurling an axe at a tree trunk. The sharp tip of the claw jammed into the Warlock's left shoulder.

A yelp of pain split from the lips of the Warlock, breaking the formation of his spell-ball. In that miraculous moment, Griffey felt his first surge of certainty that this creature was not only mortal, but vulnerable. Overcome with a competitor's thirst, the scent of advantage in the air, Griffey drew a shortsword with his right hand for the first time after what felt like an agonizing slumber.

As a Ranger, he'd been trained to wield a sword in his left hand merely as a defensive measure. It was to be complementary, filling in as needed during a fight. Still, it felt splendid to not only have his right hand taking the lead once again, but also exerting the ability to launch a confident attack.

Off-balanced from the shoulder wound and unnerved by the Ranger closing in on him, the Warlock unleashed the silver-black spell-ball slightly off course and before it was ready. The spell of *Telekinetic Blast* whipped Griffey backwards, but the range officer and Grack Washencraw received the worst of the blow. The mighty gust flung the trio weightless through the Midsummer air. They landed on their backs, the wind knocked from their lungs, but all three survived. Griffey sprawled in the dirt next to an arrow-peppered target board, groaning, sputtering, coughing.

"*Kran-tokk ye! Bell-korr!*" rasped the Warlock. Despite his distance, Griffey heard these archaic words and wished for Ramsey's translation skills. He sat up and glared defiantly back at the Warlock, just in time for the translator to appear. The Warlock twirled, dirty purple cloak cascading in a wavy flourish. The remaining people in the crowd shrank away, revealing Ramsey the Green.

The tall green Sorcerer elf looked exquisitely startled by the predicament of staring down a deadly Warlock, framed on the street of Benson village, visible courtesy of a fuzzy lantern glow.

Ramsey's attention was torn away from commitments inside a black handbag. He'd just finished applying the power of the Healer's scroll, followed by using his own spell abilities to extract the mended hand from the sub-world and replace it where it belonged. That string of deeds—coupled with the wonderful feeling of watching Konragen sit up painlessly, cured of *dragon's throat*—had combined to leave Ramsey feeling optimistic. Those feelings died fast and were replaced by fear.

Vengeful thoughts of John Parker barged through Ramsey's head. He slung the handbag over his shoulder and raised his staff, mentally preparing to cast a spell of *Protection*. It would be insanity to fight such an advanced magical enemy. *Have to hold him here, hope the others show up to help kill him.*

With timing worthy of storybook enchantment, both Marynda and Brisk hustled up to where Ramsey stood. They skidded to a halt, gulped air, and shot frantic looks over their shoulders. Marynda was wielding a large wooden club, and Brisk had a shield now, but Ramsey barely looked at them.

Marynda spied her black handbag, mouth flapping open, carelessly discarded over Ramsey's shoulder, and she felt a tidal wave of exasperation. This was interrupted by Brisk punching her in the arm and gesturing. At the purpose of their Quest. Their prey. Standing straight ahead.

All three humans—Ramsey, Brisk, and Marynda—could read what was about to happen next. It was augured in the Warlock's complicated facial expression. The Warlock knew he might not be at full-strength, but he was still a wolf in a corner, capable of ferocious violence. Yet, like any wolf with its wits intact, the Warlock knew it wasn't wise to risk his life. If his powers weren't yet fully regenerated, attempting to *Cast* away would destroy him. Staying here and fighting might also kill him.

Thus, having reached the shatter point, the Warlock knelt in the dirt, spawned a spell-ball of dazzling bright white light between his palms. It could've all ended right there, when the crouching assassin risked it all for a coward's escape. His body could've imploded. But when the Warlock uttered some guttural command his vitality must've been adequate because he vanished with a blinding snap.

Devastation bore down upon the hearts of all four Rivercrest warriors who witnessed this escape—Marynda, Brisk, and Ramsey from where they stood, Griffey from his spot over in the target field. They'd been so tantalizingly close to completing their mission, but bad decisions and distractions had doomed them. There wasn't much time to dwell on the disappointment before more danger arrived.

Two black-clothed borlogs barged up the main avenue, immensely creepy in the flickering light of the lanterns. Mothers and fathers backpedaled away from them, dragging yelping kids along in their retreats. Ulkar and his remaining associate—the cyclops, a haggard cloth wrapped around the punctured half of his skull—trampled everything in their path, kicking over tables and shoving people.

Ulkar twirled a deadly hatchet in his hand while he sauntered, breathing with the heavy determination of a soldier bent on revenge. Ulkar's face was already rippled with scars from a broken ale glass, and blood was trickling from a fresh set of burn wounds centered around his left eye, which was swollen shut. *Dual cyclopses!*

The borlog which hated Marynda wasn't able to fire his crossbow—couldn't even lift it, as one of his arms dangled with a queasy, unnatural sway, shoulder torn from the socket where it belonged.

"How'd you light that firecracker with your hands??" Ulkar demanded of Brisk as he closed in.

"A Cook works miracles when he smells a meal," Brisk explained, raising his shield and clanking Kozard's longsword against it. He would be ready for the attack this time. Brisk and

Marynda inched forward with natural, unspoken instinct, protecting Ramsey and the black handbag.

It was Ramsey, however, who saved the situation from further escalation. The green elf swung the black bag around front, reached inside, grasped his friend's arm. Konragen burst forth, red robes swirling, broad chest thrust forward, striding at his full towering height. Unhindered by bodily ills, the dragonman stomped ahead of his pals, and roared the borlogs to a halt.

Griffey Parker ambled over, winked at Brisk, and the company was fully reunited.

"You've failed in your mission, Parker," Ulkar taunted. "The First King was a fool to send a group of ragtag scraps—a Sorcerer who slays his master, a Cook who can't hold a sword, a Druid woman who kills loyal servants of the kingdom. Oh yes, oh yes, it's true, it's true. Your woman killed one of my companions with that bat of hers. And now you've got your pet dragon threatening to fry us." Ulkar shook his head, while Griffey tried to clear the fog in his. "Your Quest has failed. You've let the assassin escape. Now we're going to have to track him down ourselves. The First King sent proven assassin hunters for a reason." Ulkar spat. Then the fuming borlogs turned and stomped away.

Griffey and his friends embraced with tight smiles, troubled by the uncertainty that lay ahead.

◇ CHAPTER THE THIRTY-NINTH. ◇
◇Reshuffle.◇

Two minutes later, the dual moons crawled indifferently across the sky and the Midsummer sun blared down once again as if the intermission had never happened. Even Benson village's main avenue was reverting to the life of a non-festival day. Typical Midsummer's Eve festivals begin at dawn, peak during the midday eclipse, then conclude with an evening feast. The event lasts all day, because no one wants to work on a holiday. Today, however, frazzled parents were getting their kids off the street. Rumors were circulating about bloodthirsty borlogs. And an invisible Warlock, too.

Some said one of those borlogs had been struck dead in the street, which meant someone would have to clean up the mess. Others seethed and swore their village had also been infested with the presence of a dragon. Which meant they were doomed. The engines of their minds were already churning out smoky thoughts of just skipping next year's Midsummer event. It seemed to be cursed.

For a lengthy drag, folks milled around, pointing and whispering while trying to disguise their curiosity behind casual gestures and inconspicuous chatter. Collectively, the Rivercrest company cared more about greeting each other, but, personally, they each knew the lingering villagers required some measure of reassurance. Maybe even an explanation. But they all hesitated. In the moment, the prospect was just too daunting. No one cared to gather up the commoners, offer a cohesive narrative, then stick around for an endless volley of inquiries, responses and allegations. Instead, the gossip ran thick.

"Konragen!" Brisk exclaimed. "You saved us! All you have to do is roar and the borlogs run!"

"Heh heh, yesss," Konragen chuckled, "fire-breath is only thing borlogs fear."

"I've killed more borlogs than he has," Marynda trolled, tossing her eyes.

"Lucky no fire-breathing was actually required," Konragen said, massaging his throat, thinking of how close he'd flirted with death. He then jabbed Griffey an accusing finger. "You lost Zodak claw!"

For a blank moment, Griffey Parker could only offer a stare of sluggish confusion. Ever since getting hit with the Warlock's *Telekinetic Blast*, the world seemed fuzzy. Then, the dragonman's allegation finally sunk in. "Frishka," Griff muttered. "I did, didn't I? Well, maybe we can get it back?"

"Need to catch Warlock to do that," Kon asserted. "Zodak claw stuck in shoulder."

"How do you know that?" Marynda asked, reclaiming her black handbag from Ramsey.

"Konragen hear much and see much, even while coughing and dying in a cave."

"The bag was open…" Ramsey the Green breathed with stupefied fascination.

"You rotten ass," Marynda chastised the Sorcerer. "Leaving the bag open was careless."

"No, no," Konragen told her, "Konragen could hear long before bag was wide open."

"What the Frishka?" Brisk remarked. "You been eavesdroppin' this whole time?"

"*Incredible*," Ramsey pondered. "The noise of our voices

can reach the sub-world…"

"In under-cave," Konragen said, sounding concerned, "there was baby on floor…"

Marynda rushed to get past that touchy topic. "Kon, how did you fix your fire throat?"

"Ramsey Green pour ice-cold liquid in my mouth."

"Ramsey *the* Green," the elf corrected.

"Well, that was generous," Marynda admitted. "One score back in your favor, Sorcerer."

Their excitement faded out, and this withering coincided with the return of the tall gentlemen in black coats and top hats. Clearly in a hurry, they reeled in the paper balloons, extinguished the candles, dealt anxious glances. Boards clapped and crates scraped as the carnival folk broke down their tents. Parents gathered their howling children. Griffey noticed the range officer and Grack Washencraw climbing shakily to their feet, so he went over to help them up, his head finally clearing. The officer seemed more concerned with collecting his target boards. Washencraw thanked him with a scowl.

Griffey returned to the quiet circle of his friends and they enjoyed an uneasy respite.

"Don't think we'll be invited back next year," Brisk commented.

"What we doing?" Konragen demanded impatiently of Griffey. "Why standing around?"

"The Warlock escaped, Kon," Griffey groaned. "We failed. Ulkar was right…"

"Well, that slob seems to think he can still catch the Warlock," Brisk said. "Why can't we?"

"Figured you might've had enough adventure already." Griffey arched an eyebrow at the Cook.

"Ulkar got the better of me back there," Brisk confessed. "Now, I want to get better with these weapons."

"How we find Frishkadammed Warlock?" Konragen

thumped Ramsey's shoulder.

"We have find a way to not only track him," Marynda spoke up, "but also *Cast* after him."

"I… I, uh…" Ramsey shakily stated. Everyone was looking at him, but he managed to keep it together. "There, uh, there's someone I did business with earlier. I don't exactly want to talk to him anymore, but I think he might be able to help us out… Will someone go see him with me, please?"

"I'll join you," Marynda volunteered, "but let's make it fast. These people don't want us here."

"I go, as well," Konragen declared. "If borlogs show up, I shall scare them again."

When they all looked to him, Griffey held up a hand. "You guys go. Meet me back here."

"I shall hang back, as well," Brisk said. "If you can manage it, bring some food."

Then, given the state of the world they all occupied, Brisk did a remarkable thing. He drew out a handful of gold coins and flipped one to Marynda and Konragen, and tossed two to Ramsey.

"Hide that second coin," Brisk advised the elf. "Last ditch bargaining chip, eh?"

With grateful nods and stunned silence, the trio turned and eased up the street.

The Financier smiled smugly. Griffey noted, "Looks like you tossed some hot dice."

"I was good at the dice game, but I was terrible at defending myself." Brisk became pensive. "It wasn't a game when Ulkar attacked me. I was worthless. Had to use an old Cook's trick—finger-spark—and a short-fuse firecracker to save myself. I hated that feeling. I felt outmatched. Helpless."

"Now that I've got my hand back, I'll help you run some basic training drills."

Brisk brightened at the offer, but quickly got serious again. "Why did we stay back here?"

"Because something's bothering me," Griffey whispered. "Remember all that stuff Ulkar yelled at me? I'm tempted to think his words were just heat, but… I fear some of it may be true…"

"How will you solve that one? Find out why the First King sent the borlogs? How?"

"I need to contact someone back home," Griffey mused. "Back at Rivercrest castle."

"Even if you *could* get ahold of somebody back there, you got poor odds they got answers." Griffey nodded and shrugged and Brisk added, "Why do you care so much anyway?"

"Because, Brisk… I need to know what kind of kingdom we're out here fighting for."

Understanding dawned upon Brisk's face and it made him look sad. The Cook bit his lower lip and nodded, then glanced over, catching a pair of mothers shaking their heads and pointing at them.

"Again… how the hell you plan on doing this?" Brisk's tone was a gritty hiss.

Griffey crossed his arms and considered. "We're going to speak with my sister. Let's go."

"Frishkadammit, Parker—" Brisk exhaled, "—again— how the hell you plan on doing this?"

Griffey grasped his friend by the sleeve and led him over to a gap between two country shacks just off the main avenue. Once they were in the shadows, Griffey peeked back out and verified no onlookers still observed them. Brisk leaned out and saw the pair of mothers had turned and left.

Griffey sat down in the grass and drew a black coin from his pocket. Looking highly skeptical, Brisk sat down across from him. "This is a Grulva coin," Griffey revealed. "From Grulva valley in the southlands. My sister Sho'pa gave it to me before we left the castle. She instructed me to…"

With a fluttering purr, the coin flipped off Griffey's thumb, high in the air. For a clip, the coin cleared the shadows and glinted in the sunlight. "*Grulva Vitiera!*" Griffey called out as he and Brisk watched the coin twirl and tumble back down to a soft landing upon Griffey's outstretched palm. Upon impact, a cotton cloud of orange foggy light burst up and hovered mid-air between the two friends. The pumpkin shade quickly cleared, the glob of light flattened into a surface resembling a circular mirror, and Sho'pa Parker was staring back at them. She looked utterly shocked, then angry.

"Griffey!" she rasped. "You don't look like you're in mortal peril!"

"I thought the specifications were: *trapped with precisely no hope for escape?*"

"Well, you don't look like that either!" Though she sounded upset, she still cracked a smile. She looked puzzled for a moment, then nodded, presumably at Brisk. "Who's this fella staring at me?"

"Madam Coin-Flip." He offered up a wave. "I am called Brisk. Famous Rivercrest Cook."

Griffey's sister gave him a critical eye, then asked, "Have you accomplished your Quest? Did you catch father's killer?" Griffey blinked, struggled to respond. Even Sho'pa seemed a bit shaken by her own words. She rubbed her face. "Look, I'm very busy. I've got a class to instruct."

"Sho'pa," Griffey cut in, "I know it's a bit sudden, but I need your help." She gave him a patient look and he continued, "The night of father's death, there was a secret meeting in the First King's chambers. I'm not sure, but I think only Callister and Ulkar were in attendance. They…"

"Ulkar the borlog?" she inquired, looking appalled. "Ulkar the mercenary?"

Griffey gave an affirmative nod, then requested, "I need to know what they talked about…"

When Sho'pa did not immediately reply, Brisk got frustrated. "How the hell you expect her t—"

"I will do this for you, brother," she said. "But not until after class. I must go. Stay safe."

One blink later, and the hovering circle-mirror vanished, leaving Griffey and Brisk sitting on the grass in a shadowy alley with nothing but a coin on a hot summer's day…

◇   ◇   ◇

"How does Ramsey Green expect to track down Warlock and *Cast* after him?"

"Konragen," the elf exuded, "it's Ramsey *the* Green. Why don't you ever use the word *the*?"

"Dragon's got logic," Marynda put in. "Gold might not be enough to get what we need."

Ramsey slowed the pace of his stroll up the main avenue, eyes sweeping the haggled villagers, distraught in the aftermath of their disrupted celebration. His heart drooped within his chest. "Hey…" he ventured in a whisper, feeling his friends draw in close around him, and taking comfort from it. "Does anyone else feel bad about this? We showed up and this peaceful place got annihilated."

"Let's not exaggerate," Konragen advised. "Was Warlock who drew us here."

Ramsey was entombed with consideration. His straying eyes saw scars far deeper than broken dishes and frayed fabric and wounded pride. He thought of the black-tinted eyeglass. An object possessed of dark magic rich enough to corrupt the High Sorcerer of Rivercrest. Wicker was its puppet now. An old man running a trinket table during a festival. An old man who claimed to have once attempted Sorcery training. The implications engulfed Ramsey with horrified panic.

"What is it, Ramsey?" Marynda asked with a worried note. "You're more pale than usual."

Ramsey stopped in the middle of the street. This abrupt pause did not obstruct traffic, for the people were both few and preoccupied. Marynda and Konragen clustered close, concern in their eyes.

When nobody spoke, Marynda snapped, "Frishkadammit, Ramsey, tell us what you've done."

"I *had* to do it, alright," the elf protested, finally breaking down and severing the tension in the same swift stroke. "Remember what Griffey said before we entered the village? Huh? He declared that Kozard's black eyeglass was to be a trading chip. And, well, I found myself in a dilemma with only one viable trade partner. I needed to save Konragen *and* cure Griffey's hand, alright??"

Konragen's features went grim. He demanded to know, "Who you give eyeglass to?"

"An old merchant. Said his name was Wicker. Casually mentioned that he'd once trained as a Sorcerer." This failed to generate a reaction. "Which is significant because he wields magic."

"I still don't see how this is a problem," Marynda said. "He gave you the goods you needed."

Ramsey shook his head. "I sensed something dangerous about him. He might hurt this village."

"To be honest," Marynda spoke, "I want to get out of this place as soon as possible. It's plain the people here don't like us, so why would they trust us that this Wicker is a threat?"

"Wicker help you once already," Konragen cut in. "That's promising. Maybe he help us now."

It was hard to argue with this. Ramsey's curiosity about the silver-bearded merchant was buzzing, so he led them to the old man's trinket booth. It was a very short walk and the results were unsatisfying. They found an old frail woman with curly silver hair gently wrapping items in leather and delicately packing them in boxes. She looked up at them with cordial blue eyes. Ramsey hung his head, closed his eyes.

"Excuse me, miss?" Marynda ventured with a soothing tone. "We're looking for Wicker?"

"That old bat," the woman huffed, shaking her head. "Been married to the bat for three plateaus. He done run off to the house, claimin' he grown ill. Left his wife Jana to pack up all his precious trash."

Disappointed, Mary asked, "Jana, maybe you can help us? We're on a Quest from the castle. Here to rid your village of a Warlock infestation, but he *Cast* and escaped."

"Pesky bastards tend to do that." Jana spat in the dirt. "Probably gone up yonder." She flapped a bony hand at a trio of mountains rising on the western horizon. "Since I was a little girl, heard rumor of a Warlock colony in yonder peaks. Yessum. Ye likely wanna go chasin' up there. An' I gotta figure ye don't wanna walk the distance… My sister Java's got no love for them filthy Warlocks. She lives northwest of town. Just tell her Jana sent ye. She's got an ancient *Casting* ring on her farm…"

BOOK

◇ IV ◇

THE FARM.

◇ CHAPTER THE FORTIETH. ◇
◇Sacrifice.◇

The attacker swung a blade at his face. He raised his shield into the path of death at the last possible instant. The defender drove outward with his longsword, a clearing move to drive the enemy into a back-pedal. The attacker retorted with a low slash, smacking his shield with a *clang*.

"Acho, acho! Faster with the sword. No wild swipes, just controlled jabs."

Brisk the Cook wheezed, waved for a break, armed sweat from his forehead.

Five minutes had passed since the face of Griffey Parker's sister vanished. After securing the Grulva coin in a pocket, Griffey sprang to his feet, hauled up his friend, and proclaimed it to be the hour of training. Fortunately for Brisk, that hour only lasted a few minutes before an interruption.

"Ho there!" Konragen woofed, smacking a fist to his chest. "Let me knock him out next!"

"No... No... No one's knockin..." Brisk rasped, bent over. "*No one's knockin me out next!*"

"See? Already gettin' better," Griffey exclaimed, clapping a hand on Brisk's shoulder. He looked up to see Konragen, Ramsey, and Marynda striding over. A few Benson villagers gazed on, keeping a cautious distance yet irresistibly intrigued by the behavior of these foreigners.

"We're headed northwest," Marynda informed them, not breaking stride. "Let's go."

The respectful silence only endured until they cleared the

rows of houses, Brisk's curiosity burst forth. "Acho, acho. You must tell us where you're taking us."

"The merchant's wife sent us to see her sister," Marynda explained, leading the pack, no compass needed. "Java lives on a farm northwest of town and supposedly has a *Casting* ring on her property."

Out in the hot sun, they now trekked across a gently sprawling meadow, spotted with the occasional pine. Fragments of civilization scattered about: stone wells, busted sheds, drooping fences. Behind, there shot a row of huts and villas. Off to the left, a trio of snow-capped peaks jutted high. Straight ahead, a procession of casual humps and valleys, with the wooden slash of a barn atop one.

"I'm just pleased we're finally out of that Frishkadammed forest," Brisk commented.

"Marynda's pleased we're free of that awkward village," Ramsey surmised.

"Supposedly she's got a *Casting* ring," Griffey muttered, shaking his head. "A luxury like that must be rare around here. Ulkar will uncover its location soon enough. May be there already."

"Can't live our lives concerned with that Ulkar fella," Brisk trumpeted. "Seems to get uglier every time I see him." The Cook hustled up to the front of the line (dodging around the absent swing of Konragen's elbow spike), and fell in step beside Marynda. Without even looking at him or waiting for him to issue his request, Marynda swung her knapsack and dealt a slice of salted pork into his hands. She didn't need to verify his astonished expression. "Yes, Brisk. That's apple bread you smell."

At the rear of the line Griffey snickered to Ramsey, "Marynda's sharp right now, eh?"

"Can I get another slice?" Brisk solicited. "You bought six slices. Only five of us, y'know?"

Marynda dealt three more slices into his hands. It was now his job to distribute them to the others. She quickened her pace. Not much, but enough to keep Brisk at a social distance.

In response to Griffey's quizzical look, Ramsey offered, "I think she's on a *Focus* potion."

Up front, her hearing exquisitely attuned, Marynda allowed herself a tiny smirk. Razor senses fired through her with every step. The confidence wasn't as exhilarating as being a wolf, but it was close.

"Runter Man holds valid concern," Konragen declared. "Ulkar will try for shortcut."

This settled the group into an uneasy silence. As they strolled, Ramsey gauged the Ranger.

"Why're you so concerned about the borlogs?" the elf inquired. "Konragen's got 'em spooked."

It was a long while and many strides before Griffey replied. While he walked, Griffey's eyes strayed, first to the trio of distant mountains then to his hand. The hand which, so recently, had been bruised, broken and broken, and was now Healed and properly attached to his arm. The overwhelming concern over his hand, however, had kept him from properly mourning his murdered father. In his mind, he had heard a song with the chorus of a fixed hand equating to a fixed world. He'd always figured the first part of that lyric would be the hardest part.

Now that the hand was whole, however, he realized he had learned something from living without it. During its absence, he'd acquired something valuable. He had learned to compensate, to adapt to changing circumstances. That said, he understood the challenges ahead were still vast and terrifying.

Not for the first time, Griffey wondered how his mother and sister were coping with this.

"I first encountered Ulkar three years ago," Griffey spoke softly, subtly amazed that everyone was still attentive to him, "and I didn't see him again until the night of John Parker's death... So, one night, I was getting some torch-lit practice on the range. The rest of Rivercrest, it seemed, thought I was crazy for shooting at night. In turn, I thought they were crazy because there are no guarantees you'll always face an attacker in sunlight. When I was done, I cut down an alley to avoid the muddy street, and I happened upon a struggle in the shadows. A man forcing his way upon a woman. Her lips were wide with a scream, but I heard no sound. She must've been struck with a *Silent* spell."

Griffey paused to shake his head with a mixture of regret, distaste, and disbelief.

"Spells may do magic," Konragen sighed, "but magic can be sinister..."

A moment later, Griffey continued, "My blood already hot from the archery shots, I hollered out, fully intending to disrupt the crime. That's when they both turned to face me. In that instant, I saw more than the mind can process. This was more than a back-alley assault. This was a borlog drinking blood from a woman's throat before violating her pride. I raised my bow, drew a shaft and aimed at him. He snarled back at me. The woman slipped his grip and ran to me. Having lost her—or, having drunk his fill—the fangs of the borlog retracted, the crooked hunch of his spine straightened, and he became nearly a gentleman. She hung on me, and I hesitated to fire. The borlog just strutted away.

"Her name was Lasha and I brought her to the River Guard. Through her testimony, together with my own, we learned who the borlog rapist was. A creature called Ulkar. Now, the reason he wasn't arrested and the reason I didn't track him down and kill him, was because Ulkar wasn't just any borlog. He was the head of the mercenary clan. He'd actually organized the mercenaries into a guild. He'd tied their fortunes with the lumberjack dwarves—probably because nobody else would work with the borlogs, and nobody likes the smell of dwarves. That alliance gave Ulkar a lot of power, as Rivercrest couldn't afford to see the dwarves go on strike. Lumber is a major part of the economy."

Griffey sighed. "I got a ranting lecture on how Ulkar was too tall to topple, but I couldn't let it go. Something special formed between Lasha and I—a flame which burned less than a month, but forever special. With her encouragement, I got my father involved. He was the Second King, after all. He proceeded to entice the dwarves into a better deal, upgrading their housing. He created slots in other industries where the mercenaries could earn more pay without committing murder or thievery. Ulkar was unimpressed and rather unkind. I sometimes think it would've been better to kill him…"

Griffey sobered, as if shaken awake. "So if you see a borlog, kill it before it kills you. That's it."

While Griffey was ready to change the subject and trudge along in silence, Brisk was not so eager to let that dog nap. Figuring he wasn't going to catch Marynda anyway, the Cook stepped out and wormed over to fall in stride alongside the elf and the Ranger, with the dragonborn trotting along ahead of them. Though he could feel Brisk staring at him, Griffey did not turn. "That's why you joined the Rangers…" Brisk softly spoke.

Finally, Griffey turned to face his friend. He did not nod, but his sorrowful eyes spoke worlds.

Brisk's chest swelled with a million questions. *You joined the Rangers to hide? To let tempers settle? Ulkar must've figured out who you were, the man who interrupted his crime on the lady Lasha. He must have discovered your connection to the Second King. Were you a sacrifice in the deal? Ulkar would go along as long as you were removed from the city?* Brisk asked none of these, his lips unparted, his mind overwhelmed. His gaze went forward as the march went on.

Griffey's mind replayed his own tragic decisions. *I was bitter that John Parker sent me away. Off into the woods. But I still should have visited him sooner once I was back in Rivercrest.*

I let the past cripple me. I could have been there to protect him. At his side with my swords…

No one said anything for a while. They hiked in silence. During the void, the gentle wisp of the wind and cheeping birdsong filled the air. Embedded within the verdant countryside were vivid contrasts of orange fungus encrusted upon white tree bark and plump silver boulders stubbornly lounging in flourishing groves of fresh green grass and bright yellow flowers. Blue dominated the sky.

Konragen belched and the reverie was broken. This noisy expulsion drew critical gazes. The dragon winced, expecting a painful rebuke from his lava guts that did not happen. The relief left him to examine the taste in his mouth. The taste of salted pork. He couldn't resist another blunt observation.

"Cook Man was correct. Druid Woman got six slices of pork. Only five in our Quest."

Remarkably, Marynda stopped in her tracks, causing everyone to draw up short, more out of surprise than any real concern of colliding with each other. Marynda's head and shoulders sagged. She felt a weary sigh wheeze from her chest. Despite the blaze of the sun in this open grassy field, she felt a frosty chill within her bones. She rubbed heat into her arms, wondering if Brishtiva's red liquid had finally worn off. She no longer felt so mighty. Alone and humbled before her only friends in this world.

Her hands were in her strawberry hair and she fought back tears as she turned to face them.

My only friends in this world. The thought echoed through her mind. It held a curious ring because she did have one other friend—an infant in a different world. *The sub-world. I've left my daughter in that dreary place for far too long. It's time she had a say in her own destiny.*

"Ramsey already knows about this," she admitted, managing to meet their eyes. "And Konragen has probably guessed it… the reason I've been so protective of my black handbag is because my infant daughter is hidden there. In the sub-world. I can't take it any more. I need her with me. In our world."

"You put a *baby* in that cave?" Brisk confronted Ramsey. "Are all you elves so heartless?"

"It was a good solution," the elf replied, aghast. "Keep the baby safe, bring her with us."

"*Safe?*" Konragen rumbled. "I nearly ki—" The dragon's words broke off as the reality of what he was about to say crashed in on him. He nearly disclosed knowledge that he'd almost smothered the baby during his thrashing coughing fit on the floor of that cave. The prospect of this was heart-breaking. Of course, he'd been aware of the tiny human lying down there next to him, but he'd been powerless to stop his movements. He'd been a prisoner to the pain, awaiting his own demise, a fuming death from his own gut. *I'm a Paladin and I let myself get so close to hurting a child…*

"It's not safe for a baby to travel with us…" Griffey cautioned, voicing their collective concern.

Marynda flourished a blue liquid vial. "She'll drink this. Skip to first-plateau-plus-seven."

The Druid woman lowered the vial into her bag. She grasped something and pulled.

A moment later, her daughter emerged…

<>M. RAY ROBERTS<>

◇ CHAPTER THE FORTY-FIRST. ◇
◇Emergence.◇

Golden and warm, the sunshine was glorious. She'd basked in the summer sun before, of course, but her previous warm encounters were embedded in her mind more as nebulous sensations rather than concrete memories. Rather than recollections of a picnic in a field, she simply recalled being comforted and happy. Now, she was thrust from the dank cushy darkness of a womb-like cave, pulled by a hand—strong with the scent of *mother*—and burst into a universe of sun.

Overwhelmed by the suddenness of the experience, Hazel recoiled. She closed her eyes and rubbed them with her palms. When she peeks, the vibrancy of the *grass*—an astounding influx of bright, lush shamrock green—bathed her senses. Speaking of her senses—the smells. Oh goodness, the *smells*. The fresh scent of a countryside meadow, a lemongrass-ginger-honey aroma mixed with the pungent richness of freshly-tilled earth astride a crisp summer's breeze.

Before her nose could properly parse through this astonishing input—and before her ears could even begin to filter through the concoction of babbling birdsong and neighing horses and whistling wind—arms wrapped her in a hug. The familiar scent of *mother* was returned to her, yet, tragically, she felt the significance of that slipping away, as a rope slips from one's fingers and trundles down the dark throat of a well. Thankfully, instinct remained to her. She reciprocated the embrace and buried her face on Marynda's shoulder, her own black hair mixing with her mother's strawberry blonde.

For a long, wonderful moment she hugged the woman who'd just delivered her second birth.

Hazel caught movement at the edge of her eye. Her sharp blue eyes, an intriguing contrast to her dark hair and pale skin. She twisted to face the source of the motion, peeling herself from the sensation of *mother*, moving from that comforting embrace. Now there was a jolt of excitement. A small beginning step of adventure, out from the known and into the unknown. What she beheld were four male strangers—one tall and red, one tall and green, one plump and black, one gruff and dirty. All these men were just standing there, looking at her while she shared a special moment with her mother. She was still confused and apprehensive about her sudden change and their stares unnerved her.

She raised her arms and stared back at them, as if awaiting some explanation. The four men continued to be mesmerized by her very presence. They were enchanted by what the elixir had wrought.

Hazel, still unsure of her outward changes, turned questioningly to the person she sensed as *mother*. Marynda spoke soothingly, "These four men helped save our lives."

Just as Hazel's body had grown in an instant to that of a woman, so too had her mind grown with newfound thoughts and comprehension. As the elixir worked through her mind, she understood that Marynda was, indeed, her mother, and that her father was dead. Alkent was dead. She understood that they were on a Quest and now she recognized who these men were.

"You must be Ramsey," Hazel guessed. "You're the High Scholar who assembled the group."

Absolutely baffled, Ramsey had nothing to say, so Hazel's gaze shifted down the line.

"Judging by your cooking equipment, you must be Brisk." Hazel shook her head at him, wondering what enticed him to leave his kitchens and join this expedition.

Taking in the dumbfounded looks, Hazel offered, "Just

because I was in a cave in a bag doesn't mean I wasn't aware of the outside world." As if to prove this point, she continued to identify the rest of them. "You, with the disheveled look, you must be Griffey Parker. You're supposed to be someone special, I think. And you're a Ranger. I sense you're dealing with many conflicting feelings about that profession."

In return, Griffey could only scratch his head and shuffle his feet. This newly-sprung seventeen-year-old girl had unbalanced him. He knew he should be focusing on other matters, like locating the borlogs, but he was far too embarrassed to admit he wasn't very good at his profession. In reality, he considered himself little more than a River Guardsman forced into the Ranger ranks who would rather be alone writing song and poetry.

"Actually, he calls himself a *Runter*," Brisk blurted informatively.

Hazel reacted with some amazement, intrigued by Brisk's description. She then turned to the last of them. "You must be Konragen," she murmured. "I know you were my companion in the cave and I know you saved us all with a rash decision that almost killed you... As a Paladin, always be wary of your choices, including who you might accidentally roll over on."

These words disarmed Konragen and left him to brood.

Finally, Hazel came back to her mother. "You've built a Webber Pyramid here and it's very unsteady. You may be forgetting crucial information the green elf shared in the village. Ramsey clearly said he'd done business with a merchant who seemed both evil and threatening..." Hazel paused to let that sink in. "And where are we headed right now? We're going to some lady's farm? Who just happens to have a *Casting* ring? Upon the advice of the merchant's *wife*."

Marynda's breath caught in her throat. Her confidence in the current plan was lessening. Her newly grown daughter made good sense. Marynda looked over at the faces of the group and found weariness rather than support. This was pretty humbling, seeing that the company, given all they'd been through, hadn't thought of the things Hazel just said.

Something snagged in Marynda's mind, a persistent tickle which drew her squinting gaze back to her daughter's face. "*Webber Pyramid…*" Marynda whispered. "When you identified Ramsey, you called him a *High Scholar*… How…?" She turned her curious gaze on the others, who finally woke up.

"Ohhh," Ramsey whistled, rubbing his face. He then adopted a sheepish cringing expression. "Uh, Marynda… I may have, uh, accidentally given your daughter a classic education…"

"Meaning what?" Hazel demanded.

"*Accidentally?*" Brisk jabbed at the elf. "Huh??"

"Listen, I, uh…" Ramsey gulped, trying to regroup, trying to ignore the fact that everyone was now staring directly at him. Trying to excuse the scrolls he'd purloined from Wicker. He still couldn't believe the actions at that table had been his own. In a matter of days, he'd sunk from being a member of the Rivercrest Sorcery Academy all the way to a pathetic gutter-scraping thief. Before his thoughts could spiral into a pit of self-loathing, Ramsey tried to speak again. "I, uh… I acquired several scrolls from Wicker's table. Scrolls on History, Architecture, Mathematics and ancient Philosophy. Contemporary Philosophy, too. They were enchanted scrolls. Uh, which means they don't need to be read. Just absorbed by proximity. I just tossed them in the black handbag, not thinking…"

Not thinking about the child, his thoughts finished. *Being selfish. Being a thief.*

Here, Ramsey ran out of things to say and stopped.

While this was unsettling news for everyone present, Hazel seemed the most upset by it. She glared at Ramsey, feeling very uncertain. "Are you saying all this stuff in my head… the buildings of the dragon empires, the migrations of the troll clans, the lessons of the elves… all of that was just absorbed? I didn't actually learn any of it? It just… seeped into me??" It was disquieting to think she'd had zero control of all that input, no chance to question any of it.

"Hazel," Griffey spoke up, clearing his throat. "It's a pleasure to meet you. Welcome to our Quest. You obviously know us all, so that's good. Let's, uh, get moving. Borlogs could be after us."

Everyone (besides Hazel) was very receptive to this idea; anxious to break the tension and move. Hiking forward was about the only thing they could agree on right now. The aftermath of the Midsummer's Eve festival had left them all on a high wave. Each of them had conquered a personal challenge and recorded some significant achievements. Once they reunited, it was as if their bond had tightened. They had success and were feeling good. Now, however, Hazel's assessment of their current mission had them rethinking things.

"*Seriously?*" Hazel cried, hustling after the loose, leaderless formation. "*Still* going to the old lady's farm? Even after what we just discussed? Isn't it obvious this could be a trap??"

"We don't have much choice at the moment," Griffey explained. His tone was unsure but also strong and stubborn. "Best chance we have. We have to go take a look."

"Have some faith in humanity," Brisk advised Hazel. It wasn't long, however, before Brisk disregarded his own advice and started getting itchy. The food from Marynda had only teased his stomach (he'd watched enviously as the final slice of pork was delivered to the new girl). Coupled with his hunger was a seed of doubt, which was steadily growing. *Can't trust the group if they're making hazardous decisions. I need to be ready to escape on my own...*

"Hey, I just remembered," Brisk called out. "I lent you all gold coins. Where are they?"

As was to be expected—the members of the company shushed and kept on moving. Brisk shrugged, chuckled, and accepted his loss. What use was money out here anyway?

Their travels took them down a gentle grassy slope and up the other side. The sprawling vistas of fields, forests, and mountains capped beneath a diamond-blue sky—gorgeous, yet also somehow domineering.

In the back, mostly ignored, Hazel grew bored listening to her elders. She was still coping with the changes to her mind and body. In some ways, she felt she knew better than her blundering travel companions. However, there was also comfort being in a group with so much unknown all around, in every direction.

Marynda walked with her daughter but didn't speak. She obviously considered trying to explain her actions and trials, but the risk of misspeaking was high, and it seemed Hazel knew everything already anyway. So she just kept a cautious separation from Hazel and occasionally entertained herself with a jab at Brisk and a placating offer to return her coin, which the Cook would dramatically refuse.

At one point, Marynda turned back. She viewed the distant specks of the village of Benson. She sensed uneasiness in that place. She imagined the mysterious Wicker, now armed with Kozard's eyeglass, rising to oppress the other villagers. Only Brishtiva would be strong enough to oppose him. *But how long will Brishtiva stay around? The eclipse festival is over. Would she abandon the innocents if they end up danger?* With a sting of pain, Marynda realized she was guilty of that exact charge. She felt deeply conflicted. She was happy to be away from there, yet sad to leave it so assailable.

Hazel's heart was just as torn as her mother's. She didn't like this group, yet she had no one else. It was almost as if she'd grown up with all of them, and she felt a great fondness for them. It was a condition the ancient elf philosopher Yak would've labeled as *natural yet antithetical*.

A shadow fell over Konragen. The big dragon halted and everyone bunched up behind him. They peered up at him with puzzlement. The scene clarified. A barn was casting the shadow.

While the group clustered, gaping at the creaking, teetering barn as if it were a magnificent temple plucked from the era of dragon excess, Konragen slipped around and tromped across the threshold. A rickety fence-line dotted the left side, a system whose level of enclosure seemed more bashful than restrictive to the horses trotting and grazing lazily in the sun. On the right was a pergola and a wire trellis encasing the thick green blossom of a garden. Interwoven on the archway and fence were vines and wisteria with buzzing lilacs, pink and blue. Straight ahead was a rumpled farmhouse, but no one cared about that. They all stared at the garden. From which an old woman emerged.

She was round and pudgy, moving with a waddle. Her gray hair was short and curly, wrinkled face drooping, with a prodigious set of breasts and belly. Her piercing blue eyes were rich with suspicion.

When no one talked, Marynda called, "Greetings! Are you Java? Sister of Jana?"

After a dramatic pause to properly inspect them, the old woman nodded and spat in the dirt.

"Jana sent us here. She said you have a *Casting* ring? To help us catch and kill a Warlock?"

"May not be a trap," Hazel whispered to Brisk, "but I don't think she will help us."

"Have some faith in humanity," Brisk reminded her.

"Jana told ye I hate the Warlocks?" Java hacked. "Welp, it's true. I can help ye. I inherited this farm, and it's got an old stone ring on the north side. Ye can use it, s'long as ye use it fer killin' Warlocks." Brisk grinned at Hazel, who threw him a scowl. A moment later, their expressions reversed. "But that ain't a free service, y'hear? I got critters killin' my crops. Ye wipe 'em out for me, ye can use them stones. But them old stones need some special juice to power 'em. No *Casting* without it."

◇ CHAPTER THE FORTY-SECOND. ◇
◇Across the Crinkled Map.◇

"**J**uice?" Ramsey repeated. "What kind of stone ring *is* this?"

"What kind of critters do you mean?" Marynda asked the lady. "Which field are they in?"

Java, the old farmer woman, spat in the dirt. "Dunno what kinda critters. Ye seen the state of me? Got a bum leg an' a bum hip an' a foot made of wood. I ain't runnin' around chasin' critters. Ye go check my fields out west of here. But I need ye to kill 'em, now, y'hear? Ain't nobody usin' them *Castin'* stones until they dead and my crops are safe. As fer them stones?" Java broke off a barking cough. "Ain't nobody used them stones in twenty years. Gonna need juice to make 'em work."

Hazel frowned. "Really? No one's used them in *twenty years*?"

"She's got a point," Griffey said to Brisk. "Resource like that? So close to the village?"

"Just cuz I got a bum hip don't mean I can't *hear*," the old farmer woman snapped. "I can hear everythin' ye sayin'. Sure, ye got reason to have ye suspicions. Everyone knows I got them stones. But that don't change the fact that they been layin' dormant. Cuz no one's got the *Castin'* juice."

"Why hasn't anyone just imported some?" Ramsey inquired.

"Takes special juice." Java spat again. "Every ring of

Castin' stones takes its own unique recipe, I suppose… Ye can find some close by, though. In a cave up north of here, you'll find a stash."

"Shouldn't be problem for mighty Sorcerer," Konragen rumbled, dishing the elf an elbow.

"Java, can you tell my friends how to reach this cave?" Marynda requested.

The old woman scratched her head. "Got a map in the house," she revealed. "Gonna take me a while to hobble over there an' a while to dig through the papers. You gonna kill them critters or what?"

Assurances ensued and the deal was struck. Java started shuffling towards her house.

From the position of the sun, Griffey gauged it to be a few hours past noon. He'd learned the skill of time-keeping well enough from the Rangers, but, at this moment, he wished he had an elf's ability to be calm and meditate. In Java's absence, the amount of fretting and worrying made his head hurt.

Griffey had an innate ability to read people and, from the recent interactions they'd shared with the old woman farmer, he could tell Java was genuine. Which was why he was startled when he heard Hazel exclaim, "She may seem like a friendly old farmer lady, but she may be up to something. First, she wants us to kill some pests. Next, she may want us to rebuild her barn."

The girl was drowned out by shouts which, like Griffey, were unconcerned with Java.

"Can we trust the *Casting* ring will send us where we wanna go?"

"How do we know the Warlock is truly up in those mountains?"

"If he's strong enough to *Cast*, how can we kill him?"

"I, uh… what is a Warlock?" Everyone paused, swiveled, and stared at Hazel. With all the scroll-based knowledge she had, it was strange to hear her so uncertain about a topic. The initial reaction of all the adults was fascination—this girl who seemed to know everything, apparently did not. The flow of their questions came to a halt and they gave their attention to Hazel.

"Darling," Marynda appeased, "Warlocks aren't things a young girl needs t—"

"Mother! I'm *first-plateau-plus-seven!!!*"

"Simply put," Ramsey sighed, "they are seekers of deeper knowledge. Sounds harmless, I know, but they're far more aggressive than a library wizard. This one we're after appeared to be a goblin." The elf gave Marynda a sheepish shrug. "She's part of our Quest now. She needs to know."

"Konragen concurs with Ramsey Green," the dragonman huffed. "She may be young and naive, but she deserves truth." The hard contours of his face turned upon Hazel, who recoiled from his dragon nostrils. Konragen didn't mean to frighten her, but he hoped to appear authoritative. "Warlocks are defined by pacts they make. Make pact with a witch or a devil or a demon. A kind of apprenticeship. Goal is to learn and wield darkest powers of universe."

"What reason…" Hazel whimpered, "could he possibly have to hurt my father…?"

This left them all in silence. No one wanted to admit how little they'd discussed that question.

Java waddled up to them with loud, stumping footsteps, brandishing a wrinkled flap of paper. She thrust the far edge of the brown page into Marynda's hands, then unfolded it towards her own generous chest. Everyone clustered, leaned in, and squinted at the faded black-ink trees and rivers.

Java tapped a pudgy finger at their current position on the map. Everyone noted their position in the world, and their host began to speak. "My grandfather Kimmy told stories about them stones. Said a troupe of mystical creatures—fairies, mayhap—wandered down from up north. Claimed to be starvin' and dyin' and fleein' persecution. Bein' a generous soul, my grandpop gave 'em shelter and essentials. Nursed 'em back to health. One day, the guests paid him back a favor. They put a ring of enchanted stones on our farm. They told grandpop that a few drops from a special jug would make them stones function. Welp, Ole Kimmy used all that liquid to do so much *Castin'* that his brains got rotten. He was driven lunatic and hauled away to jail. Them creatures, before they left, put a stash of that liquid in a cave up north of here... Easy to get to, but protected by magic."

Java's finger trailed out from the tiny sketch of her farm to some nearby foothills. She tapped.

Silence followed. No one wanted to challenge the old woman on the specifics of the magical barrier installed at the cave. Griffey's eyes rose from the crinkled sheet and shaded his gaze at the sun. "Time is dying, let's get moving," he announced. "Ramsey and Konragen—you two with me. If the scale on Java's map is accurate, we can reach that cave in an hour's hike time—"

"Hold back a moment," Hazel interjected. "You're sending me, my mother, and the *Cook* to solve the agricultural problem? With borlogs likely drawing near this farm??"

"I think you severely misread the strengths of your companions, daughter of Marynda," Griffey replied, a lick defensively. "Your mother's especially equipped for the task and Brisk has training—"

"—*swordplay training?*" Hazel cut in. "I fear his training may be severely limited. No offense, mister Brisk."

As tempers flared, Java stood by, chuckling and relishing the entertainment.

Griffey held his palms for peace, yet he addressed Marynda instead of her daughter. "We'll give you Konragen, and Hazel can go with us, acho? We should keep the group sizes equal."

Marynda looked dismayed. "Today is practically her birthday and you'll take her away fr—"

"Dragons don't even have a sense of smell!" Hazel

exclaimed. "He can't sniff out pests in a field!"

"*Griffey's right!*" Brisk blurted, hushing them all. He turned his brown eyes to Marynda. "It may be good to get the child off the farm for a while. Konragen will help us clear the field just fine."

"Stop calling me a *child!*" Hazel shrieked as she gripped her black hair. "*Aaarrghhh!*"

Marynda sighed, rubbed her face, and wrapped her daughter in a hug. When they finally parted, she shot the Ranger a frustrated look. "We'll only be gone three hours," he assured her.

"One hour there, one hour to break into the cave, one hour back," Ramsey summarized.

"Acho, acho," Marynda said in surrender. "Move fast. Try and get back sooner than that."

Just before the party broke apart, Java cleared her throat. They all stared expectantly at her. "There's actually one more thing," she slowly wheezed. "The *Castin'* stones only work at midnight..."

◇ CHAPTER THE FORTY-THIRD. ◇
◇Split Quest.◇

"**J**ust to be clear," Marynda said, "I do *not* appreciate being away from my daughter."

They were out of earshot from where Java roamed, and the other trio had long since vanished over the gentle hilltops. Marynda was leading their stroll, vaguely guiding them westward, past a sloppy field of mud patrolled by broncos. As she walked, she shook her head, and seemed to be oblivious to everything. Konragen, predictably insouciant, lumbered along, shooting occasional glances for the borlogs. Brisk countered Kon's style with anxious energy.

"Let's discuss this, shall we?" Brisk submitted. "None of us know a Frishkadammed thing about exterminating beetles in the cornfield, so let's talk." He held up fingers to help illustrate his points. "We need the juice for the *Casting* ring. The juice is in a cave protected by magic. So we have to send our Sorcerer to do that. Griffey is useless on a farm. Trust me, I know him. And the borlogs will probably attack the farm any minute now, so Hazel's safer away from here."

Marynda caught herself gripping the handle of her wooden club tighter and tighter.

"It was a mistake what Griffey did back there," Marynda said with a shudder. "Why keep our groups to equal numbers? Why couldn't he and Ramsey handle the cave on their own? What in Frishka could my daughter possibly do to help them? She *should* be with her mother right now."

"She needs space," Brisk countered. "She's new to this world and needs to sort things out. She's got all this knowledge in her head—thanks to the elf putting those scrolls in her cave—but she's got no real world exposure. Trust me, time away from you will make her need you more."

"Young girl was uncertain of us," Konragen added. "Time away will make her think about that. Will give chance for her to reassess her feelings. She will warm up to us. Trust Konragen."

"Trust him, trust you," Marynda rattled. "You guys aren't parents, by chance, are you?"

While the Cook sputtered out some nonsense, Konragen redirected the discussion. "Speaking of education scrolls… how did Ramsey Green acquire those? All he had to trade was black eyeglass. Do you really think merchant took eyeglass and gave Ramsey Green a scroll to fix Konragen's throat *and* a scroll to fix Runter Man's broken hand *and* five scrolls on various academic topics…?"

"Ever the Paladin, huh," Brisk huffed. "Always need to judge people. You must be perfect, eh?"

"You insulted elf thirty seconds ago," the dragon retorted. "You called him *careless*. I asked honest question. Think about it. There was *no reason* for elf to purchase an Architecture scroll."

Marynda's mindless movement led them over the crest of an easy hill. Revealed before them was a pasture of brown-sugar-dirt, which appeared soft as a pillow, cut with dozens of vertical-running strips of leafy green sprouts. "It's a potato field," Marynda observed.

"*Potatoes?*" Brisk repeated, suddenly enthralled and comprehensively distracted from all other discussion. "Fry 'em with salt, mash 'em with cheese, slice 'em in a soup! Is this heaven?"

They filed down their own neighboring rows of powdery crunchy dirt, careful to avoid tottering and stomping an errant boot on the blossoming clumps of green. A rich, relaxing scent swelled the air.

As she strolled, Marynda rested her wooden club upon her shoulder. As is commonly done while walking, she planted her right foot without thinking about it. The ground slipped away and she nearly stumbled. She moved on, but her eyes caught upon the ground. A hole encircled with a humble mound of dirt. With her Druid's mind—ever conscious of the call signs of the creature kingdom—she noted the hole purported to be the standard size of a groundhog's tunnel... but something was *off* about it. Something about the rings down inside the tunnel, as if it were drilled, not dug.

Konragen sneezed and the whip-crack sound was honestly terrifying. This made his companions cringe and step out wide, one row further away from the big dragonman. After he'd recovered from the sneeze with a shiver and a snort, the dragon bluntly admitted, "Konragen despises potatoes."

This admission launched Brisk into a dizzy tizzy. "Whaddya mean? Potato soup? Delicious!"

"Dragonborn don't eat vegetables," Marynda recalled, throwing a sympathetic look at Kon.

Brisk was unconvinced. "Well, Frishkadammit, he needs to get over i—"

Brisk dropped. Plummeted into nothing. His yelp of surprise trailed away, "*Ayyyyooooo—!!!*"

Marynda and Konragen snapped to attention, pivoted, and ran to the spot of his disappearance. On the way, Marynda's left boot snagged on the lip of another not-groundhog-hole.

The dragon drew his axe and the Druid woman whipped her club into attack position. They met where Brisk had fallen and beheld a round pit wide enough to fit a man. Off to the sides of the hole, there lay Brisk's sword and shield, testaments to his inability to hold onto them. Down the throat, there clung only shadows—no sign of the Cook. Marynda noted striated rings etched into the tunnel walls.

"*Brisk!*" she wailed down the hole. "Brisk! Can you hear me??"

There was a pause, ripe with tension. A hacking cough echoed up to them. Then, a haggard grunt and proof of life. "Yeah yeah…" Brisk called up. "I got jammed up about ten feet down."

Konragen whipped his blade to the dirt with a tomahawk splat, then knelt beside it. He hastily unstrapped a rope from across his armored chest. Once unfurled, he linked a splay of hooks to the nub of the rope and, with a flick, opened it to a fan of fingers. "Grappling hook," he proudly stated.

Marynda raised an eyebrow at him. "Konragen… are you trying to save him or spear him?"

Konragen's brow furrowed; he looked offended. "A Paladin would never seek to harm—"

"Acho, acho," Marynda relented. The spines themselves were rounded, easy to grip, and the tips looked pretty dull, so she let it go. She hollered down a warning, "Brisk! Got a hook coming your way!"

"*You guys trying to kill me or save me??*" Brisk roared back up at her.

While the dragonman meticulously lowered the contraption down the hole, Marynda stood up and stretched. She caught sight of movement. A glimmer of something silver. And slimy. A brief flail of irregularity, sharp on the pattern of dirt stripes and veggie stripes. Just as fast as it flashed, it was gone.

"What did Java say was eating her crops?" Marynda asked. "She called them… critters?"

"Critters and pests," Konragen supplied, "descriptions severely lacking specifics."

"I have a suspicion what we're dealing with is much larger than a critter…"

"Druid Woman better not be insinuating Java lied to us," Kon growled. "Java was genuine."

"Whether she lied or not," Marynda replied, "the creatures

devouring this field might not be easy to exterminate..." Her eyes dropped to the ground. "They're big enough to make this hole..."

A snarl rumbled up from the tunnel, trembling dirt pebbles and quivering potato plant leaves.

"Oooooo Frishka," Brisk yipped. *"Get me outta here!!"*

An instant later, the grappling hook reached the Cook's station, and he hollered up confirmation, "I got the rope! I got it! I'm holding on!" Konragen stood and started hauling furiously on the lifeline.

There was a dusty ***pop*** and Brisk's waist was jostled free from where he was stuck. With Konragen pulling and Brisk scrambling up the tunnel, the Cook got moving pretty fast.

But it wasn't fast enough. Whatever creature was patrolling this tunnel caught up and gave Brisk a mighty shove in the backside. An instant later, Brisk burst up into the sunshine and flew airborne. Right behind him, a gigantic groundshark exploded against the blue sky, flinging a rainshower of dirt.

Brisk *plopped* to the field and rolled. The groundshark ***thumped*** down five feet beyond that. The beast thrashed about, righted itself onto its six stubby legs, and turned to the stranded Cook. Beady black eyes glinted hungrily in the sun. Slick, slimy silver sparkling skin. Its face was a dome slanting down to the sharp tip of a snout. A sneer split across its jaws, revealing a mouth of fangs with a growl.

Marynda saw that Brisk, sputtering face-down, was about to get eaten, and she started to run.

The ground to her left erupted as a groundshark—half the size of the first; a baby—hurled up from the dirt and lunged at her. She swung her club and ***bashed*** it mid-flight. Another surged up on her right, blinded her with dust, and bowled her over. The bat squibbed from her grip, the baby shark seized it and began to gnaw. This filled Marynda with rage. "That's ***mine***, dammit!!!" A shark thrust up from the ground and slashed her right thigh, drawing blood, demanding her attention. She dealt it a frenzy of kicks, which pummeled the monster until it collapsed back down its hole with a pitiful yelp.

For no apparent reason, Alkent flashed through her mind. Her beloved Alkent. At the log-drag river-cross contest, all those years ago. The memory filled her with warmth and sadness over his manner of death. She shot over and *socked* the shark away with a ferocious boot.

In the moment before the jaws of the adult groundshark destroyed the Cook—cracking bones, shredding limbs, spilling blood—Konragen stepped up and threw a dagger. With remarkable finesse and superb accuracy, the blade met its mark— sank into the eye of the shark with a bloody *splat.*

Konragen tugged on his end of the rope, and the grappling hook lurched Brisk to his feet.

Breathing heavy, Brisk sputtered, "Guess this is what an agricultural infestation looks like."

Marynda hobbled over to join Konragen, scowling and seething at the bite-marks in her club.

Movement. To the left and to the right. Blades popped up from the earth, spewing tiny fountains of gravel and slitting green plant stems. No, not blades. *Fins.* Usually found in bodies of water.

"Oooo no-no-no-no," Brisk stammered. "I've had enough of the field. Time to head back."

Upwards of a dozen fins rose up, slicing across the surface, circling in on the three adventurers.

"This is our task," Marynda called over, dropping to a fighting stance. "We need to clear this field."

Even as she felt the reassuring heft of the lumber in her grip, Marynda felt just as scared as Brisk sounded. Just as a bite was taken from her club, so too was a chunk taken from her confidence. She missed the sensation of Brishtiva's red liquid. Her blustering swagger and invincibility were gone.

"Dirtfish," Konragen spat, brandishing his axe, swiveling

to gauge the nearest threat. "My axe will make them miss water." To Mary, he uttered, "Must destroy nest. Will kill them all automatically."

A shark burst up, jaws gaping, aiming for Marynda's midsection. This attack drew a startled cry from her throat and set her heart racing. She swung the club in a pure defensive strike and battered the beast bloody to the turf. Another shot up at her. She pivoted, set her feet, and hit that one, too. Then she realized two things. First was how much Griffey Parker deserved to have his name cursed for not being here with his crossbow. The second was almost as shocking as a shark attack. She didn't belong in her human form right now. She was a Druid. With a job to do.

She struck another attacker, and the impact produced a satisfying **crunch**, yet the action felt unnatural. Misplaced. *We're above-ground, fighting a buried enemy.* She ran through transformation options, and felt extremely anxious. She never got nervous while selecting an animal form to fit the current challenge. Normally, the process of *choice-and-change* was a rapid whip. Something was different now, though. Brishtiva's red liquid had gifted her a taste of survival as a woman.

Her clothes fell away with a ragged flutter. For an instant, she was weightless; suspended on a cushion of summer air. Then her belly was in the dirt, tail swishing, sun upon her back— pleasantly toasty. She wasn't a traditional black mamba. In a rare Druid move, she'd achieved a *combination*. Successfully coupled a mamba's speed and agility with the size of an anaconda. No time to dwell on it.

The pink fork of her tongue flicked from her lips and the scene grew clear in her mind. A tunnel entrance five feet away. A groundshark about to surface three feet away. She paused long enough for the beast to appear, sank her venomous fangs into its guts, twisted off, slithered down the hole.

Konragen's heart nearly exploded when he saw Marynda change into a giant snake. He knew she had such powers, but it was still shocking to see. The jaws of a groundshark surfaced at his feet and snapped at him. He sank the blade of his battleaxe into the creature's skull, plucked it out again, swiveled to smash another clean in half. He then heard Brisk cry out in fear, about twenty feet away.

Brisk was battling the beasts with dual daggers—his own and Kon's, plucked from a corpse.

The dragonman acted fast. With a strategic stomp-kick, he sprang the Cook's longsword up from the dirt, snagged it mid-air, pulled tight on the grappling hook line, secured the sword's cross-guard handle atop the rope. He raised it high, then shoved the sword into a carrier pigeon air message, sliding it all the way into the bedazzled clutches of Brisk, who immediately grasped it and began hacking sharks.

Down in the dark tube of the shark tunnel, Marynda glided on her belly and hissed from her lips. The channel curved and coiled downwards in a corkscrew descent, other conduits branching off, tempting her to detour. A rack of fangs split open in the dark. They snapped at Marynda's face. She managed to slip around the bite, sink her venom into the eye of the shark, then slithered onward.

As soon as she started spying little ones, she knew she had found it. The tiny scurrying critters led her directly to the nest. A musty ovular-shaped chamber with a patch of sickly translucent eggs piled up. Without hesitating she forced her lengthy, muscular body in there, coiled, and crushed the entire stock.

Marynda was human again when her head popped into the realm of blue sky and summer air. All the sharks were dead. As victory throbbed in her veins, she sought the faces of her friends.

What she saw killed her enthusiasm. Both men were shrieking. Pointing frantically at Java's farm. Java's house and barn were burning, fuming black smoke in the air.

Both Ramsey the Green and his raincloud spell were tragically far away...

<> CHAPTER THE FORTY-FOURTH. <>
<>Distrust and Inexperience.<>

"**S**o, you've got a group of six, acho? And your *only* solution is splitting into threes?"

Griffey Parker tensed. He had to remind himself—*command* himself—that getting ruffled and angry would not be productive. Every time Hazel questioned him, his natural instinct was to protect his pride. *Gotta treat her as an equal, not as a child*

"Hazel," he managed in a flat tone of voice, "how would you split up a group of six?"

"The dragon and the Cook clear the field. My mother and the elf protect the farm. Th—"

"—you wanna be out here alone with Griffey?" Ramsey scoffed, surprised.

Hazel responded with a rhetorical stream that made Griffey grin.

"Three people on each team gave us better odds at winning both Split Quests," Griffey said.

"Yes, but you're blind in your third eye," Hazel retorted, "you forgot the borlogs."

Griffey only grunted at this claim. In every encounter they'd had with Ulkar and his goons, they hadn't exactly defeated the borlogs, but they had certainly repelled them. Which reduced them more to a persistent annoyance rather than a deadly threat. Griffey looked ahead instead.

"Why did they name you *Hazel*?" asked Ramsey the Green. "You've got black hair an—"

"—and blue eyes, I *know*. My mother's a strawberry

blonde hair with hazel eyes. I get it." Hazel gave a theatrical sigh. "That's one of the first things I need to talk to her about," she stated, as if it were obvious, "if I could ever be alone with my mother again."

Griffey was leading their march along the softly scrolling hills, with speckles of forest carved across the horizon and chunks of mountain soaring above that. They marched out north from Java's, leaving both the farm and the village of Benson behind them to the south. They'd only been trekking for about five minutes when they crested a hill and were struck into a breathless, mystified silence.

The ring was about twenty feet across, comprised of ten rocks, evenly spaced. The stones were roughly egg-shaped boulders, their surfaces smooth yet pitted by decades of wind gusts, rainshowers, and heaps of frosty snow. Scars of such endurance were worn in the faded shade of chalky dusty maroon, which ebbed thoughtfully into the hearts of the observers. Such a sight was casually expected, but the subtly elegance, the reserved, slumbering power of this place hummed with an almost physical presence. A speechless encounter with a dormant deity.

After they'd left the ring of *Casting* stones behind, there followed a short time of silence, because no one knew what to say. There was nothing more numbing and humbling than an artifact of mythical power.

Ramsey queried, "You don't have the map upside down, do you? Let me see the map."

"Not much map reading to be done, it's straight ahead," Griffey replied, irritated at Ramsey for questioning his skills. Still, he begrudged the paper over anyway.

"So... we're going to a cave on a map..." Hazel recited, "...to find some juice... to power a bunch of stones and *Cast* to catch a Warlock... whom you all have already declared guilty?"

Her implication ruffled her companions and suddenly their concern over the map was forgotten. After a great deal of self-control, Ramsey said, "The Second King was killed with a red-black assassin's orb. Konragen saw it in the western courtyard."

"Konragen is the dragonman, right?" She tried to sound innocent but it was skeptical. "I thought no one trusted their kind? And he's the Paladin, right? So, a Paladin's goal is to not impede on the freedom or happiness of others. There's nothing explicit in that code about not lying to people. Are you sure he just didn't tell you something that would reinforce your theory? What if he claimed to see something because that would help justify all the effort being put into this Quest?"

This got her companions agitated and Hazel felt somewhat satisfied.

"You've got all that knowledge in your head," Ramsey told her, "but you don't know people."

"Ramsey the Green, how exactly did she get that knowledge?" Griffey asked, shooting him a brief, heavy stare.

Dear Merciful Frishka, how Ramsey detested hearing the allegation that he was a thief.

"I *told* you…" the elf groaned, wiping sweat off his face. "The merchant gave me the scrolls."

"Thought you said you traded for them?" Griffey noted how the elf would not meet his eye. This tiny act of avoidance triggered memories of Kozard's demise. And Ramsey's involvement. In this moment, that dark impression overshadowed any esteem Ramsey had earned in healing Griffey's hand.

Suddenly, the dynamic was changed. Griffey was out here with a petulant child and a shady elf.

"I'm going to carry the Frishkadammed map," the elf declared. "I'm older than you. *Way* older."

Griffey did not object to this. The fact that he didn't made him question himself. *Am I still the leader? Did I take it for granted? Lose their trust? Do real leaders—like my father—have such doubts?*

"Do you really think it's only an hour hike to this place?"

Hazel changed the subject. She hadn't liked the way her two companions were starting to behave. They were her only source of stability and safety out here. When her question only received a gruff wordless nod from the Ranger, she tried to patch things up. "Do you think Java was really telling the truth about special juice in a magic cave?"

"Yes. She told us the truth." Though Ramsey didn't sound convinced. "Why would she lie?"

Hazel winced, realizing that her method of *patching things up* actually increased the tension. "To get us off her farm. Split our forces. So she could, I dunno, trick the others, trap 'em, and eat 'em."

The thought of the other three in peril clouded Griffey's features. The girl saw this change and couldn't resist noting, "You really care for my mother, don't you?"

"Hazel," the Ranger huffed. "Now is not the time."

They hiked on for twenty minutes, and Griffey was rather pleased that no one talked during that duration. They were now far enough out that they couldn't even see Java's farm over their shoulders.

Ironically, it was Griffey who broke the silence. The closer they got to the cave on the map, the more edgy he got. The more his palms began to sweat. "What kind of magic is defending this cave?"

"I would assume it's purely defensive," Ramsey replied. "Wards against looters and raiders."

"I'll bet you've never raided a treasure cave, have you?" Hazel said. "I'll bet you're just like me. To use your words: you've got *all that knowledge in your head* but you got no world experience."

Ramsey sputtered, exuded a classic rebuttal, "I'm *119* years old. You're only *17*. I don't th—"

"—You've *sure* done a lot with all those years, haven't you?" the girl snapped.

With this ongoing chatter, Griffey wanted nothing more than to *Scout Cast* away, thinking again how much more he preferred poetry to people.

In an abrupt shift, the soft crunchy stability of dirt and grass beneath their feet morphed into a moist, mushy sinking sensation and the ground began to tilt undeniably downhill. A rancid odor assaulted their noses and sent tears streaming from their eyes. Hazel loudly wretched.

There was a series of wispy, crinkly, shuffling sounds as Ramsey flapped open the map and peered at it. "Hmmm…" He paused, grunted, then revealed, "This marsh leads down to the cave…"

Griffey and Hazel bit back complaints over the inattentive map-reader not warning them of this.

With dragging, hesitant footsteps, they breached the swamp.

Clouds, mustard yellow smeared with ash, scrubbed overhead, blocking out the sun and dipping the temperature to a fusty chill. The elf and the girl huddled close and hung back. Griffey eased into the forward position with practiced smoothness. He was far from excited about traversing this ground but moving to the lead, feeling the others follow him, did boost his confidence.

However, having them trusting in his leadership made him responsible for their lives.

Hazel's foot sank into a puddle of black water. She shrieked, Ramsey pulled her free. Griffey was briefly held prisoner, imagining telling Marynda that her daughter drowned in black swamp water.

They crept forward and uttered audible gasps when a swirl of fog crawled up the slope and grew and expanded until it wrapped them tightly in obscurity. This was not an ordinary early morning cloud but one that was thick, pea-colored and menacing. As they advanced, trees filtered lazily through the haze; pads of flat rich green perched atop thin gnarled trunks that curved and twisted as if encircling invisible flagpoles. Toads croaked, ravens cackled.

Independently, they each harbored an absurd conviction that their current attitudes had birthed the changes in both the weather and scenery. Each battled away the urge to flee back to Java's farm.

Griffey whispered, "Ramsey the Green, invoke *Bubble* protection, please."

There was a tense pause, during which Griffey imagined the elf ignoring the request simply because it was Griffey who issued it. A moment later, Ramsey cast the spell.

As they moved, the Bubble moved with them, keeping them always in its center. The exterior of the defensive spell was usually invisible, but its edges now simmered with a soft babble of lightning as it dispelled the fog. It was mildly entertaining to watch the invisible barrier burn tree branches to a mist and slice logs and rocks cleanly in half, but no one felt like cheering, laughing, or commenting.

The caws of the ravens intensified. From somewhere nearby—a very concerning proximity—a pack of wolves unleashed a chorus of blood-chilling howls. Hazel grabbed Ramsey's arm in fright, broke his concentration, and their safety bubble burst with a dreadful *pop*.

◇ CHAPTER THE FORTY-FIFTH. ◇
◇Cave Encounter.◇

In an instant, everyone recoiled, froze up, held their breath, and peered around suspiciously. When no more wolf howls echoed through the fog, they eventually relaxed a little.

Griffey noticed how fortuitous their stopping point was, and knelt to inspect the ground. His fingertips found a smooth plate of stone, diamond in shape, large enough for a man to stand upon.

Ramsey rustled up the map once again. "The junction diamond..." he whispered. "From here, it appears we have two choices to get down to the cave entrance. Both are straight ahead from here..."

Griffey drew his shortsword and advanced. The others inched along behind him. They reached a haggard cliff. Pie slices of mossy, muddy earth hung over the precipice. Griffey looked to the right, where a path of flat rock meandered down the lip of the cliff, into the fog. It was an obvious option. In the middle, Hazel eased forward, enticed by the danger of the drop-off, equally afraid and excited by its threats. Ramsey the Green favored the left-hand option, where the rack of a stone staircase trundled down along the shoulder of the cliffside. The smoky blue-gray steps were slick with glistening moisture, yet they appeared sturdy and purposeful.

"We're not going to argue about this," Griffey husked. "I presume both of you are going to want to take the stairs. And that option makes sense. I get it. I just think they could be here to trick us." The others started talking at the same time. Griff waved them to silence, his authority gaining traction. "We're *not* going to argue. We're here to work together and we need to work fast. We take the stairs. Let's go."

Some discussion might have been helpful, as both Hazel and Ramsey could have been easily convinced to take the flat rock path. But Griffey didn't have the patience for it; didn't want to waste any more time. As he saw it, he had just demonstrated compromise without the chitter-chatter.

"*Wait!*" Ramsey hollered, halting the Ranger mid-stride en route to the stairs.

With all eyes on him, the green elf gestured to another plate of stone in the grass. A series of simple runes were carved in the surface: three diamonds, side-by-side atop a thick horizontal line. "This means we take every step together," Ramsey proclaimed, hoping he wasn't wrong about this.

Mercifully, Hazel did not complain. Griffey did not appreciate the tight formation, which would restrict his motions in case of an attack, but he gave his approval. The first few steps were incredibly awkward as they scrunched shoulder-to-shoulder and tried to stay in-step. The risers were barely wide enough to admit the trio but when no threats arose they fell into a steady pace.

Halfway down, Hazel felt both invincible and bored. She hopped ahead to the next step alone. In a violent jolt, the world tilted. The steps flipped down, as if latched to the wall on a hinge. The sturdy stone beneath their feet betrayed them to the open air, spilled them out into horrifying emptiness. Vertigo whipped them, plunged them, tore the air from their lungs, forced their stomachs up through the tight funnels of their throats. Before they splashed into the pond, they managed to scream.

Thrashing in the icy black water, their heads bobbed to the surface with gasps and sputters. The blood-taste of iron stung their tongues and crept down their throats. Their clothes were soaked deeply and instantly, as heavy as layers of armor plating upon their shoulders, arms, and backs.

Hazel was furious with herself for her disastrously impulsive step—yet she was equally distressed over having the others judge her for it. As hard as she started paddling for shore— at least in the direction she thought was shore—she paddled with equal fervor to haul her companions to safety. The sooner they reset their footing to normal, the sooner they could move on and not talk about this.

Glimpsed within the splashing, misting waves of black-crystal water, Hazel saw a flash of deep forest green. She grabbed Ramsey's arm and forced him to hold steady. After a breath, they spotted the stone-rippled shoreline, and swam at it, him thankfully still holding his staff. Something grabbed their ankles in an iron grip and yanked them rudely underwater. The convenience of sucking air was swapped for gulps of choking, rushing water. Whatever beast of the depths had captured them was obviously ecstatic over its catch—it may have been decades since its last authentic feast—and the excitement caused it to thrust its tentacles upward in triumph. Both the elf and the girl burst from the surface in a droplet gush, coughing, terrified and bewildered. The world blurred into a mindless shriek.

A half-dozen additional milky white tentacles—spotted with cancerous blotches along the tops and sickening suction circles on the bellies—exploded from the water, flexing and squiggling in a fit of glory. Right then, the Ranger surfaced with both shortswords drawn and a war cry on his lips. Griffey hacked and severed a tentacle. Ramsey crashed back down with a yelp. With another three strikes, three more arms collapsed, dropping Hazel, as well. Griff grabbed his friends and forced them to the shore.

Blood booming in his veins, pounding in his ears, Griffey bounded up and twisted back to see that the ancient octopus was sufficiently deterred. His friends were on all fours, spitting up globs of goop and fighting for breath. Once the water calmed, Griffey sheathed one of his swords and turned ahead.

The swirls of the fog shifted and he spied the cave entrance. A shadowy half-circle mouth with rocks hanging from its top in an imitation of teeth. From behind him, he heard Hazel gasp, "Let's not—*gack!*—talk about what happened on the sta—" Griffey interrupted with a bark: "Let's get moving!" To prove his point, he trotted for the opening, blood running hot.

Griffey was five feet short of the cave when Ramsey cried out, "*Wait!* Hold up hold up!"

The Ranger's advance ground to a halt, but not out of deference to the wishes of the elf. His eyes caught upon something up above and his face drooped into a gape of disbelief. A moment later, the girl and the elf stepped up behind him, shivering off the cold, rubbing their arms, and blinking a lot.

The elf and the girl followed Griffey's gaze and gasped. From the corner of his mouth, Griffey muttered at Ramsey, "Next time you yell at me to wait I don't think I'm gonna listen."

"Maybe this guy will listen for you," Ramsey replied with an upward nod.

Seated in a gap in the rock wall above the cave entrance, boots dangling off the shelf, was… Griffey Parker. An exact replica of the son of the Second King. Staring back down with the same green eyes which matched his gaze from below. The duplicate's expression was an eerie emotionless blank.

Were he to be suspended in the moment of that bizarre eye contact for many days, Griffey (the one on the ground) could have composed a dozen songs and a hundred poems over the sensation. A meeting with something more real than a mirror. He hollered up a greeting and received nothing back.

With his sharp Ranger's eyes, Griffey (the one on the

ground) noticed how the shelf his copy sat on was developing a thin jagged crack. A soft dusty waterfall poured out. *Strained by his weight.*

Without warning, Ramsey moved up beside him. An exact copy of Ramsey appeared—simply *materialized*, as if freed from invisibility—in a sitting position, feet dangling, right next to the Griffey copy. While this development elicited further gasps, the Ranger noted how the crack did not worsen.

"Ramsey… How much do you weigh?" This question was met with blunt honesty, "Not much."

Not wanting to be left out—and definitely wanting to make a copy of herself to look at—Hazel began to move forward. Griffey thrust a hand out to stop her, and turned a wide-eyed look of painful seriousness to her. He spoke softly, "If your weight gets added up there, the ceiling crashes down."

After a pause, Griffey uttered a command, "Ramsey, cast a *Hover* spell on Hazel." This elicited a number of objections, which he calmly cut off with: "It's either that or she stays out here." As if on cue, a wolf—prowling through the swamp above—loosed a wailing howl.

The trio of adventurers entered the cave. Griffey and Ramsey gaped up at their copies until drug out of sight. Hazel floated a foot off the ground, in a cross-legged sitting position. Enveloped within a weightless gossamer cloud, she ducked to avoid hitting her head. She was no longer captivated over the upstairs duplicate people; she was busy seething over the indignity of being carried instead of walking.

Down the throat, the air was chilly and the light was scarce. Still, their breath was visible, painting specters in the air. It smelled earthy, muddy, moldy. They could see the smooth ribbed texture of the ceiling, speckled with stalactites, which dripped cold darts of liquid with a persistent *pip-pip-pip*.

The ground seemed to angle downhill and this served to increase their anxieties—no one wanted to travel further from the surface, further from their friends and family back at the farm.

From somewhere behind them, Griffey heard the muffled thumps of two people jumping off something. "Ramsey... unless you think she's safer in there, get Hazel out of that thing."

When Ramsey cautioned about the weight of the copies back at the entrance, Griffey gruffly noted, "Don't worry about them crumbling the cave. I think they're in here following us."

He spoke softly enough so that his voice didn't echo, hoping the others would match his tone.

After releasing the girl to a rude smack upon the ground, Ramsey grew tense. He knew the Ranger would ask him to light the way, then demand to know which way to go whenever they hit a fork in the tunnel, then command him to disarm any and all magical traps. Since all the pressure on the roof was off, it was shifted to his shoulders. Despite the cold, dank confines, Ramsey began to sweat. Despite the misanthropic heritage of the elves, and despite how few people were with him, he feared their judgment. *I'm just a Seventh Year, not the High Sorcerer!*

But Griffey asked for nothing beyond a light source. Once Ramsey's staff produced a glowing bulb, which hovered overhead and matched Ramsey's movements, Griffey went back to quietly leading their procession. In fact, he increased their pace, ripe with impatience over this Split Quest.

In an abrupt emotional reversal, Ramsey the Green actually felt offended by this. He'd been dreading the pressure of fulfilling a larger role, and the resulting vacuum left him feeling bitter. Just as much as Griffey wanted to get out here, the obverse became true for Ramsey. His feet began to drag. He started to fantasize about slowing down, letting their copies catch them. Forcing a showdown.

"I..." Hazel stammered, "I think the air in here is... I think it's making me hallucinate..."

"What do you see?" Griffey asked, drawing out his left-hand shortsword to join the other one. Any perceived impatience from him was absolutely accurate—his movements and reactions were razor sharp. *This is all wrong. We shouldn't be here. Should be back at the farm. Danger at the farm.*

"Lizards on the ceiling..." Hazel said. "And no. Before you say it, they aren't just shadows."

Griffey only had time for a brief uptick of his eyes—and he indeed glimpsed a slash of green between the shadows of stalactite daggers. The ground disappeared. For an awful, hysteric moment, his left foot left the earth and momentum flung him feebly forward. His hyper-awareness allowed for a quick recovery. With a stuttering shuffle, he found the top step. Then the next one. Griffey stood there, huffing at the top of the stairs, concerned that their light source was lagging so far behind.

"*Ramsey...*" Griffey growled. He turned back and the intensity on his face caused Hazel to step aside. He was prepared to reprimand the elf for his lack of gumption, but what he saw in their third companion disarmed him. A cloaked figure—especially tall now that Griffey was two steps down—effectively a black shadow despite the light source bobbing directly above his head. The overhang of the hood left Ramsey's face cushioned in blackness. *Did he always have a hood?* Griffey wondered.

There was nothing to say and Griffey didn't feel like talking. He turned back around and began to trot down the stone block staircase—which soon twisted in around itself; a corkscrew descent.

Hazel followed along with a squirming, ducking motion, hesitant to go down these stairs, yet also suddenly dubious about lingering back with Ramsey the Green. One nervous backward glance revealed no features on the face of the elf. Multiplying the creepy effect was that she couldn't hear Ramsey breathing. Conversely, Hazel didn't want to stray too close to the grumpy Griffey either.

A screeching swarm of fluttering wings and gashing claws flooded at their faces. Griffey and Hazel ducked as the black bats scurried past, yet the creatures swerved around Ramsey.

After spiraling around two full circuits, their feet hit the dusty base of the cave. They were birthed into a cramped corridor. Twenty feet ahead was a display of golden twinkling candlelight. Griffey advanced in a trot and was held up short when he smacked into an invisible barrier. It was as if a perfectly clear window with no jamb outline was constructed right in the middle of this tunnel. He peered through at the treasure. Two benches, lined with alternating candles and trinkets—string-tied scrolls, shiny telescopes, bejeweled daggers, and, in the center, most prominent, a clay jug with a cork.

In the distance, just beyond this exhibit, Griffey caught sight of a tiny ghostly face staring back at him. Though it was ghostly, it was far from menacing. In fact it was feminine, and somehow both youthful and ancient. His perception of it was similar to that of a rabbit. A harmless gentle creature, wary of the clattering ruckus of the open world. "I seek to kill a Warlock who killed my father," he called. "I require the *Casting* juice." After a long moment, the fairy nodded, and he stumbled through.

There was no time to savor the moment. Griffey moved swiftly to the desk, cast a sorrowful look to the fairy—whom was cowering as if frightened, watching him. There was, of course, the impulse to take more than he bargained for, but he claimed only the jug. Back through the solid barrier—which changed to translucent jelly for his passage—Griffey emerged just in time to hear Hazel scream. The copies of Ramsey and Griffey were charging in, weapons drawn. Original Ramsey froze Copy Ramsey in a chunk of ice. That wasn't so bad, but the fate of the other enemy was immensely disturbing.

The Sorcerer elf sent a *Fire Bolt* at the charging Ranger. Griffey, clutching the jug, watched in horror as his own face melted away, peeled down to the barren bone of his skull, strands of flesh flung back in streamers, globs of blood and gore slicked away. Ramsey cackled while Griffey burned.

◇ CHAPTER THE FORTY-SIXTH. ◇
◇The Strike Back.◇

Their retreat unfolded in a blur. A hop around the frozen Ramsey copy, a shot past the atrocious *cooked meat* smell of Griffey's copy. A surge up the spiral staircase, up the slope of the cave, back outside, into the stale acidic air of the swamp. This time, they bounded up the flat rock instead of the stairs, per Griffey's original intuition. Only an Oracle could say for certain how their cave journey would have unfolded had they only followed his initial instincts to avoid the stairs. Had Hazel not flung them all down into the water, Ramsey would not have suffered a death-brush with the submerged sea monster. Had its tentacles not threatened to strangle him, Ramsey may have been less protective of his pride. Less wounded when Griffey didn't need his help to navigate the challenges of the cave. That raid should have been Ramsey's proving moment.

No one paused for a breath until their boots cleared the squishy, mossy carpet of the swamp and reached the comfort of the meadow grass. Overhead the ashy mustard clouds gave way to a blue summer sky hinting towards evening. With the departure of those oppressive clouds, the air seemed more hospitable, safer, more accommodating for breathing creatures.

No wolf pack pursued them from the marsh—in fact, *were the wolves even real? Were their howls just enchanted noise on a haunted breeze?*

Griffey Parker's mind was a chaotic swirl. He felt no satisfaction in having won the jug of precious *Casting* juice. He felt as if he'd stolen something from the frail, delicate fairy he'd seen quivering beyond the benches. He felt uncertain clutching the flask and considered asking Ramsey to stash it away in the sub-world. Yet the prospect of talking with the elf filled him with trepidation. His mind replayed the incident outside the fairy's chamber. The horrid sight of his own mirror body in flames, then the agonized scream.

*Was it **me** that screamed? Or were **both** of me's screaming at that moment?*

Why was Ramsey reacting like that? Laughing while he killed me?

Why am I acting like he's my enemy? All he did was laugh and save our lives.

The enchanted defenders were faceless chameleons who resembled any trespassers. Can't take it personal.

"Acho, acho, achoooo," Hazel exhaled dramatically, a short time after they could no longer smell the swamp. "That wasn't so bad, was it? We had some scares, but we made it out just fine, right?"

No one said anything. Griffey marched ahead at a pace approaching a trot. Ramsey hung at the rear, hood off his head once more, hair spiky and disheveled, looking haggard.

"Hey, we made it out alive," Hazel strained. "Everything's alright now, huh?"

Just as Griffey was trying to formulate some kind of response, they saw smoke. Great clouds of it. Billowing, gray and black, vomited upon the bright blue sky.

The plumes were rising from the house and barn.

Java's farm was burning.

Just as Griffey took off running, Ramsey was beginning to articulate a response to his behavior in the cave. He got no further than "sorry" when he heard his name.

"*Ramsey!*" Griffey roared over his shoulder. "*Get a raincloud on Java's barn!*"

Griffey ran. Hazel took off after him.

As the smoke reached his nostrils, Ramsey was now fully alert. He cast the necessary spell and watched as a heavy gray cloud appeared in the sky, pouring out a shower of rainwater. But it was fifty yards short of the burning structures. He would have to get closer. Mixing with the sounds of crackling of flames and pattering rainwater, the shouts of a battle reached his ears. Ramsey advanced, keeping low, pushing the cloud ahead of him, fighting to suppress his dismay.

Up ahead, Griffey was running so hard that his heart labored in his chest. He passed the ring of *Casting* stones and flicked a scathing glance at them. *If it weren't for those stones, we would never have come to this farm. Would never have split the party. Would never have drawn danger to this place.*

Down a flowing hill and back up the other side, Griffey heard the pleas of Hazel somewhere behind him. Though he didn't turn, she did occupy his thoughts. He wondered why she'd chosen to follow him towards danger, but that conversation would have to wait. Same as any disagreements he had with Ramsey.

In the dip of the next valley, Griffey spied the husk of a fallen pine tree. He stashed the jug of *Casting* juice beneath it. Emerging from the valley, he swung out wide and the scene grew clear.

Off to his right, he spied the unmistakable figures of Brisk and Konragen, ducking behind the crippled shell of a wagon. Arrows were railing at their hiding place; the bolts clanging off the iron wheels, bursting and splattering a pile of watermelons in the bed and splintering the coach. Konragen rose up and tried to get a good angle to huck a dagger. Konragen's ammo was limited; he had to carefully choose a window and there wasn't much to choose from. The distance was too far and the shooter was relentless.

Griffey spied the archer's nest—a cozy spot behind the block of an equipment shed. With one elbow jutted out to brace his crossbow, there stood one of the Frishkadammed borlogs. The attacker leaned out, jaw sagging open, tongue lapping crudely upon his chin. He was missing one of his eyes, so he didn't need to squint. The sight gave Griffey pause, then he tried to run faster.

A bark of pain echoed across the landscape as Konragen reeled and fell with an awful **thump**.

Griffey felt a renewed urgency as he pushed himself forward. When he paused to catch his breath, he saw Brisk— frantic with concern—dive over to assist the fallen dragonman.

Where he lay, Konragen writhed in pain. And his position drew Brisk out into the open.

With apprehension, Griffey watched as the borlog archer stepped free and took aim.

A streak of black-and-silver blurred into view. The furry shape galloped in, leapt with predatory grace, and sank fangs and claws into the borlog with the crossbow. The next shot fired wide, clearing both the dragon and the Cook by three feet. The snarling wolf tackled the borlog to the dirt.

Marynda! Marynda in wolf shape! Griffey felt elated.

Hazel finally arrived at Griffey's side. She'd missed everything he had just witnessed, but she did see the wolf mauling the screaming borlog, thrashing and tossing wildly on the ground. Right then, Griffey wanted to say: *That's your mother. She's a wolf and she saved our friends.* But he kept his own counsel and the moment passed.

As she was short on details, Hazel pondered the situation and reminded herself of Griffey's bravery back in the cave. Then, she said, "You've got a crossbow," as she reached over and touched the weapon. "It may be time to use it."

Regaining his wind, Griffey turned to look at her. What he saw in her face startled him. She was looking straight ahead, skin pale, eyes wide. His eyes followed hers and he saw her concern.

Java stepped into the wide grassy alley which ran between her burning barn and her burning house, capped with both the shed and the busted wagon—where the skirmish had just occurred.

Only she wasn't alone. The old farmer woman walked stiffly, rigidly, face frozen with fear—because a man walked closely behind her with a blade held to her throat. Griffey recognized him.

Ulkar forced Java to shuffle forward while he hollered demands at Marynda the wolf.

Griffey stood once again, blood roiling in his veins, drew his swords, and prepared to run again. The element of surprise, however, was stolen when the stormcloud broke overhead. The rain soaked both Griffey and Hazel, and revealed their locations to Java and Ulkar. Their faces were pressed close to each other in reproachful contrast—Java: old and gentle, against Ulkar: scarred, one-eyed, and hideous.

The drizzle departed—en route to the remaining embers of the barn. As the sky opened back up, Griffey and Ulkar locked eyes across the empty glade of farmland. When a sneer lit Ulkar's lips, Griffey's heart sank.

The borlog drew the blade across Java's throat. Blood dribbled out. Then it gushed in a sheet, drenching the fabric of Java's shirt, staining the lumps of her breasts and belly. The poor old woman's eyes rolled away as she gurgled and shook. Ulkar let her topple to the dirt.

From somewhere beside Griffey, he could hear Hazel screaming. But she sounded far away.

Griffey wasn't sure if he let loose a roar, as well, or if he just ran with silent, simmering rage.

A few seconds later, Griffey uttered the sacred words instilled in him in Ranger training, and activated his *Scout Cast* ability. In an instant, he vanished mid-stride and appeared five feet short of Ulkar—who staggered back a step, obviously startled. Griffey went at him with both swords, peeling downward with the right and swiping chest-level with the left. Ulkar's hands filled with a dagger and a hatchet. Ulkar dodged the swipe and blocked the overhand strike with his blade.

Griffey pressed forward, sweeping both weapons in constant motion. He scored a slice across Ulkar's left arm, but the borlog hooked the heel of his hatchet around the Ranger's sword, tore it free, flung it away. Griffey's attack intensified, now battling with a lone sword in his left hand—the same hand Ulkar had forced into prominence by breaking Griffey's right. Steel sparked and sang as they collided, spun, jabbed and growled. Griffey swerved, swatted Ulkar's blade away, landed a boot on the borlog's hatchet hand, then slashed Ulkar across the face. Ulkar's weapons dropped, and his hands shot up with a yelp of agony. Blood seeped from the fresh gory pit of his right eye-socket.

The sixty-second *Scout Cast* window expired and Griffey was plucked away—sent back one hundred yards. From this removed distance, Griffey watched as the freshly blinded Ulkar lurched and stumbled, then ran off in a sloppy retreat. A moment later, Griffey was reunited with Hazel and Ramsey the Green. His concern, however, was for his downed comrades, and he ran to them.

◇ CHAPTER THE FORTY-SEVENTH. ◇
◇Step Across the Bridge.◇

Looking back at it later, Griffey Parker couldn't remember much of the aftermath. What really stayed with him was the cloud of speechless sorrow. At times, the grief he felt was overwhelming.

As Griffey ran to the scene, Hazel and Ramsey tagged along behind him, each with their own private thoughts. Griffey appreciated the silence, because he didn't feel like talking. As he roamed through the farm, he noted the work of Ramsey's raincloud. The fire in the barn was extinguished, as well as that of the house. All the flames were gone, but the blackened stain of their destruction remained. Both the barn and the house were sagging skeletons of their former selves. It was all a waste. Their owned was dead on the ground.

Griffey knelt beside Java's body. Her blood was no longer pumping, but the dark liquid had pooled beside her body. As he viewed her remains, so alive only moments before, he felt moved to offer a prayer. Yet no meaningful words reached his lips, so he twisted and glared across the hills to a cluster of trees. That was the direction where Ulkar had fled. Griffey even marked a faint haphazard trail of blood in the grass, assuredly spewed from the borlog's devastated eye-socket.

Griffey took no special pleasure in knowing that Ulkar had spilled blood in the same place as his friends. He was visited by an echo of this feeling soon thereafter, when he walked over to the equipment shed. He stood there, numb, staring down at the corpse of the other borlog. His throat was ripped out; below his wide, gaping eyes and slack face, there was the strip of a gory cavity. The borlog was dead, but death would not bring back Java or cure Konragen.

With these thoughts, Griffey reached down and took the borlog's arrows.

Now, Griffey turned his attention to his company. Hazel had been following him around, alternating between looking anxious. Ramsey the Green was with Brisk, kneeling next to the injured Konragen. Marynda appeared, absently assembling the final straps of her clothing, hurrying over to help their dragon Paladin partner. Griffey noted how Marynda brushed clumps of thick black wolf's fur from her forearms. He noticed the borlog's blood was still smeared around her mouth and on her chin.

Griffey thought it was a permeating sense of helplessness which kept him from rushing to see Konragen faster. There was also an irrational avoidance; if he didn't see his friend's wounds, then maybe they would somehow prove less serious. As his reluctant footsteps carried him over to the huddle, Griffey watched as Hazel and Marynda were reunited. There was a brief hug and some quick words, but it was nowhere near the loving reception a separated mother and daughter deserved.

As he walked, Griffey saw that the borlogs had not neglected to burn Java's flower garden. The villains had set the roses and sunflowers and tulip blossoms aflame. Only dust remained.

The arrow was deep in Konragen's left shoulder. It had missed his heart by slim inches.

Konragen roared with displeasure as Brisk tried—for probably the tenth time—to remove the bolt. "You have to leave that in there." Marynda swatted at Brisk. "If the arrow comes out, he bleeds to death."

The dragonman's face was pale. Stains on his chest and in the grass made it plain the disconcerting amount of blood he'd lost already. From where he lay, on his back with everyone crouched around him, Kon looked up at Griffey. "Don't worry, Runter Man. Konragen is survivor."

The content of the dragon's words was far more optimistic than his feeble, quivering tone.

"Brisk... Ramsey..." Griffey softly breathed. "You are our Healers. Can you help him?"

"I wish nothing more," Brisk groaned, sounding defeated. "I'd give up everything if I could..."

"I will go back to the village," Ramsey spoke, more to himself than to anyone else. "Back to Benson. I can get some more Healer scrolls there... I will hurry... And I must go alone."

For some reason, Griffey was uneasy, but he didn't see any other viable options. Though no one saw him do it, he nodded his consent. "Agreed. But not alone. Who will go wi—"

Ramsey abruptly stood. He brushed himself off. Tightened his grip upon his staff, a gnarled old branch, nearly as tall as he was. Ramsey's green eyes flashed as he reiterated, "I will go alone."

Griffey forced himself to confront the tall green elf. "If you can't find the scroll we need, we will will need to freeze him and place him in the sub-world until later." Ramsey gave a brisk nod with no eye contact, then started heading back towards town. Everyone twisted and watched his departure.

"Move fast, Ramsey, sundown approaches," Griffey called, not sure how he sounded. He hoped his words carried both caution and encouragement, but he feared he sounded weak.

After a pause, Griffey spoke to the others. "We're going to set up camp near the ring of stones." He gestured up to the north. "That way we'll be in position when midnight arrives. When we can *Cast*."

Though no one said anything, Griffey could sense some reluctance to move from this spot. But he knew they needed to be close to the *Casting* site.

Griffey thought it best to keep everyone busy. "Hazel, keep Konragen comfortable. Get him anything he needs. Brisk, get a fire pit ready for dinner. Marynda, we need you in wolf form again. Get to those woods and try to track down some herb of *heaven's breath*. It smells of cinnamon. If we heat it to a mushy paste, it can act as a disinfectant for Konragen's wound. I'll track us down some food."

"Plenty of food right that'a'way, Park," Brisk pointed a finger. "Shark meat and potatoes."

"What does…" Konragen wheezed, "…Runter Man… need Konragen to do?"

Griffey forced up a smile. "You just relax. We've cured you before, we'll cure you again."

Brisk nudged the dragonman. "Seems we're constantly patchin' your medical problems, pal."

Griffey's eyes met Marynda's. From her perspective, he knew she shared his thoughts. It was, indeed, ironic how the biggest, toughest member of their squad was the most susceptible to injury.

Soon, Griffey was alone again. He scarcely remembered the hike back to the valley with the fallen pine tree, the hiding spot of the juice. He wound up dragging the plump carcass of a groundshark across the bumpy ground, lugging a sack of potatoes on his back. He thought about the last few days and how things had gone horribly wrong. Death and injury had come to good people over and over in this uncaring universe.

As he got closer to camp, Griffey thought about *Scout Casting* the remaining distance. This way he would drop off his heavy load and *Cast* right back again for a leisurely stroll back in. But Griffey wanted none of that. Rather, he wanted to experience the exertion, to feel the weight he was carrying. It helped him deal with the weight of his thoughts. The burden of his guilt.

Though his footsteps crunched upon grass and dirt, the soles of his boots touched down on the stone deck of a bridge.

That's where he was now. Where they all were. They were on the bridge. Moving across the complete their task. They had fought hard and secured what they needed to move forward, to the next step. There had been sacrifices—health, friendships, and lives— but hopefully the end result would be worth the cost.

This had been the first time he'd let his mental guard down and allowed himself to contemplate the real possibility of avenging his father's death. However, he knew much more would need to be done for him to even sniff that chance. He also knew he had a friend to help. Plus an ally to bury in the ground.

Their campsite was settled on a hill adjacent to the *Casting* stones. Konragen must've walked here under his own power, for he was now lapsed into a heavy slumber. Once Griffey arrived and placed the ingredients for the evening meal out beside the steepled sticks of Brisk's campfire, no one felt it proper to start preparing the food. Instead they trekked back down to the farm one last time. They chose a spot next to the devastated remains of the garden and began to dig. Griffey used his swords, Brisk dug with his shield. Soon enough, Marynda relented, disappeared for a moment, then a growling badger lumbered over to assist with the shoveling.

After digging the grave, they gently carried Java's body to the site and lowered her in. For a long time, they stood in a silent eulogy with their heads bowed. Hazel had been instructed to stay with Konragen at the campsite, but the dragonman was asleep, so she sneaked over to join the funeral. Hazel saw the others standing around in silence, and she, too, lowered her head. Marynda embraced her daughter and expressed regret that Java's sister, from down in Benson, could not be here for this.

After a time, they filled in the grave and headed back to camp with stars and moons lighting the way.

Ramsey was still not returned…

◇ CHAPTER THE FORTY-EIGHTH. ◇
◇Kill Your Ghost.◇

As the sun shrank away, exchanging its illumination for the crispness of Midsummer's evening, Ramsey the Green had yet to set foot in the village. From where he sat, he could see the place. In contrast to the buzzing liveliness of the festival, Benson was as tranquil as a forgotten tomb.

There wasn't much to foresee in the future of that sad cluster of shacks other than ruin. Ramsey cursed himself for having given that merchant the eyeglass of Kozard. Wicker was the man's name. A former Sorcerer's apprentice. Which was exactly what Ramsey was now. The fate of Ramsey's family and friends, staring down a plague back in his homeland, depended on Ramsey's patience and persistence in learning Sorcery. Yet that was over now. The High Sorcerer was dead because of him.

He'd contributed to the death of his instructor, the lone elf who'd been willing to guide him in the intricacies of magic. He hadn't outright killed Kozard—the Trail Guardian bushes had done that—but, through the whisper of a subversive spell, he'd rendered Kozard weak at a crucial moment. He could not avoid the truth. He'd killed his teacher. Just as he'd placed the entire village of Benson in harm's way. It was only a matter of time before Kozard's eyeglass grove Wicker mad. Perhaps he would enslave all the villagers. Or sacrifice them to some otherworldly demon, as instructed through the cosmic channel of the eyeglass.

As Ramsey sat upon the hill overlooking the village—he thought of Java's farm and its skeletal remains and his head sagged. His grip tightened upon his staff. He recalled a tense moment during the eclipse when the memory of John Parker's inauguration filled him with inspiration. He tried to recapture that same spirit but the feeling was too elusive. John Parker was dead. No replacement leader could match his promise.

This thought—perhaps more than all the others—left Ramsey feeling impossibly overwhelmed and miserably lonely. His watery eyes lifted, first to the stillness of the village below, then to the stars. As if in accommodation of this stillness, the landscape around him drooped into a hush. The soft neighs of unseen goats and horses fell respectfully silent, the wind scraped to a whisper, bats trickled across the sky but their wings flirted mutely upon the air. Ramsey's eyes found the constellation of Kraven—an omen of mighty struggle and great change. Ramsey thought it odd how that particular arrangement of stars—and all the implications they foretold—was visible just about every night of the year. Then again, maybe that was the point. This world was an incessant swirl of constant changes. When things changed, struggle ensued. And things were always changing.

Rather than continuing that thought, Ramsey's eyes shifted to a bulb large enough and bright enough to be a planet. A rock similar in size and composition to the one he was sitting on right now. Yet that one had tiny specks of flickering light orbiting around it.

Footsteps. Someone approaching. Softly disturbing the grass as they hiked uphill towards him.

As the figure drew into view, Ramsey the Green hopped to his feet and leaped backward, dragging his gnarled Sorcerer's staff along with him. Thoughts of casting a protective spell entered his mind.

Ramsey stood there, his weight leaning back upon his planted right foot, and his eyes shot wide.

Kozard, the High Sorcerer of Rivercrest kingdom, was grooving up the hill towards him, with a smirk upon his face.

Only… his face wasn't solid. Nor was the rest of him. It was as if the translucent fabric of a window curtain were imprinted with ink depicting the physical features of Kozard, and that illustrative cloth was fitted tight upon the body of an invisible person. The contours of Kozard's nose, chin, and forehead, plus the wrinkles of his cloak upon his arms, shoulders, and torso were sketches of black pencil upon a gossamer cotton white. Ramsey was staring at a ghost.

Heart hammering, Ramsey dismissed the protective *Bubble* spell—would it even keep this ghoul away from him??—and nearly turned to flee. But then, bitter feelings gurgled up within him. Recollections of how Kozard began every Sorcery lesson with an insult upon Ramsey's heritage, and how the old fat elf treated him more as a floor mat than a student. All it took was seeing Kozard up and walking around to scrub away any sadness and regret over killing him.

Kozard stopped eight feet away, his staff a glaring absence. The two Sorcerers stared in silence.

Once he decided he wasn't going to run, Ramsey stammered, "You shouldn't be here…"

The shorter, fatter elf wheezed and shook his head. "Still just a lousy Seventh Year."

"It's unnatural for you to be here," Ramsey said, feeling emboldened. "Your presence is a lie."

"Ramsey the Green. Always concerned with defending the natural world, as if it needed your help," Kozard scoffed. "Nature is the strongest force on this world. It doesn't need your sympathy or support. Magic's in your veins. Magic was put on this planet to combat nature's dominance. No super-power goes unchallenged… as you well taught me at the Trail Guardians."

Ramsey's first instinct was to recoil and deny. Perhaps shake his head in defiance and gasp with outrage over the accusation. But, in that moment, both his humility and social restraint collapsed. At the same instant, he was emboldened.

"That's right, High Sorcerer. I enabled your demise."

Kozard's face betrayed no emotion beyond his original sneer, but he did raise his hands. Tiny spurts of cottony cloud fluffed out from the tiny collisions of Kozard's soft, appreciative clap.

"Been needing to talk with you about that, actually. Been chasing you for a day and a half."

"Turn around and evaporate, Kozard," Ramsey barked, surprised by his own words, yet also relishing them. The fire in his chest made it clear: he was alive, and that was more than he could say for Kozard.

"I'm enjoying the fire of your words, Seventh Year, I really am." Kozard was examining his fingernails. "Had you kept on with your studies, you eventually would've learned that only Sorcerers killed by magic get the choice of remaining. In regrettably limited form, yes, but around no less. Even though you didn't deliver the killing blow, you were still implicated in my death. And, since you broke my staff over your knee, I really had no choice but to follow you. These are the rules, you see."

"You need my help, don't you?" Ramsey said with apprehension.

Furious anger flashed across Kozard's features. He reached out one clawed hand, his knobby, bony fingers curled, the fingernails extending into knives. Kozard locked Ramsey's throat in an invisible distance grip. It didn't hold for long, but it was enough to seize Ramsey's focus.

"It is *you* who needs *my* help, sniveling Seventh Year," Kozard snarled. He pointed at Ramsey's staff, which briefly rippled with light in response to his gesture. Ramsey felt it quiver in his grip. "We shall help each other," Kozard spoke. "You're in need of Healer's powers. You have them now. Go. Infiltrate the group, ingratiate yourself. Heal your dragon friend and—when the time is right—kill the Ranger."

Ramsey barely witnessed the dismissive gesture of

Kozard's hand. He was already turned away, at first hopping and hobbling, then, strength building in his legs, positively running back to Java's farm.

The ghost of the High Sorcerer stood there, looking at the stars, entranced by their unending numbers.

A few minutes later, a miserable groan rose from the tall grass off to Kozard's right; just what he'd been waiting for. A blind borlog with a grotesque, mangled face staggered over to him. Ulkar was a pathetic creature without eyes, yet the wretch held a working body. A body worth inhabiting. Worth taking over. Kozard's ghostly face smiled...

◇ CHAPTER THE FORTY-NINTH. ◇
◇Infiltration and Ingratiation.◇

Soft ribbons of smoke swirled above the campfire, intermingling with the starlight. The smell of roasting meat gladdened the senses, enlivened spirits and sparked conversation.

As soon as the promising scent of a meal whisked past Konragen's nostrils, the snoring dragon sat bolt upright—startling Hazel into a yelp, hand upon her chest, heart pattering. The bewildered expression of delight upon his face turned to a grimace as his fingers met the arrow in his chest. The black feathers of the bolt were in stark contrast to Konragen's deep crimson color scheme.

To distract themselves from thinking about Konragen's injury, the adventurers either stared down the gentle valley at the cluster of block-shadows comprising the sleepy village of Benson or examined the eerie ring of the nearby *Casting* stones.

"How you like your 'taters?" Brisk asked the dragon. "Lightly toasted? Boiled? Burnt?"

Konragen gave a heavy grunt. "Put potatoes back in ground. Konragen sick enough already."

The group lacked normal eating utensils, but Brisk the Cook proved both imaginative and resourceful. He gathered up a collection of sticks—firm pokers, none too flimsy—purified them in the flames, skewered up a meal, and distributed them.

It took a full minute for the chunks of groundshark meat to

cool down before everyone gained enough trust not to sizzle their tongues. Then, there was a tentative exchange where peoples' mouths gently gauged if their teeth could break the crunchy exteriors. Next came concerns of under-cooking.

"*Relaxxxx*," Brisk hummed, beginning to dish out potatoes. "Shark meat—medium rare, folks."

"You've never cooked seafood before, have you?" Hazel jeered, though she enjoyed the food.

"Could really use a beverage," Marynda commented. "Got that burn taste on my tongue."

Playful accusations flew, punctured with laughs. It all stopped when Konragen coughed, hung his head.

The mood changed again to concern over Konragen's wound, and his obvious pain. The unspoken fear of his wound worsening beyond any Healer's powers.

At one point, Griffey cleared his throat. His thoughts were weighing on him and he needed to speak. "Over these last two days, you have become some of the closest friends I've ever had," Griffey expressed. He noticed how everyone paused and gave him their full attention. "I'm not much for getting sentimental unless it's in a song, and I know Marynda's not a fan of songs." The two smiled at each other, while Hazel looked confused. "Still, we've battled through a lot together. Survived a lot of tough spots. I was wrong earlier when I insisted we should push ahead with chasing the Warlock... I was wrong to put you in danger and I'm sorry for that. When midnight comes, I'll step into that ring alone."

Griffey glanced at the moonlit stones. His fingers found the jug of juice, in the grass at his side.

After a moment, it was Brisk's turn to clear his throat. "We got your back, Griff. Always, brother. Thing is... it's just... with Konragen hurt and all, it's just not smart to go fight a Warlock."

"And I have a child now..." Marynda softly spoke. "I mean, I always did, but it's different now." Hazel bristled and

Marynda said, "Sorry. I shouldn't have said that."

Footsteps. Someone approaching from the direction of the village. Everyone was now alert. Konragen continued to wheeze rapid, raspy breaths. Griffey hopped to his feet and drew one of his swords. He thought how vulnerable their group was without Ramsey and his protective spells. A moment later, his mind was eased.

Ramsey the Green emerged from the darkness. His forest green clothes were deeply darkened by the night. His face was pale and his eyes were wide. Griffey thought he looked shaken. Terrified.

Ramsey noticed how Griffey did not sheath his sword. Griffey saw Ramsey raise his hands.

"I've got it…" Ramsey stammered, pointing at Konragen. "I've got the Healer's powers…"

"Well you damn-well-better be sharin' those," Brisk called out. "I'm gonna be a Healer, too."

This comment eased the mood considerably. Griffey put away his sword and sat down next to Marynda and her daughter, thinking of how Ramsey had raised his hands. As if he didn't belong here.

Ramsey inched over to where Konragen was seated. While the dragonman appeared close to curling up into a shivering ball, Ramsey looked as if he were totally spooked, about to shriek at the slightest rustle of meadow grass. "Konragen? It's me… Ramsey Green. How you feeling?"

"Cold…" the heap of muscle-in-red quietly replied. "Cold as a summer's day in the south."

"Just be calm," Ramsey instructed, managing to take some of his advise. The Sorcerer elf knelt down beside his patient, and this contact with the ground seemed to steady him. Privately, he couldn't stop thinking about the shock of having Kozard's ghost walk up on him. How it felt to see a familiar face. After all, he'd known Kozard for far longer than anyone else out here.

Professionally, he commanded himself to focus. With both hands, he gripped his tall, gnarled staff and aimed it at the dragon.

A thin river of blue light zapped into Konragen's shoulder. The dragon gave a mighty twitch, coupled with a hefty bark, before toppling over and laying in the dirt. Everyone gasped, made a move to go help him, then held back and watched, enraptured. A moment later, Konragen sat up and looked around, dazedly. Then, he flexed his arms, plucked out the arrow, flicked it away, and chuckled. He thumped Ramsey a rough pat and proclaimed, "I am well! And in debt to Ramsey *the* Green!"

"Glad I could finally earn my name from you," Ramsey said, settling next to Konragen at the campfire. He looked relieved, but his face turned grim. "The infection is gone, and your wound is healed, but you'll have blurry vision, indigestion, and a foggy head for a while."

Ramsey sounded optimistic, but he was scared. Kozard had infested his magic staff.

"No one play any dirty tricks on Konragen or he will clout you," the dragon warned. "Don't give him potato when his eyes bad. Dragons can't smell difference between shark meat and nasty potatoes."

Ramsey's Healing brought relief to the circle of friends. With one swift appearance, Ramsey had eliminated the most crushing, most damning concern on all their minds. It was also fortuitous that no one pressed for details of how Ramsey found Healer's powers.

"Ramsey… Thank you so much," Marynda said, across the fire. "May Frishka bless you."

A blush arose in Ramsey's cheeks, which was more alive and more encouraging than the sickly ghost-pale shade it replaced. A broad, sad smile crossed Ramsey's face as his eyes swept the area. He lit up bright and excited. "Hey, so, this wouldn't be a proper evening meal without drinks!"

The green elf nodded his staff. A circle of six ceramic

cups appeared beside the fire. Positioned at the center of the cup circle was a ceramic pitcher of dark ale, topped with a fine layer of creamy foam.

Cheers and applause rose from the group. A smile lit every face, including Hazel's—she was puzzled, yet the mood was infectious. For that blissful moment, every single one of them was happy.

◇ CHAPTER THE FIFTIETH. ◇
◇Further Mountain.◇

The six people encircled the campfire in a design matching the six cups around the pitcher of ale. Nearby, the smooth nubs of *Casting* stones sat around a pivot point where fairy juice would be poured at midnight.

"Now this ale is real," Ramsey explained. "But the cups are magic. They will vanish from your hands in an hour or so. A natural time limit, so drink well."

Griffey felt a quiver of suspicion, but his good feelings won out. He raised the cup to his lips and gulped some ale.

"You can wave that staff of yours…" Hazel recited in disbelief, "and conjure ale from nothing?"

"It is convenient, I admit." Ramsey smiled sheepishly. "But it's people who do the real magic."

"People like John Parker," Konragen reflected. "It was truly magic, what he could do."

This comment brought a reflective mood to the camp. They studied their drinks.

Griffey stood, extended his beer, and calmly announced, "I propose a toast to John Parker. As he learned in his own adventures across the world, and as he told us when we were children: *the safest path is not always the most rewarding...* Yes. I declare a toast. To my father. To Alkent Johns. To my friends."

Marynda stood next, eyes set upon Griffey. Ramsey joined the ranks, using his planted staff to haul himself up. Konragen wobbled but made it. Brisk stood next. Hazel, confused, stood last.

Each reached his or her cup of ale towards the heart of the circle, paused, then deeply drank.

Once they settled back down, Marynda was the first to speak. "Konragen was being genuine. You need to know that, Griffey. We all lived in the same city. We all saw what your father was capable of."

"Something I noticed about him…" Brisk spoke up, polishing off his ale with a gulp, then waving at Ramsey for a refill. "He was a man built on caring for people. He went out and talked with them. All sections of the city. The kitchens, the docks, the training fields. Even with the dwarves."

"He visited dragon slums, too," Konragen added. "Not as often as we would have liked, but I know he was busy. We told him how hard it was to find work, and he secured us weekly food rations."

"That's who he was," Griffey sighed. "Not just listening to worries, but actually easing them."

"Before *and* after his election, too," Ramsey added. "Those connections weren't temporary."

"What I remember most about him," Marynda said, accepting the pitcher as it was passed around, pouring herself another cup of ale, "was how well he kept his composure. I actually saw two of his debates in the gathering hall. Before he got the Second King job. What was special about him was how he would never resort to insults during a philosophical dispute. It was… it was as if he not only respected his opponent, but the art of discourse, as well. His opponent would get bitter and say awful things to him, but he wasn't tempted. He never used their personal flaws as hunting arrows."

Everyone lapsed into a companionable silence. Well, it was companionable for everyone other than Hazel. She lacked the passion the adults shared on this topic, and within that void she was bristling with questions and ideas, both discordant and radical. When nobody spoke, she simply had to.

"So... what form of government does Rivercrest have, exactly? It's a monarchy because you've got a King... or, rather, a *pair* of Kings. But one of them is freely chosen by the people. So it's got the flavor of a republic? I just... I'm sorry, but I just don't see how the common people consider that system fair to them. I mean, obviously, if one position is called *First* King, then *that* person is going to have more power than the second. I don't see why people put such strong faith in the lower person..."

A breath of shock followed this. Everyone's eyes moved to Griffey. Of all of them, Griffey had the closest, most personal connection to Rivercrest's upper echelon of power. Per that dynamic, they were going to take their social cues on the subject from him. Griffey didn't get upset. He just took a sip of ale. Perhaps his somber calm was a practice inherited from his father.

Hazel looked to Griffey, as well. This entire exercise, to some extent, was a way for her to gain attention. Hazel felt an uncontrollable urge when she looked at him. She couldn't help that feeling of attraction, just as much as she couldn't help the thoughts and questions from spilling from her lips. She registered that her skepticism did not elicit much engagement, and felt a pang of guilt.

Marynda forced a smile, as if sensing the conversational dilemma her daughter might have caused. With a hug, she explained, "The Second King is *ours*, Hazel. We have no choice in the rest."

"But why don't you—" Hazel stopped talking, feeling woozy and delirious from the alcohol.

"It's not a perfect system," Griffey admitted, rubbing his face, "but it would be considered treason to Frishka and our ancestors to dismantle what they left for us. Plus, the people are elated from having the First King lead them. Having a divine presence at the top is rather empowering."

"How about misleading? Deceptive?" Hazel retorted. "I mean… you have been on this side of the river for, what, fifty years? And all you've done is build a castle with a city around it?" Hazel failed to notice the queasy discomfort on the faces of her audience, and kept right on blazing. "Sure, you've managed to scrape a living off the river and the forest. But how much have things progressed? How far have you really gone? You don't know anything about the countries you border with. What are their kinds of government? You don't trade with any of them. Haven't conquered any of them. I'm sorry, but it just seems as if Frishka was the last significant moment for the people of Rivercrest…"

The resulting silence was deafening. All eyes gazed into the campfire.

Hazel, not knowing when to stop, resumed: "Speaking of that… what's the story of Frishka?"

Marynda cleared her throat, gave her daughter a feeble smile. "Let's talk of something else?"

"You guys say *Frishka* all the time," Hazel complained. "Who was he? Who was he really?"

A while ago, the ale pitcher landed in Brisk's possession and he just now remembered that. Seeing no reason not to, Brisk polished off his half-cup of beer and filled it back up again. "Seeing as I'm feeling rather *empowered* by this beer, I think I'll tackle this topic." All their eyes switched to Brisk. Hazel's briefly flicked to Griffey, but she was quick to follow the group.

Brisk gobbled a munch of roasted potato with a swig of beer and oozed an appreciative "*ahhh.*" Then, he proclaimed, "S'far as I know, Frishka wasn't much different from a normal fella. Rumors say that wasn't even his real name, but onward we go. Frishka was a regular guy, worked as a shoemaker, I believe. This was in the way-back days—as you said, Hazel, about fifty years ago. Back over on the east side of the Grayboulder, in the old realm of Crallum. We don't talk about them much anymore."

Brisk claimed another swig, then refined his portrait. "So, in Crallum, there was the classic arrangement of the wealthy few, at the top, running everything, with the poorer masses on the floor, running all the gears. Not much is known about Frishka before his uprising. I just know he was a tall guy with long black hair that made shoes. His reservoir of resentment must've run deep, because there came a day when he burst. Must've sniffed his own mortality, I imagine. Rallied up a mob and demanded a redistribution of power. The uppers were always quiet and cautious and shy and Frishka must've sensed their weakness. Indeed, the uppers were leery of a fight and actually agreed to his demands. Makes me suspect they were already planning a colony across the river, but, whatever…

"Frishka and a population of a few hundred were given approval and supplies to go build a new home across Grayboulder river. The deal was: the rulers of Crallum would appoint a First King to watch over the colony, and Frishka's populace could select a leader of its own, to balance things out. The uppers of Crallum installed Fred Callister as the first First King. Heh-heh. It was strange how little the rulers of Crallum cared about us escaping to the west. As if they were just happy to be freed of all the trouble-makers, grumbling beneath their feet. So, anyway, our people get across the river—that part wasn't easy; many died right there—and start to set up camp on the shoreline on a warm summer day."

Here, Brisk paused, pawed through his pack, and retrieved the final chunks of apple bread. There wasn't much left, but everyone got at least a bite. Brisk knew how to keep an audience awake.

"It was widely thought and generally accepted that Frishka would be elected as the Second King. It was just a matter of tabulating votes. That first day, people were too torn up. Feelings of joy and excitement over getting a fresh start. Feelings of crippling remorse over all the souls lost getting there. All the family members left behind, back at Crallum. When night fell, things took a dark turn.

"Shouts rang out, west of the camp. Side closest to the trees. People started hustling over to join the others and wake everybody up. A crowd of immigrants clustered by to the water, shaking with fear. The crowd watched, captivated, as a witch stepped free of the trees. She stood there in the light of the dual-moons, old and scratchy, haggard yet elegant." A shiver rustled through the group. Griffey shifted his arms and legs. Marynda flipped her hair, discreetly shot her eyes to the shadows beyond their fire. Konragen gulped his beer, a reverential sadness glowing in his orange eyes. "So, the witch boasted at the immigrants that these woods were called Shadowbranch forest and that they belonged to her. She claimed total dominion over this side of the river. Some doubted her claims, others believed it way too much.

"Inevitably, the crowd decided it needed to select a spokesperson and send that person over to talk to her. There was a lot of finger-pointing and a few bruised egos, but the debates ended pretty fast. Frishka loudly volunteered. People noted how Fred Callister did not. Frishka split from the crowd with a torch thrust high above his head and walked through the moonlight to meet the witch. Introductions were made and conversation was had, and it was all loud enough for the onlookers to hear it. Frishka introduced himself as Frishka. She said her name was Vivixtia. Strange name, no doubt, but Frishka was courteous and calm, not confrontational, surprised by nothing she said…"

Brisk gave a heavy sigh, as if retelling the tragedy wore him out. "Vivixtia demanded a sacrifice. In return she would give her blessing to the new kingdom of Rivercrest. Would even guide them to a rock quarry to help construct a castle. Obviously, not much is known about what Frishka was thinking in that moment. He was already standing apart from everyone, which left him singled out. He probably didn't want to, but he gave himself up as the sacrifice. Vivixtia uttered a call in some horrid tongue and Frishka's skull vanished from atop his shoulders and appeared in the cradle of her hands. There was no blood. No decapitation. No. The skull simply disappeared from Frishka's neck, and the skin of his head and face deflated like an empty water bag. His body crumbled to the ground. People rushed over, gasping and shrieking. Vivixtia hugged the skull to her chest, a delirious look in her eye. She pointed to the rock quarry, then sank into the woods and no one's seen her since…

"With Frishka dead, a man named Updike was elected as the first Second King of Rivercrest…"

"Updike…" Ramsey rasped in a chilling whisper. "The first Second King was also the first to be assassinated. Poison leaf of *rumjin*, from Meltrock islands. The murder went unsolved…"

A hush fell upon the group as everyone turned wary, worried glances at Ramsey.

Soon, Hazel spoke up again. "So, Frishka is a hero to you guys for his sacrifice. Do you ever think that the removal of his skull was an elaborate metaphor for the restriction of your knowledge?"

Respectively, Brisk, Marynda, and Griffey looked confused, alarmed, and affronted.

It was Konragen who rescued the moment. In a soft voice, and with a smile, he nodded to Hazel. "A nice interpretation. But, with no skull to hold it, one's mind is free to forever expand."

There was silence awhile, broken by the rustling of a critter in the grass, which triggered a memory for Griffey. "Many thanks for sharing stories of my father earlier. I have one I must share, as well. Early on, he instilled in his children a love for animals. He was always bringing exotic pets into the house. Snakes. Birds. One summer, we nursed a raccoon back to health. Hearing it screeching nearly drove our mother mad. Really, father bred in us a love of nature." This statement struck Ramsey's troubled heart, and the elf felt remorseful and sad. "In a way, I was pleased to become a Ranger. In the River Guard I was just another rank-soldier. I never felt like an individual with them. Wasn't even a person."

Griffey sobered. "I've run wild-off-track. John Parker is not the only one we should be fondly remembering tonight." He smiled at Marynda and Hazel. "Tell us of Alkent. Tell us about your husband and father."

Hazel was visibly upset. Perhaps from nervousness because she hadn't really known her father. Regardless, this was a chance for Hazel to begin to understand who Alkent was.

Marynda blushed for a moment, sipped her ale, and said, "Alkent was an unbelievably sweet man. Simple. Practical. Always bringing me flowers and treats. Goodies from the kitchens…"

Marynda trailed off and wiped her eyes. Hazel leaned in to be close with her mother.

Sitting so close, Hazel couldn't resist one more question with a twinkle in her eye. "Mother, I have to ask… I have black hair and dark eyes, why, of all things, did you name me Hazel?"

Marynda looked deep into the fire, a distant expression on her face. When she spoke, her words were to Hazel, but her eyes resided in the flames. "When you were first born, your hair was blonde and your eyes were hazel-green. Alkent and I agreed it was a lovely name. Then… well, then, you changed. Three weeks later, one morning, your complexion was suddenly dark… I quietly surmised that it was the Druid-blood in your veins. That made Alkent leave the room. He didn't like to talk about that…"

When no one said anything, Griffey ventured, "Something I've been thinking about… if we had an Oracle here, and could gaze into the future… I wonder how will Alkent and my father be perceived? Once everyone who actually knew them passes with death, when no personal witnesses remain…"

Hazel spoke again. "I know exactly what you're talking about. The African culture refers to the recently departed as the *sasha*—which means they aren't fully dead yet. Not until the last person who knew them is gone, not until that happens are they classified as *zamani*, which is fully dead. So, you see, your father still lives on…"

Where is that culture, exactly? Ramsey thought but didn't ask. He shifted anxiously. To him, John Parker was dead and no amount of talking could change that fact. His idol was gone. He was abandoned.

It was Konragen who gave a retort, and he did so in a soft, careful tone. "In culture of dragons, children are told: immortality is not a place in heavens and it is not endless life on earth. No. Immortality is a mountain. Further Mountain, we call it. Yet it is a place one never reaches. One in constant pursuit of a distant goal has no time to grow old and must become eternal. See how it works?

"Hunger of chase keeps you active. Keeps you alive. Dragon children are told: best way to pursue Further Mountain is to grow large, gain big wings, take to the skies. It motivates dragon children, you see, gives aspirations. Though, of course, big wings and sky travel are rare for us now. For us, I think of Warlock as our own Further Mountain. But is *Casting* to catch him seems somehow wrong to me…"

There unfurled a long silence, filled with the crackle of the campfire, the brush of the wind, and a delightful chorus of chirping grasshoppers. Lightning bugs glowed and melded with the stars.

Eventually, Brisk said, "I always knew there was an eloquent public speaker hiding beneath the rocky shell of this dragon." The Cook chuckled. "Usually, *he talk blunt and dumb.*"

Not picking up on the humor, Hazel looked curiously at Konragen. With a startled thrill, she noted a gap in her knowledge base, and saw a chance to fill it. "Tell us more, Konragen. Tell us more… about your people. About your culture and legends. I… I've never met a dragon before."

◇ CHAPTER THE FIFTY-FIRST. ◇
◇Almost Midnight.◇

Konragen, customarily reticent, was feeling unusually loquacious this evening. Perhaps it was his brush with death (the most recent one). Perhaps it was the ale swirling in his skull, mixing with his post-Healer loopiness. Despite his chatty mood, Konragen took a calm moment to compose himself before speaking. His orange eyes strayed to the flotilla of stars above.

"On night of killings at castle…" Konragen spoke in a hashy whisper, "in western courtyard of Rivercrest, before I saw fugitive red-black spell-ball, my eye caught upon something in sky. It hung near constellation of Kraven." (Ramsey's pointed elf ears perked up attentively at this.)

Konragen broke off and turned to Griffey. "When Konragen was in sub-world, when you put me in weird cave, I heard you talking as you walked towards Benson village." Konragen aimed a thick finger at Griffey, and the digit wavered a bit, for the dragon's balance and vision were impaired. "Even though I was a thousand miles away, I was only in Druid Woman's handbag. I heard you use a word which stuck with me… you said *planet*." Staring back at him, Griffey's eyes were intense.

"It is a word rarely spoken. You know its meaning?" Konragen waited politely while Griffey gave a gruff nod. Brisk, Marynda, and Hazel shrugged. Ramsey did not react. "Planet is what we all sit upon right now. It is collection of all continents and mountains and oceans. A big, round rock. Of gargantuan, unbelievable size. Walk as far as you want, you'll still be there." He polished off his ale.

"Now, back to what I saw. *Something* in sky. It was bright. Yet it was not a star. It was another planet. A neighbor to our own. Close enough to be seen without magic in eye." (This comment caught Ramsey's attention and he thought of the black monocle.) "It had specks of light buzzing around it. Yes, buzzing. As if it were beehive. As if it were alive."

There was a pause. Brisk began distributing leftover potatoes (to every party except their speaker, of course), and the nourishing crunch of these treats helped keep everyone engaged.

Eventually, Konragen continued, "Long ago, in glory days of dragons, before we sacrificed our size and wings, we ruled the skies. Soared above mountains…" His words hung on the soft summer air; a starlit hammock. "Some flew beyond roof of our planet. Couldn't stay up there long, but fire in their bellies kept them warm. They saw what was *out there*. Pieced it together over many years. It wasn't easy. Many trips by many dragons, way-up-beyond. They saw five other planets. Same size as ours, going around Sun Ball. Running in a circle. Forever chasing own personal Further Mountains. Equally spread around center point. Just as we sit around campfire tonight…"

A spear of heat lanced the side of Griffey's leg. At first, he swatted at it, as if it were on fire. His logical mind clamored that an ember had sprung from the campfire and ignited his trousers. But there was no burning ember there. The pain was originating from inside his pocket. Rattling, as if it were some plump insect, disgruntled by its imprisonment. Griffey slipped his fingers in his pocket, felt a thin, round shape of familiarity, and was jolted with a reminder of the Grulva coin, vibrating hot.

"We should all get some sleep," Griffey huffed soberly as he clambered to his feet and trekked to the outer limits of the campfire glow. He drew out the coin, felt it sizzle his fingertips. Unsure how to stop the angry attention-demanding heat, he decided to flip it through the air. At the peak of its arch, Griffey remembered to recite the activation phrase: "*Grulva Vitiera!*" He caught the coin in his palm.

The face of Griffey's sister materialized, floating mid-air, even with his own face. She looked unsettled, eyes flicking, as if checking to see if someone were coming through a doorway or sneaking around a corner. "Sho'pa," Griffey exclaimed, "are you acho? Are you and mother safe?"

Sho'pa's brown eyes were more intense than usual, and she quickly rubbed them, as if fighting off sleep, or discouraging tears. Nothing about that was common; she was usually very composed.

"Sho'pa, what's wrong?" Griffey had nearly forgotten why he was corresponding with her.

"I should never have agreed to this," she hissed. "Griffey, my training as a Monk isn't complete yet. I should've known there would be consequences. I should never have agreed to this."

"Slow down, be calm, tell me what's happening. Are you safe? What did you find?"

"I'm safe. We're safe." Her exasperated words seemed conflicted. "For now, I think. Look. I did what you asked. I shouldn't have. My training isn't advanced enough. Should've known I'd leave a trace. Frishkadammit, I left a trace." Briefly, it seemed as if she were talking to herself, scolding herself. "I dropped into a trance and turned back two days. The eyes of my consciousness went back across time and into the office of First King Callister. On the night of father's murder…"

Sho'pa's eyes shot away. Griffey stood rigid, wide-eyed, breathless with anticipation. Griffey glanced around, saw he was still alone, standing in a field of gently flowing valleys beneath a dazzling ink-black hearth of summertime starlight.

Sho'pa spoke, her voice a serious whisper.

"Forty minutes after father died, I stepped up to the door of Rodrick Callister's command room. It opened and four people exited into the hall. None of them could see me standing there. There was Queen Sheeva, duke Halderman, Trunk of the River

Guard, and the High Sorcerer Kozard. They all walked past me, and the door swung shut. I waited in that quiet hall for a short moment, just me and two big guards, standing there in full knight armor. A figure slipped from the shadows and approached the guards. I saw that it was Ulkar. The borlog said something to the guards, but this was my first time meditating back in time. My consciousness was there, but my ears weren't adjusted yet.

"I missed what Ulkar said to the guards, but they let him past, and I followed along. The door shut, and now I was inside the command room, staring over Ulkar's shoulder. The King was nowhere to be seen. The man was hiding under his desk. It wasn't the King who offered a greeting, but an old shaggy brown dog that waddled out from behind the crescent-moon desk. It bounded over to the guest, happily enough, given the state of its old eyes. Ulkar kicked the dog, sent it reeling back against the desk with this hideous, delirious yelping noise. Dear Frishka, that sound was awful, so so *awful*...

"Callister came up into view, this stupid, startled expression on his face. From what I could tell, he wavered between retreating beneath his desk again or becoming defiant and asserting his authority. In the end, he crumbled and Ulkar was in control.

"The King sank into his chair with a tired, defeated look, and he said '*Ulkar...*' as if he'd been dreading this meeting for a long time and had kept postponing it. '*I suppose you've heard the news...*'

"'*I understand a leader party has dissolved,*' Ulkar said. '*I see change as a positive thing.*'

"'*Ulkar, you've always been so harsh on the Parker family,*' the Fist King replied.

"Ulkar groaned and said, '*Griffey happened upon me in an alley one night. I was with a woman. Said her name was Lasha. She asked me to bite her neck. Begged me to make her a borlog. Said she needed strength to defend herself, energy to do her job everyday. We became intimate and things were progressing. Then Griffey showed up and she got embarrassed and the whole thing became a horrid mess. My reputation was tarnished. So, no, to be honest, the Parkers do not have my respect.'*

"Ulkar went on to say, '*You, my King, are smart enough and skilled enough to run this kingdom on your own, without the help of a Second King. You were born and bred to be a leader; it's literally in your blood. You weren't chosen by the brainless dirt-bred peasants.'*

"Callister finally spoke up and said, '*We're sending a Chase Quest to apprehend the assassin.'*

"Ulkar said, '*Hmmm. I presume you're sending relatives of people who were killed. Which means you're sending a Parker. Such inclusion is the law, after all. But, you must see that the Parkers aren't in power anymore. Aren't relevant anymore. You need kingdom presence in this delicate matter.'*

"That was when I saw the First King officially break. When I saw how weak he truly is. He put on this mopey face and said, '*There's not much to be gained on this Quest, anyway. What's done is done. John is dead. You may follow the Quest, take charge if necessary. Kill the assassin if you can.'*

"Callister scrawled out a decree, put his signature to it, and gave the scroll to Ulkar."

Sho'pa concluded her telling abruptly, ducked aside, peered across the room, listened intently.

Griffey felt a stone catch in his chest. He felt cold sweat on his face but he forced himself to talk. "You said you left a trace?"

Sho'pa, eyes back on her brother, gave a grim nod. "I stayed too long. My presence there left a scratch upon the fabric of meditation space. That's the dimension we ascend to whenever we meditate. The Higher Monks spend months floating there. I'm not sure, but I think they detected me. You have to understand. I broke a core rule tonight. I could be punished, expelled, tortured, killed…"

Griffey ran through a number of questions he wanted to ask—but he decided on one that was most urgent. "Can you get mother out of the castle? Get to where I am?"

Sho'pa gave him a sharp, inquisitive squint. "Where are you?"

"Further Mountain—" he caught himself, closed his eyes, shook his head, waved his hand as if to omit that, "—I mean, we're north of Benson village. Going to a Warlock colony in the mountains."

Griffey saw his sister's focus finally break. Her eyes shot wide and she ducked into a shadow. "Someone's here," she whispered, "I must go." The floating image of Sho'pa's face dissolved like a sprinkle of sugar down a waterfall. The coin of Grulva lay inert and unresponsive in his palm and did not reanimate no matter how many times he flipped it and caught it. There was no way to know for certain if his insistence on having Sho'pa talk had drawn enemy eyes upon her.

Heart hammering, Griffey looked to the skies. To the dual-moon system. He gauged the time with urgency. Pocketing the coin, he hustled back to camp, golden crossbow bouncing upon his back. Upon arrival, he found his friends—not drunk and munching potatoes—standing together around the extinguished campfire, bags on their backs, patiently awaiting his return.

Griffey halted. After a pause for everyone to gather their thoughts and breath, it was Brisk who spoke. "Listen, Park. We've been talking while you were gone. With Konragen Healed now…"

When Brisk trailed off, Griffey was awash with emotions. He felt some certainty that his friends were about to leave and trudge all the way back to the castle. He was scared they might be walking into a trap once they got back home. It was clear that the administration held little faith in their expedition. Their Quest had been assigned such poor value—Griffey felt incensed that

Rodrick Callister, the King alongside his father, was not more invested in catching John Parker's killer. Griffey was also afraid of pushing on alone. He wasn't naive. He knew he couldn't take down a Warlock. Plus, he was now heavily torn over returning to Rivercrest, as well. It agonized him to think of his sister in danger back there. With his mother assuredly to follow.

The maelstrom of Griffey's thoughts nearly drowned out Brisk's next words.

"...I guess what I'm trying to say is: we've come all this way together, survived all this danger together, and, seeing as Konragen is healed and all—thanks to our Sorcerer—we've decided that... We've decided to see this thing through. End it."

It took some time for Griffey to fully catch his breath. "I can't ask you to put your lives at risk unless you're all in this together..." One-by-one, Griffey looked at their faces and collected nods of assent. "It's almost midnight. Let's get moving." Griffey plucked the jug of fairy liquid from its spot in the grass, then led his party through a valley to the adjacent crest. He walked without saying anything. He was moved by their commitment and let any lingering thoughts of abandoning their mission fade away on the wind.

They breached the circle of *Casting* stones and clustered around. Griffey knelt at the center and popped the top off the container. Marynda crouched beside him, her presence giving him confidence. "Shake the juice, shake the juice," she suggested, and he complied. Right at midnight, with the dual moons perched directly overhead, Griffey dribbled six drops into the grass, and replaced the plug.

Nothing happened. The pause was long enough and tense enough for them to question this whole thing. This was dangerous and foolish. How were the stones to know their desired destination?

In the instant before they *Cast* away, a figure burst from the darkness and ran up on them...

BOOK

◇ V ◇

THE CASTLE.

◇CHASE QUEST◇

◇ CHAPTER THE FIFTY-SECOND. ◇
◇Surrounded.◇

From the split of his eye, Griffey saw the intruder—nothing more than a shadowy blob with shoulders and churning legs. His blood rushing, Griffey lurched to his feet and drew one of his swords. A second later, the others were startled and pivoted, as well. Griffey saw Brisk raise both his shield and sword and felt a swell of pride in that. Marynda and Hazel rushed into each other's arms. Ramsey spun on his heel and lofted his staff. Konragen, still woozy from the Healer's treatment, nearly toppled over, as if the mild flurry of motion around him had been enough to tornado his balance.

No one's reactions were quick enough to prevent the arrival of the shadowy figure, to shove him away or threaten him from the circle before it was too late. An instant after the invader breached the circle of stones, the stones began to spin. They remained level with the ground in which they were lodged, but they swirled, stretched, blurred into their fellows, forming a smeared maroon wall, dancing and racing around the people now trapped inside, inflaming their brains with an awful fuzzy dizziness.

With a sense of failure—they realized they hadn't defended the circle—Griffey fell unconscious to the dirt.

Moments later, the ritualistic spinning came to a halt, rocking the Ranger awake once again.

For an agonizing stretch of swirling intensity, Griffey's brain couldn't register his surroundings. His backside sank into the mushy ground; the surface morphed and squished beneath him. Tucked within the sand were rough clumps of rock, nudging at his forearms. He planted his sword as deep as he could, heaved to his feet. The sister moons were no longer directly overhead. They were distant now, looming high behind him somewhere. In addition to the beach, the lunar position change was solid confirmation. They had *Casted.*

Griffey sheathed his sword armed himself with the golden crossbow. He figured the long-range weapon might better serve the current situation and he didn't trust his wobbly legs to support much sword fighting. He focused on finding enemies.

Marynda was next to her feet, at Griffey's side, wooden club held high, a bit wobbly on her feet. Together, the pair spun in formation, backsides pressed. Nervous sweat trickled into their eyes. Pulses increased to a persistent pounding. Kindred lookouts; a slow twirl in the thick darkness. No words passed between them, but their thoughts were matching: *Are we near the Warlock colony?*

The immediate area drew into focus first. Though Griffey's eyes were sharp during the daylight, his night vision needed improvement, and Marynda was the first to see significant features.

Lumps appeared in the darkness, the shapes of bodies sprawled out and curled up and sleeping. Marynda recognized Konragen and was concerned that he wasn't moving. Then she saw Konragen thrown an arm as he groggily thrashed about. Relieved, she darted her eyes and marked the rest of their party, all still down on the sand.

At her back, Griffey's field of vision encompassed a beach pattern, speckles of obsidian chunks atop a brown crinkle-spread of sand. He saw the seventh member of their *Cast.* The shadow invader. A man cloaked in darkness was rising shakily to his feet—ten feet away, attempting to stand with a series of graceless, wretched hitches. Griffey ceased his half of the defensive spin and Marynda matched him.

Griffey raised the golden crossbow and took aim.

Marynda was in mid-twist—en route to join Griffey in facing down the villain—when strange lights caught her eyes. Upon the sliver of shoreline just beyond the *Casting* stone boundary, orbs lit up, a rich red-orange. The absurd thought of pumpkins on Hallow's Night entered Marynda's head. She looked closer, and saw that wasn't far off. Glowing human skulls lined the circumference of the island.

◇ ◇ ◇

Dashing into the *Casting* ring had been a daunting challenge. For the creature which carried a borlog's body and an elf's corrupted soul, none of it had been easy. There'd been the challenge of laying quietly in the tall grass, springing to his feet, then the exact timing needed to sprint into the circle. Above all else was the ferocious need to be in control.

At first, Ulkar the borlog agreed to the accommodation; at the time of their agreement, he would have done anything. He was blind, howling, and staggering through a world stripped of color. Blood was seeping down his face and dripping off his chin. Altogether, it was the most maddening, frantic sensation Ulkar had ever experienced. There was no question he would consent.

Suddenly, their thoughts had merged, occupying the same skull. Kozard's thoughts soared triumphant—he was a ghost no longer. He now had the body of a seasoned fighter. A borlog mercenary. However, he was still without sight. Tapping into his remaining magic, Kozard was able to conjure up a pair of eyes. The left one was without vision, but the right held promise. A blissful vestige of the black eyeglass.

Kozard held control of Ulkar's body. Ulkar was a passenger, an observer, who could now clearly see that the High Sorcerer intended to pledge himself to the Warlock everyone was chasing. It would be a humiliating exercise, but Kozard sought to be reborn. The fat old elf was willing to become a Warlock himself, if necessary.

Ulkar cared little about assisting Kozard's spiritual rebirth. He was now nothing more than a puppet on a string. One thing was certain: he was grateful for the one good eye. The painful takeover of his body had at least returned his sight.

Unfortunately, the first thing he saw was encroaching danger...

<> <> <>

"You here to kill me, Ulkar?" Griffey called, crossbow ready to kill. The figure was still dark, but Griffey knew who it was. And the borlog somehow had his eyes back. "I may just kill you first."

A rumbling cackle whipped from Ulkar's mouth; the shrill noise of a rabid hyena. A glint of moonlight drifted across the island and briefly illuminated the villain in all his hideous glory. The borlog's hands were gnarled claws, shivering with an unnatural sickly shake. Ulkar's face was in its regular state of horrid disarray, displaying scars atop tattoos. His skin was ghostly pale, his left eye was a milky white bulge and his right eye was black speckled with tiny glitter-dots of gold.

"So consumed with death you are, Ranger," Ulkar cried— though he didn't speak with Ulkar's voice. It sounded different, ugly and familiar. "All this time, you've been chasing our beloved Warlock with the intent of killing him. Never did your overwrought mind consider the value of catching him alive."

"Parker..." Marynda whispered, her tone harsh. "There's something in the water..."

The Druid woman's words proved prophetic an instant later. In the background, behind Ulkar, beyond the *Casting* stones, beyond the ring of orange skulls in the sand, Griffey saw waves disrupting the black water. A clear thrashing indicator of something fighting to the surface. Multiple somethings.

A hefty breeze brought the fresh salty scent of an ocean tributary past their faces.

"You haven't shot me already, it's clear you're not going

to," Ulkar barked. "Still, there will be plenty of death. Even some for you. The water rogues might kill you. If not, death will strike from closer to home. How deliciously tragic that will be. Well then, I'm off to catch a Warlock!"

Fifty feet out, on the water, the wooden shell of a naval ship bobbed to the surface, sails unfurling. Water discharged from valves in the hull as it became a surface-craft. The vessel sat there, rocking idle on the tide, eagerly waiting to gorge itself on prisoners and treasure.

The activity in the water increased with a rapid churning. Things resembling squirming pinkish tentacles broke from the surface, recklessly splashing. With rapid movement, an array of tentacles shot up onto the shore, slithered past the glowing skulls, latched around the bulk of the *Casting* stones. There was a visible tightening strain, then whatever lurked at the other end of those fleshy ropes began to grind up into the air. Dozens of figures forced their way free of the water and began lurching onto the sand.

"Frishka's broken skull," Marynda hissed. "*Squid-pirates!*"

The rogues matched descriptions from worker's tales on the Rivercrest docks. Seeing the pirates in person was a massive shock. They were half-squid/half-people. Bipedal, same as women and men, with a flock of additional appendages. Their tattered black jackets and trousers were peppered with holes admitting the muscular tendons of tentacles, exuding from their hips and ribcages. They stood broad-shouldered and tall, with greedy sneers on their faces—the salmon skin of which was a crusty, grungy texture, deeply grooved and wrinkled from too much time spent underwater. They drew cutlasses from their belts, fat blades with golden handles. The squid devils had footholds on every inch of the shoreline, stepping amongst the skulls. With the island surrounded, they began the inward march.

Excess liquid sloshed from their waterlogged boots.

Drawling footsteps, shaky yet determined.

Griffey saw Ulkar draw out a blade and twirl to face the onslaught. For some reason, that released a hold upon Griffey's tense trigger finger. It was a conscious decision not to shoot Ulkar in the spine and drop him dead—Griffey would save the ammunition and trust the pirates to kill Ulkar. First, the Ranger swept his sights out to the left. He socked a bolt into the right eye-socket of a squid-man, watched him reel backwards and go down. With swift action, he drew back the cable, slid another arrow in the barrel-notch, and slugged another villain in the chest. That one dropped with a flapping, wailing roar.

Attempting a rapid re-load, Griffey's fingers slipped slightly on the roller release. A trio of tentacles lashed up from the sand—a flashback of the Trail Guardians exploded in his brain. All three worms wrapped snug around the calf of his left leg and immediately hauled him off balance. His weight thrust him forward and his fingers fumbled yet again with the crossbow. His heart was pounding.

Marynda stepped up and swatted down at the offenders with her trusty wooden club. The impact of her bat severed right through the tentacles with a series of bloody, quivering *snaps*. The head of her bat ***thumped*** to the sand, amongst the wriggling worms of broken tentacles.

The success of Marynda's attack surged confidence back into Griffey's veins. Not only did he have his friends here to back him up, but the squid-pirates were suddenly less intimidating now that he'd seen their tentacles get broken and severed. He finally threaded the bolt properly in-place, raised the weapon, fired, and dropped another of the growling approaching creatures. Griffey, however, sensed the reality of their situation—soon they would be overcome by a flood of ravenous squid-pirates.

Griffey aimed, fired, killed another staggering squid. He started the fumbling process of reloading the crossbow and realized it was pointless. The fishermen horde was now shuffling past the *Casting* stone borderline. Close enough to smell. A rancid, fishy smell assaulted Griffey, springing tears to his eyes. He heard their watery boots scraping on the sand.

Four tentacles slashed up and snagged hold of Marynda's club. The bat was wrenched from her grip and went skittering across the beach, consumed in the puddle of shadows swarming at the feet of the muttering, rasping, advancing squid-men. Marynda was an adaptable fighter, for she grabbed the shortsword from its slot on Griffey's left hip and brought it up to defend herself. (Though she kept her eyes on the enemies, she was keen to not deal Griffey an accidental cut in the process.) Following her lead, Griffey threw the strap of the crossbow to his back, and drew up his other shortsword.

Now, the water-walkers were a mere ten feet away. The swarm of tentacles cut that gap short.

A squid-limb darted at Griffey, he hacked it in half. Marynda split another at her feet. Black-purple blood spewed from the severed, thrashing arms, tagging their clothes. The recent enemy casualties were pitiful compared with the fresh swarm of arms advancing on them. Their optimism was waning as they backpedaled absently into their sleeping friends.

A sudden heat rose up directly behind them, a warm handprint on the backs of their necks.

Both Marynda and Griffey twisted around and gaped in amazement. Ramsey the Green, was perched on one knee, aiming his gnarled Sorcerer's staff, launching *Fire Bolts*. The fists of fire hit four villains—one after the other, rapidly down the line. They fell, screaming, arms flailing in the flames.

Reinvigorated, Marynda and Griffey stepped up to defend their other companions on the sand. Marynda and Griffey hacked and swatted and split a relentless flurry of fleshy, waving tentacles. A combination of the warriors' churning feet and the chunks of blood-splattering meat smacking the sand was enough to jolt Hazel, Brisk, and Konragen awake, up onto their elbows, eyes wide, faces aghast.

"**Ramsey the Green!**" a voice bellowed. "**Do your duty! Kill the Ranger!**"

Despite the fish-arms slapping at his face and throat, Griffey twisted. He saw Ulkar lower his shoulder and bash into the twisted shadows of the pirates. Griffey thought he heard a *splash* as Ulkar escaped. Griffey turned back. Ramsey, eyes blaring, face contorted, aimed his deadly staff at Griffey...

◇ CHAPTER THE FIFTY-THIRD. ◇
◇You Have My Blood.◇

In a swirl of mental activity, the Sorcery words which would draw forth a *Fire Bolt* coalesced within Ramsey's mind. Ramsey's fingers tightened upon his gnarled wooden staff. He felt hot breath seething between his teeth. Cold sweat slicked his face. His wide eyes burned.

Before him, five feet away, stood the Ranger. The man reminded Ramsey of John Parker, yet Griffey had no hope of achieving such greatness. Ramsey saw Griffey for what he was: the spoiled son with none of his father's talent, charisma, or ambition. Griffey was a pale imitation; his life a meandering march leading nowhere. Which was why Ramsey felt so heavily, so mercilessly *judged* whenever Griffey tasked him with something. Or didn't trust him with something.

The words of Kozard echoed in Ramsey's mind: *Kill the Ranger when the time is right.*

In Ramsey's estimation, Kozard was a complicated knot, in need of intricate untying. Indeed, Kozard had delivered into Ramsey's possession a collection of Healer's powers, enough to cure Konragen, enough to fix his friend. By helping him save Konragen's life, Kozard had earned a measure of vindication. The value of the old High Sorcerer's influence went beyond even that. In the field of the Trail Guardians, when Ramsey enabled Kozard's death, Ramsey tasted what he was truly capable of.

Ramsey wanted that feeling again. The sensation of eliminating another soul from the living realm. Not just an unnamed squid-pirate, but someone significant. Ramsey had slaved for seven years in Sorcerer's studies hoping to impact the world, yet now he could do it in a vengeful moment. Maybe he, too, could follow Kozard and join forces with the Warlock. All he needed to do was kill Griffey. A flashback rippled through his mind. The image of Griffey burning, down in the fairy cave.

Skin stripping back in roasted tatters, bloody flapping rags clinging to Griffey Parker's skull.

That memory gave Ramsey encouragement. He'd already killed Griffey once.

Ramsey the Green needed to act fast. His thoughts were a battleground and they were making him hesitate. He saw a pink squid-pirate tentacle flick toward Griffey's throat. If Ramsey's lips didn't say the command so recently formed in his mind, then the Frishkadammed pirates would kill Griffey first. This consideration put a crack in his resolve. There were other enemies. Danger, close.

"Ramsey the Green..." Griffey wheezed in a rattling voice. "You don't have to do this..."

This statement caused Ramsey to redouble his grip and step forward. Yet, still, he did not fire.

From their vantage on the ground, at the feet of the standing characters, Brisk, Hazel, and Konragen watched with pale, shocked faces. Despite the overwhelming smothering blanket of the pirates closing in, the three in the sand stared up at Ramsey and Griffey. It was Brisk who managed the courage to say something. "Ramsey. Brother. We're the closest friends you've ever had..."

Griffey's blue-green eyes were frantic. They locked with Ramsey's crystal green eyes. A tear slid from Ramsey's eye. The elf's resolve wavered. Nonetheless, a *Fire Bolt* slipped free with a hiss.

From the tip of Ramsey's staff, the arrow of fire whisked over Griffey's shoulder and torched a squid-pirate whose blade was raised at Marynda's backside. This action broke the tension and sparked them all to service. Griffey ducked and spun away, a trio of grasping tentacles missing his head by a hair. The squid-pirates were close enough now that Griffey jabbed and slashed and struck solid bodies instead of fleshy tentacles. Marynda spun away, as well, striking at a foe who hit back with a blade of his own. Konragen hobbled to his feet, found he was still woozy from the Healer's treatment, and plopped right back down. Brisk bounded up, hoisted his rusted-brown trapezoidal shield just in time—swords and tentacles smacked against it with a series of shuddering **clangs**. Brisk stepped back to gather himself, then urged back at them, dicing over the top of his shield and drawing some screams.

Ramsey the Green continued to shell out *Fire Bolts*. His victims either fell dead in the sand or shrieked and fled for the water. The rest of the company managed to hold off the attackers long enough for Ramsey to work all the way around. The barrage of tentacles and steel finally relented. Breath returned to their lungs. They regrouped in a cluster at the heart of the sandy blood-soaked skull-ringed island.

There was only a fleeting instant of reprieve. Then, they all sensed something amiss.

"Hazel…?" Marynda asked with a choke. "Where's Hazel! *Hazel!*"

The Druid woman twisted, her heart speared with terror. Then she saw it. The most appalling thing imaginable. Apparently, one squid-pirate had failed to fall down dead or slink into the water. This final enemy was not only still here, but he held Hazel before him as a shield with a dagger at her throat.

"Such anger, such hate," the pirate observed, his voice a wretched gurgle. His prisoner kicked and squirmed, but his tentacles easily wrangled all her limbs. She was locked solid, wide eyes staring back at the bewildered gang. "I know your kind, yes I do. You live in castles. Have your food brought to you. Doesn't matter what castle you're from; you're all the same. You hate my kind because we look different than you do. You won't hire us. Won't trade with us. Force us to steal to feed our families."

"Ramsey," Griffey whispered aside, eyes on the enemy. "Think you can burn him?"

Ramsey the Green considered the options. Firing straight-away would fry the squid-man, but Hazel would be the first one burned. Ramsey was still only a Seventh Year Sorcerer and couldn't bend a *Fire Bolt* up and around to strike from an elevated angle. Ramsey didn't want to admit any of this aloud. His emotions were still in turmoil from the murderous temptation he'd just resisted. Plus he was surprised and profoundly humbled that Griffey had already disregarded it all, and was now asking for his help. If his mouth opened, he thought he'd scream. Ramsey shook his head.

"Seeing as we're about to become family, I believe introductions are in order!" boomed the squid-man, who wore a tight skull-cap above his eye-patched, severely water-wrinkled face. "Grok is my name!" He emitted a maniacal cackle—"*ehh-heh-heh-HAA!*"—coupled with a mocking bow.

"Let her go!" Marynda cried. "*Let my daughter go!*"

Marynda's heart slammed in her chest. She saw the fear in her daughter's eyes. She could only imagine Hazel's agony. Chained by tentacles. Overwhelmed with the squid's reeking fishy odor.

"Ahh, you must be the mother! *Heh-HAH!*" A giddy grin cracked and splintered across Grok's face. "Oh don't worry, dear mother. I won't be taking this fine lass as my bride. Oh no no. I meant we'll be family soon, because all are family in our guild. Oh, this fine lass will learn *so much* with us."

"Let the girl go," Griffey commanded. "If it's food you want, if it's trade you want, whatever it is, let the girl go and we'll work something out." Griffey's muscles strained as he tensed and waited.

"What we *need* is a new crew member," Grok explained. "One with youth. One still alive, as well. Considering the number you've run on us tonight, replenishing the ranks seems reasonable. Ha!"

"Let the girl go—*or I'll destroy your ship!*" Ramsey growled, aiming his staff out on the water.

For a moment, Grok looked alarmed. Then a mischievous smile spread rumpled hillocks across his ghastly, gnarly cheeks. The pirate extended a hand with a claw and flapped out at his ship. With instant compliance, the vessel retracted its sails and began to sink to safety. Ramsey was startled for a moment, but recovered and shot a *Fire Bolt* blazing across the water. The yellow-orange dart reflected starkly upon the glistening, rippling mirror of the black water. Everyone on the island turned away from their standoff to watch the missile fly and the target retreat. Breath was held and eyes did not blink as the drama unfolded. The spear of fire was splitting very fast through the air, spewing embers in its wake, which trickled down to sizzle-kiss the water.

Suddenly, the spear seemed to lose speed. The bulk of the ship sank beneath the surface, leaving only its mainmast visible above. The *Fire Bolt* sagged down to the water, as well, but not because it was in pursuit. Exhausted, the spear sputtered and died in a harmless crackle of steam.

Back on the island, the questers sagged their shoulders. Ramsey felt defeat settle heavy upon his eyelids and thought he might perish beneath the weight of such guilt-ridden failure. Grok's wicked grin was broader than ever, tobacco-stained teeth on full display. Marynda's motherly eyes shot back to her daughter and the sight of her still in the pirate's grip caused her to take an involuntary step forward. In response, the grinning pirate tightened his grip on Hazel, reasserted the knife at her throat.

"Peace, dear mother, peace!" Grok called. "You have my assurances, the lass will be well treated. The Warlock gave our tribe strict rules for prisoners. She will be one of us. She will learn to steal. Learn to survive. She will thrive. Such fine education we offer. Now don't panic, dear mother—I can see it in your face. You look so pitiful with that look on your face. One of my tentacles is going in the lass's mouth. Oh, I know how it sounds, dear mother. This will help her breathe underwater. In time, she will grow gills of her own. What a day that will be! Oh yes, *so much* will she grow with us."

Alarmed, the gang stepped forward, looks of disgust and outrage upon their faces. They raised their weapons, but their hearts went the opposite direction, sunk to unbearable depths.

As promised, one of Grok's crusty purple tentacles wriggled its way up Hazel's leg, brushed past her hip, slithered up her stomach, slid between her breasts. The pointed tip of the snake reached Hazel's chin. She tried desperately to twist and turn her face away, but the blade at her throat restricted her movements. At first, she valiantly pressed her mouth closed and refused to allow entry to the serpent. When tiny hooks stabbed into her lips, she resisted a wail of pain, but couldn't resist her jaw being yanked open with a dribble of blood. After that, the fat wrinkled worm drove inside her mouth and down her throat with ravenous gumption. Hazel's dark eyes shot impossibly wide in revulsion.

Grok trembled with lunatic laughter. Marynda nearly collapsed to her knees, tears streaming down her cheeks. Griffey stepped out wide, swapped sword for crossbow, tried to get a shot on Grok.

"*It's only fair!*" Grok screamed, suddenly viciously serious. "You slaughtered my guild-brothers! My guild-sisters! Yet I am not vengeful! Not killing her! I am giving her a life! A career!"

"Oh dear Frishka," Marynda moaned. She felt the sadness and helplessness with a crippling force. Her knees sagged to the sand. Strength drained from her sword-arm and the blade fell to her side. Maybe it was better this way. Smarter to not be raising a weapon at the bastard holding her daughter captive. She didn't want to provoke him any further, didn't want to propel him past the line of reason. She would be a more palatable negotiator if she was harmless and broken.

A jolt of desperation burst through Marynda's veins, lighting up her senses as if she'd just awoken at sunrise from a thorough night's sleep. She snapped up straight, strawberry blonde hair thrown back as her shoulders squared and eyes narrowed with focused, relentless intensity.

From the brink of collapse and despair, a primal awakening shocked Marynda back to life.

Marynda wasn't exactly sure why she called out words to her daughter. Wasn't even exactly sure where the words originated from. But she trumpeted them with a sprawling, confident force.

*"Hazel Alkent, you have my blood! Never forget that! **You have my blood!!**"*

There was a slit of silence when nothing happened. It didn't last long, but it was there.

Either Grok had nothing else to say or Marynda's words pierced a tick of unease into his triple-system of squid-hearts. The pirate whirled on his heels, boots spitting up a spray of sand, and hurled face-first into the water—powering Hazel out before him, slapping her down with the sickly sound of a stone smacking wet stone. In the flash of a blink, both were gone beneath the surface…

◇ CHAPTER THE FIFTY-FOURTH. ◇
◇Vile Training.◇

Marynda ran to the shore, eyes wide with inconceivable terror. She may have unleashed a single shriek, she may have been shrieking for the entire trek across the island. Her friends probably dashed right along with her, but she didn't see them. She only saw the water. And her gone daughter.

Marynda didn't stand around for long. As she ran to the water's edge with hair flowing atop her head and blood racing in her veins, she made her decision. Her clothes dropped off her shoulders in a flutter and the shortsword toppled to the sand. Her body formed into a streamlined spear with a fin on her back and glistening milky-blue skin.

In the midst of changing, Marynda dove forward, off the shore and out into the air. Before she splashed down, the Druid woman's transformation into a shortfin shark was complete.

With anger fueling her momentum, Marynda shot forward in the water, her fin slicing the surface above. Her sleek black eyes brought the scenery into focus. A chalky layer of dirt lay at the bottom, from which there jutted rocky uneven castles of coral coated in a crust of nipples, monuments interspersed with wavy green ribbons of seaweed. Above those decorations, there hovered a school of mackerel. The crowd dispersed with a dozen flourishes as Marynda's snout punctured their bubble. As the mackerel dissipated, her forward path grew clear.

The water was murky but she could still see a half-dozen squid-pirates lingering ahead, bobbing in the water and leering back at her. Some were partially burned from the battle on the island, but others seemed to be a reserve force covering the retreat for those on land. No matter, below the surface they were more squid than man. Their human limbs brandished swords and kicked as they swam, but their tentacles powered their agile mobility and fanned into broad intimidating cages around each of them.

Up the middle of this enclosing tunnel, Marynda saw Grok. Paddling away, Hazel in his arms.

With a twitch of her tail, Marynda sped up, gliding through the water with lightning quickness. The first pirate rushed her from the right, trying to ensnare her with its tentacles and gut her with a blade. She snapped her jaws, crushed the attacker, and the water churned red. She felt her progress slow. Two more pirates converged from the sides. She clamped her jaws on both, pouring more blood in the water. These encounters slowed her even more; she was not moving as quickly as she needed and thoughts of her daughter—with Grok's tentacle down her throat— greatly distressed her. In addition, the blood in the water was playing on her shark's natural instincts. She had to suppress the need to feed. She had to *keep moving*.

Marynda made fast work of the next three adversaries— mashing flesh and crunching bones—but it wasn't fast enough to please her. Nothing short of reclaiming her daughter and killing Grok would please her now. She surfed past the final ink-blot of blood and spied her target ahead. She was making headway, for Hazel was kicking and resisting and slowing the advance of her captor. The excitement of closing in was balanced with dread. The submerged husk of the squid-pirate ship was hovering up ahead, and Grok was dangerously close to it. He would reach it soon.

Before they got there, there rang back an explosion. As if Grok and Hazel were thrust headlong into some invisible barrier, a shudder rocked through their bodies. The shimmer rippled back in a shockwave like an underwater earthquake. Marynda felt the vibration peel along her cartilage body with a sting of icy cold. From tip to tail, snout to caudal fin, she was frigid. She shook it off but was alarmed. Grok and Hazel had vanished. The wooden bulge of the ship—presently converted to a submarine vessel— was still bobbing up ahead, but Grok and Hazel were gone.

Marynda's jaws tore open in a silent scream of desperation. She powered forward and watched with agonized astonishment as the husk of the pirate ship began to waver and wash and fade and slip out of focus, as if the depth of its framework were paint-strokes being cleansed from a canvas. It was hard to focus on that when the world became a breath-stripping shroud of frigid chill. Marynda shivered, felt her entire body clench and falter, as if it were shutting down to die.

Her shark avatar wasn't meant to endure such extreme cold. She was afraid she might die right along with her shark body. Marynda changed back to her human form and was instantly greeted with the same punishing cold. Now she couldn't breathe. A gulp of icy water—sucked down during a gasp—froze over her throat and filled her lungs and sent her thrashing towards the surface in an urgent climb. Her head burst up into the black of night, but the grip of cold still remained.

Without much thought, she morphed into the form of a grizzly bear—anything to keep warm—and distantly noted that the pirate ship was gone. It was no longer waiting patiently underwater or sailing atop the waves. The ship, and Grok, and her beloved daughter were all completely gone.

The worst part of it—the most insulting, most humiliating—was the fact that she had no time to worry over Hazel's disappearance. The water was cold upon her thick brown fur and the air was rushing past her face as the tide swept her along. The rapids of this river were remorseless, crashing on rocks and spouting up spray with a serpent hiss. Marynda's right hip bashed against a hidden boulder, a bark of pain tore from her throat, she spun out of control, head dunking below the water.

There was a sprawling, mindless stretch of kicking and flailing and insanity and suffering.

Once Marynda's mind settled back in, her powerful paws took charge and she paddled safely to shore. Her grizzly bear body collapsed upon the pebbles, she rolled onto her back, but her rolling didn't stop right there. She kept on tumbling. Bouncing and scraping. Reverberating up the beach.

It was a painful journey. Especially after she lumbered over to where the island was. The sandbank encircled with *Casting* stones and glowing skulls. It was daytime by now and she could clearly see the island. It was disconcerting to see no smoldering squid corpses laying charred upon the sand. And all her friends were gone. Brisk and Kon weren't snoozing there. The rest weren't clustered, awaiting her arrival. They weren't splashing in the water or posted on the riverbank, either. Lonely abandonment swelled in her chest. Her powerful bear jaws gaped with a bellow of anguish.

Finally, her gaze shifted to the riverbank. The beach was a strip of brown-blue-black utterly dominated by what loomed beyond it. The grim plate of a hundred foot cliffside ran along the riverbank for a few hundred yards. The sheer smoothness of the rock was an intimidating scream. Perched atop that rise, shooting high to scrape the clouds, was the boastful fortifications of a castle. The black stone formed a round casing, taller than it was wide, split into three towers with the mightiest one in the center. For any sad soul who wanted to get up there, hope grew upon the river bank with fat, twisted roots. A giant pine tree rose from the sand to monumental heights, thick branches gnashing defiantly against the rock face all the way up. The green cone of the tree actually bested the cliff-top by fifteen feet or so. But, of course, despite the magnificence of a tree able to grow so massively tall, it was outshone by the castle.

This was all too much for Marynda to absorb. She turned and galloped away, heavy paws pounding ruts and shooting up sand behind her. Her rumble along the beach continued.

She ran in the direction she'd come from, keeping the cliffside to her left. Marynda went that way naively hoping to run into either Hazel or the ship of the squid-pirates. Neither happened. Distraught, she barely noticed how the ledge of the cliff sank into an impassable hillside of jagged enormous boulders—a deterrent for anyone seeking to raid the castle from the side. She was far more intrigued by the forest of pines which burst up from the dirt once those rocks receded.

The Druid Mother's tumble along the beach stopped at that snag; she bounded up into the trees with gruff, thoughtless determination. Her shoulders bounced off tree trunks. She slobbered, snarled, scattered critters at her feet, scared birds into flight. She roamed that forest for a year. She hunted, slaughtered, and dominated, utterly devoid of mercy. When the rampage was over, she didn't remember sleeping at all. Could only recall what she could procure from the blood on her face and claws, and construct from the scars torn deep in her hide. But she did entertain flashbacks of trampling in the moonlight, crashing through branches, shredding flesh, breaking bone, tasting blood. When she finally shambled back down onto the riverbank, her pretty brown coat was ragged, war-torn, and filthy.

She splashed gratefully into the water, soaked in the rapturous river, washed in the warmth. The warmth. Yes. The water was warm. Because the squid-pirates were gone; the horrid exhaust of their ship was no longer polluting and distorting. When this thought struck, Marynda's face slackened, she melted from grizzly bear back to human form, and was left bobbing and sobbing and gaping at nothing.

After cleaning her hair as best she could, she staggered up onto the beach and stood there, naked, and hollering for her daughter and her friends. She cursed herself a fool. Suddenly, she remembered what she knew about squid-pirates. It wasn't much.

No one knew very much about the patrollers of the waterways. Still, she'd heard persistent rumors that swimming in the wake of a squid ship was apt to kick the swimmer to a time that wasn't their own.

Marynda didn't know how to define it any better than that, and trying to do so only made her head hurt. That headache chopped the flood-gates and she felt a dozen pains flare up across her body. More than all her wounds, it was pure exhaustion that drove her up into the bushes to curl up in the shade. Luckily, hunger wasn't an issue, for she must've eaten well. She slept the rest of the day.

When she awoke, she fashioned an imitation of clothing from vines, twigs, and leaves. She was hesitant to use her Druid powers; feared losing control again. Her ramble along the beach resumed in an orderly manner. She waged an internal battle to keep her composure. To keep the panic away. She focused on finding the giant tree and the castle. She could feel time slowing back down again…

◇ ◇ ◇

More than being kidnapped, more than being separated from her mother and her friends and protectors, Hazel was scared of the intrusion in her body. The squid tentacle currently lodged down her throat. She could feel the lumpy texture upon her tongue, could taste raw, slimy seafood. Her mind recoiled at the damage the intruder could be wrecking upon her insides.

Then, the reeking pirate flung her—*splat*—face-first to the river. Fully dunked, her terror accelerated. The imminent threat of drowning was as sharp as a blade and worse than death itself. She felt her captor grab her and begin to drag her along as he swam. She kicked and thrashed in protest, and these movements made her lungs demand a breath. Just as her internal hysteria reached its apex, Hazel found plenty of air already in her lungs. The tentacle in her mouth was still repulsive, but, without it she'd be dead. In shock, she quit struggling, which made her easier to drag.

Their progress took them into a pocket of surprisingly clod water and this snapped Hazel into her natural state of resistance. She twisted her head back and glimpsed a shark following them. She felt somehow confident that it was her mother. Then the shark vanished in a curtain of silky, watery vapor and time seemed to rush forward. Her body still felt the pains and strains of being hauled aboard the pirate ship, yet her mind saw it all unfold as if hours were only fleeting moments. Time was still moving with activity and emotion, yet it went by fast. She felt fear and suspicion when Grock introduced her to his crew, but she continued hopeful, constant glances over her shoulder. The tentacle was removed from her body—unneeded when sailing above the waves—and, although she appreciated its absence, it made her long even more for her mother.

With her ankle shackled to a post, Hazel slept out under the stars, scrunched into the shadows beside a crate with a net secured around it. She wondered if the squid-people were experiencing the same rapid slippage of time as she was. She wondered if they wanted it that way. Under the sun, she was forced to tie knots in thick, thorny rope, scrape crust off the hull, and got yelled at by beastly men with rotten fish breath. Whenever someone noticed her subtle acts of defiance—kicking over a bucket of mop water, peeling splinters from the wooden planks—the pirates warned her that, if she were to escape, jump down into the water, then her mind would be destroyed, churned to raving mush.

One day, she worked up the courage to ask Grok about the magic in the water. The old pirate shoved her to the deck and she came up with blood splitting from her nose and lips. Hazel had fully expected this assault, for Grok's lessons always came in pairs. First, there would be pain—she'd get clocked in the face, or kicked in the shin—and then Grok would answer her question. That was how it worked. Grok would never initiate any of her training; he always waited until she asked a question before engaging with her. With consistency and reliability, Grok answered painfully and truthfully.

She never asked, but suspected the episodes of pain were student humility before a mentor.

The rest of the crew either ignored Hazel or barked at her with sudden rage whenever she got in the way. Other than that, they left her alone. There were no unwanted midnight advances (she figured they weren't attracted to human women). They mostly left her to her training with Grok.

After Hazel asked about the magic in the water and was rewarded with gashes on her nose and lips, Grok extended one of his humanoid hands and helped her to her feet. They both resumed their scrubbing duties, side-by-side in the hot sun, the ship rocking gently on the river, and Grok gave her an answer. He explained that their species was cursed. Ten years ago, they were nearing death, shrunken with starvation, such that the helmsman was away from his post and their ship ran absently aground. The hull crunched to a halt upon the little island with the skulls and *Casting* stones. Their ship sat there, their people teetering on extinction, for the rest of that day and the night that followed. No one had the strength to get them adjusted and sailing again. The next morning, the Warlock descended from his castle on the cliff. He introduced himself as Revelt, but that could've been a lie.

Revelt adopted the squid-people into his service and placed a green-glowing jewel at the heart of their ship. Not only did this jewel gift the pirates regeneration, but it spewed mysterious matter into the water wherever they traveled. Gloriously rejuvenated, the pirates sailed the river-ways, plundering villages, burning civilian vessels, leaving a trail of liquid madness wherever they went.

During the first raid opportunity in her time aboard, Hazel was locked in a cellar filled with crabs clicking and clattering in the musty darkness. Eventually, she was permitted back up into the light, and asked Grok to train her as one of his own. Grok responded by sweeping her legs out from under her, slamming her to the floor, and booting her in the ribs. After that, he helped her stand back up and began to train her. Taught her the art of sneaking in the night, and going undetected in the day. Instructed her in picking locks. Stealing coins. Throwing knives. Swimming without breathing.

Hazel didn't need to calculate how long she stayed on that creaky, slimy ship. She simply asked Grok, received an elbow to the ear, then learned she'd been part of the crew for nearly a year. The contents of that year felt like *more* than a year, all gone in a blink. Not only was her life stolen by pirates, but her own time didn't belong to her either. With a renewed sense of urgency and frustration she recalled the last words her mother spoke to her.

Right then, her Druid's blood surged.

In a snap, she had feathers, her arms were wings, her ankle slipped free of the cuff. Grok and the other pirates gaped in shock as Hazel became a falcon and flew away. Instinct guided her back to the island of skulls and stones. She landed on the riverbank at midnight and saw a figure approaching...

◇ CHAPTER THE FIFTY-FIFTH. ◇
◇Choice and Punishment.◇

The dash to the shoreline was a breathless run swollen with screams. Their feet struggled with the mushy instability of the sand as they battled to get to the island's edge.

In the grip of panic, Griffey's mind replayed the last few moments. At Grok's first hint of movement—a turn towards the water which proved unbelievably swift—Griffey's crossbow trigger-finger loosed an arrow. Griffey thought he glimpsed a flick of purple blood and felt satisfied that he'd hit his mark. Yet the squid's body featured any number of swarming appendages. *Did I hit one of those instead?*

Griffey didn't even notice when he kicked over a jug in the sand—the *Casting* juice, brought along with them to this place. All his focus—as well as his friends'—was given to rushing towards the spot where Hazel was stolen.

When they got there, the company smashed some of the glowing skulls to dust and kicked others out into the water. With gaping eyes, they saw the writhing water, the rippling aftermath of the abduction. When no squid body bobbed to the surface, Griffey knew he'd missed.

Dual sources of midnight moonlight rippled upon the black inky water and betrayed no secrets.

Marynda paced the shoreline, a shriek erupting from her lips. Her movements sent the others into awkward backpedals of deference, clearing the way for her march. Then she dove into the water—in the split of her mid-air passage, her body flipped into a silver shark. Under other circumstances, the theatrical reaction from the men would've been mildly humorous. In unison, Griffey, Brisk, Ramsey, and Konragen all gasped, recoiled one step, then pounded forward, war cries booming.

With their weapons flailing and legs kicking and mouths bellowing, the men crashed down into the river. The summertime water was a hot greeting, yet their blood ran far hotter.

Despite entering the water simultaneously, they advanced at wildly different paces. With an athletic vengeance, Griffey powered forward, arms and legs and lungs working with precision. He'd swiftly sheathed his lone remaining shortsword— its mate surrendered by Marynda back on the island—and his golden crossbow now surfed the strap on his back as he swam.

After Griffey, there came Ramsey the Green. The tall elf weighed far less than the others, which made it easier to swim yet also left him susceptible to getting shoved by the current. Plus, he gripped a staff which was trim yet substantial and its weight threw off his balance. Soon, he learned to hold the staff in his left hand, braced against the tide at his left side. He was getting tired fast, panting already.

Behind Ramsey the Green, was the bulk of Konragen the dragonman. Normally he was an efficient swimmer, able to use his strength to compensate for his size. However, Konragen had recently traded his battle wounds for a Healer's haziness. The spell had left him with a foggy head and weak biceps. He would urge forward through the waves in a spurt, go limp and sink down as if suddenly sleepy, then streak back to the surface. It was a cry for help which cleared his head.

When he jumped in the river, Brisk didn't jump as far as the others, and with good reason. That reason was why he lived in a city with a floor beneath his feet. There was a reason he cooked seafood instead of catching it. Being in water was a perversion, an unnatural state. It stripped people of all their senses. You can't see underwater, can't hear, can't function, and certainly can't breathe.

The first time Brisk got dunked by a wave, he resisted crying out. He suppressed childhood memories of a riverside picnic when he paddled out, got caught in a whirlpool and was flung away from his family. He silently insisted that his new shield was sagging his progress. He was busy hacking and sputtering and wiping his eyes when the second wave dunked him. Once he surfaced, he wailed.

It was as if a chord of transference struck across the water. Brisk accepted his watery demise, the fight drained from his arms and legs, and he sank below the surface with a hideous gulp of salty mossy water. At the pitiful sound of the Cook sinking, Konragen's focus and spirit soared suddenly high. Konragen rattled his head, pivoted around, and streamed back towards the island. Spurned with a chomping kick, the dragonman dove, snagged Brisk beneath his arms, and hauled him up with a misting burst. Konragen slung the Cook securely across his shoulders and swam after the others.

Konragen was back to life! Energy ran through his limbs, his eyes were unclouded, the water was a refreshment. While he swam, he was tossed back to the glorious day when he crossed Grayboulder river in the Log-Drag River-Race. The four years between this moment and that event were an easy bridge to cross. His arms latched around the trunk of a tree, the waves undulating playfully, people cheering and waving from the shore. Bofork behind him, Rivercrest before him. Konragen finished in second place by a hand's length and was still many paces ahead of the third place finisher.

Caught in the trance of physical exertion, Konragen thought of what the Druid woman had told him. Her man Alkent had not only swam the river race—*he won it*. Konragen considered Alkent one of his clan. His new clan. These people in the river with him—right now, in a contest of death and life. He felt a feverish desire to preserve them and protect them. He'd never felt at home in the dragonfolk slums. Though he was supposed to have been among equals there, they always reminded him of his sinful crime of arriving in town four years ago and not being a lifelong resident. No, no, these people—those in the Chase Quest with him—they were all he had. All he had to fight for.

Konragen—with Brisk on his back—caught up to Ramsey in the river. The green elf was thrashing and sputtering and clinging to his Sorcerer's staff as if it were a life raft. With a burst of self-assurance, Konragen plucked the elf by the collar of his robe and hoisted him onto his back to join the Cook. This, Konragen instantly learned, as he sank and choked, was a foolish over-step.

After getting his face engulfed with water, Ramsey sensed something was wrong and peeled away to fend for himself and swim for himself. Brisk remained on the horse and the three swam on.

Up ahead, a squid's tentacle snared hold of Griffey's ankle and drug him underwater. For a long, horrid moment, Griffey couldn't see and writhed as a fish does on the shore. Without thinking, he drew his sword and dove. With a blind yet mighty hack, he cleaved the interloper from his leg and sprang back to the surface. With the shake of a dog, Griffey swam on, sword still out, and peered ahead.

In the moonlight, he saw the back of Ulkar's head and shoulders as the borlog streamed towards the shore. Beyond Ulkar, off deep to the right, there loomed the shell of the squid-pirate ship. He marked Marynda's shark fin tearing for the ship.

Griffey despaired. There was no way to win. Despite how rapidly it passed in reality, that moment hung around for a long time, and Griffey sensed it would torture him for a long time after. He could choose the righteous path and follow Marynda to save her daughter. Or he could go after Ulkar. And the Warlock beyond that.

If Marynda failed to rescue her daughter, Griffey would be

haunted forever by the knowledge that he could've helped. His assistance and his sword could save Hazel from slavery. And if Marynda *did* succeed, then Griffey could be right there when it happened. A comforting presence at that crucial reunion. In that embrace, he would prove himself as something more than Marynda's friend, and more of a father than a protector to Hazel. Simply *being there* would make all the difference.

If he followed Ulkar, he might be able to disrupt a union of a darker kind. Griffey knew for certain that having Ulkar reach the Warlock first would be disastrous. If that were to happen, he would lose his grip on being able to alter events. That sensation of losing his grip had started back on the island. When he'd seen that Ulkar had gained his eyes back. That was impossible, unless Ulkar was somehow merged with dark magic. Which meant that Ulkar might now be whole enough to join forces with the Warlock. Griffey would never survive a showdown against that united pair of villains. Another possibility was that Ulkar might destroy the Warlock. Might catch the assassin with his guard down, during a meditative trance or something. If that happened, the question burning in the furnace of Griffey's heart would go eternally unanswered. *Why was my father killed?*

Griffey swam after the borlog. Committed to it fully. There was no other way. He would never catch his quarry if he was worrying about something else he could be doing. He had to trust that Marynda would handle her business and Hazel would find her own outlet of resolve to free herself.

Only a short time later, Griffey was doubting his choice. He saw Ulkar disappear. At one moment, the borlog was creeping through the water. The next moment, the shape of his body melted away as if he were feathers and the tide were a breeze. (Griffey wasn't looking at the squid-pirate ship and Marynda's shark fin, but both of those vanished, as well.) With a yelp of defiance, Griffey charged towards Ulkar's last vantage. The water grew cold, as if he'd breached a glacier melt.

Griffey was whipped away with the strength of an insurmountable tide. He imagined flipping up and out of the water then crashing back down, and that may have actually happened. His world spun out in a whirl that stretched like a blanket and then folded him into it. When that blanket opened, it spilled him onto the beach, retching. Griffey sensed a rapid movement of time.

At first, he thought it was a hallucination resulting from his recent sickness. But it didn't let up. The cycle of sunrises and sunsets rushed past, as if hurrying to resolve business elsewhere. As the days bled by, Griffey knew there were things he needed to do, goals he needed to accomplish, but he could never focus all the way through. He would set out to do something simple, such as yelling for Konragen and Ramsey and Brisk. But his own voice seemed to leave his lips and spread across the horizon. He would try to stare at the opposite shore, or the *Castling* island with the skulls around it, but the landscapes drew across his eyes with unending visual detail. When he grew hungry, Griffey managed to focus intently enough to shoot fish with his crossbow. The act of hunting, for some primal reason, increased his awareness, but that focus would flutter away as soon as the catch was made. Catch. Yes, the catch. He needed to catch someone.

He needed to catch the Warlock. And Ulkar, as well.

When his eyes tried to find the castle, standing tall against the bright blue sky, he could only see a scrape of its outline and color. Trying to get up there, he hiked around to the side, found a field of sharp boulders and a forest next to that. From the depths of the forest, there boomed the horrifying echo of a roaring bear. The dominance of those roars did not let up, day or night, and Griffey turned back.

By the time Griffey strode up and stood at the base of the giant pine, he'd lost all desire to keep track of the days. The pattern of sunrise and nightfall passed as if each episode equated to empty hours.

Despite the fleeting nature of his thoughts, Griffey recalled his time on the River Guard. Keeping things at bay in a group like that was impossible. Rumor stabbed through any shield. Rumors persisted that the squid-pirates could be killed but their ship could never be captured. No matter how many times the pirates attacked the docks of Rivercrest castle, no matter how many harpoons and catapults the River Guard launched, and no matter how many times the navy pursued the ruffians, their ship was never seized. This was because the water around their ship was deranged. Water was scooped from the wake of a departing pirate raid and the cup was brought to scholarly examiners. All of the examiners ended up disappearing. Some didn't return for a year, others for five, and some ended up gone forever. At least that's what the rumors said. Standing there, staring at the pine, watching the sun race across the sky then rise again after the barest blink of darkness, Griffey was inclined to believe all of it was true.

In Griffey's first attempt to climb the pine, he ascended five levels of branches, which brought him some distance high. Then he slipped. After lurching and bouncing off thick tree arms, he grabbed hold of the final one available. He dangled, dropped, and got the wind battered from his lungs. Then, he sat in the sand for a long, dreadful stretch. On his second try, he made it just as far—only, this time, he happened to look up and see somebody. It was Ulkar. Ten levels above him, also climbing towards the top. Ulkar peered down at him and sneered. Griffey looked into his old adversary's eyes—black with glittering gold—and recognized those eyes. Then, Griffey slipped again. Pretty much the same result happened—he hung from a low branch, then fell, and was lucky not to break any bones.

When he awoke, Griffey saw the dual moons in a sky of velvet blackness skittered with starlight. This was the first time he remembered seeing the moons since he first swam through the cold water in the river. He even heard the hoots of owls, roosted in the giant pine. Time was slow enough for him to hear the owls. He sat up on his elbows, twisted around, and was flooded with relief.

Griffey saw his friends paddling to the shore. Ramsey with his staff. Konragen with Brisk on his back. At first, Griffey was wobbly on his feet, but he dashed over and helped each of his three friends to their feet and gave them hugs. "Where have you been? Where's Marynda? Hazel?"

"Parker..." Brisk sputtered, wiping his face, rubbing his arms, "...we just swam from the island to the shore. The trip was so Frishkadammed long, that we all got hungry. Ramsey used his Sorcery to catch fish and fry them for us. Day and night bled together, and onward we swam. We swam so much, I don't think I'm afraid of the water anymore. It went by fast, but it felt like a year to get here..."

From above them, lost in the expanses of the giant pine tree, Ulkar's evil laughter tore out...

◇ CHAPTER THE FIFTY-SIXTH. ◇
◇Beckoning Death.◇

Griffey bounded up the tree. He now had a practiced familiarity with this climb, and he flew up the branches with ease. The strongest, most convenient branch on the lowest level was at four on the clockface, then a path resembling a ladder rose up-to-the-left from there. Griffey felt a thrilling urgency to stop Ulkar from getting to the Warlock and he blocked out everything else. He was not that far into his climb when he stopped.

Through the screen-maze of branches and pine needles, Griffey caught sight of his friends, still on the beach, watching his progress. As had been the case earlier, he was face with two conflicting choices. One, to get past his previous high point and then try to stop both Ulkar and the Warlock on his own. Two, descend to gain the needed support of his friends, and then lead them up the unforgiving tree.

It was Ramsey the Green who resolved all his conflicts with a few shouted words.

"Go, Parker! Catch the scoundrels! We're with you! Right behind you!"

Griffey was incapable of speech. He gulped and gave a nod in response. All he could do was hope his friends saw that nod. Then, with a twist, Griffey sprang to the next branch. A split-Y up-to-the-right. From there, a gnarled thatch of branches thick enough to hold him. He pulled himself up, taking care not to disturb a bird's nest where his right hand slotted in. Balanced with his boots upon a branch, he leaped a four-foot clearing—his feet landing shaky yet safely, arms wrapped on a chest-level bar.

Griffey squirmed up a few notches more, his efforts met with a sharp jab to the forearm and a scratch to the face. He reached the spot of his previous failures.

This was a crossroads with no other options. Around to his right and left, Griffey saw nothing but the trunk's smooth curve, rippling bark with occasional knots. There were no other branches to bail him out, and only one bar overhead. The gravity of his predicament became real. Griffey felt the allure of a fall, hands growing sweaty, legs going weak. The world expanded from a simple branch-to-branch climb to one of beckoning death.

Griffey jumped high. He grabbed hold. Slipped. Eyes wide, he fell. Feet kicking nothing…

◇ ◇ ◇

"No more water!" Brisk trumpeted with a clap of his hands. "I can tree-climb all night!"

"Brisk has got the right idea," Ramsey said. "We need to get up there."

"Konragen no problem swimming, but…" The dragonman's speech faded into a cave and his feet remained rooted where they were. Even as Brisk and Ramsey hustled to the tree, trying to see in the dark where Griffey had climbed, Konragen hung back in the shadows, hesitant and upset.

Konragen had no doubt that Brisk's assessment was correct—they'd literally just been trapped swimming in a river for an entire year. Yet, despite the implications of that, Konragen wasn't tired. His blood was still running with exhilaration, and he actually wished there was more swimming to be done. Konragen would have gladly swam with a person on his back for another year rather than climb this tree.

"Konragen," Brisk called over his shoulder, "either get to talkin' or get to climbin'."

"Konragen not want to climb tree," the dragon blurted. "Tree is hundred feet high!"

"Think of your ancestors," Ramsey exclaimed. "They

soared higher than that on their wings!"

"With wings, no need to climb anything!"

Brisk and Konragen finally gave up scouting for convenient branches and ran to Konragen.

"Ramsey," Brisk huffed, "you're gonna have to levitate him or something. Now, let's go."

"If I'm concentrating on levitating him, then I'm not concentrating on climbing."

"Acho, so, you stay down here, float Konragen all the way to the top, then you climb up."

Ramsey shook his head. "It doesn't work that way. I need to keep close or else the spell breaks."

"Ramsey the Green," Konragen said, commanding attention. "How much do you weigh?"

While Ramsey looked confused, Brisk's eyes got wide with realization.

"He's right," Brisk wheezed. "The elf is feather light. I'm gonna have to carry him."

"What? Car—no, no way," Ramsey objected.

There was no time to address the elf's complaints. Konragen unstrapped the rope from around his shoulders. *The rope is wet*, Ramsey thought, too shackled with anxiety to speak. *No matter how tight you tie it, I'm gonna slip out!* Ramsey closed his eyes, forced his mouth shut. Brisk strapped his shield to his back, then stood back-to-back with Ramsey. Konragen tossed the rope around them and began blending furious knots. Both Brisk and Ramsey wheezed when the final knot rocked home.

The dragonman stepped back and spread his arms, wide and inviting. Ramsey knew that the urgency overrode his own reservations and obliged by aiming his staff at Konragen's chest. There were definite flashbacks of the time—so very recently—when Ramsey pointed his deadly staff at Griffey. Ramsey felt shame and remorse. *I just traveled through time but I still can't change the past.* At that moment, more laughter from Kozard (in

Ulkar's body) rattled out from up above. It was that direction where Ramsey's future resided. And that was all that mattered now.

If Konragen held any concerns about being betrayed and murdered, he did not outwardly show them. That display of trust from his dragon friend helped embolden Ramsey. But first, he needed assurances. He turned his head and was reminded of how awkwardly close Brisk was to him now.

"Brisk. Listen. Will you be able to climb this thing in the dar—"

"—Get the dragon levitated so we can get moving."

All Ramsey needed was the Cook's iron tone of voice. Ramsey twitched his staff and hit Konragen with a buoyant invisible bubble which froze him as he stood. All the way up, Konragen would be struck motionless, his clear outer coating batting aside limbs and sizzling pine needles.

Brisk leaped and grabbed the starting branch, felt the weight on his back begin to heave his balance, but he recovered and drove upward. Brisk accepted the weight as a challenge. He'd backed down from too many challenges in his life and it was about time to accept one. He climbed on. Dipping through gaps, springing up splits, firing through forks, ascending with gumption, Brisk climbed on.

Ramsey felt the waterfall of branches try to spill the staff from his hands, but learned fast to play the game. He talked to Brisk as little as possible, kept his eyes locked on Konragen. Making good progress, Konragen simply floated along for the ride, and Ramsey occasionally lost sight of him in the wash.

To reach the next limb, Brisk had to lean uncomfortably far to his left. Whether he was feather-light or not, Ramsey's body tilted, as well. That's when the elf slipped from the wet rope around him. Ramsey cried out as he fell. Before he dropped away, Ramsey managed to snag the crook of his right arm in the rope. This extreme shift pulled Brisk harshly off course and he loosed a cry of his own.

Together they plummeted. Screams were ripped from their throats. Air rushed past them and then the barrage began. Fists of pine needles slashed their faces and tore their clothes as they thrashed and wailed in freefall. Brisk snared a sturdy branch, then caught Ramsey's arm. They hung breathless.

The spell of *Levitation* broke and Konragen dropped right along with them, only he was on the outskirts of the giant pine and the only things to grab onto were flimsy twigs. With a blind snag, Konragen gripped a flexible limb which didn't snap and actually swung him inward, towards the trunk.

There wasn't much time for ragged breathing; no one was comfortable enough for that.

"Konragen!" Brisk hollered out. "If you survived, if you're still in the tree, then you've gotta start climbing on your own!" Brisk heaved Ramsey over to relative safety, then pulled himself up. Konragen called out a confirmation which was more of an angry snarl, but little attention was paid to it.

Separated now, the three adventurers rightfully should've felt defeated. But the sudden isolation actually made them focus. The collapse of support enhanced their survival instincts.

Brisk, now unburdened with weights and pressures, wove his way up with ribbon fluidity.

Ramsey the Green found climbing with his staff to be unbelievably cumbersome, but he soon secured it to a rope on his back. The elf's lightweight framework empowered an agile ascension.

At the back end, Konragen forced himself to concentrate. The dragonman didn't care for climbing trees (especially not the tall ones), but he reduced the exercise to one-branch-at-a-time.

Not long later, the trio completed the circuit. The top was the region where the pine arms grew feeble and barren, yet the generous ledge of a cliff offered some hope to hop to. Their arrivals were staggered, but they waited (impatiently, for sure, yet they still waited) for each other.

Standing upon the firm assurance of grass and rock and dirt, they stared up at the stone blanket of a castle wall. There were three large entrances available. Drawn naturally to the middle one, they inspected it first. Same as its mates, this door was burgundy red, built of oaken planks, with wrought iron window grills. It was both promising and present, so they tried to shove at it. Their fingers couldn't get close enough to push it open; got stopped a few inches from its surface. An invisible barrier repelled their every advance and also resisted Ramsey's (admittedly limited) arsenal of spells. The sensation reminded Brisk of a pan of obdurate dough. It was curiously warm to the touch.

They headed for the option to the left. They found they could touch this one, but it was locked. Ramsey dealt a pair of *Fire Bolts* to the hinges on the left, then one to the lock. After Konragen kicked the door down and they stepped inside, the crumpled remains of the shattered door actually crinkled to life. In the fashion of a mangled rag smoothing itself flat, the door knitted back together with a series of awful creaks. Then, the reformed plank rose from the floor with a rumble and filled the frame with a slam. Outside, an invisible barrier sealed that one off, too.

In mid-air—at the last second before falling away and cracking his spine upon some unforgiving obstruction—Griffey drew his sword and stabbed it deep into the tree. Hanging from the handle, he clambered up, then reached down to retrieve the blade. As he ranged vertical, Griffey found climbing at night to be quite the challenge, but the his renewed desire sent him upward.

Griffey hit the upper region of sparse branches and jumped out. His boots hit the ground and he ran for the castle. The distance was short, yet his body was numb with strain, legs and forearms burning from exertion in the tree.

Griffey approached the middle door of the three. After hacking at the lock, Griffey shoved the gate open and entered. Behind him, the door flapped shut once again. Crawling up the exterior of the door, there rose a see-through mold which was still warm by the time Brisk, Ramsey, and Konragen got there.

◇ CHAPTER THE FIFTY-SEVENTH. ◇
◇Reunion.◇

Fresh off her slumber, belly filled with rabbits and squirrels, with tattered clothing fashioned from forest detritus, Marynda shambled up the beach. She felt hot tears threatening to gush down her cheeks, leaving tracks on her muddy face, making her eyes red and her vision blurry.

She didn't know how much time had passed, but she was certain with the bitter finality of a dungeon grate slamming shut, that she'd been out of it for a long time. Emotionally distraught by the loss of her daughter, Marynda had laid waste to an entire forest.

It was the sight of the giant pine that brought her back around. The pine which stretched all the way from the riverbank up to brush the feet of the castle. By now the sun was gone and the big tree was aglow in the double moonlight. She battled back the tears and her vision was sharp. Marynda spotted movement. The shape of a falcon swooping in to roost on the lower branches of the wooden behemoth.

Marynda started running. Her legs were wobbly and her balance was haggard and her breath was a series of pale shrieks. Her calves were aflame, the leafy clothing felt flappy and ridiculous upon her hips and breasts. Her legs groaned as if she were running downhill after descending a mountain. She was a flail of exhaustion. Every step was an invitation to smack her cheek on a rock.

She didn't want to run. Didn't feel like running ever again. It brought back alarming memories of her time as a bear. The shredding of defenseless creatures when she didn't even need to feed. The destruction of animals' homes, just because she was too enraged to recall her own home. That's what running reminded her of. Yet she ran. Ran so she could get there.

To the bird. The bird in the tree.

On some distant, foggy level, Marynda recognized the brutal irony of this moment. She was running—in human form—to go greet a bird. She knew she was doomed to startle the Frishkadammed thing as soon as she showed up, sending it fluttering up through the pine. That result would be a blatant waste of her effort in running over there. It would be frustrating, especially given that Marynda could become a falcon and avoid scaring it away. Yet, still, she was proud to be human again. She felt more in control. The feeling was a remembrance of her beloved Alkent. She didn't want to use her Druid powers ever again. Because she knew Alkent didn't trust those Druid powers.

Marynda grunted to a wheezing, staggering halt within the hollow chamber around the base of the tree trunk. She forced herself to stand tall and she was rewarded for it. The bird had not fled. In fact, it seemed to be awaiting her arrival. She saw Alkent's daughter up there on that branch, staring down with falcon's eyes. This was Marynda's daughter, too. But something was different now.

Marynda had never seen Hazel in animal form, yet she could sense—was, in fact, overwhelmed by—the mastery of her daughter's falcon aura. It was a throbbing sisterhood recognition which thudded in every Druid's heart. Yet her intuition quietly insisted that there wasn't any Frishkadammed *mastery* on display here. Rather, Hazel's intimidating stare was governed by anger. Furious anger. She was a rumbling mountain. It put Marynda on edge, thinking about all that boiling anger.

"Hazel…" Marynda coughed out, feeling both worried and elated.

Hazel said nothing for a long moment. She only looked

down at her mother.

Then Hazel's beak snapped and her voice spoke with intensity. "Where were you, mother? I felt so alone and abandoned…"

"I thought I lost you," Marynda gasped. "I lost your trail."

Hazel reflected, and said, "My time with the pirates was hard, but it allowed me to think. To think of our lost time together and what I have missed not growing up with you."

Marynda's heart ached for her child. She looked at Hazel and said, "I am also saddened by that missed time, but proud of the woman you have become. And I am also proud of the Druid you have become."

Hazel gave a look of understanding which only Druid's would recognize.

"I love you," said Marynda.

"I love you, as well, mother," replied Hazel.

They both looked up to the castle and Hazel said, "I know a year has passed since the night we *Cast* onto that island. What I *don't* know is what's really in that castle up there. I don't know what happened to our friends. If they ever made it…" Her wings ruffled and her beak snapped. "Mother, I have work to do."

Hazel flew away and disappeared in the pine needles, leaving Marynda down there alone, staring up after her daughter.

◇ CHAPTER THE FIFTY-EIGHTH. ◇
◇Ominous Chasm.◇

Griffey was barely inside the castle when he met the first death trap.

After the door slammed shut behind him, Griffey's energy seemed to drain. He reminded himself that he had once again barged into a dangerous situation… alone. His sword grew heavy in his hand. *I should have waited for the others to join me. If I face down the Frishkadammed Warlock on my own, I'm dead.*

Now that he had steadied himself and was thinking clearly, he understood another thing. The prospect that he was not only too late but he was also in the wrong place. Griffey agreed with Brisk—a full year had probably passed since they landed on the *Casting* island. If that were true, then Griffey's mad dash up the tree and into this castle was certifiably stupid. If the Warlock ever actually lived here or operated here, a year was plenty of time for him to escape. This thought spawned an offshoot which was just as depressing. Griffey recalled Java, the farmer woman north of Benson village, mentioning a Warlock colony in the mountains. *She never said anything about a castle by a river. But what if she was wrong?*

"None of that matters," Griffey assured himself, trying to shake the insecurity. He just needed to be more careful from here onward. "Ulkar is in here. *That's* what matters."

Griffey was stymied, however, as he found no visible tracks.

With a cautious pace, the Ranger advanced through a hallway with fat stone blocks in the walls and an arched ceiling. He passed glowing torches, mounted on the walls every ten feet, alternating on his left side and right side. Though these flames were spread out, they gave enough light to detail the floor. Ulkar had just swam a river, climbed a massive tree, then ran through dirt to enter the castle—he should have left traces of his passing.

As he deemed no assailants about, Griffey bent over and studied the floor while he walked. His eyes swept the offset-block-pattern, searching for a lump of mud clinging to the crack outline of a brick. Or a splinter of tree bark jutting from a pillow of shadows. Or a shred of fabric, caught in the firelight, still wet and reeking of river water. Even a footprint would have been nice.

Wherever they roamed, borlogs shed a fetid stench, and not even that lay upon the air.

As his current methodology was proving fruitless, he quit inspecting the floor and walked upright. He tried to keep his guard up. He tried not to be bothered and disappointed by losing Ulkar.

He even thought about turning back, trying to find his friends. But he wasn't ready to give up.

When he'd walked the hall for some time, with the scenery remaining monotonous and unchanging, he started to get wary. The sweat upon his neck and forehead brought him to again consider that a year had passed and there was nothing to find.

Then he spotted something. His breath caught in his throat, a shred of fabric flung in a gust, snared upon a spiky tree branch. Seven feet ahead, a familiar shape lay upon the tile, framed in an orange block of wavering torch-light. It was the black cone of a Zodak claw.

The same claw Konragen chopped from the giant iguana in Shadowbranch forest. The same hunk of armor with a hook that Griffey used to win an archery contest in Benson village. This was it.

The last time he'd seen the Zodak claw was in Benson village during the archery contest. When the Warlock had attacked, Griffey flung the claw and impaled the Warlock in the shoulder. Then, the Warlock had escaped and *Cast* away to safety. All the way to this castle.

Griffey's increasing heartbeat confirmed this reality. The Warlock had walked this very hallway, stepped on these very stones. The blanket of dust upon the shell made it conceivable that the Zodak claw had been discarded and left here for a year. Griffey walked over, reunited with his past, picked it up, dusted it off. He had no way to carry it but to slip it on his left forearm. He moved on.

His left boot crunched down upon something. It wasn't an object that didn't belong there. Rather, he'd stepped on a stone tile which sank beneath his weight. A dark liquid seeped out from the edges of the square and filled it like a bowl. Griffey retracted his boot with reflexive disgust and that's when he saw the crimson tint of the liquid. Even more alarming than that—the blood didn't quit rising once it filled the dropped tile. It seeped and spread across the floor with serpent quickness.

Griffey didn't intend to stick around and gawk at the flood; he dashed ahead. Then, as if in validation of his decision to run, the ceiling began to fall. The cave-in started twenty feet back—sealing off his escape—and the collapse moved with violent fever. With thundering destruction in hot pursuit, Griffey ran. His boots slid in the blood and his shoulder rammed the wall.

As a mushroom blob of dust shuddered up around him, choking his throat and stinging his eyes, Griffey spotted hope ahead. The timing was so fortuitous, he instantly distrusted it. Cursed it as an enchantment. But he had no other options.

It was a door. An arched passageway, carved into the stone twenty feet ahead on his right. No torch flickered inside, which meant the gap was hiding in the shadows until he got close enough. Still, it was foolish to think the falling ceiling might not kill him just because he entered a doorway.

Slick upon the blood, Griffey's boots betrayed him. Nearly paralyzed with a horrible whip of vertigo, Griffey pitched forward and fell. The Zodak claw moved naturally into position but did little to cushion his chin. He was lucky to keep hold of his sword. His knees and elbows smacked off the tile. The encroaching storm did not wait for him to gather himself and rise to his feet again. Chunks of discharged mortar popped against the backs of his legs, providing mighty insistence that he get moving. Griffey shot to his feet with no time to spare and ran. His boots slid again—but this time he took advantage of it and swung right into his target.

With a sweep inside the doorway, he flopped down and covered his head. An ugly moment of clenched teeth and crippling terror ensued. The thunder roared out in the hallway but nothing crushed him in here. The falling debris, however, did spray a mist of blood in from the corridor. A few seconds after the ceiling was done falling down and silence crept back in, Griffey was still too shaken to climb to his feet just yet. Then the wetness began to creep up his pantlegs to his stomach to his chest. An offshoot from the rising river of blood. That got him moving.

It was totally dark in here and he was lucky to see the cliff before he ran over it.

Grinding to a halt—boot-tips hissing over the edge— Griffey paddled his arms for balance and staggered back a few feet. It took a few moments for his eyes to adjust, but a flashing blue lightning helped the process. Griffey stared out across a wide cavern with a ceiling so high he couldn't see it. Off to his left and right, the walls swung out in a wide sloping curve—matching the round graduation of the castle's central tower. The blue flashing lightning was too bright and too dramatic for his eyes to focus on just yet, so he inspected his more immediate environs. He stood upon a ledge which wrapped around in a broad circle, right along with the castle walls. From what he could see, the drop-off fell at least fifty feet and the bottom of the ominous chasm was obscured with a sheet of thick black shadow.

Along the ledge to his right, Griffey spotted a pair of posts end-capping a wooden suspension bridge, hanging and swaying across the canyon. He hustled over to it and that's when he gagged so bad he nearly tripped. This entire chamber was filled with stale, fusty air and it had taken a few seconds to punch him in the face.

The bridge was simple, built of planks and rope, with maintenance assuredly neglected for the past few decades. The drooping runway featured a single support rope on each shoulder of its frame. These single ropes didn't offer much to grab onto, but he grabbed on anyway.

Allured by the source of the blue lightning, Griffey eased out onto the rickety bridge. He felt the wood creak beneath his weight and imagined the pad of a potato struggling to support him without getting squashed. With a rush of alarm he heard a trickle as the flowing blood reached this chamber and scrabbled across the ledge behind him. The crimson liquid actually dribbled out onto the bridge next to his boots, teetering along the bristles of the ropes, spilling out across the boards. He got moving.

Griffey's path across this delicate, drooping bridge would dip him down into the shadowy marsh which coated the nadir. On the far side of the cavern, the bridge reappeared from the darkness and rose to meet another arched doorway carved into a wall over there. Inside that doorway was the source of the blue-purple lightning. A single word entered his thoughts: *Warlock.*

Not long later, he cursed himself for his naivete.

Finally approaching his prey was never going to be an easy task.

Strolling into the final showdown was never going to happen without sacrifice...

◇ CHAPTER THE FIFTY-NINTH. ◇
◇Sacrificial Descent.◇

Suddenly, Griffey saw a spectacular strata of golden clouds. An astral plane with the texture of fluff sprawling out to kiss a bright sunny horizon. Gone was the gloom of the cavernous interior of the castle, and gone was the uneasy bridge holding his life aloft. Also gone… was his body. Gone were his boots, balanced on the bridge. Gone was his left hand, pocketed inside the Zodak claw, and gone was his right hand, gripping the support rope. Only his mind remained.

Imprisoned with wonder, Griffey felt the sublime *extraction* of his conscious mind. Griffey wasn't even sure what earthly definition could fit the mystical concept of a *conscious mind*, but he nonetheless felt swept away. Freed from physical restraints, he elevated across an impossible vastness of earth and knowledge. Mountains and legends, oceans and fables. Humbling to a breathtaking degree.

He pitched abruptly off-course and tumbled into a pocket hidden within the bright sunlit air. It was a dark cushy sanctuary, backlit with a wash of red, connected to others of the same through a web of tunnels. *This is a meditation chamber.* The thought was planted in his mind. By a familiar voice.

"Griffey…? Oh dear Frishka… Griffey, is that you?"

He hesitated. He was accustomed to speaking with his mouth, but such a contraption was no longer in his employ. "Sho'pa…?" he managed to say. "I recognize your voice. But I can't see you?"

"Where we are, we're not people anymore. We can't be seen," his sister explained, in her typical matter-of-fact tone. "I told you about this place, long ago. This is something the Monks call meditation space. It's where the Super Monks spend most of their years. Transcended from their bodies."

There they were, brother and sister, reunited at last. Disembodied voices conversing.

Griffey was so overwhelmed—by this and all leading up to this—he was numb to the shock.

"Uh…" Griffey stammered. "Is it safe here? Are you acho? Where's mother? Is mother safe?"

"Yes to all your questions—for the most part. For now." Sho'pa didn't let this shaky answer linger long. "I've been searching for you, brother, ever since we spoke over the Grulva coins."

"That night we spoke of King Callister… That was a year ago…"

Griffey felt a stab of shame. No longer shielded by the impulses of his physical body, he felt clearer. A full year had passed, but he'd never considered the effects beyond himself. On his home, on his family. As if he'd expected everything to remain bottled dutifully in a jar, unchanged and waiting to interact with him. And there was even more shame than that. The last time they'd spoke, Sho'pa had risked her life to help him and he'd been too preoccupied to spare much concern for her.

"Mother escaped the castle, just in time. She's been living in seclusion. No one will find her."

"Seclusion?" Griffey strained. "Sho'pa… how am I here right now? How are we speaking right now? How did I get here? I'm not a Monk, I don't belong here…"

"You won't be staying for long, I will see to that. You'll get trapped if you stay too long."

"Uh…"

"It's the Warlock. He made a pact with a powerful being, and that benefactor has established a channel of dark magic down into the heart of this castle. That dark magic is keeping the Warlock alive, feeding him, while he's worked, without rest, for the past year on building this machine. Areas of high magic—especially sustained over a long period of time—attract meditation space. Meditation space actually moves to encircle places like that. Where meditation space is thick and concentrated, it's easily accessed. Just by walking into that cavern, you were able to breach this plane and find me."

Griffey's head hurt. He didn't understand how he—a modest Ranger from a modest kingdom—could possibly enter the realm of the Super Monks. "Anyone can enter meditation space," Sho'pa explained, as if reading his mind, "but it takes years of training to reside here and avoid detection."

Griffey was still befuddled. He forced himself to move on. To finally admit some of his personal shame. "Last time we spoke, I could tell you were scared, and that was my fault... I..."

Sho'pa spoke in a voice so bland it was scary. "That night we spoke through the Grulva coins, I broke monastery rules... You didn't care when I told you that. Breaking rules never bothered you.

"You asked me to go back a few days to spy on Ulkar and the First King. To do that, I had to break into a special realm of meditation space. And I left a trace there. It... it marked me..." Her voice cracked. "I made those choices to help *you*, Griffey, and it was my doom..."

"Frishka..." Griffey wheezed. "I'm sorry. I didn't know. What... what happened to you?"

"I lost my body, that's what happened," Sho'pa coldly replied. "I am now no more than my conscious mind. And I am forever trapped in meditation space. Chained to a world where no chains exist. I will forever flee my Super Monk masters, who seek to destroy me for betraying the convent."

"I'm sure it's not *all* bad," Griffey rebounded. "And you're *not* trapped here. I will get you out."

She paused. Then, when she spoke, Griffey felt idiotic. "I am an entity of the boundless mind. I have accessed unparalleled knowledge from the universe. But, I lost my body to get here. I wasn't just a Monk. I insisted on cross-training as a Warrior Monk because the physicality of that lifestyle filled me with confidence. I thrive on meditation, but it's only half of who I really am. I've been reduced."

If Griffey had shoulders to sag, they would've sagged right now. "I will get you out. Oh sister, I promise, I will get you out of here..." Griffey trailed off, cursing how hollow his assurances sounded.

Up here, hovering in the clouds, freed from all physical tethers, an honest evaluation finally clicked into Griffey's mind. In that moment, he was no longer bloodthirsty for catching his father's assassin. There was no more drive for constant movement; his appetite for persistent progression was just as gone as his physical body. All that remained was cold, measured analysis. With a hint of hope.

"Sho'pa... we've lost our family. I see that now. Father was killed by the Warlock. Mother was taken from our home, fleeing whatever happened there. You've gotten stuck in the otherworldly clouds. I've been absorbed with chasing vengeance... Yet I don't think all of those fates are permanent..."

"You have a new family now, brother," Sho'pa told him. "The friends you've bonded with in pursuit of father's killer. That's your family now. Our family was sacrificed for you to get to this point."

"I didn't ask for any of this, and I will fix it if I can..." Griffey realized he was flirting with fantasy once again. With that, he reverted. "Tell me about mother. Tell me about the Warlock..."

"We've stayed here too long," Sho'pa said sharply. "Not only do I sense the Super Monks closing in on my position, but I think if you stay much longer you'll get trapped in meditation space."

Before Griffey could protest, Sho'pa pressed on: "Get

across the bridge. Get to the chamber at the heart of the castle. You will find the Warlock there. Before you enter the chamber, we will reconvene and I will tell you what I know. You will have your answers on the other side."

Griffey was subjected once again to that perplexing sensation of *extraction*—only this time he was removed from the current moment, suspended in the heavens, chatting with his invisible sister.

As if he'd never left, Griffey's nostrils once again picked up the stale, grimy cavern air. His left hand in the Zodak claw, his right hand on the flimsy rope railing. The soles of his boots planted upon the frail planks of the suspension bridge. Ahead, the signature blue lightning of the Warlock's operations flashed once again, too sudden and too bright for Griffey's eyes, and he looked down. He saw blood. The flow from the collapsed castle hallway had slunk all the way in here. He saw streams of the sickly red liquid dancing across the suspension cables on each edge of the bridge. The blood was not only surfing along the ribbed surfaces of the ropes, but staining each of the boards.

Disturbingly, he could hear the drip-drip of blood falling off this rope bridge. It was the only sound in here, echoing across the wide silent graveyard. Griffey wasn't quite sure why he would label this place a graveyard, yet he felt confident in the description. After his meeting with Sho'pa, he felt he belonged in such a place. Clinging to memories of that talk, as if awakening from a dream and desperately reviewing it, he uncovered scant optimism. *My family is destroyed. Sho'pa is a prisoner.*

Griffey thought of what else his sister had told him. How his companions on the Chase Quest were, in fact, his new family. He was overjoyed by that, elated with the comfort and reliability of friendship. Yet he was also filled with sorrow for his namesake family and its untimely demise.

It was too much to think about. He would fall off this bridge if he thought about it any more—

—his right boot met a slick of blood on a plank and his balance flung backwards. His momentum obliterated two cross-boards, which cracked with bursts of dust. For an ugly instant, his stomach fell away and his breath froze into ice crystals as it was expelled from his lungs up the tube of his throat. Only the grip of his right hand on the support rope saved his life.

For a moment, Griffey hung in that awkward position—upper back on the bridge, his hips and rear hanging down in the broken gap, legs and boots fighting for purchase. It was when he felt the tickle of blood seeping down his shirt collar to lick the back of his neck that he shot to his feet with a shiver.

Griffey moved forward cautiously—board to board, section to section, one grip of the rope to the next—all the while praying for the rope bridge's continued stability. His meticulous, unhurried approach to the crossing of this bridge stemmed not only from his fear of crunching through another plank or slipping on the blood again but rather a palpable hold-over from his meeting with Sho'pa in meditation space. After rushing impetuously into so many dangerous situations in his life—that always seemed like the most constructive option—he now moved without a rush, with only a calm precision.

He traversed the sagging bridge. Soon, he approached the circuit's lowest point. The toes of his boots breached the thick black shadow that coated the floor of the cavern. The shadow dissipated with an ominous hissing whistle. In a gradual wash, a layer of green soupy fog spread out from his position, dispelling and replacing the black shadows. Griffey could tell he was close to the floor and was no longer afraid of falling yet there was plenty to fear about the floor itself. The trail of blood tracking along the bridge's suspension ropes was audible as it dribbled to the floor. As the droplets landed, they emitted a soft whispering *pat-pat* sound which made Griffey imagine a fat carpet of pasty bone dust.

The reek of a dead bird in a rotten cheese cellar pricked

his nose. Cold sweat rippled his skin.

He stepped forward with his accustomed slightness and his right foot bashed clean through a plank. The landing was a soft one, vindicating his mental image of a puffy nasty floor. The pea soup fog went *hash-hash* at his arrival, his intrusion. Eyes wide, teeth in a grit, Griffey set the Zodak claw on the bridge, grabbed the ropes and tried to haul himself up with a grunt. The pressure on his left foot broke that board, as well. He smacked his shin in a bark of pain, then planted both feet in the dust.

In the past, even the recent past, Griffey Parker would've found this position to be stifling and infuriating. Though he was nothing more than a short hop away from mounting the bridge again, that distance was still daunting. The distance from here to there was the gap between right and wrong, righteousness and disgrace. It was as if the slats of the bridge represented civilization and it was grossly improper to be distanced from the light when it was available in such a dark place.

This was not the Griffey of the past and he did not wriggle and thrash and obliterate this section of the bridge in a flurry of frustration. Instead, he breathed deep, then began gauging how best to climb back up. His eyes caught upon a tiny waterfall of blood, seeping down in sheets and strings from the ribbed curvature of the suspension rope. He followed this deposit downward and caught a break in the eerie green fog. The blood spit onto a pad of chalky maroon dust mounded on the floor. Beneath the bloodstains, the dirt shifted and twitched. A pair of bony human fingers flicked free from the sand.

Rapidly following this emergence was a bony hand and forearm. Then a shoulder, then a skull.

Instead of a startled yelp and a flail for his sword, Griffey only gasped, stood back up, and quickened the process of regaining the bridge. He didn't want to rush, didn't want to tear it all down.

All around him, he heard the sickening *pops* of skeletal

monsters extricating themselves from dusty tombs. He heard the gruesome crinkles of joints and sockets reconnecting, old bones clicking. He even heard the call of a gristly yawn. In a dizzying spiral, he saw the ribcages, shoulders, and skulls of a dozen skeletons rise above the green shimmer-fog. Blank faces gaping, the pits of their eyes and noses and mouths gorged with inky blackness. Their hungry growls echoed across the cavern.

Griffey tried to climb back onto the bridge and slipped. Back down in the dust, a hand grabbed his ankle. With a kick, he tore loose. With a stomp, he crunched the attacker's skull. He saw the undead clearly now. Their bones were a foul dark purple shade, speckled with bits of clinging flesh. Some of them wore helmets mounted with horns. Others wore raggedy armor and carried knives.

With a calm reassurance—which he secretly feared would get him killed down here—Griffey swung his golden crossbow around to the front. Thankful for the shine given off by the layer of green graveyard fog, Griffey could see his targets well enough to aim. His first shot exploded a zombie skull in a puff of bones and dust, dropping the walker below the fog again. His second shot delivered the same result, same with the third, but he missed on the fourth. Watched it sail into the tragic dark.

There were now eight walkers instead of twelve, but he was down four arrows. With a hammer of fear, he realized he'd neglected his backside. Dragging footsteps behind him, a grating rasping snarl. He dropped the crossbow to its sling, slotted the Zodak claw onto his left arm, drew his sword. He turned to face the walker and barely raised his claw-arm in time to deflect a strike from an ancient rusty blade. The stench of the gathering skeletons built a putrid womb. From all directions, death closed in...

◇ CHAPTER THE SIXTIETH. ◇
◇At the Corridor's End.◇

With a gurgling rush, the castle door reconfigured itself and slammed shut. Not only did it lock Brisk, Konragen and Ramsey inside this place and cut off their escape, but the ensuing silence left them with their own thoughts. Tragedies, doubts, regrets, fantasies and fears.

They inched forward, through the arched-ceiling hallway of stone with far less gumption than they'd barged in here with. It was Brisk, Cook of Rivercrest, who eased into the forward position.

Brisk was rather pleased he'd climbed all the way to this castle without dropping his sword and keeping his shield secured to his back (the latter accomplished with an elf clinging to his back).

Brisk held his shield and sword out strong ahead of him— and everything behind him in life was just about forgotten. Since setting out from the castle into Shadowbranch forest, Brisk had barely thought at all about his family, friends, and job back home. If he did spare thoughts on it, he would consider his own obscurity, his own invisibility. A Cook in the kitchen, creating a meal for someone else to deliver to the table for someone else to enjoy. While back there, in that world, he'd found it easy to judge and disparage Griffey for striking out into the wilderness with those irrational Rangers. Now, Brisk could see he'd been secretly jealous. There was liberation and adventure beyond the kitchens.

Brisk was always someone who would shudder at the thought of camping in the woods. But, Frishkadammit, he'd already survived two overnights with the rocks and the mosquitoes. He decided he wasn't going to let some creepy hallway intimidate him. Beyond that, he thought of his friend Griff, raiding this place on his own somewhere. At least Brisk wasn't here alone, and that was a boost.

The Cook stepped into the lead because sometimes a default leader happens, and sometimes it's just as good as a regular one. A lack of retort from his fellows helped the process greatly.

In the back-left position, Konragen's feelings were nearly the opposite of his leader's. Konragen hated climbing that tree to get up here and that entire exercise left him frazzled. Kicking in the castle door had been fun, absolutely. But the enchanted rubble had reformed itself; an insult to Konragen's punishing kick. It was as if the damage Konragen inflicted was easily remedied.

Speaking of remedies, Konragen had required far too many of those things lately. He'd exhaled with his own fire-breath and torched his own throat. The rest of the group was forced to carry him, stash him, and cure him. Then, later, he'd been hit with a borlog arrow and laid meekly in the grass with magma tears dribbling from his eyes. Konragen shook with embarrassment.

The dragonman hoped Ramsey the Green didn't see him shake just now. Every single time Konragen went out and got himself afflicted, the elf had to step in and bail him out. It wasn't hard to feel indebted or somehow subservient to the Sorcerer after all that. Konragen knew other dragonmen and dragonwomen wouldn't think that way. His brothers and sisters would accept the gift of a remedy, perhaps offer a gruff nod of wordless gratitude, then move on with life, resume bashing elbows with the world. In that, Konragen saw what made him different. He respected and appreciated Ramsey for helping save his life twice. It went beyond that. Konragen felt as if he somehow needed to make up the debt. As if he weren't pulling his own considerable weight. Double shame on a dragon for that.

Of course, there was no hiding the fact that Ramsey recently almost executed Griffey Parker. Essentially everything in the script of the Paladin ethical code went against murdering the main leader of their Quest, killing their friend. This mandate was embedded deep in the Paladin pledge; it was in the ink, in the very fibers of the scroll-paper which that ink lay scrawl to. Back on that sand-and-skull island, Ramsey was a whisper away from treachery. That complicated Konragen's thinking. It didn't feel right to be indebted to someone so recently duplicitous.

Just as his health flickered between extremes, Konragen could tell his heart was equally jostled. He needed to concentrate on events at hand. Like his dragon brothers and sisters, too much thinking would hamper his fighting prowess.

Konragen raised his dual-bladed battleaxe and the strength and exertion felt good. Hanging upon his chest, the crimson jewel of his necklace flashed in the torch-light. His orange eyes swept the barren stone hallway, ever alert for any impending assault.

From the split of his eye, Ramsey the Green saw Konragen give a slight shiver, as if it were cold in this musty, humid hallway. The elf watched as Konragen recovered then braced his battleaxe for action. He was relieved that Konragen was focused elsewhere.

Striding cautiously to the back-right of Brisk, Ramsey was in deep thought, still mulling over his actions against Griffey. Though neither Brisk nor Konragen wanted to talk about that right now, Ramsey could feel the tension in the air. He wanted to break the silence and explain how his mind was deceived at that time by the dark Sorcerer Kozard (who was somehow inhabiting the body of Ulkar the borlog). Something that now appeared to have occurred a year ago.

Regret claimed Ramsey, leaving him feeling similar to

Konragen. Ramsey felt indebted to his friends. His value had yet to be proven. If they could find Ulkar/Kozard and Ramsey helped kill them, that would go a long way towards freeing his conscience.

Ramsey recognized his personal flaws and past mistakes, yet his sense of curiosity and wonder was heightened. His mind whirled with the possibilities and implications of the full calendar year which they had so deftly leaped over. He thought of Willowflow forest, of his family back home. Another year without a cure for the disease which was ravaging their lands. This was dreadful to consider, yet he forced himself to consider it. It was painful to think about how unhelpful he'd been for his suffering people.

For Ramsey, as he saw it now, both recognition and pain were penitent actions he demanded of himself. Being conscious of the struggles of the people he cherished, yet knowing he could only help himself in the present moment. *If* and only *if* he managed to stay focused and help his friends survive this ordeal, then he would earn the opportunity to save his people and set everything right in the future. If he conquered the present moment, instead of getting flung away with musings on yesteryear's cryptic passage, then he would defeat the imposing tidal wave of time and all its threats and weapons.

Ramsey's mind cast him back to the trail he'd walked alongside his Quest mates. To the time they'd been discussing what to do with Kozard's black eyeglass. Griffey had mused, almost dreamily, "Perhaps we need to consider the entire *world* differently." Ramsey took that and applied it to just about everything—not just the face of their planet with its rocks and rivers, but the people and the politics and the machinations of power. Even more, the laws of their universe and time itself. Even further, remarkably so, it encompassed how Ramsey would perceive obstacles and challenges.

Now, his boots padding the stone hall floor, staff raised,

close on the tail of Brisk, massively grateful for the balance Brisk provided, Ramsey was free to see what lay ahead and only what lay ahead. There was a hideously distorted figure, the Kozard-Ulkar hybrid. Ramsey was confident that Ulzard held the advanced Healer's powers he needed. Kozard's ghost supplied the talents Ramsey used to save Konragen's life. Within that old nasty elf's arsenal could also be the elixir for Ramsey's home.

"Ramsey..." Brisk's voice whispered in the silence.

"I'm here," the elf replied.

"Cast a *Detection* spell, let's see what's ahead."

Examining what lay ahead was exactly what Ramsey wanted and he was glad for the task.

"No trace of the goblin Warlock," Ramsey reported. "A glimmer signature of the borlog Sorcerer, ahead fifty yards and two floors up... As for this hallway... a trap twenty yards ahead..."

"Can't Ramsey the Green," Konragen growled, "provide more clarity than that."

"The trap is above my *Detection* grade. Get past the trap, we're at the stairs."

"I don't want to try and sneak by it," Brisk rasped at the others. "Get ready for anything."

At the fifteen yard mark, Brisk held up his shield arm for a halt. Brisk then knelt, plucked a chunk of rock off the floor and chucked it forward. There was nothing subtle about what happened. The rock struck the floor and a giant figure burst through the right-hand wall with a thunderous **crash**. The encroaching boisterous beast booted and batted the blocks of stone as if they were butterflies. Brisk and his companions took a step back not from fear but because the booming entrance was so incredibly loud.

Standing in the resulting rubble heap in a swarm of dust, with the bulb of its bald misshapen head scraping the ceiling, the castle troll roared. The frame of the big dumb beast was nearly wide enough to fill the throat of the hall and it was a miracle it had room to raise its giant stone hammer.

"Ramsey," Brisk exclaimed, "can we get a *Fi*—"

Before the request was even completed, Ramsey aimed his staff and launched a *Fire Bolt*. The missile crossed the gap very quickly and slammed into the troll's chest. The troll slid back a few feet and it roared with painful rage. But its body did not catch on fire and the *Bolt* only sizzled on its skin. Baring down, the troll charged forward at them, its footfalls sending shudders up the hall. Brisk ran forward to meet the monster. The Cook dodged a hammer-strike which pounded to the floor, then he slashed in to sever the muscles of the troll's right calf. With a swipe of its paw, the troll knocked Brisk aside, just in time for Konragen to leap forward and hack the troll's right arm clean off at the elbow.

Though it was consumed with wails of suffering, the troll spied Ramsey dashing in on its left. The troll brought its hammer down to Ramsey's head. But the Sorcerer invoked a *Shield* spell, and the stone striker imploded on impact with a flash. Konragen jumped up and lopped the troll's head off.

The hulking headless body toppled with a thump. After some heavy breaths, they went to Brisk.

"I'm alive, I'm acho," Brisk assuaged his friends, standing and dusting off his pants.

"Let's get to the stairs," Ramsey suggested. "The troll corpse is already starting to reek."

Brisk led them in a hustle over the mound of rocks, to the door, and up the stairs. Their leader was proud of how they followed along. Their movements spoke of people who had abandoned self-interest and were invested in the common goal. They'd set aside their personal turmoils.

The stairs wound up in a spiral for two stories. There was no torch-light on the stairs, so Brisk snapped his fingers and sparked a candle flame hovering above his lifted fist. Brisk had to sheathe his sword to do this, so Ramsey moved up front. This

position exchange happened without pause, as they had graduated
to collective understanding. Perhaps their maturity was
attributable to the full year which just passed. Yet that year had
raced past, almost thoughtlessly. Still, they were all wiser for it.

Out from the stairs into a hall, Brisk was back in the lead
and was wise enough to hold distance when they saw the man. At
the corridor's end there stood a tall figure framed in blue
crackling light.

Knowing Ramsey possessed better long-range weapons,
Brisk once again waved him to the front. As they steadily
approached, the hall widened, granting generous breathing room.
Soon enough, it was obvious. It was Ulkar standing there, head
bowed, maybe frozen, wreathed in a wash of blue.

"*You're covered!*" Ramsey hollered, pausing ten yards
short, his staff on the target.

Ulkar detached himself from the screen of blue light
which sealed the end of the hall and he whirled to face them. The
tails of his black trench coat swirled dusty by his boots, nasty
scars shone bright upon his crazed, pale face. His right eye was
red and wild. There he stood, cornered and trapped.

Brisk saw the vile Ulkar; vampire who'd broken his friend
Griffey's hand.

Konragen also saw Ulkar; evil borlog who'd executed the
old woman Java on her farm.

Beneath it all, Ramsey saw Kozard; wicked elf teacher
who'd nearly made him a murderer.

"*The Warlock won't admit me,*" Ul-zard howled, his voice
insane, "*until I've proved my worth!*"

Though Ulkar had lost both his hatchet and his dagger in a
duel with Griffey on Java's farm, Kozard had enough magic
strength left to generate new weapons. And these had a twist to
them.

From his right hand, Ul-zard threw his hatchet. The blade
duplicated as it chopped through the air—as if they were after-

images imprinted on a blinking eye, a dozen deadly copies of the hatchet ran at them in a string. Ramsey hesitated. Perhaps he was stunned by the presence of his old Sorcerer tormentor. Perhaps he was numbed by the furious rage on Ul-zard's face. Either way, he froze.

It was Brisk who leaped forward, shield raised high. With the ugly persistent drum-beat of steel rain-drops, the blades crashed against his shield. Brisk was driven back with a cry, but he kept the protection braced. The shield withstood the barrage for eleven blows, but the last one slipped through.

Konragen sprang forward and flung a blade of his own, which stabbed into Ul-zard's shoulder.

Ul-zard recoiled in pain and Ramsey didn't miss this chance. In rapid succession, the green elf launched three *Fire Bolts* and each one blazed home. The *Bolts* thumped Ul-zard's chest and smacked his face and encased him in a gorge of red-orange flames. He screamed in terror as he fell to the floor.

Ramsey ran to Ul-zard, desperately seeking the vestiges of evaporating magic.

Konragen, hot tears in his eyes, knelt beside Brisk, laying there, coughing, shaking, bleeding…

◇ CHAPTER THE SIXTY-FIRST. ◇
◇Flight of Falcons.◇

Marynda ached for her daughter. She hoped the force of her emotions might carry from the roots she stood upon all the way up the giant pine. All the way to her daughter's heart.

The Druid woman was tired. Marynda lay down and put her hands to her face. Her daughter was gone. Hazel had just flown up from this tree to the castle, with important errands to attend to. Off to become an independent woman and find her own way. Again, Marynda took pride in the daughter and Druid Hazel had become.

Though she might have a year ago, Marynda didn't understand what drew Hazel to an empty place that wasn't important anymore. She had been hoping to continue their encouraging conversation and become more acquainted with her daughter. Instead, Hazel had flown away.

Her daughter was a falcon now; drawn by the Druid inheritance from her mother's side of the family. The side of the family that slept in the woods. In the penultimate moment before Hazel was abducted by the pirates, Marynda screamed: "*You have my blood!*" She'd said that with hopes that Hazel actually *did* have her Druid's blood and would be able to somehow use that to escape. Marynda never expected a year to go by, leaving Hazel to struggle with her Druid abilities. Hazel hadn't even stepped down from that branch as a human to speak with her mother. Just as her daughter refused to not be a falcon anymore, Marynda had been a rampaging bear for an entire year.

Marynda's mind flooded with horrid memories of rampaging through that innocent forest. Her strong paws crushing the life out of playful chipmunks and elegant sparrows. A shudder rippled through her body and the quake dislodged the shoddy bra she'd hung upon her shoulders. She thought of the promise she'd made to Alkent, after emerging bloody and haggard from the devastated forest. With tears on her muddy, gory face, she'd sworn to her departed beloved that she was done. She would never change into an animal again. Her Druid's powers had always spooked Alkent; he'd thought it some unholy witchcraft. *Maybe he was right.*

I'm descended from witches. That's why I deal with witches in tents. That's why I'm cursed.

Couldn't Hazel see that witchcraft was deadly? Hazel wanted to act so advanced, so mature, *so Frishkadammed* **wise**, but she had no concept of discretion. A girl could get lost in the Druid world; could get trapped there and commit irredeemable atrocities. Marynda demanded that her daughter be different. If only she'd been strong enough to make her daughter listen. To make her **understand**.

Marynda's breath quickened. The tears in her eyes dried. She felt her hands curl into fists, mushing globs of dirt and rock harshly in her palms. A growl began to gurgle in her throat.

Hazel had left for the castle and Marynda now sensed that it wasn't vacant. With that thought, she knew what she must do.

My daughter needs my help.

Marynda rose to her feet.

Alkent forgive me.

Marynda transformed in an instant. She stood tall, a human woman with no grassy bra to cover her breasts, head held defiantly high, eyes valiant and ferocious. And then, she was a human no more. Her arms were wings, her skin was sleek with feathers, she was off the ground and shooting through the branches. She was a falcon to match her daughter and she tore through the tree with a vengeance.

The target was her daughter and her daughter was flying fast. If there was time for criticism, Marynda would've cursed the precious time she'd spent weeping on the ground.

The doubts still pricked at the edges of her brain—the threat of once again falling into a blind rage, losing track of weeks, losing control. When she burst out into the open in a pine needle flurry, all her worries receded. Crisp and strong and invigorating, the night air swept it all away.

Settling in from the sides of her eyes, painting a scarlet shade, was a narrowing focus. There was only the Chase. That's what they'd been doing ever since leaving Rivercrest; they'd been on the hunt. It was almost easier not to think about the target. There was only the next thrust of her wings.

Marynda's trajectory was nearly vertical, her belly facing the tree. In no time, the pine thinned to a husk of spiky-top twigs. The tree ended and a lip of grass and dirt bled past and a gap fell out on her belly-side. Above her and ahead, the bulb of the world filled with an inky ocean of twinkling starlight. Glow from the dual-moons gleamed off the stone curvatures of the castle towers—the reflection almost disagreeably bright for her sensitive falcon eyes. There were three castle columns, looming broad and stepping to the sky. The one in the middle was the highest.

If the fog of the moonlight hadn't been blurring her vision, she would've spotted it sooner. The flow of dark winged creatures streaming perpendicular with her path. A hideous chorus of screeches filtered down to her in the same instant she ducked into a spin. Screeching objects whipped past her; she heard claws slicing the air as if shredding sheets of fabric. A rancid stench stabbed at her.

Marynda leveled out, facing inward, gaining on the castle midway-up. She marked the flow of leathery shadow-creatures streaming out from a dark window in the castle's exterior. As if mimicking a fountain spray, the spew was thin as it emerged, then spilled back in a buzzing, pulsing swarm.

Two of the bats swiped at her from above, but their forward momentum didn't let them slow down for a proper attack. The three bats on her tail, however, closed in for the kill. Marynda dropped into a cork-screw, then shot back up, out wide to her right. In a clumsy display, two of her pursuers bashed their skulls together, but the third kept after her. Marynda grinned. She was faster—but they had the numbers. She saw three more racing in at her, aiming to cut her off.

Before any of her pursuers could reach her, another screamed up at her from below. She was lucky to veer directly vertical and miss getting killed by a mere whisper. She now saw these weren't bats. Their heads were knots, their faces were scrunched, their eyes were beady, their snouts were snarls. They were gargoyles. Each of their wings were lined with a dozen spikes, and her closest attacker tried to *clamp* on her as if its wings were jaws. As she dodged this embrace, Marynda dealt her own claws to the membranes and tore a streak of flesh, flinging silver blood in the moonlight.

In a swift decision, Marynda settled into a relentless upward flight. There was still pressure zipping up behind her (*getting closer now*) and the blanket crashing down on her was also concerning. Yet she stuck with her course. Kept her belly a few feet from the castle stone. It was a race to the top.

Marynda was going to lose. The swarm would overwhelm her. Would slam her up against the wall and shred her until she shrieked and plunged, broken, to her death. Her eyes grew frantic-wide.

Something tore in from outside the scene. It was a streak in the moonlight; something separate from the black jittery gargoyle horde. This airborne arrival slashed in and gnashed its claws in two rapid swipes. Two gargoyle heads were lopped from shoulder mounts in jets of blood and went toppling to oblivion.

As if the swarm shared a hive connection, all of them rasped and cringed with outrage.

Seizing on the disruption, Marynda broke from her course and charged right to the heart of the gargoyle mob. Marynda hit a gap in the screen and decapitated one of the beasts just as Hazel had.

It took but a moment for the gargoyle swarm to regroup, and this gap birthed another reunion between mother and daughter. Their wingspans swung into formation and, together, they raced for the castle top.

"That was close, mother!" Hazel called. "Your stealth needs work!"

For a stunned, breathless moment, Marynda couldn't reply. All she could do was fly.

While her mother continued her flight, Hazel was already thinking of other things. Thinking ahead. To whatever obstacle she would encounter next. The span of Hazel's entire childhood was leeched away with a sip of blue liquid. That Frishkadammed vial of blue liquid. Tilted to her lips by her own mother. Contained within that single gulp were all her years of wonder and amazement. Her teenage loves and mistakes and heartbreaks. Even the little kisses and triumphs that were so small in reality yet felt monumental. She got none of that.

Hazel's real memories contained her year spent with the wretched squid-pirates. It was a brutal learning experience, yes, but there was profit in there. The tentacle vagabonds thought of life in terms of equations. They weighed opportunities based on investment and return. Hazel had learned that lesson.

Both mother and daughter voiced displeasure over the year they had spent apart. Hazel, over the tortuous treatment at the hands of the pirates, and Marynda over her blindly vengeful assault on the forest.

Now, Hazel flew in silence, feathers ruffling in the wind.

The castle top was drawing closer. Before they got there,

Marynda chanced a look-back.

"We're past their breathing altitude," Hazel stated. "Gargoyles can't fly this high."

"You've learned a lot since we lost each other," Marynda said.

"I learned enough to never get trapped again."

"You're a strong woman, Hazel. I'm proud of you for surviving. Your father is, too."

"We need to survive tonight." Hazel lofted her wings, prepared for landing. Life was moving fast.

The rooftop was a circle of brick with seven-foot walls of stone ringing the outside. At the heart of the keep was a round well entrance, thirty feet across. The area was deserted. For now.

"What's your plan?" Marynda hissed as they roosted on the ring-wall.

Hazel stabbed with her beak. "Get down that hole. Kill everything we find inside."

"Be careful you don't kill *yourself* inside. Unleashing destruction doesn't give satisfaction."

"Don't lecture me, mother. I forgive what happened, but you need to treat me as an equal now."

With that, Hazel lifted off and soared through the air, leaving Marynda to scramble after her.

Hazel flew only a handful of feet, hadn't even reached a moderate speed, when a trio of apparitions fired up from the throat of the well entrance. Figures in robes with tall hoods that held the black gape of a cave's upper lip. They floated without the trouble of legs and feet. Their motions were ghostly sputters. Screens of glitter washed their back-trails wherever they hovered. Both Marynda and Hazel surmised those slimy curtains would smell of rancid milk and would probably paralyze you.

One of the ghoul-witches shot to meet Hazel's falcon with a mid-air death-blow. Hazel veered off, a jolt of shock hitting her system. As she dodged the apparition's swiping fingernails, she saw the hag-fairies wore ragged, bristly brown robes and the skin on their bony arms was a pale soupy green.

Enraged that her prey would be so brash as to try and escape, the witch howled icily. Another hag pressed out her palms and fired a net of magic which hit Hazel and knocked her to the brick floor.

Marynda evaluated the scene as fast as her daughter lived her life. These shadow-witches were the Mistresses of the Warlock. A lover who'd given them no affection for a year. Their love for him led the presumptuous witches to fancy themselves as goddesses. *Ancient, overconfident, and not unstoppable.*

Talons jutting, Marynda raced at the nearest witch, who swiveled to face her with a devilish grin. At the last possible second, as the witch-fairy's jaws snapped wide, Marynda twisted into a dive and became a jaguar. The claws of her powerful left paw slashed the witch across the stomach, doubling the gnarly woman over with a shriek. Marynda swiped the net off her daughter's body.

"*These witches are old!*" Marynda roared. "Can't handle surprises!"

Hazel looked frazzled and clueless. Marynda knew she would have to clear these ghouls herself. It was her motherly duty. She bolted for another witch, who zig-zagged in response, zipping from spot-to-spot, painting a glitter canvass. Once again, at the last second, Marynda changed. The jaguar leaped, then shrank into a poison wasp, slipped the ghoul's defenses, put a stinger in her throat. That witch fell and the remaining fairy was bearing down on Hazel, about to crush her. Marynda, still a wasp, shot over, dropped into a gorilla and booted the final witch over the side of the castle with a shattering wail.

Back in human form, naked and breathing heavy, Marynda looked to her daughter. Hazel was still a falcon. *The squid-pirates taught her much. But not how to control the powers of her bloodline.*

◇ CHAPTER THE SIXTY-SECOND. ◇
◇Graveyard Canyon.◇

Another blow from the rusty, ancient blade rained down at Griffey with deadly intent. Griffey ducked back and took the hit on his left-arm Zodak claw. The impact sent a quiver through the claw and left a gnarly scar, but the shield held up. Whistling through the air, the wrist of the skeleton rose once again, and Griffey imagined its antique sword finally breaking with this next hack. There was no such luck, as the chop landed and the skeleton snarled. A mustard tooth toppled from a crack in its jaw.

Griffey crouched, claw-arm raised, with a cold, grimy sweat creeping across his arms and the back of his neck. Looking up at his attacker from a lowered vantage, he felt a ripple of fear. A body of bones coated in a moldy purple sheen, fingers bent into claws, skull-face agape with mindless hunger.

The next strike from the skeleton sword slapped off his claw-arm and Griffey made a quick decision. He easily could have sent blows from his own sword to the skeleton's exposed rack of ribs, but he wasn't going to do that. The goal wasn't to stay in place and count dead skeletons. He needed to get back on the bridge, get top-side of the canyon. He needed to reunite with his sister in meditation space. Sho'pa would be waiting for him there. Waiting with information he desperately needed. Plus, the Warlock was beyond that. And the Warlock needed killing.

Grotesque yowls seeped from the gang of skeletons as their dragging footsteps converged on Griffey. Though their bones were as cold as dead winter, he could feel the heat of their advance.

As his immediate attacker lofted its sword once again, Griffey sank beneath the fog. There was a hiss as he breached the plane, and, from down here, everything up above was obscured. He lay flat upon a mounded carpet of black-powder bone-dust and his movements ruffled up a rotten stench. He saw the bone ankles of his nearby attacker and slammed a boot into them. The bones snapped and the zombie crashed down through the fog with a startled yelp and planted in the dust.

Griffey didn't stick around and allow it to swipe at him some more. He was off and crawling, through the reeking dust beneath the fog. He could see nothing above him but a frosting of mist, but he did his best to stay on track with the bridge. He wanted to squirm at least ten feet before resurfacing and getting back on the bridge. With every elbow churn, he stirred up more crystals of stench.

Two skeletal hands thrust up spurts of powder and seized his ankles. In an effort to kick away their grip, Griffey rolled over, which sent his crossbow jabbing painfully into his back. Gasping for air, Griffey kicked free. Then another hand burst up and slapped down tight upon his mouth. Packed in that nasty palm was a cake of black bone ash. In a panic, he coughed and kicked and lurched away, spitting out the char.

Back up on his hands and knees, sucking air, Griffey kept moving. He didn't peek up through the fog, but stuck to his natural instincts. He stayed true, kept low, and crawled on.

He reached his preferred distance then poked his head up through the fog and peered out. He was perfectly in-line with the bridge—maybe he was a natural Ranger, after all—but he was at the point where the angle of the sagging bridge started veering upwards again. If he went any further, the slats would be out of reach. It was either climb on right here or go backwards.

He wasn't alone. Two skeletons staggered past, one immediately next to him and the other on the flip-side of the bridge. Both creatures wore spiky shoulder pads, helmets with horns, and wielded cutlasses which were aged centuries yet still looked sharp. They migrated, with agonizing slowness, to where the others were gathering, where Griffey had left one of them crippled and howling for help.

The shambles of the undead soldiers came to an alarming halt. Both turned, old bones groaning, to look where he was kneeling. Having been found, Griffey adjusted his plan. He bounded up through the fog, drew his sword and slashed the closest zombie in half, dispersing bones in a clattering spray. In one smooth action, Griffey threaded his shoulders between the bridge ropes and heaved up onto the hovering wooden pathway. As if it had anticipated this, the walker on the far side scrambled up onto the bridge, then rose up to face him in a fighting stance.

This skeleton was more spry than the others, and announced this by twirling the sword as it advanced. Griffey blocked its first two rapid blows with his Zodak arm, then swung low. The zombie's cutlass *clanged* against his sword, leaving its face open for a skull-popping punch from Griffey's claw.

With no further thoughts, Griffey turned and bolted up the bridge. He moved fast, yet with caution, fully expecting the worst to happen any time now. He figured the cluster of skeletons would feel left behind and would begin hacking at the bridge's suspension. This would send the severed bridge flapping against the canyon wall and force him to climb up the rope. Mercifully, that didn't happen and he hustled on. His left boot crashed through a rotted board, he toppled, recovered, and moved along.

As he gained elevation, the flashes of blue lightning returned. Signatures of the Warlock's ongoing work inside the chamber at the heart of this castle. He reached eye-level with the source, but the contrast of the bright light against the dank shadowy canyon made it hard to see clearly.

Just as abruptly as last time, his vision breached an astral plane of spectacular golden clouds.

◇ CHAPTER THE SIXTY-THIRD. ◇
◇The Ranger and the Warlock.◇

Griffey's body was gone. Only his curious mind remained. His path diverted into a den of seclusion with a scarlet shade, soft surroundings, velvet cushions lining the walls of a sultan's tent.

He was returned to meditation space and struck with profound weightless awe.

"Brother, you made it," Sho'pa's voice broke into his mind.

They were reunited. Brother and sister, bodies abandoned, particles in the heavens. There wasn't much time to enjoy this imagery. Time was drawing dreadfully short.

Griffey tried to nod, then remembered he couldn't. "You escaped the Super Monks?"

"I will never escape them," she stated. "One day I hope to be strong enough to fight them."

"Sho'pa… I must know… What happened to mother? What happened to Rivercrest?"

His sister obliged with meticulous efficiency, and without emotion.

For Griffey it was a visceral blow and required no follow-up questions. He then asked, "Please tell me about the Warlock… Who is he? Why did he kill our father?"

"He is from Meltrock Islands," Sho'pa revealed. "He goes by many names, but, in your region of the map, he is called Revelt. He is aged 205 years old, that's twenty-plateaus plus-five. He is one of the few goblins to ever grow curious about the world, and he did not fit in well with his people. His kind are traditionally raised to be fodder on a battlefield, so his life is something of a success story. An outcast who wanted to lead his own life. He didn't see mindless destruction as the solution to everything, as is goblin culture. Still, he is no harmless, carefree inquisitor. His pursuit of knowledge is a violent obsession. It got him expelled from his clan at the age of seven-plateaus. Thrust out upon the world, he pledged his life as a Warlock. In service to a demon."

"Why did he kill John Parker...?" Griffey pressed in a tight, quiet voice.

"To understand that, we must first understand much else," Sho'pa stated cryptically. "You have dragon-blood in your Quest. Recently Konragen recited for you the wisdom of his ancestors. Those who could fly high enough to see Beyond... Ours is not the only planet, brother. It has five siblings; twins, the same size and same age. The whole family orbits the same distance from what Konragen called the *Sun Ball*. Those six planets planets are the ring and the sun is the knuckle it sits around. A collection called a *solar system*. All of them have life—trees and fish and people, just like we have. Some of those people can even travel between planets. Visit the sibling rocks. People built carriages that traverse the heavens. Remember when Konragen described seeing a planet near the constellation of Kraven that reminded him of a beehive? The dots he saw flickering around it are ships."

Sho'pa let that sink in for a moment. "Not all of these other planets have advanced machines, but some of them do. Some of them have used it to wage wars upon their brother and sister planets. There was once a war fought for possession of an entire planet; the Battle of CrunchTop Ridge. These people out there have their own name for the neighborhood of our solar system. They call it Spiral Pit."

"Why has our world seen no such action?" Griffey cut in. In human form, he would've rubbed his forehead. Apparently, being sacrificed to nothing but a conscious mind did not eliminate headaches.

"It has. Recently, actually. Ah—" Sho'pa hesitated, as if the toe of her boot just inched upon a cliff, "—ah, you must understand that our home world has been insulated because it was identified as an opportunity for an isolated experiment. Long ago, a golden cube was discovered on one of the many moons throughout Spiral Pit. Unsure what else to do with it, the finders deposited it in the middle of a forest on our world, five hundred years ago. All the magic possessed by our Sorcerers and Wizards and Druids grew out from that mysterious cube, which remains hidden to this day. Without talking about it, everyone in Spiral Pit kept away, waiting to see how it worked out. We faded into the background.

"Until recently. Two weeks before father's death, a pair of explorers touched down in the mountains far north of Rivercrest. They encountered a scout and introduced themselves as Glavinich and Walker. The scout had been dispatched to those mountains by John Parker. They engaged in conversation and the explorers from the sky revealed the details of Spiral Pit. This behavior makes me presume the explorers were not from this system and did not know of its hands-off approach to our planet. Also, I have my doubts that this meeting in the mountains was entirely by chance...

"After the two explorers departed, back to the sky, the scout sat immediately down and scrawled out a journal of that splendid interaction. He sealed the scroll and hiked urgently back to the castle. En route, he joined ranks with a group of Rangers. It is unclear how he was killed, but that scout died along the way. With his dying breath, he passed the scroll to a Ranger, who eventually delivered it."

"Delivered it to father..." Griffey breathed in a hush.

"On the night he was killed, John Parker received that scroll. And he correlated it with a map drawn for him by his allies in the Rivercrest dragon village. It was a map of Spiral Pit. A structure foretold in dragon legends passed through the ages. They trusted father enough to share it with him.

"What did father feel in that moment? In the moment of glorious revelation when he learned there was life—*active* life— beyond our world? Even here, in meditation space, where it is possible to know so much, we cannot be sure exactly what he felt. But I have a belief beyond a guess, dear brother, that he felt wonder and amazement and hope. He thought not of going to war with those other planets. He thought of the promises and possibilities. He thought of contacting them. Working with them. Trading with them. Learning from them. He thought of the industries that relationship could build. Industries which would benefit his people. The people of Rivercrest, whom he loved so much… Yet, sadly, he also felt fear. He was smart enough to know this information held the power to hurt people. Others less virtuous than he held the potential to reject it. Or abuse it. Use it to start a war."

"That's why he was killed…" Griffey said in a somber tone. "Not by some neighboring empire looking to topple the Rivercrest power structure… because he knew what the Warlock knew…"

"It is unclear how Revelt learned of the secret scroll," Sho'pa went on, "but it is obvious that Revelt wanted no competition in his enterprise to the planets. He must've recognized that John Parker was ambitious enough to mobilize the magic and make it happen. I know it doesn't make it any easier, or any less painful, but at least there was respect there. Revelt assassinated him out of respect…"

Griffey said nothing. Her assumption was correct. The heavy pain in his chest was just as severe with or without the Warlock's admiration for his father. But Griffey wasn't ready to dash off and do something about it. His life-approach was changing. He would stay here with his sister and learn everything he could before rushing off to maybe get himself killed. Off to join John Parker.

Sho'pa resumed, "To finish the story of Revelt… He committed unspeakable horrors in service to the demon. That went on for years and years. When he'd finally achieved moderate Warlock status, he was rewarded with the same knowledge John Parker got. The Warlock learned about the solar system. Spiral Pit. He learned that people could travel across it. Revelt's aspirations grew large.

"The Warlock became enthralled with the idea of escaping his home planet and venturing elsewhere. Since the demon could not offer that, Revelt terminated the partnership. He proceeded to pledge himself to an other-world intelligence. For the next four plateaus, he committed more unfathomable crimes, earning the goodwill of his benefactor, gradually amassing the knowledge—"

"—knowledge to construct a flying carriage," Griffey cut in. "A ship to sail Spiral Pit."

"That's what he's working on." Sho'pa paused, and Griffey sensed an intruder behind her words. Sho'pa spoke faster, drawing their talk to an urgent conclusion. "Brother, what you need to understand is that Revelt is fully consumed with his goal. Since his birth in the goblin colony, he's felt insulted by everything and everyone on our home world. He thirsts to escape more than he thirsts to continue living. If it weren't for his other world benefactor keeping him alive, he would work day and night and starve and die. All to build his precious flying carriage… I hope you see his vulnerability there."

"Sho'pa…" Griffey said softly. "Endless thanks to you. I am sorry you're stuck here…"

"Stay safe, brother," Sho'pa replied, preparing to vanish. "Please avenge our family."

Instantly, Griffey was *retracted*. Back down, out of the cloud-realm, away from meditation space, freshly provisioned with phenomenal knowledge. His feet—housed, once again, in boots—landed and bounced lightly upon the wooden slats of the hanging bridge. The cozy weight of the Zodak claw was returned, slotted upon his left arm. Beneath him, the bridge swayed and his balance nearly toppled over the side. His right hand grasped the rope and the strength of his grip felt good.

Flashes of dazzling blue mesmerized him. Griffey now stood ten feet from the entrance to the central enclosure where the Warlock's lightning crackled. The door was an arched passage and there were others to match it, spaced with twenty yards between them as they marched a circle around the Warlock's work zone. A strip of flat rock served as a doorstep, running around to all these doorways.

Way back down below, the shambling skeletons realized their prey'd slipped away and grew agitated. With their ancient blades, they hacked the suspension ropes, and Griffey felt the vibration only a few seconds later. Beneath his feet, the bridge wobbled, then fell clean away, stealing his stomach. He grabbed hold, gritted his teeth as his lifeline swung in for an inevitable *whap* against the cavern wall.

As he climbed, his mind did not falter over this barrier to his progress. In fact, this had been expected. The zombies were tasked with defending their Warlock master and Griffey had skirted them. It was only natural they would strike back at him in some form. There was a parallel to be drawn with the Warlock, whom had hurt Griffey's family yet stayed blind to the inevitable counter-strike. His climb was a focused effort, and he hit the summit just before the ropes snapped an fell.

Gone was the anger throbbing in his chest—the voracious demand for *immediate resolution*.

Griffey's attention was strict as he struggled up onto the landing and got briefly blinded by a flare of blue light. It took a bit to blink it away and recover, but that period was not stuffed with panic. He simply waited it out. Shading his eyes with the Zodak claw, he went to the doorway and peered in.

The expanse was a broad cylinder, at least fifty yards across and stretching high—presumably, all the way to the top of this castle tower. The scenery was dominated by a column of light, hazy robin's egg blue, streaming down from above in a piercing blur. That stream touched down upon a vast silvery disc, at least fifty feet across, and Griffey's face sagged a little when he saw it. The Warlock's sailing ship was forged of metal; a sculpted plate, glossy and sleek. From this distance, the top-side looked unerringly smooth, and the ridge curving along the circumference was equally flawless.

Down below, where objects were dangling, that's where the operation was more grungy than elegant. Lurking in the belly-shadows of the disc, scurrying around, uncorking paneling and unraveling strange-looking ropes, was the black-robed figure of Revelt. The Warlock assassin from Meltrock Islands.

Even from way up here, Griffey could hear Revelt panting as he hustled busily about, spine furiously hunched, pale face twisted with focus upon his elongated hairless skull. He dashed about, twisting tools and casting spells with a fever that suggested his assassin's errand to Rivercrest was one of the very few breaks taken in a very long time. (*He was never running from our Chase Quest. He was rushing back to his escape project.*) Sho'pa had mentioned magic keeping the Warlock alive, and Griffey figured that was the blue ceiling light. The blue lightning flashes, bright enough to spill out and fill the skeleton cavern, were emitting from the Warlock's fingertips each time he threw a spell.

Griffey's survey shifted to how he was going to get down there. A stone walkway, devoid of hand-railings and fifty feet high, extended all the way down to the floor. Even though he was in a trance, the Warlock would most certainly spot a person, out in the open, strolling down the block. Griffey's eyes shifted and he noted matching pathways of stone descending from the other chamber entrances like fingers into a bowl. This mirrored more rope bridges across the canyon on the outside.

A plan formed within Griffey's mind with the efficiency of a Ranger on the hunt. *Runter Man.*

Down below, at the base of the chamber, in the shadows where the blue ambrosial light didn't shine but its restorative effects still seeped through, the Warlock's work continued. The bony claws of his goblin hands hurried in their business, snapping the vitals into place. The process looked hectic and unorganized, but that was because each step needed to be completed in a certain order and the components were spread out across the vessel's underside. On some secret level of his mind, buried beneath decades of repressive dust, the Warlock feared he might be working too fast. He feared he would miss some essential connection and be forced to a humiliating back-track. He also sensed an intruder presence but didn't much concern himself with mortal interference. The job was almost done.

The Warlock sensed the arrival before he saw it and spun to face the threat. A snap tore from his fingertips as he fired a spell of *Paralysis* at the attacker, but an arrow struck him in the shoulder and threw off his timing. He dissolved the arrow and healed the wound, but his attacker disappeared.

Using *Scout Cast*, Griffey whipped away, right back to the arched doorway gazing down into the chamber. While drawing back the latch on his golden crossbow and fitting a fresh arrow into the groove, Griffey dashed along the exterior walkway to the next entrance. He paused there and peeked in to find the Warlock absorbed with his project yet again, despite having just been shot. The last few days, Griffey was concerned about the Warlock regaining his full power. Perhaps his concerns had been misplaced, as the Warlock's full strength didn't stop his focus from abandoning the practical.

Griffey *Cast* down again, shot the Warlock in the back, and elicited a shriek this time. He retreated again, and found he felt no shame at his strategy. This foe was superior to he, and he would seize every shot. He ran to the next door and pounced again. The Warlock was lit with such feverish preoccupation that he had yet to remove the arrow sticking from his shoulder blade. Even more disturbing: the Warlock was replacing the final disgorged panels. After all this time, the ship would be ready to fly seconds from now. The threat was maddening, yet Griff stayed close to calm.

A chuff of dust flung from Griffey's boots as he landed his next *Cast*. He raised the crossbow, but the Warlock was ready. The Warlock vanished. Went invisible. Griffey's heart raced. A blade zipped at his face. He raised his Zodak arm and deflected it. The next dagger slit across his temple. The next one shot clean-through his left shoulder. With a bark of pain, Griffey *Cast* back to safety. With a grim certainty that the Warlock was about to escape, he cursed this ill-timed retreat. His left shoulder was volcanic agony, so he tossed the crossbow. He kept the claw because it hurt to twist the shield from its snug position. His eyes closed and he drew a breath. *I've fought one-handed before.*

He *Cast* down to the puddle of shadows beneath the disc. A door-flap swung down on his right, dropping a rack of stairs from a glowing rectangle on the ship's belly. His pulse pounded, his palms grew sweaty. He twisted and scanned the area beneath the ship. Despite his practiced mood of calm, it was impossible not to feel nervous right now. His father's face flashed through his mind. A memory of a puppy; a childhood gift from his father. A bloom of warm sympathy and comfort. His eyes locked on the stairs. His target. Griffey charged that way with a roar on his lips, sword held high.

At the crucial second, he dove and rolled. The crack of a *Paralysis* spell flew over his head. Griffey sprang up and lunged with a mighty cross-hack. The blade connected with an unseen body and blood gashed the empty air. The Warlock flickered to visibility. Lurched. Gurgled. And fell.

BOOK

◇ VI ◇

EPILOGUE.

◇M. RAY ROBERTS◇

◇ CHAPTER THE SIXTY-FOURTH. ◇
◇Righteous Path.◇

$\mathbf{A}$ rustling hashed out from the bushes. The leaves scraping together were a symphony of rusted hacksaws. Dusk was drawing near, and it wasn't time for the birds and grasshoppers to ease their singing, yet all the critters of the forest fell silent. It was like nature took a collective gasp.

From where he was kneeling at the edge of camp, unrolling his sleeping sack and patting it flat into a tolerable cushion, the Sorcerer's gaze twisted slowly over his shoulder. He planted his staff in the dirt and pressed to his feet, even daring to shift his eyes from the encroaching foe to the campsite. Everyone was gone. Off hunting dinner or collecting kindling or filtering water or scouting the grounds. Keeping busy. Working as a team. Which left Ramsey here. Alone with the monster.

They hadn't planned on camping directly on the trail. That wasn't the plan when they'd first set out. Yet the path was broad and roomy and the trees weren't the kind to hover and menace. The last two nights camping on the trail had birthed no threats worse than mosquitoes. Plus, everyone on this expedition had faced so much recent danger that they weren't too intimidated by a tranquil trail.

Ramsey attempted to squint through the greenery screen of branches and brambles, hoping to gauge the threat as early as possible. One thing he didn't have to gauge was the loyalty of his friends. Several times along the way, during their Chase Quest, Ramsey had faltered and flirted with making a great mistake. Yet he'd avoided such tragedy, and his companions rewarded him by never bringing it up. They never offered outward judgment worse than jokes. This was treatment Ramsey felt deeply humbled by, and he didn't deserve it. Yet he tried to earn it. Every minute, he would earn it.

A snort huffed out from around the corner and two raptors slid into view. The sleek scales of their long snouts slit from the leaves and Ramsey even saw the glint of six-inch claws. He considered hurling a *Fire Bolt* but the thought of accidentally burning the forest down brought that up short. Setting the trees ablaze would not endear his friends. So he clicked his tongue, nodded with his staff, and cast an illusion. The distant scent of a wounded deer drew the raptors away, clear of their camp.

From behind Ramsey, there rose a chorus of voices and bustling movement. They were back.

Ramsey the Green took one more look into the bushes and felt pleased the raptors would be distracted the rest of the night. He smiled to himself and turned back to camp. He would cast illusions at the animals, but never again would he cast them on his friends. He felt too indebted to their kindness.

It was Ramsey who dealt the fatal blow to High Sorcerer Kozard—who was merged with the borlog Ulkar at the time. Ramsey ran up the hall and got there just before the corpse disintegrated into dust. The remainder of the High Sorcerer's magic supply nearly evaporated into the ether, but Ramsey caught it and absorbed it. Then, he'd ran back up the hall. Brisk lay cradled in the thick arms of Konragen, bleeding from a knife wound, inflicted on him by Ulzard. It was a very emotional moment as Ramsey pointed his staff at Brisk. At that time, Ramsey wasn't used to advanced Healer's powers, and he was afraid something might go wrong. However, the spell worked and the wound melted away. Brisk was left loopy and dazed for a few hours, but he managed to mumble out a demand, "Ramsey, if I live through this, you're teaching me those Healer's powers."

The members of the Chase Quest—all of them, alive and breathing—reunited out front of the Warlock's castle, as if drawn by some subliminal force. It must've seemed safer to get outside. Two falcons swept down and landed with them, squawking excitedly. The group assembled on the lawn just as the first rays of sunrise splayed down from the highest branches of the great pine rising from the river below. That dawn harmonized with the company's origins in the western Rivercrest courtyard.

Griffey Parker was injured and bleeding and coughing, laying on the ground, his left arm immobilized with pain. Ramsey went immediately to this patient and explained that he'd been the recipient of a vast Healer's knowledge. While he was willing to accept such hospitality, Griffey waved for a pause, and spoke. He, like Brisk, was aware he would be struck groggy and useless for the next few hours, and uttered two requests. "Get this claw off my arm," he said, "give it to Konragen."

It was his second request that nearly brought tears to Ramsey's eyes. Just before the spell was cast and he fell asleep, Griffey said, "…we need to go to your village, Ramsey. Need to help them…"

Ramsey was simply awestruck. He didn't even remember telling Griffey about his family.

Once Griffey and Brisk were rolled up in blankets and snoozing and recuperating, something similar to a minor debate developed over Griffey's proposal. First, however, Marynda and Hazel flew to the pine and fashioned clothing from branches. The men who remained awake politely turned their backs while the ladies returned to their human forms and dressed. Hazel hesitated a few seconds longer than her mother before reclaiming her human body. She feared losing the freedom of a falcon's wings. She feared getting too comfortable as a person and with these other people. Yet she saw her mother was right. The squid-pirates may have taught her much, but not how to control her Druid's blood. The squid-pirates were nothing but cruel teachers. These people were her friends. She could trust them.

Konragen conducted the ceremony of gently removing the Zodak claw from Griffey's mending left arm. The dragonman hugged the shield to his chest, the flicker of a smile on the rocky contours of his face. There was no question the Paladin would follow the Runter Man's request.

Then, the debate began. Which was more of a heated discussion—heated because the implications of Griffey's proposal were pressed up against them getting caught up on the latest. Hazel and Marynda told of their airborne battle with the gargoyles, then their destruction of the ghostly hags atop the castle. Marynda did the talking, of course. After that, Ramsey and Konragen told how they'd defeated a lumbering troll and then faced down Ulzard in that hallway. Ramsey did the talking, of course.

Both Ramsey and Marynda were confused as to how Griffey knew about Ramsey's elf village suffering from a plague. Neither Ramsey nor Marynda had told him about that. It was as if the information was given to Griffey by some ethereal source. As if he'd convened with the supernatural.

Committing to Griffey's plan would be a definite implication that their time together wasn't over yet. Their Quest to destroy the Warlock was complete—Griffey assured them of the villain's death before giving his final requests. They didn't openly discuss splitting up and going their own ways, but each pondered it briefly, independently. Once Ramsey and Marynda explained to Hazel and Konragen how the elven people of Willowflow forest were stricken with a mysterious disease, it didn't take long for them all to agree. Ramsey was one of them, and they couldn't let his people suffer.

Though they agreed on the virtues of the mission, concerns were raised about its viability. Hazel pointed out that they'd all been tossed through a window of time distortion. A full year had passed briefly for all of them, but had passed in reality for the rest of the world. What could such a lapse mean for a village full of sick elves? Ramsey also wondered if his new Healer's powers would carry the necessary elixir. What if they hiked all the way to Willowflow, found his people barely holding on, and he couldn't deliver their lives? These were heavy questions and no one had satisfying answers for them.

They didn't have to accept the mission. The man who suggested it was passed out and would be a groggy toad all day tomorrow. They easily could've chosen some other course and left Ramsey the elf to go resolve his own peoples' problems. But they chose instead to go with him and get him there safe.

Before they gathered up their things and prepared to leave, Marynda wandered over to the castle doors and found them curiously sealed once again. The magic locking them had relented after the death of the Warlock, but, after they'd all exited, some other force seemed intent on keeping them out.

They developed a plan for transporting everyone down to the riverbank below. The resulting episode actually allowed them to skip the task of climbing down the giant pine tree and it was rather entertaining. Marynda and Hazel became falcons once again, clasped their claws on Ramsey's shoulders and buoyed the featherweight elf out into mid-air. From that comical position, the Sorcerer elf was able to gradually levitate Konragen and the slumbering forms of Griffey and Brisk safely down.

From there, they set out. Proceeding on-foot because no one wanted to risk trying the island with the skulls and *Casting* stones again. They marched northeast, with the Ranger and the Cook hovering in a peaceful nap behind the troop. They'd hiked for six nights and days to get to this current point.

With camp set up on the trail and the threat of raptors averted and dusk creeping in.

Konragen stacked and steepled sticks for a campfire. Griffey presented a pair of rabbits for Brisk's inspection. The Cook then sparked a fire, positioned his kettle, and began to prep some stew.

Ramsey noticed Hazel lounging off to the side, reading one of the scrolls from the sub-world stash hidden inside Marynda's handbag. Hazel ignored all the grunts and jokes of the men as they prepped supper and unstrapped their weapons and began to settle in for the night. She was too engrossed with the glories of some ancient civilization to care about their antics. Distant, withdrawn, invested.

All the men in the group treated Hazel as either a daughter or a younger sister, and she would match their teasing with insults carrying the salt of a squid-pirate's tongue, often drawing wide-eyed appreciative nods from her companions. On the surface, those exchanges felt cursory and fun, yet everyone sensed Hazel was more removed than she used to be. She was always sharp and critical and curious, but now she was matured. And that wasn't the only change about her.

It was mostly little things. Things that went *missing*.

First night on the trail, Brisk laid out a trio of silver spoons upon a red silk cloth. During supper, he leaned back to admire his cherished utensils. No one really noticed as Hazel got up and went to refill her bowl. There was no indication that she knelt down in front of Brisk, or went anywhere within arm's reach of Brisk at all. Yet, when Brisk blinked, he found one of his spoons was missing. There was a stretch of consternated babbling before Brisk noticed Hazel. The girl was calmly and obliviously slurping broth from the Cook's missing spoon. Another time, Konragen's gold necklace with the red eye actually ended up hanging around Hazel's neck for a few minutes. No one even speculated on how she did that one. How could anyone get that close and avoid the dragon's detection?

That first night, the spoon incident during dinner, Brisk made a joke about the whole thing. From there, whenever someone noticed something odd they would be quick to label it "Hazel interference." These jokes would prompt smirks and nods from the group, but no one ever laughed too loud or too long. Everyone recognized they had a budding Thief growing within their ranks. No one really knew whether to discourage it or encourage it. So they left that to Marynda, who was just so endlessly proud to have her daughter back that she loved the child no matter what the child was.

The flutter of wings from overhead marked Marynda's return to camp. Everyone (except for Hazel) looked up to watch the falcon land upon a branch and announce her arrival with a squawk. Konragen, humble, dutiful Paladin, clambered to his feet, scooped a stack of Marynda's clothes and trotted over to a pair of trees. He put the clothes on the ground, removed his crimson robe and strung it between the trees. As Konragen returned to the others, the falcon swept down behind the curtain, became a human woman with strawberry-blonde hair, then got dressed, and came out to join them.

As Marynda sat down to a spot near the others, she met each of their eyes and, in turn, offered them each a nod. But her eyes lingered on Griffey's the longest, and his lingered right back.

"What did you find out?" Ramsey asked, unable to hide the anxious twitch in his voice.

"We will arrive at the elven village tomorrow by noon," Marynda revealed. Everyone gave approving nods, and before Ramsey's urgency spilled over, Marynda continued her scouting report. "Ramsey, the elves in your village live. Even though we lost a year in the squid-pirate water, your people still live. They're in rough shape, the disease has infected nearly all of them. But I think they'll hold out until noon tomorrow for their Healer to arrive." She shot Ramsey a wink and he sat back with a heavy sigh. The green Sorcerer elf gave her a smile of tearful relief that warmed Marynda's heart.

Ramsey the Green thought of what lay ahead. Tomorrow at noon, he would see his father again. For the first time since their ugly argument, almost a full plateau of years in the past.

Ramsey was ready to remedy that interaction. He'd proven himself and his Sorcerer's powers beyond the classroom, had succeeded in the field. And tomorrow he would bring his talents home and save his people.

Marynda turned to Griffey next. "Tonight's our last night on the trail. You promised."

A chorus of tiny cheers arose around the circle. Even Hazel rolled up her scroll and came over to join, settling in next to her mother. Griffey had, indeed, promised to finish his story, and it was time.

Griffey smiled around the circle, to each one of his Quest mates. "So... where did we leave off last night? I was doing battle with the skeleton zombies, right? Yeah, that's it. So, I get away from that, climb up this wooden suspension bridge to the other side of the cavern. When I get to the top, I find myself in meditation space again. Remember how I described that? Mystical? Cloudy?"

Nods went around the ring. The sun was down by now, the duo of sister moons aglow with a shaft of starlight seen through a gap in the trees above. Their campfire crackled, an owl hooted.

"Again, my body was gone and nothing but my mind remained. Once more, I was speaking with my sister, Sho'pa, and we were talking with our thoughts. Apparently meditation space is this higher realm where all earthly knowledge is accessible. And Sho'pa knew how to navigate up there, because she learned a great many things. She learned what happened at Rivercrest castle..."

His friends erupted: "*Yes!*" "*Yes, that's what we want to hear!*" "*Go on, Frishkadammit!*"

Just because he could—or because he needed to—Griffey claimed a moment of melancholy silence. "Our Chase Quest departed the morning after John Parker was killed," Griffey spoke. "Days went by, the Second King's funeral happened, he was put to rest in the commoners' burial grounds. Soon after the funeral, the people of Rivercrest started getting restless. While unease whispered through the castle, there came no word from the First King as to what would happen next. During that time of uncertainty, my mother escaped the city and has been living safely, peacefully on some undisclosed farmland. My sister wouldn't even tell me the location. Back in the castle, cries from the people steadily mounted. They demanded a new Second King be elected, chosen by them to represent them. They demanded answers for why such an election hadn't happened already. Yet the office of the First King had no answers. It became pretty clear in the minds of the people what was happening. The First King was consolidating power. Without a counterpart to muddy the waters, he was the one true King.

"The rebellion happened fast. The soldiers of the navy and the River Guard were the same as the common folk. The Second King was a position meant for them, too. The minority groups of the dwarves, elves and dragons joined the revolution without hesitation. The First King's tower was raided and Rodrick Callister was eventually banished from the kingdom. The monarchy was ended, and an oligarchy was established. A council of wisdom. It seems that people thought leadership was best administered from a group of people, rather than just one or two. From what Sho'pa told me, life in Rivercrest is getting back to normal and people are happy with the new system of rulers."

"A council, huh?" Ramsey uttered. "Who's on it?"

"It's a rather diverse collection," Griffey replied. "It's built of one dragon, one elf, one dwarf, one woman, and one man. Curiously, the man on the council is called Garver. He was the leader of the gang which freed me from the dungeons on the morning our Chase Quest began." Griffey shrugged.

"No borlogs made council roster, eh?" Konragen noted with a grunt and a smirk.

"That's pretty startling," Marynda breathed. After a pause, she ruffled her strawberry blonde hair with a *whoosh*. "Enough government talk. Don't you have something else for us?"

Griffey grinned at her. "I thought you hated being forced to endure poetry?"

"I'm sure it won't be terrible," Marynda oozed, making Hazel roll her eyes.

"Acho, acho," Griffey called when the others hooted. "I wrote one today, short and simple…

"Across the country, on a dangerous Quest,
For John Parker and Alkent, stand high above the rest.
Always remembered, leaders aspired to,
From their legacy seeds, a family grows anew."

A moment of awestruck, appreciative silence ensued.

Gradually, their eyes lifted to examine the stars.

"Do you think the other planets of Spiral Pit have councils leading them?" Brisk wondered.

"We could always go find out," Hazel said excitedly. "We could take the Warlock's sky carriage…"

Griffey's eyes met Marynda's again and they smiled at each other. "I think we should leave the carriage where it is for now," Marynda submitted. "Leave it locked up inside that castle."

"It's nice to know that carriage is there," Griffey agreed, before they shared supper with contentment in their hearts. "Nice to know we could escape and go explore if we wanted to. But, for now, I think Marynda's right. Our home world needs us here. Needs us fixing ills and fighting evil."

M Ray Roberts has worked a full host of interesting jobs.
The jewels of the bunch include: a golf course,
a pizza joint, a video store, a bookstore, a hardware store,
Kansas capitol building tour guide, DoorDash delivery driver,
cartographer, and one hot summer as a softball umpire.
◇◇◇
If you need him, you can find him hip-deep in his next novel,
nose-deep in a book, or nine-deep on a disc golf course.
◇◇◇
Kindly leave a review on
Amazon.com or Goodreads.com.

◇M. RAY ROBERTS◇

The adventure continues in…

Doom

Quest

Sequel available now on Amazon.com.

No pressure, but lots of fun!

Thank you so much for your support.

Made in the USA
Monee, IL
19 July 2023

39229705R00252